Tom Holt was born in 1961, and studied at Westminster School, Wadham College, Oxford, and the College of Law. He produced his first book, *Poems by Tom Holt*, at the age of thirteen, and was immediately hailed as an infant prodigy, to his horror. At Oxford, Holt discovered bar billiards and at once changed from poetry to comic fiction, beginning with two sequels to E. F. Benson's *Lucia* series, and continuing with his own distinctive brand of comic fantasy in *Expecting Someone Taller*, *Who's Afraid of Beowulf?*, *Flying Dutch*, *Ye Gods!*, *Overtime*, *Here Comes the Sun*, *Grailblazers*, *Faust Among Equals* and *Odds and Gods*. He has also written two historical novels set in the fifth century BC, the well-received *Goatsong* and *The Walled Orchard*, and has collaborated with Steve Nallon on *I, Margaret*, the (unauthorised) autobiography of Margaret Thatcher. Thinner and more cheerful than in his youth, Tom Holt is now married, and lives in Somerset.

Praise for Tom Holt:

'Literate, light fiction, an under-appreciated genre of which Tom Holt has made himself a modern master.'

Washington Post

'A rival to the comic throne'
Starburst

Also by Tom Holt

GRAILBLAZERS

Tom Holt

ORBIT

An *Orbit* Book

First published in Great Britain in 1994 by Orbit
This paperback edition published in 1994 by Orbit
Reprinted 1994, 1995

Copyright © Kim Holt 1994

The moral right of the author has been asserted.

A CIP catalogue record for this book
is available from the British Library.

ISBN 1 85723 191 0

Typeset by Solidus (Bristol) England
Printed in England by Clays Ltd, St Ives plc

Orbit
A Division of
Little, Brown and Company (UK)
Brettenham House
Lancaster Place
London WC2E 7EN

For G L H
Thanks

1

It is quite some storm.

It had started out with a perfectly ordinary squall on the strings, but then the brass had joined in, followed shortly afterwards by the entire woodwind section, and now the tubas and the double-basses are in full cry, with the trombones in the background doing the lightning effects. It is also slashing down with rain.

A flash of brilliant electric whiteness cleaves the darkness and reflects, painfully bright, off a man in armour staggering up the steep escarpment of the fell. His visor is up, and his face is lined with agony. He is an idiot. You can tell, just by looking at him. It's not so much his tall, youthful, athletic build or the sopping wet golden hair plastered like seaweed down his forehead that gives him away; it's just that nobody with anything substantial between his ears would climb up a steep mountain in full armour in a thunderstorm.

True, there is supposed to be a sleeping princess at

the top of this mountain, whom a kiss will awaken from a century of enchanted sleep. True, this princess is alleged to be beautiful, wise and extremely rich, and quite likely to be well-disposed towards the man who wakes her up. But common sense, even if it can handle the concept of sleeping princesses on mountain-tops, must surely insist that if she's been up there for a hundred years she's probably still going to be there in the morning, when it'll have stopped raining and a chap can see where he's putting his feet.

The knight stumbles on, and something – fool's luck, probably – guides his footsteps clear of the anthills, tussocks of heather and other natural obstacles which would send him and his fifty pounds of sheet steel slithering back down the hillside like a heavy-duty toboggan. The lightning forks from the sky again, and instead of electrocuting him chooses to illuminate the mountain-top. In fact it goes further, setting a wind-twisted thorn tree nicely on fire, so that the knight can make out the figure of a sleeping human under the lee of a rocky outcrop. Short of providing an illuminated sign saying YOU ARE HERE, there's not much more anybody could do to make things easy.

'Ha!' says the knight.

He lays down his shield and his spear and kneels for a moment, lost in wonder and awe. A sheep, huddling under a nearby gorse bush and chewing a ling root, gives him a look of utter contempt.

The sleeper remains motionless. The funny thing is that, for somebody who's been asleep on a mountain-top for a hundred years, she's in a pretty good state of preservation. When one thinks what happens to a perfectly ordinary pair of corduroy trousers when they inadvertently get left outside on the washing line overnight, one is amazed at how tidy she is. But of course, the idiot doesn't notice this. In fact, he's praying. He doesn't half choose some funny moments.

And now it has stopped raining, and the dawn pokes its rosy toe outside the duvet of the clouds and shudders. A single exquisite sunbeam picks out the scene. The knight's armour rusts quietly. Somebody is going to have to go over it later with a wire brush and a tin of metal polish, but you can guess, can't you, that it isn't going to be the knight.

Finally, having said quite a few paternosters and the odd Te Deum, the knight rises to his feet and approaches the sleeping figure. Dawn is now in full swing, and as he lifts the veil off her face – please note that some unseen force has protected the veil from mildew and mould for over a century – the sun lets fly with enormous quantities of atmospheric pink light. Creaking slightly, the knight bends down and plants a chaste, dry little kiss on the sleeper's cheek.

She stirs. Languidly, she opens her eyes. Consider how you feel first thing in the morning, and multiply that thirty-six thousand, five hundred times. Correct; you'd feel like death, wouldn't you? And the first thing you'd say would be, 'Nnnggrh,' surely. Not a bit of it.

'Hail, oh sun,' she says, 'hail, oh light, hail, oh daw...'

Then she checks herself. She blinks.

'Hang on,' she says.

The knight remains kneeling. He has that utterly idiotic expression on his face that you only see in Pre-Raphaelite paintings.

'Who are you?' says the princess.

The knight clears his throat. 'I,' he says, 'am Prince Boamund, eldest son of King Ipsimar of Northgales, and I have come—'

'Who?'

The knight raises both eyebrows, like someone by Burne-Jones who's just trodden on something sharp. 'I am Prince Boamund, eldest son of King—'

'Boamund?'

'That's right,' says the knight, 'Boamund, eldest son of—'

'How do you spell that?'

The knight looks worried. Where he comes from you can take advanced falconry, or you can take spelling; not both. Guess which one he opted for.

'Bee,' he says, and hesitates. 'Oh. Ee . . .'

The princess has a curious expression on her face (which is, of course, divinely beautiful). 'Are you being funny or something?' she says.

'Funny?'

'Kidding about,' she replies. 'Practical joke, that sort of thing.' She considers the situation for a moment. 'You're not, are you?'

'No,' says Boamund. He thinks hard. 'Look,' he says, 'I am Boamund, eldest son of King Ipsimar of Northgales, and you are Kriemhild the Fair, and you have been sleeping an enchanted sleep on top of this mountain ever since the foul magician Dunthor cast a spell on you, and I've just woken you up with a kiss. Agreed?'

The princess nods.

'Right, then,' says Boamund.

'So?'

'What do you mean, so?' says Boamund, flushing

pink. 'I mean, it's supposed to be . . . well . . .'

'Well what?'

'Well . . .'

Kriemhild gives him another peculiar look and reaches under a nearby stone for her cardy. It is, of course, pristinely clean.

'I mean,' she says, 'yes, you qualify, yes, you're a prince and all that, but . . . well, there seems to have been some mistake, that's all.'

'Mistake?'

'Mistake. Look,' she says, 'who told you? About me being here and everything?'

Boamund thinks hard. 'Well,' he says, 'there was this man in a tavern, if you must know.'

'A knight?'

Boamund scratches his head. Imagine a knight by Alma-Tadema who's somehow managed to fall off the picture and is wondering how to get back in without breaking the glass. 'I suppose he might have been a knight, yes. We were playing cards, and I won.'

Kriemhild's roseate lips have set in a firm line. 'Oh yes?' she says.

'Yes,' replies Boamund, 'and when I asked him to pay up he said he was terribly sorry but he didn't have any money. And I was just about to get pretty angry with him when he said that he could put me on to a pretty good thing instead, if I was interested. Well, I reckoned that I didn't have much choice, so . . .'

'I see,' says Kriemhild icily. 'Tell me, this knight, was he sort of dark, good-looking in a blah sort of way, long nose, hair fluffed up at the back . . .?'

'Yes,' says Boamund, surprised. 'Do you know him? I mean, how can you, you've been asleep . . .'

'Just wait till I get my hands on him, the treacherous little rat,' says Kriemhild, vigorously. 'I should have guessed, I really should.'

'You *do* know him, then?'

Kriemhild laughs bitterly. 'Oh yes,' she says, 'I know Tancred de la Grange all right. The little weasel,' she adds. 'I shall have a thing or two to say to Messire de la Grange when he finally condescends to get here.'

Something sinks into Boamund's slowly grinding brain. 'Oh,' he says. 'So you're going to, er . . .'

'Yes.'

'And you're, um, not going to . . .'

'No.' Kriemhild takes off her cardy, rolls it into a ball and puts her head on it. 'Please replace my veil before you go,' she says firmly. 'Good night.'

'Oh,' says Boamund. 'Right you are, then.' He stoops awkwardly down and picks up the veil, not noticing that he's standing on one corner of it. There is a tearing sound. 'Sorry,' he says, and drapes it as best he can over the face of the princess, who is now fast asleep once more. She grunts.

'Damn,' says Boamund, faintly; then, with a shrug which makes his vamplates crunch rustily, he sets off slowly down the mountain.

He's about a third of the way down when it starts raining again.

Fortunately there is a small cave nearby, its entrance half hidden by a wind-twisted thorn tree, and he squelches heavily towards it. Just inside he sees a dwarf, sitting cross-legged and munching a drumstick.

Promising.

'Hello, dwarf,' says Boamund.

'Wotcher, tosh,' replies the dwarf, not looking up.

'Still pissing down out there, is it?'

'Um,' says Boamund. 'Yes.'

'Rotten bloody climate, isn't it?' says the dwarf. 'I suppose you're coming in.'

'If you don't mind.'

'Suit yourself,' says the dwarf. 'I suppose you want a drink, an' all.'

Boamund's face lights up under his sodden fringe. 'Have you got any milk?' he asks.

The dwarf favours him with a look of distilled scorn and indicates a big leather bottle. 'Help yourself,' he says, with his mouth full.

It's a strange drink. Boamund thinks there are probably herbs in it; cold herbal tea or something. Then he suddenly feels terribly, terribly sleepy.

When he's fast asleep the dwarf jettisons his chicken leg, grins unpleasantly, makes a cabalistic sign and gets up to leave. A thought crosses his mind and he turns back. Having stolen Boamund's purse, penknife with corkscrew attachment and handkerchief, he leaves, and soon he has vanished completely.

Boamund sleeps.

Quite some time later he woke up.

Localised heavy rain, perhaps; or else someone had just emptied a bucket of water over him. He tried to move, but couldn't. Something creaked.

'It's all right,' said a voice somewhere overhead. That was probably God, Boamund thought; in which case, what he'd always suspected was true. God did indeed come from the West Riding of Yorkshire.

'You're not paralysed or anything like that,' the voice went on, 'it's just that your armour's rusted solid.

Really solid,' the voice added, with just a touch of awe. 'We're going to need more than just tinsnips to get you out of there.'

Boamund tried to see who was talking – probably not God after all – but the best he could do was crane his eyes. Result, a close-up of the bottom edge of his visor. 'Where am I?' he asked.

'In a cave,' replied the voice, and then continued, 'You've been here for some time, actually, sorry about that.'

Boamund cast his mind back. A fiery mountain. A maiden. A dwarf. Milk that tasted funny. Something his mother had told him, many, many years ago, about not accepting milk from strange dwarves.

'What's going on?' he asked.

'Ah,' replied the voice. 'You're the perceptive type, I can see that. Maybe all it needs is a dab of penetrating oil. Hold still.'

This injunction was, of course, somewhat redundant, but at least Boamund caught a very brief glimpse of someone small, in a purple hood, darting across his restricted line of vision. 'Here,' he said, 'you're the dwarf, aren't you? The one who . . .'

'Close,' said the dwarf, 'but not quite.'

'Hang on,' Boamund remonstrated. 'Either you are or you . . .'

'I'm not the dwarf you're thinking of,' replied the dwarf, 'but I'm a relative of his.'

'A relative . . .'

'Yes.' A small, ugly, wide grin floated across Boamund's sight-plane for an instant and then vanished again. 'A relative. In fact . . .'

'Yes?'

'Um.' A scuttling noise. 'A direct relative.' There was a curious swooshing sound near Boamund's left knee. 'Try that.'

Boamund made an attempt to flex his leg, without results.

'Give it another go,' said the dwarf. 'Brilliant stuff, this WD-40, but you've got to let it have time to seep through.'

Something began to tick inside Boamund's head. 'How long *have* I been here, exactly?' he asked. 'If my armour's really rusted solid, I must have been here . . .' He considered. 'Weeks,' he said.

'Try that.'

'Nothing.'

'Sure?'

'Of course I'm . . .'

Sound of intake of dwarfish breath. As well as being notorious for their alliance with enchanters, sorcerers and other malign agencies, dwarves are celebrated blacksmiths and metalworkers. This means that they have that profoundly irritating knack, familiar to any-one who's ever taken a car to a garage to have an inexplicable squeak sorted out, of drawing their breath in through a gap in their teeth instead of answering questions. The gap in the teeth, so current research would indicate, is usually the result of getting a smack in the mouth from telling a short-tempered customer that you can't get the parts.

'You're stuck solid there, chum,' said the dwarf. 'Absolutely solid. Never seen anything like it.'

Boamund felt a tiny twinge of panic, deep down inside his digestive apparatus. 'What do you mean,' he said, 'solid?'

The dwarf seemed not to have heard him. 'Not really surprising, though, amount of time you've been here. Suppose we could give it a try with the old cold chisel, but I'm not promising anything.'

'Hey!' said Boamund; and the next moment the entire universe began to vibrate loudly.

'Thought not,' said the dwarf, after a while. 'Helmet's rusted solid on to your vambrace. Looks like a hacksaw job to me. Stay there a minute, will you?'

In an ideal world Boamund would have pointed out, very wittily, that he didn't have much choice in the matter; however, since the world he was in fact inhabiting was still badly polluted with the after-effects of the dwarf attacking his helmet with hammer and chisel, Boamund didn't bother. What he in fact said was, 'Aaaagh.'

'Right then,' said the dwarf at his side. 'I've got the hacksaw, the big hammer, crowbar and the oxyacetylene cutter. Hold still a minute while I just . . .'

'What's an oxy-whatever you said?'

'Oh yes.' The dwarf was silent for a moment. 'You know I said I was a relative of that other dwarf?'

'Yes?'

'Well,' the dwarf replied, 'the fact is, I'm his . . . Just a tick.' The dwarf muttered under his breath. He was counting.

'You're his what?'

'I'm his great-grandson,' said the dwarf, 'approximately. I'm basing that on, say, fifteen hundred years, thirty-five-odd years per generation. You get the idea.'

There was, for the space of several minutes, a very profound silence in the cave, broken only by the sound of the dwarf having a go at the hinge-bolt of Boamund's visor with a triangular-section rasp.

'What did you just say?' Boamund asked.

'I'm the great-grandson of the other dwarf,' said the dwarf, 'the one you mentioned just now. And my name is Toenail. Ah, that's better, I think we're getting somewhere.'

Boamund made a gurgling noise, like a blocked hotel drain. 'What was that you said,' he asked, 'about fifteen hundred years?'

Toenail looked up from his raspwork. 'Say fifteen hundred years,' he replied, 'give or take a year or so. That's your actual oral tradition for you, you see, handed down by word of mouth across forty generations. Approximately forty generations, anyway. Hold on a second.'

There was a crash, and something gave. A moment later, Toenail proudly displayed a corroded brown lump. 'Your visor,' he explained. 'Now for the tricky bit.'

'I've been here for fifteen hundred years?'

'We'll call it that,' said the dwarf, 'for ready money, so to speak. You got enchanted.'

'I'd guessed that.'

'It was the milk,' Toenail continued. 'Big tradition in our family, how Toenail the First put the Foolish Knight to sleep with a drugged posset. About the only exciting thing that's ever happened to us, in fact. Fifteen hundred years of unbroken linear descent we've got – there's just the three of us, actually, now that Mum's passed on, rest her soul, that's me, our Chilblain and our Hangnail – fifteen hundred years and what've we got to show for it? One drugged knight, and a couple of hundred thousand kettles mended and lawnmower blades sharpened. Continuity, they call it.'

'I . . .'

'Hold still.'

There was a terrific creak, and then something hit Boamund very hard on the point of his chin. When he next came to, his head was mobile again and there was something looking like a big brown coal-scuttle lying beside him.

'Your helmet,' said Toenail, proudly. 'Welcome to the twentieth century, by the way.'

'The what?'

'Oh yes,' Toenail replied, 'I forgot, back in your day they hadn't started counting them yet. I wouldn't worry,' he added, 'you haven't missed anything much.'

'Haven't I?'

Toenail considered. 'Nah,' he said. 'Right, it's the torch for that breastplate, I reckon.'

In spite of what Toenail had said, Boamund felt he'd definitely missed out on the development of the oxy-acetylene cutter.

'What the hell,' he said, when his voice was functional once more, 'was that?'

'I'll explain it all later,' Toenail replied. 'Just think of it as a portable dragon, okay?' He lifted off a section of breastplate and tossed it aside. It clanged and disintegrated in a cloud of brown snowflakes.

'Basically,' Toenail went on, 'you've had your Dark Ages, your Middle Ages, your Renaissance, your Age of Enlightenment, your Industrial Revolution and your World Wars. Apart from that, it's been business pretty much as usual. Only,' he added, 'they don't call it Albion any more, they call it Great Britain.'

Boamund gurgled again. 'Great . . .?'

'Britain. Or the United Kingdom. Or UK. You know, like in Kawaguchi Industries (UK) plc. But it's basically the same thing; they've changed the names a bit, that's all. We'll sort it all out later. Hold tight.'

Boamund would have enquired further, but Toenail turned the oxy-acetylene back on and so he was rather too tied up with blind fear to pursue the matter. At one stage he felt sure that the terrible white-blue flame had gone clean through his arm.

'Try that,' Toenail said.

'Grr.'

'Sorry?'

Boamund made a further noise, rather harder to reproduce in syllabic form but indicative of terror. 'Don't worry about it,' said the dwarf. 'Just count yourself lucky I didn't think to bring the laser.'

'What's a . . .?'

'Forget it. You can move your arms now, if you like.'

For a moment, Boamund felt that this was a black lie; and then he found he could. Then one and a half millenniums' worth of pins and needles began to catch up with him, and he screamed.

'Good sign, that,' Toenail shouted above the noise, 'shows the old blood's beginning to circulate again. You'll be up and about in no time, mark my words.'

'And the first thing I'll do,' Boamund yelled at him, 'I'll take that oxy thing and . . .'

Toenail grinned and went to work with the torch on Boamund's leg-armour. Wisely, Boamund decided not to watch.

'Anyway,' Toenail said as he guided the terrible flame, 'I bet that what you're dying to ask me is, *Why* was I put to sleep for fifteen hundred years in a cave with all my armour on? I'm right, aren't I?'

'Aagh.'

'Well,' said the dwarf, 'oops, sorry, lost my concentration there for a minute. The armour was a mistake, I reckon, personally. Bit slapdash by old Toenail the First, if you ask me.' The dwarf grinned pleasantly. 'The actual going-to-sleep bit, though, that was your destiny.'

'AAGH!'

'Butterfingers,' muttered the dwarf. 'Sorry. The way I heard it, anyway, you're destined to be this, like, great hero or something. Like the old legends, you know, Alfred the Great, Sir Francis Drake—'

'Who?'

'After your time, I suppose. Like the great national hero who is not dead but only sleeping and will come again when his country needs him, that sort of thing.'

'Like Anbilant de Ganes?' Boamund suggested. 'Or Sir Persiflant the—'

'Who?'

'Sir Persiflant the Grey,' said Boamund wretchedly.

'You must have heard of him, he was supposed to be asleep under Suilven Crag, and if ever the King of Benwick sets foot on Albion soil, he'll come again and . . .'

Toenail grinned and shook his head. 'Sorry, old son,' he said. 'Guess he forgot to set the alarm. Anyway, you get the idea. That's you.'

'Me?'

'You. Not,' Toenail admitted, 'that there's much going on just at the moment. I mean, they say on the telly that unless someone does something about interest rates pretty soon it's going to mean curtains for small businesses up and down the country, but that's not really your line of work, I wouldn't have thought. Maybe you're going to do something about standards in primary school education. That it, you reckon?'

'What's a school?'

'Maybe not,' said Toenail. 'What else could it be?' He paused. 'You're not a fast left-arm bowler, by any chance?'

'What's a . . .?'

'Pity, we could really do with one of those. Anyway, whatever it is we need, apparently you're it. Try your feet.'

'Ouch.'

'Champion,' Toenail said. 'We'll give it a minute, and then you can try getting up.'

Boamund shifted slightly and discovered that he'd spent the last fifteen hundred years lying on a small but jagged stone. 'Ow,' he said.

Toenail was packing tools away in a small canvas bag. 'I'll say this,' he said, 'they made stuff to last in those days. Fifteen-hundred-year-old steel, eh?' He picked up a massive armguard and poked his finger through it. 'Should be in a museum or something, by rights. There's probably people who'd pay good money...'

Boamund gave up the effort and lay back, wondering if you could die of pins and needles. Outside there was a noise; it had been there a while but he now perceived it for the first time. A low, ominous growling, like an animal – no, like a huge swarm of bees. Only these bees would have to be eight feet long to make a noise like that.

Toenail grinned at him.

'What you can hear,' he said, 'is the M62. Don't worry about it.'

'Is it safe?'

Toenail considered. 'Depends,' he said. 'But as far as you're concerned right now, yes. Try standing up.'

He reached out a hand and Boamund grabbed it. A moment later he was putting his weight on his fifteen-hundred-year-old shoes. Oddly enough, they were fine. A spot of polish wouldn't hurt, mind.

'My clothes,' said Boamund. 'Why aren't they...?'

'Enchanted,' Toenail replied. 'Keeps them all nice and fresh. Come on, we're running late as it is.'

Boamund followed Toenail to the door of the cave, looked out, and screamed.

A year or so back, a television producer, one Danny Bennett, made a documentary which implied that the poet T.S. Eliot was murdered by the CIA.

According to Bennett's hypothesis, Eliot was killed because he had, quite by accident, stumbled upon highly secret metaphysical data which the Pentagon was in the process of developing for military use. Not aware of what he had done, Eliot published his findings in the *Four Quartets*; twenty-nine years later, he was dead, yet another victim of the Men in Grey Suits.

According to Bennett, the fatal lines were:

Time present and time past
Are both perhaps present in time future

and Bennett's argument was that this was taken by the nasty men to be an exposé of the strange things that people seem to get up to in the parts of ancient monuments and historic houses which are never open to the public.

Take, Bennett said, Hampton Court Palace, or Anne Hathaway's cottage. More than half of the rooms in these jewels of England's heritage are permanently shut. Why? Is it, as the Government would have us believe, simply because there isn't the money to maintain them and pay attendants? Or is there a more sinister explanation? Could it be that top secret experimental research into the nature of time itself is being carried out behind the nail-studded doors – research that, the nasty men hope, will lead to the perfection of a super-weapon that will allow NATO forces to zap back across the centuries, assassinate Lenin, and so prevent the storming of the Winter Palace? And was it his unfortunately ambiguous statement in the opening lines of 'Burnt Norton' that signed Thomas Stearns Eliot's death warrant?

Shortly after completing the filming of the documentary, Bennett was promoted sideways and appointed to be the new head of BBC local radio on

Martinmas Island, a small coral reef three thousand miles due east of Sydney. Interpretations of this outcome differ; Bennett, on his mid-morning phone-in *Good Morning, Martinmas*, has proposed the view that he has been muzzled, and this only goes to prove that he was absolutely right. The BBC, on the other hand, say that he was posted there because he had finally, irrevocably, fallen out of his tree, and although the next three years were likely to be tough going for the two marine biologists and six thousand penguins who inhabit Martinmas, short of having the wretched fellow put down there wasn't much else they could do.

Oddly enough, and by the purest coincidence, there is something extremely fishy about the back rooms of ancient monuments. These areas are used, as one would expect, for administration, storage and similar purposes; but nobody as yet has come up with a satisfactory (or at least comfortable) explanation for the fact that, when the staff come in every morning, they tend to find that someone's been using the typewriters and the kettles are warm.

'That's it?' Boamund said.

'Basically, yes,' the hermit replied.* 'I've left out Helmut von Moltke and the Peace of Nikolsburg, and maybe I skated over the Benelux customs union a bit, but I think you've got the essentials there. Anything you're not sure about, you can look up in the book.'

Boamund shrugged. He had learnt that, in the one

---

*He was short, round, fiftyish; and Boamund had an uncanny feeling that his beard was stuck on with spirit gum.

and a half thousand years he'd been asleep, Albion had indeed changed its name and they'd invented a few labour-saving gadgets, but basically things were very much the same. In fact, to be absolutely honest, they were worse. He was disappointed.

'My dad used to tell me,' he said, 'that by the time I was grown up, mankind would have grown a third arm it could use to scratch the small of its back.'

The hermit smiled, a tight-lipped, well-there-it-is-and-it's-too-late-now sort of smile, shrugged, and examined the crumpet on the end of his toasting fork. Outside in the street, small children rode up and down on bicycles and smacked the heads off flowers with plastic swords.

'I know,' agreed the hermit sadly. 'We've tried, God only knows, but people just won't listen. You try and guide them in the right direction, and what do you get? Apathy. You drop heavy hints to them about harness-ing the power of the sun, the wind and the lightning and they go and invent the vacuum cleaner. Nobody's the slightest bit interested in mainstream technology any more.'

Boamund looked sympathetic. 'It must be hard for you,' he said.

'Not really,' said the hermit. 'I get by more or less. It's not like the old times, but as far as I'm concerned, the main thing is to try and blend into the landscape, as it were, and bide my time.'

'Bide your time until when?'

'I'm coming to that,' said the hermit. The in-substantial red glow had burnt the crumpet, and the hermit impatiently dismissed them both and opened a packet of biscuits instead. 'Have one?' he asked. 'You must be starving after all this time.'

'Thank you,' Boamund said, and took a mouthful of Rich Tea. A moment later, he made a face, spat out a mouthful of crumbs and coughed.

The hermit apologised. 'I should have warned you,' he said. 'It's organic, I'm afraid. Made from ground-up grass seeds and processed sugar-beet, would you believe. The art of synthesising food was lost centuries ago. You get used to it after a while, but it still tastes like eating your way through somebody's compost heap. Here, have a doughnut.'

A doughnut appeared on the arm of Boamund's chair and he ate it thankfully. With his mouth full, he asked, 'So how do you manage it? Blending into the landscape, I mean?'

'Simple,' replied the hermit, 'I pretend to repair televisions. You won't credit it, but this country is full of little old men with their elbows showing through the sleeves of their cardigans who make a living mending televisions.'

Boamund considered. 'Those are the little box things with pictures in them?'

The hermit nodded. 'I've been here forty years now,' said the hermit, 'and nobody's taken the slightest notice of what I do. If anyone hears strange noises or sees flashing green lights late at night, the neighbours say, 'Oh *him*, he mends televisions,' and that seems to satisfy them. I imagine that, since they expect you to work miracles, they aren't too bothered if you do. In fact, I do it so well that some of them bring them back afterwards and complain that they still aren't right, even when I've hexed the dratted things so hard they'd withstand a nuclear attack.'

'That sounds like a really good cover,' Boamund said. 'Actually, while I'm here, I'll get you just to have a quick look at my astrolabe. I think it's the bearings.'

The hermit ignored him. 'I'm fortunate, of course,' he continued, 'in still having a dwarf.'

'You mean Toenail?'

'That's right. They're getting a bit thin on the ground, dwarves, though it's not as bad as it was. I think it was the free milk they used to give out to schoolchildren. Plays havoc with calcium deficiency, milk.' The hermit frowned. 'I'm drifting off the point a bit, aren't I? You and your destiny, all that sort of thing. I expect you want to know what your destiny actually is. Well . . .'

'Atishoo!' Boamund said.

'I beg your pardon?'

Boamund explained that he'd just spent the last fifteen hundred years in a draught. 'Sorry,' he said, 'you were saying . . .'

'What you've got to do,' said the hermit, 'is go to Ventcaster-on-Ouse and discover the Holy Grail.'

Boamund thought for a moment.

The curriculum of chivalry is selective. It consists of, in modern terms, A-level heraldry, genealogy, religious instruction and falconry, horsemanship and weapon-handling to degree level, and the option of post-graduate studies in either mysticism or dalliance. Essential as all these disciplines are to the profession of arms, none of them tends to stimulate the rational faculties. If you can't kill it, hit people with it or worship it, then as far as chivalry is concerned it clearly can't be all that important. To set a knight thinking, therefore, a proposition has to be fairly startling.

'If you know it's in Ventcaster-on-Ouse,' said Boamund carefully, 'how come you need me to go and look for it? Couldn't you just send a dwarf to fetch it or something?'

The hermit smiled kindly. 'Sorry,' he said, 'perhaps I could have put that better. I'm not saying the Grail is in Ventcaster. In fact, it's a pretty safe bet that that's one place on earth that the Grail isn't. But if you're going to look for it, going to Ventcaster is an essential preliminary step, because that's where the rest of the Grail Knights are. They need a new Grand Master. That's you.' He paused. 'Better?' he asked.

Boamund nodded. He was still thinking. 'Yes,' he said, 'that's fine. But why me, what's a Grail and why?'

Maybe the hermit smiled again, or maybe it was the original smile winched up another eighth of an inch.

'When the powers that be decided that Albion was finally going into Europe and we had to start changing over to continental ways,' said the hermit with obvious distaste, 'a few of the more far-sighted of us reckoned that it would be a good idea to ... how shall I put it? We salted away a few essential personnel – knights and hermits and sages and the like – just in case. They had to be fairly low status, or else they'd have been missed, but with potential nevertheless. You were one of them.'

'Oh,' Boamund said.

'What you might call low-flying high-flyers,' the hermit explained. 'Bright lights under heavy bushels. Anyway, from time to time, when we need you, we wake you up. The Grail Knights have just lost their leader, and so ...'

'Killed?'

'Not exactly,' said the hermit, sourly. 'He left the Order to start a window-cleaning round in Leamington Spa. So, of course, we need a replacement. It's a good posting,' the hermit added, as Boamund gave him a look you could have broken up with a hammer and put in a gin and tonic. 'Grade C status, company horse, makes you eligible for the pension scheme.'

'That reminds me,' Boamund started to say, but the hermit frowned at him.

'Also,' he went on, 'actually finding the Grail immediately qualifies you for a place in Avalon, remission of sins and a legend. If I was a bright, ambitious young knight wanting to make my mark, I'd jump at it.'

Boamund looked at him.

'And,' the hermit continued, 'if you don't I'll send you back to sleep until you do. Right?'

'Right,' said Boamund.

'Splendid,' said the hermit. 'Toenail!'

The dwarf-flap in the living-room door pushed open and Toenail appeared. His arms were oily to the elbow and he was holding a spanner.

'What?' he said.

The hermit frowned. 'Are you fiddling about with that motorbike again?' he asked.

Toenail looked shiftily up over the footstool. 'What if I am?' he said.

The hermit gave him a despairing look. 'Why, that's what I want to know,' he said. 'If the wretched thing doesn't work, then I'll hex it for you, and then perhaps we won't have so many oily fingerprints on the tea-towels.'

The dwarf scowled. 'You leave my bike alone,' he

replied. 'I'm a dwarf, fixing things is in our blood.'

'Putting new washers on taps isn't,' replied the hermit pointedly. 'I was soaked to the skin, that time you—'

'That's plumbing,' replied the dwarf. 'If you want plumbing done, call a plumber. Anyway, what can I do you for?'

The hermit sighed, and stared the oily footprints out of the carpet. 'Sir Boamund will be needing some new armour,' he said, 'and a sword and a shield and all that sort of thing. Have a look in the cupboard under the stairs, see what we've got.'

'Ah,' said the dwarf. 'Now you're talking.' He bowed and hurried away.

'He's a good sort, really,' said the hermit. 'I just wish he wouldn't keep trying to put a saddle on the cat and ride it round the house. It doesn't like it, you know.' The hermit got up, shook Boamund by the hand and clapped him on the shoulder. 'Anyway,' he said, 'best of luck, pop in after you've found the Grail, tell me how you've got on.'

Boamund nodded. Chivalry is like that; one minute you're sitting under a tree, chewing a blade of grass and dreaming of nothing in particular, and the next you're in the middle of some peculiar chain of adventures, which may end up with you marrying the king's eldest daughter but is just as likely to end up with you getting knocked off your horse and breaking your neck. You learn to go with the flow in chivalry. In that respect at least, it's a bit like selling door to door.

'Bye, then,' Boamund said. 'I'll leave the astrolabe with you, just in case you've got a moment to look at it.'

'Yes indeed,' said the hermit. He was gradually sinking into a pool of blue light, drifting away into the heart of the great Glass Mountain. A pair of carpet slippers crackled suddenly into flame, and then there was nothing left but an empty chair. Boamund turned to go.

'Oh yes, I forgot to mention,' whispered a faint voice. 'Whatever else you do, make absolutely sure you don't go near the . . .'

'Sorry?' Boamund asked. He waited for three minutes, but all he heard were the chimes of an ice-cream van, far away in the distance.

'What's this?' Boamund asked, puzzled.

Toenail sighed. He had this feeling that Boamund was going to turn out to be a difficult bugger, and resolved to do his best to be patient. Unfortunately, patience isn't one of the Three Dwarfish Virtues*.

'It's a zip,' Toenail replied. 'Look, it does up.'

'Does up what?'

'Does up like this.'

'Ow!'

Toenail sighed. 'It's sort of instead of a codpiece,' he explained. 'You'll get used to it.'

Boamund rubbed himself painfully, and muttered words to the effect that he thought it was a bloody silly way of going about things. Toenail smiled brightly and handed him the helmet.

------

*Honesty, manual dexterity and, would you believe it, dental hygiene.

'What's this?' Boamund asked. Toenail was getting sick of this.

'It's a helmet,' he replied.

Boamund stared at it. 'Look,' he said, 'I know I'm new to most of this, but don't try being funny with me. A helmet is heavy and shiny and made of the finest steel. This is made of that stuff . . . what did you say it was called?'

'Plastic,' Toenail replied, 'or rather, fibre-glass. It's a crash helmet. They're different from the ones you know about.'

'But . . .'

Toenail decided to be firm, otherwise they'd never get anywhere. 'Look,' he said, 'in your day, you had jousting helms and fighting helms and parade helms, and they were all different, right? Well, this is a helm for riding on a motorbike. That's why it's different.'

Boamund started to sulk. He'd already sulked twice; once when Toenail had handed him a bike jacket and Boamund had tried to make out that only peasants and archers wore leather body armour, and once when he'd been told that he was going to be riding pillion. He'd started to say that the knight always rode the horse and the dwarf went on the pillion, but Toenail had managed to shut him up by dropping a toolkit on his foot. He anticipated big trouble very shortly.

'And here's your sword,' he said, 'and your shield. Grab hold, while I just . . .'

'Here,' Boamund said, 'why're they in a canvas bag? It's not honourable to go around with your sword cased.'

Toenail decided it wouldn't be sensible right now to try and explain why it would be injudicious for

Boamund to wear his sword. Terms like 'arrested' and 'offensive weapon' probably didn't form part of his vocabulary. Instead, he made out that the quest demanded that he travel incognito, to save having to fight lots of tiresome jousts on the way. Oddly enough, Boamund swallowed that without a murmur.

'Right,' Boamund said. 'Where's the horse?'

'It's not a horse,' Toenail replied tentatively. 'Not as such. Look, follow me.'

He led the way out the back. There, under the washing line, stood his treasured Triumph Bonneville, the only thing in the whole world that he really and unreservedly loved.

'What's that?' Boamund asked.

Toenail clenched his fists tightly and replied, 'It's a motorcycle. It's like...' He closed his eyes and ransacked his mind, pulling out the drawers and throwing their contents on to the floor. 'It's like a magic horse that doesn't need shoeing,' was the best he could come up with.

'Does it fly?' Boamund asked.

'No,' said Toenail, taken aback. 'It goes along the ground. Downhill, with the wind behind her, she'll do a hundred and fifteen, no worries.'

'A hundred and fifteen what?'

'Miles.'

'Oh.' Boamund frowned. 'And then what do you do?' he asked.

'How do you mean?'

'After you've gone a hundred and fifteen miles,' Boamund replied. 'Do you get another one, or ...?'

'No, no,' Toenail said, screwing up his eyes and resisting the temptation to take a chunk out of

Boamund's kneecap. 'A hundred and fifteen miles an hour.'

'Hang on,' Boamund said. 'I thought you said it didn't fly.'

'She doesn't.'

But Boamund didn't seem convinced. 'All the magic horses I ever heard about could fly,' he said. 'There was Altamont, the winged steed of Sir Grevis de Bohun. She could do three hundred and forty-two, nought to a hundred and six in four point four three—'

'Yes, well,' Toenail said. 'Now—'

'My uncle had a magic horse,' Boamund went on, 'he did from Caerleon to Tintagel once in an hour and seven minutes. You could really give it some welly on that horse, he used to tell me.'

'Um . . .'

'Had all the gear, too,' Boamund continued dreamily. 'Monoshock stirrups, power-assisted reins, three-into-one hydraulically damped underneck martingale, customised sharkskin girths with three-position auto-adjusted main buckles . . .'

Toenail stumped across to the bike and unscrewed the filler-cap. 'Come on,' he said, 'we haven't got all day, you know.'

Boamund shrugged. 'All right,' he said. 'Where do I sit?'

'Behind me,' Toenail said. 'Up you get. Got the bag?'

Boamund nodded and pulled on his helmet. Muttering something or other under his breath, Toenail opened the choke, flicked down the kickstart, and stood on it and jumped.

Needless to say, the bloody thing wouldn't start.

Boamund tapped him on the shoulder. 'What are you doing?' he said.

'I'm trying to get her to start,' Toenail replied.

'What, by pulling out its whatsit and jumping on it?' Boamund replied. 'What good's that supposed to do? You'll just make it cross, and then it'll bite you or something.'

I could try and explain, Toenail thought, but why bother? He located the kickstart under the ball of his foot, lifted himself in the saddle and jumped again. As usually happened, the kickstart slipped from under his foot and came up sharply against his shin. Toenail swore.

'Told you so,' said Boamund. 'Why don't you just say the magic word?'

'There isn't a magic word, you pig-brained idiot!'

Boamund sighed and said something incomprehensible. At once the engine fired, revved briefly and then fell back into a soft, dreamy purring. Of the usual wittering of maladjusted tappets there was no sign. Toenail sat, open-mouthed, listening. Even the camchain sounded good.

'Can we go now, please?' Boamund said. 'It'll take us at least an hour, if all this thing does is—'

'How did you do that?' Toenail demanded. 'She *never* starts first time. Never.' He felt betrayed, somehow.

'Simple,' Boamund replied, 'I said the magic word. I'm not a complete ignoramus, you know.'

Right, Toenail thought, enough is enough. You've asked for it. He flipped up the sidestand, trod the gearlever into first and opened the throttle. The front wheel hoisted itself gratifyingly skyward and, with a squeal of maltreated rubber, the bike careered down the drive and out into Cairngorm Avenue. By the end of the road, Toenail was doing nearly fifty, and as they went round the corner he slewed the bike down so hard that the right-hand side footrest touched down with a shower of sparks.

Magic horses be buggered, he thought. I'll give him magic horses, the cocky little sod.

They were doing a cool seventy down Sunderland Crescent, weaving in and out round the parked cars like a demented bee, when Boamund leant forward and tapped Toenail on the shoulder.

'All right?' he shouted back. 'You want me to slow down?'

'Certainly not,' Boamund replied. 'Can't you get this thing to go any faster?'

Toenail was about to say something very apposite when Boamund muttered another incomprehensible phrase and the road suddenly blurred in front of Toenail's eyes. He screamed, but the wind tore the sound away from him. There was this furniture van, right in front of them, and . . .

And then they were flying. It had been a near thing; the front tyre had skimmed the roof of the van, and quite probably he was going to have to go the round of the breakers' yards to get another rear mudguard (you try getting a rear mudguard for a '74 Bonneville and see how you like it), but they were still alive. And airborne.

'Put me down!' Toenail shrieked. 'How dare you! This is a classic bike, I've spent hours getting it up to concourse standard. You crash it and I'll kill you!'

'But it's so slow,' Boamund replied. 'You hang on tight, we'll soon be there.'

Toenail was beginning to feel sick. 'Please,' he said.

The laws of chivalry, which are as comprehensible and practical as the VAT regulations, ordain that a true knight shall have pity on the weak and the feeble. Boamund sighed and mumbled the correct formula, and a moment later the bike touched down on the southbound carriageway of the M18, doing approximately two hundred and forty.

Jesus Christ, thought Toenail to himself, I could write to *SuperBike* about this, only they'd never believe me. He exerted the full strength of his right hand on the brake lever, and slowly the bike decelerated. He made his way across to the hard shoulder, cut the engine and sat there, quivering.

'Now what is it?' said Boamund testily.

Toenail turned slowly round in the saddle and leant towards Boamund until their visors touched.

'Look,' he said, 'I know you're a knight and I'm only a dwarf, and you've got a Destiny and know all about the old technology and your uncle had some sort of drag-racer that could do the ton in four seconds flat, but if you pull a stunt like that ever again, I'm going to take that sword of yours and shove it right up where the sun never shines, all right?'

Three foot seven of shattered dreams and injured pride can be very persuasive sometimes, and Boamund shrugged. 'Please yourself,' he said. 'I was just trying to help.'

'Then don't.' Toenail jumped on the kickstart, swore, tried again and eased the bike out into the slow lane.

In the course of the next fifty miles he was overtaken by three lorries, two T-registration Mini Clubmen, a scooter and a Long Vehicle with a police escort transporting what looked like a pre-fab bridge; but he didn't mind.

'If,' as he explained to Boamund when the latter implored him to try going a bit faster, 'God had intended us to travel quickly and effortlessly from one place to another, He wouldn't have given us the internal combustion engine.'

As far as Boamund could see, there was no answer to that.

'Where are we going?' Boamund asked.

Toenail took his left hand off the bars and pointed.

'Yes,' Boamund said, 'I can read. But what does it mean?'

This puzzled Toenail; to him, the words 'Service Station' were self-explanatory. He made no effort to explain, and drove into the car park.

'I mean,' Boamund said, taking off his helmet and shaking his head, 'service is what you owe to your liege lord, and a station is a military outpost. Is this where knights come to bow down before their lords and beg favours of them?'

Toenail thought of the palaver he'd been through the last time he tried to order sausage, fried bread, baked beans and toast without the fried egg, and replied, 'Yes, sort of. You hungry?'

'Now you mention it,' Boamund replied, 'yes. All I've had in the last fifteen hundred-odd years is a cup of poisoned milk and a biscuit.'

'Not poisoned,' Toenail pointed out, 'drugged. If it'd been poisoned you wouldn't be here.'

'Must just have been wishful thinking, then.'

Toenail took great pains to explain the system. 'You get your tray,' he said, 'and you stand in line while they serve the people in front of you, and then you ask the girl behind the counter for what you want. Food-wise,' he added. 'And then she puts it on your tray and you take it up to the cash desk. Got that?'

Boamund nodded. 'And then what?' he asked.

'Then we sit down and eat,' Toenail said.

'Where?'

Toenail looked up at him. 'You what?'

'Where do we sit?' Boamund repeated. 'I mean, I don't want to make a fool of myself by sitting in a dishonourable seat.'

Jesus flaming Christ, thought Toenail to himself, why didn't I just bring sandwiches? 'You sit wherever you like,' he said. 'It's a service station, not the Lord Mayor's Banquet.'

'What's a—?'

'Shut up.'

To do him credit, Boamund waited very patiently in the queue. He didn't push or shove or challenge any of the lorry drivers to a duel if they trod on his foot. Toenail's stomach began to unclench slightly.

'Next,' said the woman on the Hot Specials counter. Toenail asked for steak and kidney pudding and was about to move on when he heard Boamund's voice saying:

'I'll have roast swan stuffed with quails, boar's chine in honey, venison black pudding, three partridges done rare and a quart of Rhenish. Please,' he added.

The girl looked at him.

'I said,' Boamund repeated, 'I'll have roast swan stuffed with . . .'

One of the few advantages of being a dwarf is that you can walk away from situations like these without anybody noticing, if necessary by ducking down between people's legs. Very carefully, so as not to spill his gravy, Toenail started to walk . . .

'Toenail!'

He stopped and sighed. Behind Boamund, quite a few people were beginning to get impatient.

'Toenail,' Boamund was saying, 'you told me to ask the girl behind the counter for what I wanted to eat, and she's saying all I can have is something called *lassania*.'

'You'll like it,' Toenail croaked. 'They do a very good lasagna here.'

Boamund shook his head. 'Listen,' he said to the girl, whose face was doing what concrete does, only quicker, 'I don't want this yellow muck, right, I want roast swan stuffed with quails . . .'

The girl said something to Boamund, and the dwarf, whose genes were full of useful information about the habits of insulted knights, instinctively dropped his tray and curled up into a ball on the floor.

But Boamund just said, 'Suit yourself then, I'll get it myself,' muttered something or other under his breath, and started to walk away. Against his better judgement, Toenail opened an eye and looked up.

Boamund was still holding his tray. It contained a roast swan, a boar's chine in honey, some peculiar-looking slices of black pudding, three small roast fowl and a large pewter jug.

'Here,' said the girl, 'that's not allowed.'

Boamund stood very still for a moment. 'Sorry?' he said.

'Eating your own food's not allowed,' said the girl.

Toenail felt a boot digging into his ribs. He tried ignoring it.

'Toenail, I don't understand this at all. First they don't have any proper food, only *lassania*, and now she says I'm not allowed to eat my food. Does that mean we all have to swap trays or something?'

Toenail stood up. 'Come on,' he said, 'we're leaving. Quick.'

'But . . .'

'Come on!'

Toenail grabbed Boamund by the sleeve and started to drag him doorwards. Behind them somebody shouted, 'Hey! Those two haven't paid!'

Boamund stopped dead, and try as he might Toenail couldn't induce him to move. 'What did you say?' Boamund enquired.

'You haven't paid for that.'

'But I didn't get it from you,' Boamund was saying, very patiently, very reasonably. 'Your people didn't have anything I wanted so I got something for myself.'

Toenail betted himself that he knew what was coming next. 'You're not allowed,' said the voice, 'to eat your own food in here.' Oh good, said Toenail to his feet, I won.

'Look.'

'No,' said the voice, 'you look.'

Honour, its cultivation and preservation, are at the very root of chivalry. It is thus highly unwise to say something like, 'No, you look,' to a knight, especially if he's hungry and confused. Although Toenail had deliberately averted his head, on the slightly irrational grounds that anything he didn't see he couldn't be blamed for, he didn't need eyes to work out what happened next. The sound of an assistant cafeteria manager being hit with a trayful of roast swan is eloquently self-explanatory.

From under his table, Toenail had a very good view of one section of the fight – roughly from the feet of the participants as far as their knees – and as far as he was concerned that was quite enough for him, thank you very much. You had to say this for the lad, fifteen hundred years asleep on a mountain, you'd think he'd be out of practice, but not a bit of it.

After a while, Toenail could only see one pair of feet, and they were wearing the pair of motorcycle boots he'd bought specially, after measuring the sleeping knight's feet about a week ago. How long ago that seemed!

'Toenail!'

'Yes?' said the dwarf.

'You're not particularly hungry, are you?'

Toenail put his head out. 'Not really,' he said. 'Let's have something when we get there, shall we?'

'Good idea,' Boamund replied. He wiped gravy off his face and grinned sheepishly.

They got to the bike and got it started about four seconds before the police arrived. Fortunately, the police had omitted to bring helicopters with them, so when the bike suddenly lifted off the ground and roared away in the direction of Birmingham there wasn't very much they could do about it, except take its number and arrest a couple of students on a Honda 125 for having a defective brake light.

2

'Yes,' Toenail replied.

'Are you sure?' Boamund said. 'Give me that street map a second.'

Toenail did so, and Boamund studied it for a while. 'Looks like you're right,' he said. 'It just doesn't look like any castle I've ever seen before, that's all.'

Toenail was with him there a hundred per cent. It looked far more like a small, rather unsavoury travel agent's office. Closed, too.

'Maybe it's round the back,' he suggested.

Boamund looked at him, 'I think you're missing the point rather,' he said. 'The thing about castles is . . .' He paused, trying to choose the right words. 'Well,' he said, 'you just don't get castles round the backs of things. It's not the way things are.'

'Maybe it is in Brownhills,' replied the dwarf. 'Have you ever been here before?'

'I don't know,' Boamund confessed. 'Things have

changed a bit since my day.'

'Well,' said the dwarf, 'there you are, then. Maybe the fashions in castle architecture have changed too. The unobtrusive look, you know?'

Boamund frowned and got off the bike. It occurred to Toenail that this was probably one of the best opportunities he was going to get for quite some time to jump on the bike, gun the engine and get the hell out of here before something really horrible happened to him; but he didn't, somehow. What he told himself was that the bike wouldn't start, and that knights took a dim view of attempted desertion. The truth of the matter was that his dwarfish genes wouldn't let him. Stand By Your Knight, the old dwarf song goes.

Boamund was knocking on the door. 'Anybody home?' he called.

Silence. Boamund tried again, with the air of a man who knows that the proper way to do this would be to sound a slug-horn, if only he had such a thing about his person. Still nothing.

'It must be the wrong place,' Toenail said. 'Look, let's just go away somewhere and think it over, shall we?'

Boamund shook his head. 'No,' he said. 'I think this is the right place after all. Look.'

He pointed at something, and Toenail stood on tiptoe and looked. He could see nothing. He said so.

'There,' Boamund said, 'can't you see, on the doorframe, very faint but it's there, definitely.'

Toenail squinted. There was, he had to admit, the faintest possible pattern or design, crudely scratched on the paintwork. He stared at it for a while, until his imagination got him thinking that it could be mistaken for a bunch of roses, their petals intertwined. 'Oh yes,' he said. 'What's that, then?'

'It's a waymark,' Boamund replied. 'Part of the Old High Symbolism. Must mean that there are knights here.'

'Is that what it means, then?' Toenail demanded.

'Strictly speaking, no,' Boamund replied. 'What it actually means is, "No insurance salesmen or Jehovah's Witnesses; beware of the dog." But reading between the lines . . . Here, what's this?'

'Another one?'

'Maybe,' Boamund muttered. 'Let's have a look.' He rubbed away a dried-on pigeon dropping, scrutinised the doorpost carefully and then chuckled to himself. 'It's definitely a waymark,' he said. 'Look.'

'This time,' Toenail said, 'I'm going to have to take your word for it.'

'It's the ancient character designed to let bailiffs know that you've moved,' Boamund observed. 'We call it the Great Self-Defeating Pentagram. This is the right place, I reckon.' He thumped on the door so hard that Toenail reckoned he could feel it wince, and then called out very loudly in what Toenail would ordinarily have guessed was Bulgarian.

Several seconds of complete silence; and then a window above their heads ground open.

'We're closed,' said the voice. 'Go away.'

Boamund was staring, open-mouthed. 'Bedders!' he yelled out joyfully, and waved. 'Bedders, it's me.'

Toenail looked up at the man in the window; a round-faced, bald head with a big red nose. 'Bo?' it replied, and its tone of voice implied that this was better than pink elephants or spiders climbing the wallpaper, but still uncalled for. 'It can't be.'

'Bedders!' Boamund repeated rapturously. 'Come and open this door before I kick it in!'

This, Toenail surmised, was entirely consistent with what he knew of the way knights talked to each other. Apparently, under the laws of chivalry, the way you expressed warm sentiments of friendship and goodwill to another knight was to challenge him to put on all his armour, be knocked off his horse, and get his head bashed in with a fifteen-pound mace.

'You touch that door,' the head replied, 'and I'll break both your legs.' An expert on courtly repartee would immediately have recognised this as being roughly equivalent to our, 'George, you old bastard, how the devil are you!', but Toenail decided to hide behind the bike, just in case.

'You and whose army, you drunken ponce?' Boamund replied tenderly. The head grinned.

'Stay right there,' he said, and the window slammed. Boamund turned round.

'What are you doing down there?' he asked.

'Hiding,' said a voice from behind the bike's rear wheel. 'What does it look like I'm—?'

'You don't want to take any notice of old Bedders – that's Sir Bedevere to you,' Boamund replied. 'Soft as porridge, old Bedders. Here, quick, where's that sword?'

He rummaged around in the luggage, and when the door opened (to reveal a huge-looking figure completely covered in steel, Toenail couldn't help noticing) he had found the sword and the shield and had put his crash helmet back on. For his part, Toenail, having assessed the various options available to him, jumped into the bike's left-hand pannier and pulled the lid down over his head. There are times when it feels good to be small.

'Ha,' he heard someone saying. 'Abide, false knight, for I will have ado with you.' Toenail shuddered and closed his eyes.

'I will well,' said the other idiot. 'Keep thee then from me.'

Then there was a noise like a multiple pile-up, followed by the inevitable sound of something metal, as if it might be a hub-cap, wheeling along the ground, spinning and then falling over with a clang. And then shouts of boisterous laughter.

And then someone pulled open the lid of the pannier and extracted Toenail by the collar of his jacket.

'Toenail,' Boamund was saying, 'meet Sir Bedevere. Bedders, this is my dwarf, Toenail.'

'Pleased to meet you, Toenail,' said the armoured lunatic. By the looks of it, the thing that had come off and rolled about on the floor must have been his helmet, since he was bareheaded and bleeding from a cut over his left eye. 'Well, then,' said Sir Bedevere, 'you'd better come in. The others,' he added, 'are all out, and it's muggins' turn to do the kitchen floor again.' A thought occurred to him. 'Hang on,' he said, brightening, 'your dwarf can do it, can't he?'

Toenail was just about to protest violently when Boamund said, 'Good idea,' and clapped Toenail heartily on the back. Much more of this, the dwarf muttered to himself, and I'm going to be sick. However, as it transpired, things could have been worse. Bedevere did show him where the mop and the Flash were kept, and it was a smaller kitchen than, say, the one at Versailles.

'Anyway,' said Bedevere, showing his guest to the comfortable chair, 'sit down, make yourself at home, tell me all about it.'

'About what?' Boamund replied, helping himself to peanuts. 'That reminds me,' he added. 'I'm starving. I haven't had any food – *proper* food, that is – in ages.'

'Help yourself,' said Bedevere politely, and Boamund, having recited the necessary formula, set about eating his way through a side of venison which obligingly materialised in front of him. In fact, thought Toenail to himself as he crouched on his hands and knees trying to shift a particularly stubborn stain, if all knights can do this, what do they need a kitchen for, let alone a kitchen floor?

'You were saying,' said Bedevere.

'Was I?'

'Yes,' Bedevere replied. 'About what you've been doing and, er . . .'

'Yes?'

'How come you're still alive. I mean,' Bedevere assured his friend, 'wonderful that you are. Spiffing. But it's rather a turn-up, don't you think?'

Boamund put down a pheasant's wing and looked at him. For all that they'd been through basic training, Knight School and the Benwick campaign together, that still didn't entitle young Fatty to go asking him personal questions. 'What about you, then?' he demanded. 'You're the one who was always stuffing himself with honey-cakes and second helpings of frumenty. If anyone should have pegged out . . .'

Bedevere winced. 'It's a long story,' he said.

Boamund gazed at him defiantly over a roast quail. 'Go on, then,' he said, 'I'm in no hurry.'

'All right, then.'

The gist of what Bedevere said was this:

Boamund no doubt remembered how sticky things were getting towards the end of Arthur's reign, what with the Saxons and everything . . .

Well, no. Boamund was asleep at the time, but he'll take your word for it. Do go on, please.

. . . what with the Saxons and everything, and the last thing the King wanted was for his knights to offer any resistance to the vastly superior Saxon forces. This could only make things worse, and was fundamentally a bad idea. On the other hand, chivalry would undoubtedly forbid the knights to do nothing while a lot of Danish bacon entrepreneurs took over the country and drove small shopkeepers out of business.

Arthur therefore decided on a diversion; and since chivalry was about to end, he felt it only right and proper that it should go out with a bang. He therefore summoned his knights to Camelot, told them a little white lie about the Saxons all having gone home, leaving money to pay for all the broken doors and windows, and suggested that they might all like to go and look for the Holy Grail.

The knights accepted the challenge with enthusiasm, for all that none of them had the faintest idea what a Grail looked like, and agreed to reassemble at Camelot a year and a day later and bring the Grail with them.

The idea succeeded beyond Arthur's wildest dreams. When the court reassembled it turned out that of the hundred knights who had set out on the quest, fifty were dead, fourteen had been arrested, twenty-two had defected to the court of the king of Benwick, and eight had given up chivalry and gone into personnel management. The remaining six, King Arthur reckoned, were unlikely to bother anyone. He therefore provided them with a chapter house and a pension scheme, named them the Order of Chevaliers of the Sangrail, and left by the fire escape while they were all in the bar.

The Chevaliers of the Sangrail continued with the quest for a while; but it should be obvious from the fact that they alone had survived out of the original hundred that they were all knights who held quite firmly to the rule that discretion – or, even better, naked fear – is the better part of valour, and besides, none of them knew what a Grail was. For three years they toured Albion on the off-chance that the Grail was to be found either in an inn or a greyhound track, and then decided by a majority of five to one to abandon the quest. Their reasoning was that Albion was a small place and in their travels the chances were that they'd probably come across it; find it, His Majesty had told them, there was nothing in the fine print about recognising it once found. They then put the chapter house on the market and went to draw their pensions. All would probably have been well, had not the chairman of the trustees of the pension fund been a diehard magician and reactionary Albionese nationalist by the name of Merlin. He insisted that the Grail had to be brought to Camelot in order that the quest be fulfilled; and until it was they could whistle for their pensions.

The Chevaliers decided to make the best of a bad job. Instead of actively searching for the Grail, they resolved in future to look for it passively; that is to say, to do something else, hopefully something more interesting and profitable, while waiting for the thing to turn up. After investing all their spare capital in a scheme to dig a tunnel connecting Albion with Benwick, which was frustrated by the fact that Benwick disappeared into the sea when they were five miles short of it, they moved into the chapter house, let the ground-floor premises to a man who arranged bucket-shop pilgrimages, and got jobs in the local woad factory.

The woad factory is, of course, long gone. The knights are still there.

'Except,' Bedevere said sadly, 'for Nentres, of course.'

Boamund surreptitiously wiped a tear from his eye and murmured, 'Dead?'

'Not quite,' replied Bedevere. 'About six months ago he announced that he'd had enough and was going south. Apparently he'd met this chap who was starting up a video shop somewhere. The blighter,' said Bedevere savagely, 'he buggered off with our outings fund. Seventy-four pounds, thirty-five pence. We were planning to go to Weymouth this year.'

'Where's Weymouth?'

Bedevere explained. 'So,' he went on, 'here we all are, and here you are too. It's a small . . .'

Then the penny dropped. Bedevere had been in the process of raising a glass containing gin and tonic to his lips. He spilt it.

'I see,' Boamund was saying. 'That would account for it, I suppose.'

Bedevere picked a slice of lemon out of his collar. 'Always delighted to see you,' he gabbled, 'and it would have been nice if you could have stayed for a while, but if you're really busy and in a hurry to get on with whatever it is you're here to do, which must be really important, then please don't let us . . .'

'Actually,' Boamund said.

'. . . stop you. After all,' he wittered frantically, 'we're just here, minding our own business, or rather businesses – Turquine delivers pizzas, you know, and Pertelope's got a really nice little window-cleaning round, shops and offices as well as houses, and Galahaut's an actor, though he's resting just now, and Lamorak buys things and sells them in street markets and I . . .' He broke off and, unexpectedly, blushed.

'Go on,' said Boamund, intrigued. 'What do you do?'

'I . . . I'm an insurance salesman,' Bedevere muttered into his beard. 'It's a really interesting job,' he said hurriedly. 'You've no idea what a wide cross-section of society . . .'

'An insurance salesman,' said Boamund.

'Um,' Bedevere mumbled. 'You wouldn't by any chance be interested in a . . .?'

'I see.' Boamund was frowning. On his broad, plain, straightforward, honest and, well yes, stupid face a cold look of displeasure was settling, like ice on the points of a busy commuter line. 'You know what we used to call you back at the old Coll, Bedders?'

'Er, no,' said Bedevere. Actually he had had a fair idea and he'd always resented it. The way he saw it, a chap can't help it if he's born with big ears.

'Li chevalier li plus prest a succeder,'* replied

---

*Since Bedevere's father was the Duke of Achaia and ninety-seven years old, the term 'most likely to succeed' might be interpreted rather more literally than Boamund thought.

Boamund, severely. 'Double first in tilting, I seem to remember. Honours in falconry. Dalliance blue. Captain of courtesy three years running. And now,' he sighed, 'you're an insurance salesman. I see.'

'It's not like that,' Bedevere growled unhappily. 'Times change, and—'

'I remember,' Boamund went on obliviously, 'I remember when your father, rest his soul, came to Sports Day one year, and you were jousting for the Deschamps-Mornay Memorial Salver. He was so proud of you.'

Bedevere snuffled. 'Look,' he said, 'they don't have jousts any more. It's all your televised snooker, your American football—'

'And when he heard you'd been selected for the Old Boys match,' Boamund continued cruelly, 'well, I've never told you this before, Bedders, but—'

'Look!' Bedevere was close to tears. 'It's not as simple as that. We tried our best, honest we did. We looked all over for the wretched thing. We even went to,' and the knight winced, 'Wales. But we just didn't have the faintest idea of what it was we were looking for. Chivalry doesn't prepare you for things like that, Bo. Chivalry is all about finding someone who's big and strong and mean sitting on a ruddy great black horse and clouting him around the head till he passes out. In chivalry, you leave all the planning and the thinking to someone else. You're just there to do the important bit, the bashing people up side of things. We couldn't manage it on our own, Bo, with nobody to tell us what to do. There's no place for knights in the modern world, you see. We're . . .' He searched for the exact term. 'I suppose you could say we're over-

qualified. Too highly trained. Over-specialised. You
know what I mean.'

'Useless, you mean.'

'Yes,' Bedevere agreed. 'It's just that there aren't any
dragons left any more. And no damosels to rescue,
either. Young Turquine tried to rescue a damosel the
other day. It was some sort of a party, and he was
delivering pizzas. He walks in through the door and
there's this terrible barbaric music and all these men
pulling girls about by the arms and . . . Well, he jumped
right in, like a true knight, sorted a few of them out,
I can tell you. And then this damosel kneed him in
the—'

'I see, yes.'

'Then they called the police,' Bedevere said. 'Luckily, Galahaut and I happened to be passing, so we were
able to pull him off before he did any of them a serious
injury, but . . .'

'Nevertheless,' said Boamund. His face looked like
something rejected by Mount Rushmore for excessive
gravity. 'I think it's probably just as well I've come to
take charge here, don't you? Delivering pizzas! Selling
insurance! Old Sagramor would turn in his grave if he
knew.'

Bedevere, remembering their old venery tutor, sec-
retly agreed, and hoped that this would involve his
brushing up against something sharp. 'But . . .' he said.

'What I was about to say,' Boamund went on, 'is that
I've been woken up from a fifteen-hundred-year sleep
to take charge of this Order, and by God, take charge
of it I jolly well will!'

Just then, the door of the Common Room flew open
and a large, round man with a red face bustled in,

holding a portable telephone in one hand and a huge stack of thin styrofoam boxes in the other.

'Bedders,' he called out, 'there's a dwarf in our kitchen. I went in there to heat up the pizzas and the nasty little thing was making the floor all wet. I chucked him in the bin, naturally, but the damage was done. How many times have I told you about leaving the back door open in the . . .'

He froze, and stared. The pizzas fell from his hand and started to roll around the room like slow, anchovy-garnished hoops.

'Bloody hell,' he said at last. 'It's Snotty Boamund!'

'Hello, Turkey,' replied Boamund coldly.

Sir Turquine went, if anything, redder than before. 'Hell fire, Bedders, a joke's a joke, but what the hell do you think you're playing at? I was only saying the other day, things may be a bit smelly these days, but at least we don't have to put up with that sanctimonious little toad and his incessant wittering on about ideals any more. And you agreed with me, I remember. You said—'

'Er, Turkey,' said Sir Bedevere. 'I—'

'And now,' Sir Turquine protested, 'you get some-one all dressed up with a mask on or something, just to give me the fright of my life! Look at my pizzas, you stupid idiot, they've got fluff all over them . . .'

'It's me, Turkey,' Boamund whispered, in a tone of voice that would have frozen helium. 'How are you keeping?'

Turquine now dropped the portable telephone as well. 'My God,' he said, 'it is you! What in the name of . . .?'

Bedevere swallowed hard, stood up and, as briefly as

he could, explained. The other two knights exchanged looks that would have had a sabre-tooth tiger yelping for joy and growing an extra thick winter coat.

'Bollocks,' said Sir Turquine at last. 'He's got no authority. If he'd got any authority, he'd have a commission or something, sealed by that bastard Merlin. He's just having us on.'

Without speaking, Boamund reached inside his jacket and produced a thick, folded parchment, from which hung a seal. The odd thing about the seal was the way it glowed with a strong blue light.

Sir Turquine, whose mouth had suddenly become extremely dry, took the parchment and opened it. He stared at it for a moment and then said, in a kind of quavering roar, 'Nuts. It's in gibberish. He's just written it himself.'

'Tell Sir Turquine,' said Boamund quietly, 'that he's holding it the wrong way up.'

Sir Turquine glowered at him helplessly and turned the parchment round, so that the seal hung from the bottom. Boamund sniffed; Turquine could remember that damned supercilious sniff as though it were yesterday. He glanced down at the writing.

'Although,' Boamund went on, 'as I seem to remember, Sir Turquine was never exactly adept at reading. One seems to recall that when the rest of the class were halfway through the *Roman de la Rose*, Sir Turquine was still sitting at the back of the room saying "Pierre has a cat. The cat is fat. The fat cat sits on the—"'

'All right,' shouted Sir Turquine, 'commission or no commission, I'm going to kill him.'

Sir Bedevere hastily placed a hand on Turquine's

chest while Boamund said 'mat', very deliberately, sat down and ate an olive. Turquine gave a last infuriated snarl, threw the commission on the ground and jumped on it. Since it was, of course, enchanted parchment, all that happened was that his shoelaces broke.

Boamund smiled, that same smug, teeth-grindingly infuriating smile he'd had when he was Helm Monitor back in the sixth form, and made a little gesture with his left hand. Turquine, bright red in the face, snorted like a horse, knelt down, and extended his hands, their palms pressed together. Boamund, looking down his nose like an archbishop, stepped forward and pressed his palms to the backs of Turquine's hands, as lightly as possible; thus signifying that he had accepted Turquine's fealty. It didn't help to soothe Turquine's feelings to find that he'd knelt in one of his own pizzas.

'Arise, Sir Turquine, good and faithful knight,' said Boamund, obviously enjoying every moment of it. Turquine gave him a look you could have roasted a chicken on, made an obscure noise in the back of his throat, stood up and made a great show of brushing mozzarella off his right knee. Boamund turned to Sir Bedevere and made the same gesture.

Sir Bedevere hesitated, muttered, 'Oh, all right then,' and performed the same simple ceremony.

'And now, Sir Turquine,' said Boamund, 'you will kindly oblige me by retrieving my dwarf from wherever it was you put him.'

'I might have guessed it was your dwarf,' Turquine grumbled as he plodded to the kitchen. 'Funny the way that even when we were at school, some of us always seemed to have dwarves when the rest of us had to polish their own armour. 'Course, that came of some of us having great soft-hearted sissy mothers who wouldn't have their dear little boys hurting their hands with nasty rough . . .'

The kitchen door slammed behind him, and Boamund sighed. 'He always was inclined to whine a bit,' he observed, and Bedevere, never a man given to nostalgia, found himself harking back to the happy days of boyhood, when he'd gladly have given a whole week's pocket money for the chance of doing something unpleasant to young Snotty.

And then it occurred to him that, although young Snotty was exactly the sort of pompous little swot that Authority invariably made a prefect, nevertheless there was a sort of malign justice that had always ended up by landing him in the smelly, right up to the vambrace, even when (as was generally the case) it wasn't actually his fault.

Bedevere, having checked that Boamund wasn't looking, smirked. The way he saw it, the mills of the Gods may grind slow, but they don't half make a mess of you when the time comes.

Dwarfish society is well ordered and stable to the point of inflexibility, and the average dwarf generally knows his place* to within 0.06 of a micron. As a result, sudden promotion is something that dwarves are ill-equipped to deal with.

---

*Which is either in the kitchen or the armoury, depending on status, and, in either case, set behind a very big jar of metal polish.

Toenail was no exception. From being a lowly hermit's gopher, he had, at a stroke, risen to being Chief Factotum to a whole order of chivalry. The only other dwarf in the oral tradition of the race who'd ever achieved that distinction was Lord Whitlow King of Arms, who superintended the household of King Lot of Orkney in King Uther's time. It was an honour.

On the other hand, Toenail couldn't help feeling, Lord Whitlow probably had a few lesser dwarves to help him out, or at the very least a vacuum cleaner. And he couldn't be positive about this, because oral tradition can be a right little tease when it comes to matters of detail, but he had a feeling that Lord Whitlow probably got paid.

Boamund was all right, of course, as knights go – and Toenail was rapidly becoming an authority on knights. Not only had the new Grand Master paid him back for the petrol and the damage to the rear mudguard of the bike as soon as Toenail had found him the old teapot which served the Order as its exchequer, but he'd expressly forbidden Sir Turquine and Sir Pertelope (who was nearly as bad) to put him in the dustbin without authority, on pain of dishonour. Toenail wasn't sure what dishonour now meant in the context of the Order, but he guessed it was something to do with not being allowed to use the van at weekends. Given the trades which Turquine and Pertelope now followed, this was clearly a sanction of the utmost weight.

Of course, it was now Toenail's job to clean out the van every morning (which meant scrubbing caked-on tomato purée off the back seat and occasionally unloading cartons of Hungarian training shoes which

Lamorak had bought cheap and somehow forgotten to disembark himself), but that in itself was an honour, if one translated it into the terms of the Old Days. You'd had to be a pretty high-ranking dwarf to be Chief Groom and Lord High Equerry.

On balance, the first fortnight of the new state of affairs had gone off all right, so far as Toenail could judge. There had been a few tricky moments; Turquine, Lamorak and Galahaut the Haut Prince had mutinied and tried to ambush Boamund on his way back from the newsagent's, with a view to loading him with chains and casting him in the toolshed, but Bedevere (rather, Toenail had felt, against his better judgement) had betrayed the conspiracy, with the result that Boamund had foiled the plot by getting the number 6 bus instead of the number 15a. He had given them all a very stern talking-to in the Common Room after tea, following which Turquine had stalked out of the room and been very ostentatiously sick in the kitchen sink. Apart from that, however, a routine was developing. Basically, it consisted of the other five going out to work as usual, while Boamund sat in the Common Room with his feet up on the sofa and watched the snooker on the television. Boamund had taken to snooker very quickly, Toenail had noticed, and was talking freely of having a table installed in the garage, which would mean Lamorak finding a home for seven hundred pairs of flood-damaged Far Eastern jeans, fifty one-handed alarm clocks and all the rest of his stock-in-trade.

Toenail sighed and dipped his cloth in the metal polish. So far, Boamund's main effort in the direction of starting the quest up again had been ordering him to get all the armour and weapons from the cellar and polished up to tiltyard standard. That seemed to suit the other five, who he knew had no intention of giving up their settled if unprofitable lives just to go looking for that damned Grail thing; but Toenail, with a degree of perception that is not uncommon among dwarves, had a shrewd suspicion that things might change once the Embassy World Snooker Championship was over. Call it, Toenail said to himself, astrology.

He breathed a fine mist on to the surface of a shining gauntlet, polished it off on his trouser-leg, and added it to the pile. There was enough armour there to equip an army, and he hadn't even started on the horse-furniture yet. Mind you, he couldn't really see how there was going to be much call for that. A couple of sheets of corrugated iron welded on to the sides of the van was probably all that would be needed.

From the direction of the Common Room he could hear raised voices, and his genes told him that the Lords were holding a High Council.

Racial memory is very powerful among dwarves. Putting down his cloth, he tiptoed to the linen basket, raised the lid and jumped in.

'No,' said Turquine.

Boamund glowered at him and struck the table with his mace of office. Lamorak, who had forty-two others just like it in the lock-up, sighed. As he'd suspected at the time, they weren't solid teak at all.

'This,' Boamund said grimly, 'is mutiny.'

Turquine grinned. 'Well done, young Snotty,' he said. 'You're learning.'

'Mutiny,' Boamund went on, 'and treason. Unless

Sir Turquine immediately repents of his words, I shall have no alternative but to declare him dishonoured.'

'You try it,' Turquine replied, 'and see how far it'll get you. Because,' he added, with the confidence of strength, 'I don't need that clapped-out old scrapheap of a van any more. Look at this!' And, with a magnificent gesture, he threw a set of keys on the table. 'They're so pleased with me,' he said, 'they've let me drive the company van. And,' he added conclusively, 'it's a Renault. So you can take your honour and you can . . .'

Boamund's expression did not change. He simply leant forward, took the keys from the table, and put them in his pocket.

Turquine nearly fell over.

'Here,' he said, 'you can't do that, it's not my—'

'Agreed,' replied Boamund. 'It has now become the property of the Order. And you, Sir Turquine, are dishonoured. Now, then . . .'

There was uproar for a moment, what with Sir Turquine trying to explain that it didn't work like that, and Sir Lamorak and Sir Pertelope both simultaneously asking if they could have it for the weekend. Boamund silenced them all with a blow from the mace, the top of which came off and rolled under the sofa.

'Since Sir Turquine is no longer entitled to speak,' Boamund said, 'is there anyone else who wishes to express an opinion?'

There was a long silence, and then Galahaut the Haut Prince got up, rather sheepishly, and looked around.

'Look, Bo,' he said, 'you know, in principle I'm with you all the way about finding the Grail. One hundred per cent. I think finding the Grail is right for us, so let's do it, yes, fine. Only,' and he drew a deep breath, 'timing-wise, perhaps we could, you know, readjust our schedules a bit, because my agent says there's this bit in a dog-food commercial coming up . . .'

Boamund's face became ominous, but Galahaut seemed not to have noticed. 'It's a real opportunity for me,' he went on, 'to get myself established in dog-food work generally. They say they want me for the tall, good-looking man of mature years in a chunky Arran sweater who says that top breeders recommend it. Play your cards right, they said, this could be a second Captain Birds Eye.'

'No,' said Boamund. 'We leave in a week.'

Galahaut looked round the room reproachfully; but everyone happened to be looking the other way, apart from Turquine, who was sulking. 'Come on, Bo,' he said, 'this could be the break I've been waiting for. One really good commercial, it's better than a West End hit these days. Look at the Oxo woman,' he added.

'Who's Oxo?' Boamund asked.

The flame in Galahaut's eyes kindled for a moment, and then died away, to be replaced by an unmistakable flicker of guile. 'All right, then,' he said meekly, 'you're the boss. You can count on me.'

Very true, Boamund thought; I could count up to two on your faces alone, you devious little toad. I know what you're thinking, and we'll see about that. 'Anyone else?' he said.

Lamorak was getting to his feet, and Boamund narrowed his eyes. He'd been practising it in front of the mirror for days.

'And before Sir Lamorak addresses us,' he said, 'I should like to make it plain that I don't think we're going to find the Grail down the Portobello Road. So Sir Lamorak can jolly well unload all those boxes and things he put into the van when he thought my back was turned.'

Lamorak groaned. 'Oh, come on,' he said. 'It's got to be worth a try, Bo. You go to a street market these days, there's all sorts of old junk . . .'

'The Grail,' Boamund replied icily, 'is not old junk. It's—'

'Yes,' said Pertelope suddenly. 'What *is* it exactly? I'm sure we'd all be fascinated to hear.'

'Ah yes,' said Boamund, drawing the tip of his tongue around lips suddenly dry as sandpaper, 'I was hoping someone would ask me that.' He paused; and as he did so, a tiny snowflake of inspiration drifted into his mind.

He could lie.

'The Holy Grail,' he said, smoothly and confidently, 'is the cup, or rather chalice, from which Our Lord drank at the Last Supper. No doubt you remember the relevant passage in scripture, Pertelope? Or did you spend that lesson drawing little dragons in the margins of your breviary?'

The Grail Knights were sitting with their mouths open, staring at him. It was easy, this lying business. Gosh, yes . . .

'Anyway,' Boamund went on, 'the Grail is a fluted, double-handed cup wrought of the purest gold. Its body is inlaid with the richest gems, amethyst and chrysophrase, diamonds and rubies, and across the rim is engraved in letters that shine like fire . . . er . . .'

Five stunned faces watched him move his lips desperately, as he ransacked his brain for something appropriate. He closed his eyes, and the words came. In fact, they came so easily that you could almost believe . . .

'In letters,' he repeated briskly, 'that shine like fire:

IE SUI LE VRAY SANC GREAL

. . . if memory serves me correctly,' he added smugly. 'Any questions?'

There was a long, long silence. Finally, Pertelope stood up again. He was trying to look sceptical but his heart wasn't in it, you could tell.

'What was that again?' he asked.

Boamund repeated the text of the inscription. It sounded better and better. Maybe this was a what-you-call-it, miracle.

'Why's it in French?' Pertelope demanded. Something wobbled inside Boamund's stomach. He was about to say 'Er' when Pertelope continued.

'I mean,' he said, 'it ought to be in Latin, shouldn't it? All your religious stuff's always in Latin, so . . .'

Boamund smiled. He'd had time to think, and the words came smoothly from him.

'You forget, Sir Pertelope,' he said, 'that at Our Lord's passion the Grail was taken by Joseph of Arimathea and borne away by him to Albion, where,' he added cheerfully, 'as everyone knows, we speak French. Satisfied?'

Pertelope growled unhappily and sat down. In his place, Turquine got up. Although he was dishonoured and not allowed to speak, Boamund felt that a magnanimous Grand Master could allow himself to be flexible, especially if he could make old Turkey look a prize ass in front of the others. He nodded, therefore, and smiled.

'So this whacking great gold cup thing,' said Sir Turquine slowly, 'with all these jewels and what have you stuck in it, is the cup from the Last Supper, is it?'

Boamund's smile remained fixed, and he nodded. Much more of this, he thought, I could get a job hanging from someone's rear-view mirror.

'I see,' said Turquine. 'Times must have been good in the carpentry business back in Our Lord's time, if they could afford huge great gold cups with jewels and—'

'Thank you,' said Boamund, 'I think you've made your point. Naturally,' he said, 'at the moment of Christ's transmutation of the wine, the chalice too underwent a similar metamorphosis. Hence its present nature.'

Turquine sat down again, red-faced as a traffic light, while someone at the back sniggered. This time, however, Galahaut was on his feet.

'Great,' he said, 'that's clarified that one for us, no problem. But,' he added, nastily, 'you don't happen to have any idea where the thing is, do you? I mean, yes, it was brought to Albion by Joseph of – wherever it was you said – we're all agreed on that, but that was all rather a long time ago, don't you think? I mean, it could be anywhere by now.'

Boamund's smile became, if anything, a little bit wider. He really had hoped someone would ask him that.

'Sir Galahaut,' he said, with the air of a man who's just about to find his way into the dictionary of quotations, 'if it were not lost, we should not have to find it.'

There was silence again, and then a buzz of Yes-buts from the assembled knights. Boamund silenced them with a bang of the mace.

'Brothers,' he said, and ignored the voice at the back who asked who'd appointed him shop steward, 'when the ancient hermit gave me my commission, he also entrusted me with a parchment of great antiquity, which will surely guide us to the resting place of the Holy Grail. I have this same parchment . . .' He patted his inside pocket, frowned and started to rummage. Just then the kitchen door opened, and Toenail trotted through.

'Here it is,' he whispered. 'You left it in the back pocket of your brown cords. Just as well I looked through them before I put them in the washing-machine, because otherwise—'

'Yes, thank you,' Boamund said, 'you may go now. This parchment,' and he held it up for them all to see, 'will surely guide us to the spot.'

Pertelope was up yet again. 'Hold on,' he said. 'If that thing's so old, and says where the bloody thing is, then how come . . .?'

But the mood of the assembly had changed. Bedevere kicked him on the shins, while someone behind him told him to stop being such a clever little devil and sit down. With an appropriate flourish, Boamund broke the seal, opened the parchment and read it.

'Oh,' he said.

The Order of the Knights of the Holy Grail were not the first adventurers to seek out this fabulous and evocative item. Far from it.

To give only one example: in the seventeenth year of

the reign of King Ban of Benwick – Benwick, it should be explained, was a kingdom lying between Albion and Europe which to a large extent shared Albion's isolation from the rest of humanity and her devotion to magic and chivalry; it vanished into the sea shortly after Arthur's abdication, and tradition has it that this was a deliberate decision on the Benicians' part, to save their nation from ever becoming a mere federal part of the united states of mediocrity that made up the World. Since all known Benicians vanished with their kingdom it would be interesting to learn where this attractive little tale is supposed to have originated – a young Benician knight by the name of Sir Prime de Ganys was riding forth upon errantry one day when he came across a castle in the middle of a desolate land.

Since night was rapidly closing in and the young chevalier had strayed far from his path, he knocked at the gate of the castle and was admitted by the duty dwarf.

It turned out that the castellan of the castle was a beautiful damosel without a lord, who lived there all alone apart from twenty-seven tall, well-built young esquires and a small colony of dwarves, who had spacious and well-appointed quarters of their own at the bottom of a disused wellshaft. Sir Prime was ushered in to a splendid banquet, feasted on broiled duck with lapwing, and entertained by a quartet of dwarfish minstrels playing all the bits they could remember out of *Ma Beale Dame*.

Happening to fall into conversation with the castellan, Sir Prime discovered that the castle, which was large and rather a nuisance to keep up, was supposed to be the repository of the Holy Grail, left there hundreds of years previously by Joseph of Arimathea as security for a substantial Snakes and Ladders debt. The only problem was that, what with the castle being so big and so many of its rooms having to be shut up for most of the year, nobody could remember where the dratted thing had last been seen. Naturally, periodic attempts were made to find it; but since these searches tended to reveal nothing more cheerful than further outbreaks of dry rot and death-watch beetle, they were usually abandoned at an early stage. What was needed, the castellan continued, was a fearless young hero who wasn't easily cowed by the sight of huge patches of purple fungus growing out of the walls, who would make a thorough search of the place, find the Grail and thus provide the damosel with a nice capital sum with which to finance her dream of turning the old place into either an eventide home or a sports complex.

Sir Prime's imagination was fired by this entrancing tale, and he pressed the castellan for further details. She obligingly produced a complete set of plans and elevations, builders' estimates, grants of outline planning permission, detailed budgets, profit-and-loss projections prepared by her accountants, and a joint-venture agreement by which, for the investment of a paltry seventy thousand marks, the knight would be entitled to a forty-per-cent share in the equity, together with interest on capital and fifty per cent of net profits. Delighted, Sir Prime produced his cheque book, wrote out a draft for seventy thousand marks, signed the contract and at once fell into a deep slumber.

When he awoke, he found himself lying on the cold

fells. All trace of the castle, the castellan and his signed part of the contract had vanished. Furthermore, he seemed to have misplaced his gold crucifix and a number of other trifles of personal adornment.

As he rode homewards, he encountered an ancient hermit, to whom he related his strange and terrifying adventure. The hermit, controlling his laughter by stuffing the sleeve of his robe into his mouth, mumbled that Sir Prime would have appeared to have had the ill fortune to wander into the fabulous castle of Lyonesse. If that was the case, then the damosel was none other than La Beale Dame de Lyonesse, and the knight should count himself lucky to have got away with just being ripped off for seventy grand. Some poor fools, he explained, had fared far worse than that. Really stupid knights, for example, had been known to buy two weeks in July and August at Lyonesse for the rest of time; fortunately really classic suckers like that were as rare as virgins in a . . .

Predictably, Sir Turquine was the first to break the silence.

'What,' he asked, 'does it say?'

'Um,' Boamund replied.

'It says Um, does it?' replied Turquine. 'Gosh, how helpful.'

Boamund stared at the paper in his hands, oblivious even to Turquine. At last he cleared his throat and spoke, albeit in a rather high voice.

'I think it's probably a riddle of some sort,' he said. 'You know, like My first is in—'

'What,' said a voice from the back, 'does it say?'

Blushing fit to shame Aurora, Boamund replied, 'It's

a ... I don't know. It's like a sort of list. Or a recipe.' He thought for a moment. 'Or a receipt, maybe.' He scratched his head.

Turquine grinned. 'Give it here,' he demanded, and Boamund made no effort to resist when he grabbed at the paper. It was almost as if he wanted someone else to have the job of reading the thing out.

'Now,' said Turquine, 'what have we ...? Good Lord.'

Various knights urged him to get on with it. He bit his lip, and then read out:

'LE SANC GREAL: INSTRUCTIONS
The Apron of Invincibility
The Personal Organiser of Wisdom
The Socks of Inevitability

The first may be found where children are carried in pockets, and came with the *first* First Fleet.

The second may be found in the safe haven where time is money, where money goes but never returns, and in the great office under and beyond the sea.

The third, God's gift to the Grail Knights, may be found where one evening can last forever, in the domain of the best-loved psychopath under the arch of the sky, in the kingdom of the flying deer.

Armed with these, let the Grail Knight reclaim what is his, release Albion from her yellow fetters, and enjoy his tea without fear of the washing-up.'

At the back somebody coughed. At moments like this, somebody always does. 'I think young Snotty is right,' said Turquine at last. 'It's some sort of riddle.'

Bedevere closed his mouth with an effort, blinked and said, 'That bit about the safe haven. Rings a bell, don't you know.'

Five knights looked at him and he swallowed.

'Well,' he went on, 'reminds me of something I read once. Or perhaps I heard it on something. It's on the tip of my . . .'

'It's a tricky one, isn't it?' Lamorak ventured. 'Maybe there's someone we could ask, you know, a hermit or something. Anybody know a good hermit?'

'Read it again.'

Turquine obliged and this time there was a hail of suggestions, all made simultaneously. Eventually, Boamund restored order by hammering on the table with the mace.

'Gentlemen,' he said, stretching a point, 'we obviously can't decipher this. It's not our job. The cardinal rule is, knights don't think. So the next step is to find someone who can make sense of it all. Now then, in the old days, you'd ask a hermit, or an anchorite, or else you'd be riding along through the woods one morning, minding your own business, looking for a stray falcon maybe, and there'd be this old crone sitting beside the road. "Prithee master," she'd say, "carry me across yon river to my cottage." And you'd say . . .'

Somebody at the back urged him to get to the point. He pulled himself together.

'Anyway,' he continued, 'the point I'm trying to make is, that's what we'd have done *then*, but that was *then* and this is *now*. Right?'

Five heads nodded cautiously. This was either wisdom or the bleeding obvious, the problem is always to tell the two apart.

'So,' said Boamund, 'you lot know all about now. Who do you go to nowadays when you've got something you don't understand that needs explaining?'

'Yes?' said Miss Cartwright, briskly. 'Can I help you?' She smiled that toothpaste smile of hers, which any of the seasoned timewasters of Ventcaster would recognise as an invitation not to try her too high this morning. 'Something about a form you'd like me to explain to you?'

'That's right,' said Boamund, blushing slightly. Apart from the girl in the service station, who was clearly a person of no status, feudally speaking, and so didn't count, this was the first woman he'd spoken to in fifteen hundred years. 'Actually,' he said, 'before we get down to that part of it, there's just one thing . . .?'

It's one of them, Miss Cartwright's inner voice said to her, I can feel it in my water. 'Yes?' she said.

'Um,' Boamund replied. 'Only, do you have to be a citizen to get advice, or . . .?' He bit his lip, obviously embarrassed. 'You see, I'm not sure I qualify, because if a citizen's the same thing as what we call a burgher or a *burgoys de roy*, I'm not really one, being more your sort of knightly . . .'

One of the maxims that had always guided Miss Cartwright in her job was that the good adviser always answers the correct question, which may not necessarily have been the question the enquirer originally asked. Focusing on the word 'citizen', therefore, she reassured Boamund that the services of the Bureau were available to all, regardless of race, creed, nationality or colour, and it followed that you didn't have to be a British subject to use it.

'Ah,' said Boamund after a while, 'I think that's all right, then. Mind you,' he went on, 'I don't think I am a, what you said, British subject, because I'm not British, I'm Albionese, and as for the other part I don't really think I'm a subject, more a sort of—'

'What exactly was your enquiry?' asked Miss Cartwright. 'Something to do with a form, was it?'

'Oh yes,' Boamund said, 'that's right.'

Miss Cartwright looked at him. Sometimes you just have to guess. 'Housing Benefit?' she asked, basing the assumption on the leather jacket. 'Income Support?'

'What's Income Support?'

Now, said Miss Cartwright to herself, we're getting somewhere. She explained. She was used to explaining, and she did it quickly, clearly and concisely. When she had finished, there was no doubt that Boamund understood; but his reaction was – well, odd. It was as if he was surprised. Shocked even.

'Really?' he said at last.

'Yes,' said Miss Cartwright, breathing through her nose. 'Do you wish to claim Income Support, Mr . . .?'

Boamund's eyes showed that he was sorely tempted, but that his mother or someone like that had warned him about accepting money from strange women. He shook his head. 'It's this paper we've got,' he said. 'We'd like someone to—'

'A summons, maybe? A writ?'

Boamund nodded. He knew all about summonses and writs. Summonses and writs were the only way things got done in Albion. If, for example, King Arthur wanted the windows cleaned, he issued a summons by the Herald of Arms challenging all the window-cleaners of Albion to meet under the town cross at Caerleon on midsummer day and elect a champion. Or if he wanted an extra pint of gold top instead of silver top, he'd leave a writ for the milk-knight.

'Probably,' he said. 'Have a look and see what you think.'

From the inside pocket of his jacket he produced a thick parchment with what looked like a seal hanging off it. Miss Cartwright stared at it as if it were alive.

'Um,' she said, and opened it.

Some time later, she put it down and looked Boamund in the eye. She hated to admit it, even to herself, but there was something about this lunatic that gave her the horrible, creeping feeling that he was for real. You couldn't *pretend* to be as weird as that and still be convincing; it would be like trying to pretend you were dead.

In circumstances like these, there is a well-established procedure. One finds the most junior member of staff and leaves him to get on with it. Miss Cartwright rose, smiled, asked Boamund if he'd mind waiting, and walked hurriedly into the inner office.

'George,' she said, 'be a love and see to that man in the leather jacket for me.'

Oddly enough, George was grinning from ear to ear. 'Sure,' he said. 'Thanks.'

As he jumped down from his chair and scampered across to the door, Miss Cartwright scratched her head and wondered. It was all very well, she said to herself, making a conscious effort to recruit handicapped and disabled people, but she still couldn't get used to working with someone who was only three foot four. You were always worried about, well, treading on him.

Boamund was just starting to wonder what was going on when he caught sight of a dwarf coming out of the back office. He smiled. It had been the right place to come to after all.

'Hello,' said the dwarf, 'You're a knight, aren't you?'

'Yes,' said Boamund.

'It's not hard to tell,' replied the dwarf, 'if you know what to look for. My name is Harelip, but you'd better call me George while there are people about. People can be very funny about names, Mr . . .'

'Boamund,' said Boamund. 'Look, we've got this document thing and we can't understand it.'

'By we,' said George, 'you mean . . .?'

'Me and my Order,' Boamund said, 'Knights of the Holy Grail.'

George raised an eyebrow. 'You don't say?' he said. 'My great-uncle-to-the-power-of-thirty-seven was dwarf to a Sir Pertelope who was a Grail Knight.'

'Still going strong,' Boamund assured him. 'Fancy that.'

'It's a small world,' George agreed. 'Well,' he added, looking down at the gap between himself and the floor, 'not as far as I'm concerned, obviously, but you know what I'm driving at. Can I see the document?'

Boamund nodded and handed it over. George read it carefully, occasionally making notes on his scratch-pad. Finally he handed it back and smiled.

'Fine,' he said. 'Congratulations. So what's the problem?'

Boamund blinked a couple of times. 'Well, what does it mean, for a start?' he said.

'Oh, I see,' said George, 'I was forgetting, yes. I can

see that to a knight it might present problems.'*

'So?'

'So,' said George, 'basically, it's a list of three things which you and your knights have got to find before you can hope to recover the Grail. They are an apron, a personal organiser – like a sort of notebook – and a pair of socks. They're hidden in remote and inaccessible places. Okay so far?'

Boamund nodded. He had the glorious feeling that at last things were getting back to normal.

'There are cryptic clues as to where these things are to be found,' George went on, wiping his nose with the back of his wrist. 'Now I'm not really allowed to help you too much . . .'

'Why not?'

'King's Regulations,' explained the dwarf. 'However, I can drop hints.'

'Such as?'

'Such as . . .' replied the dwarf, and he went on to drop several very large hints. In fact, compared to the dwarf Harelip's hints, the Speaking Clock is a paragon of obscurity.

'I see,' said Boamund. 'Right. Thanks.'

---

*Dwarves are, of course, naturally gifted at solving riddles, explaining conundrums, cracking codes and doing crossword puzzles. Partly, this is because they are, by their very nature, fey and uncanny creatures, much more at home inside the Glass Mountain than outside. The other reason is that, being too short to reach the pool table and too weak to be able to throw a dart, there's nothing else for them to do in the pub on their night off.

'Don't mention it,' said the dwarf. 'A pleasure. Remember me to Sir Pertelope. Tell him he owes my great-uncle-to-the-power-of-thirty-seven three farthings.'

'How is your great-uncle-to-the-power-of-thirty-seven?'

'Dead.'

'I'm sorry to hear that.'

'These things happen,' replied the dwarf. 'Anyway, never mind. Could you just sign here?'

From his inside pocket he produced an official-looking form.

'What's that?' Boamund asked.

'My discharge,' the dwarf replied happily. 'You see, my family's been indentured to the Grail Knights for generations. We're obliged to do so many hours of service before the indenture is up. My great-uncle-to-the-power-of-thirty-seven had done all his time except for ten minutes when King Arthur abdicated and the Orders of Chivalry came to an end. We've been . . .' The dwarf shuddered slightly. '. . . hanging about ever since, waiting for an opportunity to get all square. And now, thanks to you, we can call it a day and retire. Lucky you came along, really.'

'Very,' Boamund agreed, signing the form with a big X.

'Or rather,' George said, 'Destiny. Yours and mine. Ciao. Good hunting.'

He folded the form, reclaimed his pen (which Boamund had absent-mindedly put in his pocket), bowed thrice to the Four Quarters and jumped off his chair. In the middle of the room, where just a moment ago there had been a display of Family Credit leaflets, the Glass Mountain appeared, blue and sparkling. A door slid open and the dwarf stepped in, waving.

'Fancy that,' Boamund said, and smiled. The way he saw it, the world he was in now was a huge, muddled heap of inexplicable things with just the occasional glimpse of normality showing through. Still, it was nice to know it was still there really; important things, like Destiny and the Unseen. He was, deep down, a rational man and it would take a damn sight more than the odd microwave oven and radio alarm clock to get him really worried.

He picked up the Instructions, smiled at a bucket-mouthed, gibbering Miss Cartwright, and left.

'Right,' said Boamund.

Leadership is a volatile, almost chimerical quality. The same aspects of a man's character that tend to make him a natural leader of men usually also conspire to make him an unmitigated pain. Cortes, for example, who overthrew the fabulously powerful empire of Mexico with four hundred and fifty men, fifteen horses and four cannons, was an inspirational general, but that didn't prevent his devoted followers from wincing in anticipation every time he rubbed his hands together, smiled broadly, and said, 'All right, lads, this is going to be easier than it looks.' In Boamund's case, all his undoubted drive and energy couldn't make up for the fact that he prefaced virtually every statement he made by hitting the palm of one hand with the knuckles of the other and saying, 'Right.' That, in the eyes of many of his men, was calculated to raise their morale to lynching-point.

'The plan,' Boamund went on, 'is this. We split up into three parties of two, we find these three bits of tackle, we bring them back, we find the Grail. Easy as that. Any questions?'

'Yes,' said Lamorak. 'Who's having the van?'

'Which van?' interrupted Pertelope. 'We've got two now, remember?'

'No we haven't, you clown,' shouted Turquine. 'I keep telling you—'

'Shut up, you, you're dishonoured.'

'Don't you tell me . . .'

Boamund frowned. 'Quiet!' he shouted, and banged the top of the orange box which had been brought in to replace the table. 'If you'd been listening,' he went on, 'it'd have sunk in that it's really academic who gets the van, since we're all of us going thousands of miles beyond the shores of Albion. The van is neither here nor—'

'All right,' Lamorak replied, 'except it's my turn, *I* haven't been dishonoured, so I think it's only fair . . .'

Boamund sighed. 'Nobody's getting the van,' he said. 'All right?'

There was a ripple of murmuring, the general sense of which was that so long as nobody had it, that would have to do. Boamund banged the orange box again.

'Now then,' he said, 'the next thing to do,' and he turned up the radiance of his smile to full volume, masking the disquiet in his heart, 'is to decide who's going to go with who. Shut up!' he added, pre-emptively.

The knights stared at him.

'The pairings I've got in mind,' he said, 'are: Lamorak and Pertelope; Turquine and Bedevere; me and Galahaut. Any objections?'

He braced himself for the inevitable squall of discontent. It would, he reckoned, be school all over again. I'm not playing with *him*. We don't want *him* on *our* team. Wait for it . . .

Nobody said anything. Boamund blinked, and went on.

'Deployment as follows: Lammo and Perty, the apron; Turkey and Bedders, the personal organiser thing; Gally and me, the socks. Any objections?'

They're up to something, Boamund thought. They've never agreed to anything without a fight in their lives. They must be up to something.

His mind wandered back to the Old Boys Joust of '6, when he'd been Vice-Captain of tilting, and the Captain, old Soppy Agravaine, had twisted his ankle in a friendly poleaxe fight with the Escole des Chevaliers seconds, leaving him, for the first and only time, to pick the teams. As his memory swooped back on that day like a homing pigeon, he could almost feel the hot tears of shame and humiliation on his cheeks once more as he'd watched them going out, in deliberate defiance of his Team Orders, wearing their summer haubergeons with rebated zweyhanders and Second XI surcoats. They'd pretended to agree with him, he remembered, and then when the moment came, they'd just gone and done as they jolly well chose. Well, not this time. He was ready for them.

'Well,' he said, 'that's fine. Now, here are your sealed orders,' he went on, handing out the envelopes, 'and you're all to promise on your words of honour not to open them until after you've left the chapter house. And,' he added, 'the three parties will leave at fifteen-minute intervals, just to make sure.'

'Make sure of what, Snotty?' asked Turquine innocently. Boamund let his lip curl just a millimetre or so, and smiled.

'Just to make sure, that's all,' he said. 'Any questions?'

No questions.

'Splendid,' he said. 'All right, dismiss.' He sat down and started to go over the packing list one last time.

The other knights filed out, leaving him alone. He was halfway through his list when Toenail came in. He looked furtive.

'Psst,' he whispered.

There are people who simply can't resist conspiratorial noises, and Boamund was one of them. 'What?' he whispered back.

Toenail looked round to see if any of the knights were listening, and then hissed, 'You know those envelopes you gave them?'

Boamund nodded.

'You know,' the dwarf went on, 'they weren't supposed to open them until after they'd left here?'

Boamund nodded again.

'Well,' said Toenail, 'they're all out there now, reading them. I, er, thought you ought to know.'

Boamund smiled. 'I thought they'd do that,' he said. 'That's why I didn't give them the *real* envelopes.'

'Oh.' Toenail raised an eyebrow. 'They looked like real envelopes to . . .'

Boamund frowned. 'Yes, of course they're real *envelopes*,' he said impatiently. 'Only the message in them isn't the real message.'

'It isn't?'

Boamund allowed himself a sly chuckle. 'Oh no,' he

said. 'All it says is, *Shame on you, you're dishonoured.* That'll teach them.'

Oh God, thought Toenail to himself, and I've got to go on a quest with these lunatics. 'Then why,' he asked, as nicely as he could, 'did you give them the envelopes now?'

'Because I knew they'd open them.'

'But,' replied the dwarf cautiously, 'if you knew *that . . .*'

'And,' Boamund went on, 'this way, they'll know that I knew they'd open them, and that way, they'll know they're all rotters, and then we'll all know where we are, do you see?' And Boamund grinned triumphantly. 'I think they call that man management,' he added.

Not where I come from they don't, sunshine, Toenail said to himself. 'Ah,' he replied. 'Man management. Right, sorry to have bothered you.'

He bowed slightly and went back into the kitchen, where the other knights were sitting on the worktops waiting for him.

'You're right,' he said. 'He has gone stark raving bonkers.'

'Told you so,' said Turquine. 'Right, the way I see it, there's nothing in the book of rules says that you've got to obey a Grand Master who's gone round the twist. I vote we tie him up, chuck him in the cellar and get back to normal.'

Bedevere held up his hand.

'Okay,' he said, 'point taken, he's acting a bit funny. But—'

'A bit funny!' Turquine snorted. 'Come on, Bedders, face facts. Young Snotty's finally broken his spring. Had to happen, sooner or later. Trouble with

Snotty is, his head's too small for his brain. Leads to an intolerable build-up of pressure, that does, and you end up going potty. I'll just go and get some rope, and ...'

Bedevere remained firm. 'Hold on, Turkey,' he said quietly. 'Just because Bo's behaving a bit oddly, that doesn't mean we should abandon the quest, does it, chaps?'

Four pairs of eyebrows lifted as one. Having got their attention, Bedevere slid down off the worktop, helped himself to a biscuit from the jar, and went on.

'What I'm getting at,' he said, 'is, sooner or later we've got to find the ruddy thing, or we're all going to be here for ever and ever. Right?'

Silence. Bowed heads. Bedevere cleared his mouth of crumbs and continued.

'Precisely,' he said. 'So, just when we're all getting a bit slack and not really with it any more, what with Nentres going off like that and taking the ... Anyway, who should turn up but young Bo, with this really quite exciting clue thing, and actually knowing what a Grail *is*, for Heaven's sake. You've got to admit, it gets you wondering. Well, it does me, anyway. Can't be co-incidence.'

From the unwonted silence, Sir Bedevere deduced that his colleagues conceded he had a point. He continued briskly.

'What I'm trying to get at, chaps, is that, all right, Bo's as potty as they come, but so what? We've got the clue, we know what a Grail is, let's all jolly well go out and look for the blessed thing. And,' he added forcefully, 'I for one think the best way to go about it is the way Bo says, splitting up and getting all these socks and things. Must be right,' he said. 'That clue thing said so. Well?'

The knights looked at him shame-faced.

'But Bedders,' said Pertelope, almost pleading, 'he's barmy.'

'So was Napoleon,' Bedevere replied.

'No he wasn't.'

'Well, then,' Bedevere answered, 'Alexander the Great, then. Lots of great leaders are a bit funny in the head, well-known fact. That's what makes them great. Not,' he added, 'that I'm saying Bo's great. All I'm saying is, we don't want to make asses of ourselves just because he's an ass. That'd be silly, don't you think?'

Turquine growled. 'So he's let you have the van, has he?' he snarled contemptuously. 'Typical.'

Bedevere ignored him. 'Come on, chaps,' he said, 'let's vote on it. All those in favour.' Four hands, including his own. 'Against.' One hand. 'That's settled, then. Go on, Turkey, be a sport.'

'All right, then,' Turquine grumbled. 'Just don't blame me, that's all.'

Bedevere grinned. 'Certainly not,' he said, 'we can blame Bo. That,' he said, sagely, 'is what leaders are for.'

It was a ship.

Oh *good*, said Danny Bennett to himself, now I won't have to die after all. What a relief that is.

For the last six days, ever since the pirate-radio ship *Imelda Marcos* hit an iceberg and sank, Danny had been wondering whether, career-wise, his sideways move from BBC television into commercial radio had been entirely sensible. On the one hand, he told himself, as he lay on his back in the inflatable dinghy and stared at the sun, I had my own show, complete editorial freedom, unlimited expense account and the chance to develop a whole new approach to radio drama; on the other hand, Bush House didn't start shipping water the moment anything hit it.

In the last few panic-stricken minutes of the ship's life, Danny had been so busy choosing his eight gramophone records that the rest of the crew got fed up waiting for him and shoved off with the lifeboat. To make things worse, there was no portable record player. They don't make them any more, apparently.

And now, just as he was reproaching himself for neglecting to pack any food and water, here was a ship sailing directly towards him. How reassuring, Danny muttered to himself, as he propped his emaciated body up on one elbow and waved feebly. Somebody up there must like me.

The ship drew closer, and a head appeared over the side. 'Ahoy!' it shouted. 'Excuse me, but am I all right for the International Date Line? There hasn't been a signpost or anything for simply ages.'

'Help,' Danny replied.

'Sorry?'

'I said help.'

The head was female, thirtyish, blonde, nice eyes. 'Fair enough,' it said. 'Would you like to buy some unit trusts?'

Danny made a peculiar noise at the back of his throat; imagine the sound of a bathful of mercury emptying away down the plughole, and you might get some idea.

'Unit trusts,' the head repeated. 'It's a very simple

idea, really. You pay a capital sum to the fund managers, and they invest your money in a wide range of quoted equities, which . . .'

'Yes,' Danny croaked, 'I do know what unit trusts are, thank you very much. Have you got any water?'

The head looked round at the infinite vastness of the sea. 'I think there's plenty for everyone,' it said. 'Why?'

'Fresh water,' Danny said. 'Drinking water.'

'Oh, *that* sort. Perrier, stuff like that?'

'It'd do.'

'Sorry, we're right out, all we have is gin. If you're not interested in unit trusts, how about a personal equity plan? There are several really excellent products available at the moment which I would unhesitatingly recommend. For instance . . .'

'All right,' Danny said, dragging breath into his lungs, 'food. I haven't eaten for three days.'

'Oh.' The head frowned. 'Does that mean you haven't got any money? Because if you don't, I can't see that there's a great deal of point in continuing with this discussion, do you?'

Danny cackled wildly. 'I've got plenty of money,' he said. 'I've got two years' back pay from Radio Imelda, for a start. What I haven't got is—'

'A flexible pension scheme tailored to *your* needs and aspirations, I'll be bound,' interrupted the head, nodding. 'Now I think I can help you there, because it so happens that I'm an agent for Lyonesse Equitable Life, and there's one particular package . . .'

'Can you eat it?'

The head emitted a silvery laugh. 'Alternatively,' it went on, 'I could do you a very nice index-linked Lyonesse Provident Flexible Annuity Bond, which would provide access to capital as well as a guaranteed rate of income, paid monthly, with a very competitive tax position. Interested?'

Danny shook his head. 'Maybe you're missing the point here,' he said. 'Here I am, cast adrift in an open boat, dying of hunger and thirst . . .'

'Ah,' said the head, 'got you. What you're really concerned about here is some really constructive inheritance tax planning, possibly involving the creation of an offshore trust. Silly of me not to have realised that before.'

'But I don't *want* to die,' Danny screamed. I—'

'Well,' said the head patiently, 'in that case we can adapt the package to allow maximum flexibility by making the fullest possible use of the annual exempt giftable sum. I wish you'd said, by the way. I hate to rush you, but time is money, you know. Now . . .'

Danny sank back into the dinghy and groaned. The head peered back over the rail at him.

'Hello?' it said. 'Is that a deal, then?'

'Go away.'

'Pardon?'

'I said go away. Bog off. Sink.'

'I don't think I quite heard you. You do want the pension policy, don't you?'

'No.'

The head looked shocked. 'You *don't*?'

'No.'

'Really?'

'Really.'

'Well!' The head wrinkled its brows. 'Suit yourself, then. Look, if you change your mind, you can always fax us on 0553 . . .'

Danny rolled over on his face and started to scream; he was still screaming nine hours later, when he was picked up by the captain of an oil tanker. When he told the captain of the tanker about his experiences with the strange ship, the captain nodded grimly.

'I know,' he said, and shuddered. 'I've seen it myself. *The Flying Channel-Islander*, we call it.'

Danny was half-dead from dehydration and exposure, but he was still a journalist, and a story is a story. 'Tell me about it,' he said.

'It's horrible,' the captain replied, crossing himself. 'Really terrible things happen to people who sight her.' He paused, his eyes closed. 'Terrible things,' he repeated.

'Such as?'

'Well,' the captain replied, 'some of them die, some of them go mad, some of them live perfectly normally for five or six years and then run amok with machetes. Some simply vanish. Some of them . . .'

'Yes?'

'Some of them,' said the captain grimly, 'even go and buy the insurance.'

3

 Between the town of Giles, to the north of the Tomkinson Range, and Forrest in the Nullarbor Plain, lies the Great Victoria Desert. It is hot, arid, desolate and merciless; and whatever the Creator had in mind when He made it that way, it most certainly wasn't human beings.

It's a really awful place to be if you've got toothache.

'I've got some oil of cloves in my rucksack,' said Sir Pertelope. 'Supposed to be very good, oil of cloves. Never seemed to do me any good, mind you, but maybe I'm just over-sensitive to pain.'

'Mmmm,' replied his companion.

'There's some aspirin in the first-aid kit, of course,' Pertelope went on, 'but I wouldn't recommend that, because it's water-soluble, and since we've run out of water . . .'

'Mmmm.'

'Needless to say,' Pertelope continued helpfully, 'if

84

we found some water it'd be a different matter altogether. But somehow...' He looked up briefly into the steel-blue sky and then turned his head quickly away. 'Now my aunt Beatrice used to say that sucking a pebble—'

'Shut up,' said Sir Lamorak.

Offended, Pertelope shifted his rucksack on his shoulders and pointedly walked a few yards to the east. Then he stopped.

'If that's north,' he said, pointing due south, 'then England is seventeen thousand miles away over that big jutting rock over there. Fancy that,' he added. He stood for a moment in contemplation; then he shrugged and started to walk; for the record, due west.

They were trying to get to Sydney.

For two men who had alighted from an airliner in Brisbane several months before, this shouldn't have been too great a problem. True, neither of them had been to Australia before, but they had taken the precaution of buying railway tickets, advance-booking their hotels and securing copies of *What's On In Sydney* before leaving England. Their problems had started at Brisbane Airport, when Pertelope had left the little bag containing all the paperwork behind on the airport bus.

No problem, Pertelope had explained. All we have to do is hitch a lift. The Australians are a notoriously friendly, hospitable people who take pleasure in helping travellers in distress.

Sixteen hours along the road, they had indeed managed to hitch a ride on a truckful of newly slaughtered carcasses as far as St George, where the lorry driver had finally thrown them forcibly from the cab after Pertelope had insisted on singing *Vos Quid Admiramini* in his usual nasal drone. After a short pause to regroup and eat the last of the bag of mint imperials that Lamorak had bought at Heathrow, they had set out to walk as far as Dirranbandi. It's hard to explain concisely how they came to be thirteen hundred miles off course; the best that can be done without embarking on a whole new book is to explain that in the back of Sir Pertelope's National Trust Diary was a map of the world; and that although Pertelope had heard about Columbus and the curvature of the earth, he had never been entirely convinced. The central premise of his navigational theory, therefore, was that the centre of the world lay at Jerusalem, and that maps had to be interpreted accordingly.

Pertelope looked at his watch. 'What do you say to stopping here for lunch?' he asked. 'We could sit under that rock over there. It's got a lovely view out over the, er, desert.'

Although Death had been trailing them pretty closely every step of the way, in the manner of a large fat pigeon outside a pavement cafe, the nearest he had come to cutting two more notches in his scythe handle had been fifty miles west of the Macgregor Range, where Pertelope had inadvertently knocked over the rusty beer-can containing the last of their water while doing his morning exercises. They had wandered round in circles for two days and collapsed; but they were found by a party of wandering aborigines, whom Lamorak was able to persuade that his library ticket was in fact an American Express card, and who had sold them a gallon of water and six dried lizards in return, as it turned out, for the right to borrow three fiction and three non-fiction titles every week from the Stirchley Public Library in perpetuity. From then on, it had simply been a matter of lurching from one last-minute borehole to another, and sneaking up very quietly indeed on unsuspecting snakes.

Pertelope had, however, refused to harm the Paramatta horned python they'd finally caught after a six-hour scramble among the rocks of Mount Woodroffe, pointing out that it was an endangered species. It was shortly afterwards that Lamorak's upper left molar started to hurt.

'Now then, let's see,' said Pertelope. 'There's . . .' He unslung his rucksack and started to go through its contents (three clean shirts, three changes of underwear, a copy of *What's On In Sydney* with a bookmark stuck in to mark the details of the New Orleans Jazz Festival, a Swiss Army knife with six broken blades, an electric razor, a pair of trousers, a tennis racket, a mouth organ, two flannels, a towel, Germolene, oil of cloves, a packet of plasters, a bottle of dandruff shampoo, entero-vioform tablets, nail scissors, a quantity of ladies clothing . . .).

'What have you got in your pack, Lammo?' Pertelope enquired. 'I seem to be fresh out.'

Lamorak unshipped his head from his hands, said, 'Nothing,' and put it back.

'Oh.' Pertelope frowned and scratched his head. 'That's awkward,' he added. 'I suppose we'll have to look for roots and berries and things.' He looked round at the baked, sterile earth. It had been a very long time since anything had been so foolhardy as to entrust its roots to so hostile an environment.

'Pertelope.'

Sir Pertelope looked up. 'Yes?' he asked.

'There's always cannibalism, you know.'

Pertelope blinked. 'Cannibalism?' he repeated.

'That's right,' said his companion calmly. 'You know, eating human flesh. It used to be quite popular at one time.'

Pertelope thought for a moment, and then shook his head.

'I wouldn't dream of it,' he replied firmly. 'Not after all we've been through together. You'd stick in my throat, so to speak.'

Lamorak stood up. 'That's all right,' he said quietly. 'I quite understand. Now then, if you keep absolutely still it won't hurt a bit.'

A small cog dropped into place in Pertelope's brain. 'Hold on,' he said. 'A joke's a joke, but let's not get silly. I mean, people can get hurt larking about, and . . .'

Lamorak smiled, and lunged at him with a small stone. Hunger, thirst and toothache had taken quite a lot out of him, but he only missed by inches. He landed in the dust, swore and raised himself painfully from the ground.

'Lizards,' Pertelope was saying. 'I'm sure there're plenty of lizards about, if only we knew what we were supposed to be looking for. Trouble is, the little so-and-sos are masters of camouflage. Would you believe it, there's one species of lizard in the New Hebrides . . .'

He leant sideways, and the haymaking blow Lamorak had aimed at him wasted its force in the dry air.

'Shut up about sodding lizards and help me up,' Lamorak growled. 'I think I've twisted my ankle.'

'It's your own fault,' Pertelope replied, 'lashing out at people with whopping great rocks like that. Anyone would think . . .'

Lamorak jumped to his feet, thereby giving the lie to his own earlier statement, and tried a full-length tackle. As his full length was only a little more than five feet, he failed.

'Lamorak,' said Pertelope sternly, 'you do realise you're making a most frightful exhibition of yourself. What would a passing stranger think if he saw you now?'

'Depends,' Lamorak panted in reply. 'If he knew what I'd had to put up with from you ever since we left Birmingham, *Bloody good luck to you*, probably.' He hurled the rock, which landed about two feet away, and then sat heavily down.

'Really!' said Pertelope, offended.

Lamorak drew in a deep breath, looked for a moment at his scuffed and bleeding palms, and sighed. 'Tell you what,' he said. 'We'll make a deal. You take the compass, the map, your rucksack, my rucksack, the whole lot, and I'll stay here and die in peace. How does that sound?'

Pertelope shook his head. 'Don't you worry,' he said cheerfully. 'I'm not just going to up and leave you, you can count on that?'

'Really?'

'Really.'

Lamorak nodded, and then stretched out his trembling hand for the rock once more. Pertelope kicked it away, and then went and sulked under a sand dune.

It didn't last, though; Pertelope's sulks never did. Thus, when Lamorak had just fallen asleep and was already dreaming rapturously of a swimming pool full of frosted beer surrounded by club sandwiches, Pertelope sat down a few judicious feet away, extended his right leg and prodded his companion in the ribs.

'Never mind,' he said. 'Something'll turn up, you'll see.'

Lamorak groaned feebly and turned on his side. Pertelope shuffled a little nearer.

'Apart from lizards,' he said, 'there's snakes, and a sort of small bird. Actually they're quite rare these days, because of the erosion of their natural environment by toxic industrial waste; so we'll only eat those as a *very* last resort. But like I said, there's lizards and . . .'

'Mnnn.'

'Or perhaps,' Pertelope continued, 'we'll be rescued by a party of wandering aborigines, although really you shouldn't call them that, because really they're a very ancient and noble culture, with a very sophisticated neo-mystical sort of religion that makes them in tune with the earth and things. Apparently . . .'

'Pertelope,' Lamorak said, 'I'm lying on a packing case.'

'Well then, move a bit. I read somewhere that they can walk for days at a time, just singing, and come out precisely where they intended to go, just by harmonising their brainwave patterns to the latent geothermal energies of . . .'

'It says Tinned Peaches, Pertelope.'

'Sorry?'

'On the lid,' Lamorak replied. 'There's a label saying Tinned Peaches.'

There was a momentary pause.

'What did you say?' Pertelope enquired.

'Oh for Christ's sake,' Lamorak shouted. 'Come over here and look for yourself.'

Between them they scrabbled the half-buried case out of the ground, and broke the screwdriver blade of Pertelope's Swiss Army knife levering off the lid.

The crate was full of tins of peaches.

'Quick,' Lamorak hissed, 'Give me the bloody penknife.' He grabbed it and feverishly flicked at the tin-opener attachment with his brittle thumbnail.

'Hang on,' said Pertelope, turning a tin round in his hands. 'I'm sorry, Lammo, but we can't eat these. It's a pity, but . . .'

Lamorak froze. 'What the hell do you mean, we can't eat them?' he said. 'Okay they're a bit rusty, but . . .'

Pertelope shook his head. 'It's not that,' he said firmly. 'Look, see what's written here on the label. Produce of South Africa. I'm afraid . . .'

Lamorak gave him a very long look, and then put the penknife down.

'That's it,' Pertelope said. 'I know it's hard luck, but what I always say is, principles are principles, and it's no good only sticking to them in the good times, because . . .'

He was still talking when Lamorak hit him with the tin.

The Fruit Monks of Western Australia are one of the few surviving branches of the great wave of crusading monasticism that originated shortly after the fall of Constantinople in 1205. The Templars, Hospitallers and Knights of St John have largely disappeared, or been subsumed into other organisations and lost their identity; but the *Monachi Fructuarii* still cling to their ancient way of life, and their Order remains basically the same as it did in the days of its founder, St Anastasius of Joppa.

Legend has it that St Anastasius, inspired by the example of the soldier who gave Christ the vinegar-soaked sponge on the cross, set up his first fruit-juice stall beside the main pilgrimage route from Antioch to Jerusalem in 1219. By the middle of the thirteenth century, the brightly coloured booths of the Order were a familiar sight the length and breadth of the Holy Land; and after the Fall of Acre ended the Crusader presence in the Middle East, the monks turned their attention to the other desert places of the earth. Dwindling manpower has, of course, severely limited their operations, so that nowadays they have to be content with depositing cases of canned fruit at random points, relying on Providence to guide wandering travellers to them.

In 1979, the Order was taken over by an Australian-based multinational food chain, and coin-operated dispenser machines are gradually replacing the simple wooden packing cases; but the process of rationalisation is far from complete, even now.

It was a suitable moment for reconciliation.

'Have a tinned peach,' Lamorak said. 'If it helps at all, it doesn't *taste* South African.'

Pertelope raised his head, and lowered it again almost immediately.

'What hit me?' he enquired.

Lamorak shrugged. 'You're not going to believe this,'

he said through fruit-crammed cheeks, 'but it was a tin of peaches.'

'It was?'

Lamorak nodded. 'Probably fell out of a passing aeroplane. Or maybe they've got a serious peach glut problem here, something to do with the Common Agricultural Policy. Anyway, it fell on you, and out you went like a light. Pity,' he added, 'that Sir Isaac Newton's already scooped you on gravity, otherwise you could be quids in. Never mind,' he concluded, and burped.

'Lammo,' Pertelope whispered, 'I'm hungry.'

'I can believe that,' his companion replied. 'Pity you can't eat these peaches, really, because . . .'

There was a silence, broken only by the sound of Lamorak's jaws. For a man with serious toothache, he seemed to be able to cope perfectly well with the chewing process.

'I've heard it said,' Pertelope ventured cautiously, 'that a lot of tinned stuff that's supposed to come from South Africa is only tinned there. It's actually grown in the Front Line states, apparently.'

Lamorak nodded. 'Well-known fact,' he replied. 'I read it somewhere,' he added confidently. 'Dirty trick, if you ask me.'

'Absolutely,' Pertelope agreed; and then said, 'How do you mean?'

'Economic sabotage,' replied his companion, shaking his head. 'The Pretoria regime puts their fruit in South African tins so's nobody'll buy it, thus undermining their economic development. It's time people did something about it.'

'Yes. Um. Like what?'

'Like eating the fruit,' said Lamorak, handing him the tin. 'That'll teach them, eh?'

About half an hour later the two knights collapsed, surrounded by empty tins, and lay still.

'We'd better bury them, you know,' Pertelope murmured.

'Sorry?'

'The tins. Can't just leave them lying about. Pollution.'

Lamorak thought about it. 'In theory,' he replied.

'I mean,' Pertelope continued, 'this is one of the few completely unspoilt natural environments left. We owe it to the next generation . . .'

'Yes,' Lamorak muttered, casting an eye across the desert landscape, 'right. Unspoilt.' He shuddered slightly. 'You get on with it, then. I'm just going to get a few minutes' sleep.'

He rolled on to his back and closed his eyes. Then he sat bolt upright and grabbed Pertelope's arm.

'Bloody hell fire,' he hissed, and pointed. 'Look, Per, over there.'

Pertelope narrowed his eyes. 'Where, Lammo?'

'There.'

'Oh, yes, right. What am I supposed to be looking for?'

Lamorak ignored him. 'We've found one, Per. We've found a bloody unicorn.'

Pertelope's jaw dropped. 'Where?' he whispered.

'Oh for crying out loud.'

On the edge of a small escarpment, about five hundred yards away, the unicorn stopped, lifted its head and sniffed. For a minute or so it stood like a statue, its ears and nostrils straining; then its head dropped once again, and its tail swished rhythmically to and fro, although there were no flies for it to dispel. Its lips brushed the sand at just the level grass would have been growing at, had any grass been so ill-advised as to try and survive in a totally dehydrated environment.

'Oh, I see,' Pertelope gasped. 'Lammo, it *is* a unicorn. That's the most incredible—'

'Yes, right, fine,' Lamorak muttered. He was trying to get his binoculars out of his rucksack while at the same time remaining perfectly still, and the strap had caught in something. 'Just keep quiet, will you, while I . . .'

'It has a golden horn,' Pertelope crooned, 'growing out of the middle of its forehead.'

'Really,' Lamorak mouthed darkly. 'How unusual. Maybe it's an experimental model or something. Look, can you just free the strap of these glasses? It seems to have got wound round the . . .'

'Its coat is milk-white,' Pertelope drivelled on. 'Look, Lamorak, it's got gold hooves as well, isn't that just—?'

'*QUIET!*' It's amazing how loud you can shout when you're whispering. The unicorn's head jumped up like the handle of a low-flying rake, and the animal stood poised for a moment, a paradigm of nervous grace, before bounding away out of sight.

There was an ominous silence.

'Oh dear,' Pertelope said. 'We must have frightened it off.'

Lamorak made a gravelly noise deep in his throat and rubbed the vicinity of his protesting molar. 'You think so?' he growled. 'You're sure it hadn't just remembered an appointment somewhere?'

'It was your fault,' Pertelope retorted, 'yelling at it like that. That's the trouble with you, Lammo, you're out of tune with Nature.'

From his pack, Lamorak had fished out a length of rope, a bundle of cloth, a small bottle and a box of sugar-lumps. 'Come on,' he said. 'It should be easy enough to follow its hoofprints in the sand.'

Pertelope nodded and stood up. They filled their bags with tins of peaches, scraped sand over the empties ('Though really we should take them with us, you know, until we can find a proper litter-bin. This sort of can is fully recyclable.') and trudged off towards where the unicorn had put in its brief, perfectly staged appearance.

Once upon a time, unicorns were extremely scarce.

So elusive were they that there was only one way to catch a unicorn ... Well, in fact there were two. The simple way was to collect a bag of leftover scraps, soak them in cherry brandy, put them in a perfectly ordinary dustbin bag and leave it outside the back door overnight. The unicorn would then rip open the dustbin bag, gorge itself silly and fall asleep. That only worked for the urban unicorn, however; and since urban unicorns were scruffy, tallow-caked, marlinspike-nosed killing machines standing about twelve hands high and entirely devoid of fear or compassion, it was more a case of not catching them if it could possibly be avoided. An urban unicorn with a hangover was capable of doing more damage to life and property than most bombs.

When it came to the white unicorn, however, only

one method stood any chance of success. It required a maiden of unspotted virtue, and six foot of stout hemp rope. The rope was usually no problem.

As time went on, and for various reasons connected with the decline of moral standards and the spread of Humanism, the annual unicorn cull became harder and harder to achieve, so the unicorns grew more and more plentiful. In fact, they became a pest. Their natural habitat could no longer support the huge herds of migratory unicorns sweeping down from the Steppes each spring, and as the cities grew, more and more unicorns drifted into them, gradually evolving into the urban mutation noted above. Fortunately for the human race, they were entirely wiped out by a form of myxomatosis in the early twelfth century; but the disease never took hold among the white unicorns of the plains, which continued to devastate crops and strip the bark off young trees at an alarming rate. Finally, the Holy Roman Emperor reached an agreement with the Great Khan and Prester John, whereby the unicorns were herded across Europe into Asia, down through China and across into Australia, which at that time was still connected to the mainland by a narrow isthmus. Once the last unicorn had crossed over, the land bridge was immediately destroyed, and the very memory of Australia was deliberately erased from the memory of the human race.

It didn't take long for the unicorns to devastate their new environment, and now they are once again a comparatively rare and elusive species. To get an idea of what would have happened to Europe if this step hadn't been taken, one only has to look at the arid deserts of central Australia and consider that, before the coming of the unicorns, they were the most fertile and productive grasslands on the face of the earth.

As time passed, however, times also changed; and although unicorns are by no means common, there are other species rarer and more elusive still. Thus there is only one sure-fire way of catching a maiden of un-spotted virtue. It requires a unicorn and six feet of rope.

'You know,' muttered Pertelope, as they limped to the top of yet another escarpment and looked down across a thousand acres of emptiness, 'I'm still not sure we're going about this the right way.'

'Shut up,' replied Lamorak.

'It's all right for you,' Pertelope protested. 'You've got sensible heels on.' He sat down, removed his left shoe and shook sand out of it.

'Don't start,' Lamorak sighed. 'We tossed a coin, remember, and—'

'Yes,' said Pertelope, 'and I've been thinking about that.' He put the shoe back on his foot. It was a patent navy court shoe with a two-inch heel and a rather smart brass buckle, and it rubbed like hell. Still, as Lamorak had pointed out, it did go very nicely with the plain halter-neck navy dress, pill-box hat and matching handbag that now made up the rest of Pertelope's outfit. 'You remember,' Pertelope added, 'you said call, and I called heads?'

Lamorak looked away and nodded. 'Quite right,' he said.

'I recall wondering at the time why you insisted on using a Portuguese coin,' Pertelope went on, 'and it's just occurred to me that, what with Portugal being a republic . . .'

'Time we were on our way, Per.'

'. . . there isn't a head on a Portuguese coin,' Pertelope continued, 'only a sort of coat of arms thing on one side and a number on the other. *I* think . . .'

He broke off. In the far distance there was a tiny speck. They froze, and Lamorak raised his binoculars.

'That's it,' he hissed. 'We're in business. Now then, stay absolutely still and do what I told you. And for God's sake put your veil down.'

'I still think—' Pertelope whispered, but Lamorak cut him short.

'Actually,' he said, 'I didn't want to have to say this, but I wouldn't be, er, suitable anyway, so . . .'

Pertelope frowned. 'Well, I'm hardly suitable either, Lammo,' he replied. 'I mean, I'm not a woman, am I?'

Lamorak bit his lip. This was embarrassing. 'It doesn't actually specify a woman,' he said, 'not as such. Just a . . . Hold on, it's coming this way. Right then, action stations.'

'I still think . . .' Pertelope said, and he was still speaking as Lamorak crawled away over the sand and hid himself behind a large boulder.

Forty-five minutes can be a long time.

It wasn't, of course, a unicorn that they had been sent to get. If all they'd needed was a unicorn, they could simply have strolled into Harrods' or Bloomingdales' pet department and ordered one.

In other words, this was the easy bit.

'Stone the flaming crows,' exclaimed the unicorn, 'it

isn't a bloody sheila after all.'

But by then it was too late; the noose, cast by Lamorak's well-practised hand, was already flying through the air. There was a brief struggle, some extremely colourful language from the unicorn, and it was all over.

'Quick,' Lamorak grunted, 'grab the rope while I get the chloroform. And watch out for that horn.'

'Pommy bastards,' snarled the unicorn, hurling its weight vainly against the rope. Pertelope dug his heels into the sand and strained backwards, while Lamorak emptied the bottle on to his handkerchief.

'You didn't tell me they could talk, Lammo,' he gasped. 'Just imagine that, a talking animal.'

As if to confirm his statement, the unicorn said something else. It was largely to do with how this particular unicorn's father had been right in his warnings about the extreme effeminacy of the English; and for all his naturalist's curiosity, Pertelope was quite relieved when Lamorak managed to stuff the handkerchief up its nose. Slowly, and still muttering imprecations under its breath, the unicorn sagged to the ground and passed out.

'Well,' Lamorak said, 'we did it. Next time, though, we use a tranquilliser gun and the hell with tradition.' He knelt down and set to work with the rope.

'Can I get out of these clothes now?' Pertelope said. He was bright red in the face, only partly as a result of his exertions.

'In a minute,' Lamorak snapped. 'Give me a hand over here first, quickly, before the blasted thing wakes up.'

Pertelope sighed and grabbed a length of rope. He

wasn't sure that what they were doing wasn't a gross interference with a majestic wild animal in its natural habitat. He firmly disapproved of such things, along with zoos, circuses and leaving dogs in cars with the windows done up. 'Don't tie it so tight, Lammo,' he said at intervals, 'you'll hurt the poor thing.'

'Right,' said Lamorak at last, standing up and breathing heavily, 'we've done that. Now I suggest we have five minutes' sit-down and a rest.'

Pertelope brushed the dust off his skirts. 'After,' he said firmly, 'I've got out of these dreadful clothes.'

'Go ahead,' Lamorak replied. 'I'm just going to sit here and . . .'

Pertelope blushed furiously. 'I need you to unzip me,' he snarled.

'Sorry.' Lamorak hoisted himself to his feet again. 'This time, for pity's sake hold still. You nearly put my eye out with your hairclips last time, remember.'

But before he could make any further movement, a bullet hissed through the air, just missed his eyebrows and lifted Pertelope's hat off his head. The two knights remained where they were, standing very still indeed.

'Thtick 'em up,' said a voice somewhere behind their backs, 'or I'll blow your headth off.'

The Australian wilderness is a place of many strange and terrible noises. There's the unmistakable yap of the dingo, the screech of the kookaburra, the soft bark of the kangaroo, the rasping growl of the mezzo-soprano gargling with eggs beaten in stout – all these can be disconcerting, and to begin with, even terrifying. But there's one sound guaranteed to fill even the hardiest heart with fear and turn the brownest knees to water;

and that's the sound of a hearty contralto voice singing:

> *Onthe a jolly thwagman camped bethide a billabong*
> *Under the thade of a tumpty-tum tree . . .*

over and over again, apparently through a megaphone.
The repetition is attributable to the fact that the singer
doesn't know the rest of the words. The amplification
effect, on the other hand, is due to the large metal
drum that covers the singer's head.

'Can we put our hands down now, please?'
  'Thorry?'
  Lamorak closed his eyes, and then opened them
again. 'I said,' he reiterated, 'can we put our hands
down now, please?'
  'Oh. Yeth. Only nithe and eathy doth it, right?'
  'Yeth. Yes. Sorry.' Lamorak lowered his arms experimentally, and ran quick checks over himself to discover
whether he'd been shot yet. All clear. 'How about
turning round?' he suggested.
  There was a pause. 'Go on, then,' said the voice. It
sounded like a cow at the bottom of a deep, steel-lined
pit.
  The proprietor of the voice looked at first sight like
the after-effects of the sorceror's apprentice run riot
in a breaker's yard. Starting from the top, there was
a big round drum, with two tiny holes. Under that,
unmistakably, what had once been the bonnet of a
Volkswagen Beetle, before someone with a degree in
design flair and enormous biceps had beaten it into
a vaguely anthropomorphic shape with a big hammer.

Two steel tubes stuck out from the sides at right angles, and there was a rust-mottled revolver at the end of one of them. Finally, two more tubes projected out from the underside and linked up with a pair of old-fashioned diver's boots.

'Ith either of you laughth, I thall be theriouthly angry,' it said.

Pertelope blinked. 'Excuse me,' he said, 'but why are you wearing those funny clothes?'

The ironmongery quivered slightly. 'Look who'th talking,' it replied.

'Please,' Lamorak said hastily, 'you mustn't mind my friend. It's just that he's an idiot, that's all.'

There was a dubious, rusty sound from inside the drum. 'You're *thure* that'th all?' it said. 'I mean, that ith a *throck* he'th wearing.'

Pertelope winced. 'There's a perfectly good reason—' he started to say, but a sudden pain in his foot, the result of Lamorak inadvertently stamping on it hard, cut him short.

'Anyway,' Lamorak said brightly, 'it's been very nice meeting you, and the very best of luck with whatever it is you're doing, but I'm afraid we've got to be getting along. Cheerio.' He started to walk purposefully towards the unicorn, but the muzzle of the revolver followed him.

'Not tho fatht,' said the ironclad. 'What're you two doing with that 'roo, anyway?'

The two knights looked at each other. 'That *what*?' Lamorak enquired.

'The kangaroo,' replied the voice from inside the drum. 'Come on, thpit it out.'

'Excuse me,' Lamorak said, in the very recherché

tone of voice one uses when pointing out the blindingly obvious to a heavily armed idiot, 'but strictly speaking, that's not a kangaroo.'

'It ithn't?'

There was something in the modulations of the voice that gave Lamorak the clue he'd been looking for. 'You're not from these parts, are you?' he said.

The ironmongery didn't reply; but it shuffled and clinked in such a way as to confirm Lamorak in his belief. 'Or this time, come to that,' he added slowly. 'You're from the future, aren't you?'

'Oh thit,' mumbled the ironclad. 'How did you know?'

Had Lamorak been truthful, he'd have replied that it was the logical conclusion when you came across someone who'd heard of kangaroos but didn't know what they looked like, and had the idea that in the Outback, the way to dress inconspicuously was to make up as Ned Kelly. Instead, he said, 'Lucky guess.'

Pertelope, meanwhile, had been doing a very good impersonation of a man swallowing a live fish. 'How do you mean, from the future?' he finally managed to say. Lamorak smiled.

'Allow me to introduce you,' he said. 'Sir Pertelope, this is the Timekeeper. Timekeeper, Sir Pertelope.'

For his part, Pertelope looked like someone who has just been told that the sun rises in the east because of horticulture. He furrowed his brows.

'Excuse me,' he said, 'but could somebody please explain what's going on?'

The Timekeeper shrugged – a gesture which would have been rather more elegant if it hadn't involved the movement of quite so much rusty sheet metal – and removed the iron drum to reveal a young, freckled and quite unmistakably female face; fourteen going on fifteen, at a guess, and with braces on her teeth.

'It'th all right,' she said, 'I'll ecthplain. I'm uthed to it,' she added. 'But thirtht, can I get out of all thith bloody armour?'

There was a confusing interval while she peeled off the metalwork. It was like watching a destroyer getting undressed.

'That'th better,' sighed the Timekeeper. She was now dressed in a scarlet boiler suit and silver trainers, and stood about five feet two in them. The revolver was still in her hand, but probably only because there wasn't anywhere to put it down that wasn't covered in sheet steel. 'I'm throm a thpathethip,' she said.

'I see,' commented Pertelope unconvincingly.

'It'th very thimple,' the Timekeeper went on, standing on one foot and massaging the other vigorously. 'There'th ten of uth, and we were put into orbit in a time capthule travelling at just over the thpeed of light.'

'The Relativity Marketing Board,' Lamorak interrupted. 'It was the biggest scientific experiment ever attempted. Years ahead of its time,' he added.

'Yeth,' said the Timekeeper, bitterly, 'ecthept the thools went and thent uth off in the wrong direction. Inthtead of going into the Thuture, we went into the Patht.'

'Sheer carelessness,' said Lamorak sadly. 'Somebody forgot to read the instruction manual, apparently.'

'And they thorgot to pack any thood,' the Timekeeper added, 'which meanth every tho ofen one of uth hath to take the ethcape capthule down to thome detherted thpot on the Thurthathe and forage for provithionth. Gueth whothe turn it wath thith time.'

Pertelope gave Lamorak a bewildered look. 'How do you know all that, Lammo?' he asked.

'Simple,' the knight replied. 'I met one of them – oh, two hundred and fifty years ago now, maybe more. Not you,' he added to the Timekeeper, 'one of your, er, colleagues. He was about nine years old, with sort of carroty red hair.'

The Timekeeper nodded. 'That thoundth like Thimon,' she said. 'I'll warn him to ecthpect you.'

Pertelope was about to say 'But—' again, but Lamorak forestalled him.

'Our past is their future, you see,' he explained, 'so although I've already met – Simon, was it? Yes, I remember now – he won't meet me for another two and a half centuries, or whatever it is in his timescale. And of course, where we get older as time passes, they get younger.'

The Timekeeper nodded. 'I wath thorty-thicth onthe,' she said savagely, 'and now look at me. And having thethe thodding thingth on my teeth doethn't help.'

'It must be awful,' agreed Lamorak. 'Why don't you take them off and the hell with it?'

'Becauthe,' the Timekeeper replied sadly, 'when I wath thorty-thicth I had really thraight even teeth and no thillingth. Which meanth I've got to wear thucking bratheth and bruth three timeth a day, otherwithe it'll cauthe a temporal paradocth. It'th a real bummer.' She paused for a moment, as something jammed in her mind. 'Hold on,' she said. 'How can you have met Thimon two hundred and thithty yearth ago? You'd be dead by now.'

It was Lamorak's turn to sigh.

'Let me explain,' he said.

Not far away, a real kangaroo – one without golden hooves or a horn in the middle of its forehead – was bounding happily along, its mind occupied with the one great mystery which obsesses the consciousness of the species; to the extent that it has stopped them dead in their evolutionary tracks and prevented them from developing into the hyper-intelligent super-lifeforms they would otherwise have become.

Namely; how come, no matter how careful you are about what you put in your pockets, in the end you always find two paperclips, a fluff-covered boiled sweet and a small, worthless copper coin at the bottom of them?

It had just come to the conclusion that the Devil creeps up and puts them there while you're asleep, when a terrifying apparition shot up out of a hollow in the rocks, waved its arms and grinned fearfully. The kangaroo stopped dead in mid-hop, landed awkwardly, and twisted its ankle. The force of the landing jerked a shirt button and a scrap of peppermint wrapper out of its pouch, and the wind bore them away.

The monster advanced, slowly and with infinite menace. Behind it, a man with a camera and another with a big tape-recorder put their heads up above the escarpment. The monster was talking, apparently to itself.

'These spectacular creatures,' it was saying, 'the world's largest true marsupials, hounded by mankind to the verge of extinction in some parts of the Outback . . .'

The kangaroo cowered back on to its hind paws and raised its forepaws feebly; whether to make a show of aggression or to hide behind them was far from clear. The monster continued to advance.

'And now,' it was saying. 'I'm going to try and get in close to the kangaroo, and if we're really lucky we might for the first time ever be able to show you . . .'

The kangaroo tried to move; but completely without success. It fought the urge to grin feebly and wave into the camera with every fibre of its being. It failed.

'The largest species – Barry, can you zoom in on the little bugger's head please –' the largest species of kangaroo, the Red, can leap twenty-five feet at a single bound and clear objects six feet high,' said the monster. 'I'm going to see if I can get close enough for you to see in detail . . .'

The spell broke. With a shrill bark of terror, the kangaroo launched itself into the air, twisted frantically round and bounded away, pursued by strange and distinctly unfriendly cries from the monster. Only after half an hour's high-speed bounding did it stop, crouch down and drag breath into its heaving lungs.

And then stiffen in cold despair; for just behind its shoulder it could hear the sound of human breathing, and that terrible voice, saying:

'And if we're extremely quiet, we might just be able – Kieron, if you scare the bugger this time I'll make you swallow your polariser – we might just be able to get a glimpse of its . . .'

A single massive jump might just reach the edge of that rock over there, but why bother? There was clearly no point.

With a soft, despairing cough, the kangaroo turned,

faced the camera and waggled its forepaws, hating itself almost to death.

'Let'th get thith thtraight, thall we?' said the Timekeeper, after a long, long pause. 'You're really ecthpecting me to believe that you're a pair of Arthurian knighth on a quetht to find an *apron*?'

'Yes.'

'Fine.' A sharper than usual pair of eyes would have seen her suspended disbelief bobbing for a moment above her head before drifting away on the breeze. 'And that'th what you need the tied-up horthe for?'

'The horthe?'

'*Horthe*, yeth.'

'Oh I see, the horse.' Lamorak scratched his head. He was hot, tired, confused, overdosed to the eyebrows with tinned peaches and dying of toothache. He didn't really want to do any more explaining just at the moment. 'It's not a horse,' he said, 'not as such.'

Just then the unicorn woke up, struggled ineffectually in its bonds, and embarked on a stream of invective.

'Hey,' said the Timekeeper, 'the horthe jutht thaid thomething.'

'Yes, only it isn't a—'

'Listen, you bastards,' screamed the unicorn. 'Tell that flamin' sheila that if she calls me a bloody horse just one more time, then so help me—'

Pertelope, showing more intelligence than anyone would have given him credit for, grabbed a sugar-lump and slapped it into the unicorn's mouth. The tirade broke off abruptly, and was replaced by a crunching sound.

'If it'th not a horthe,' whispered the Timekeeper, 'then what ith it?'

Lamorak sighed. 'It's a unicorn,' he said. 'Satisfied?'

'Oh.'

'And now, we've got to get on with what we were doing, and I'm sure your colleagues are getting very hungry up there in orbit, so . . .'

'What do you need a unicorn for?'

It took Lamorak just over six seconds to count to ten slowly under his breath. 'If you must know,' he said, 'we want it as bait to catch a maiden of unspotted virtue.'

The Timekeeper looked at him. 'You'th got that the wrong way round, you know.'

Lamorak prised his lips apart into a smile. 'Have we? Oh *damn*. That *is* a nuisance, isn't it, Per? Oh well, it's back to the drawing board for us, then. Thanks for the tip, anyway. And now we really must be getting along.'

'And bethideth,' continued the Timekeeper, 'you thaid you were questhting for an apron, not a maiden of unthpotted . . .'

'It's her apron,' said Sir Pertelope.

'Ith it?'

'Yes.'

After the unicorns came the convicts.

There were two waves of them. The second wave arrived with the First Fleet in 1788, seven hundred years after the first wave.

The aborigines, whose permission nobody bothered to ask, had a phrase for it. One damned thing after another, they said.

***

The first man in the first wave to set eyes on Australia had been the overseer. His first reaction was to shudder slightly. Then he jumped down from the observation platform and told the drummer to stop marking time.

'Right,' he shouted, 'everybody out.'

Nobody moved. Two thousand dragon-headed prows bobbed silently up and down in the still waters of Botany Bay.

The overseer blinked. 'Did you lot hear what I said?' he yelled. 'Everybody off the ships, now.'

'We're not going.'

The voice came from behind an oar in the third row back. It was backed up by a mumbled chorus of That's Rights and You Tell Hims. The overseer started to perspire.

'What did you just say?' he demanded. The faint blur of grey smoke behind the oar coruscated in the sunlight. If it had had shoulders, it might well have been shrugging them.

'I said we're not bloody going,' it replied evenly. 'We can see into the future. It sucks. We stay here.'

In the back of the overseer's mind, a little voice nervously started asking around to see if anyone had any ideas about what should be done next. The overseer's hands were more positive. They reached for the big knotted whip hanging from his belt.

'We'll soon see about that,' he said, and he aimed a ferocious blow at the cloud of smoke.

'Idiot.'

With aggravating slowness, the wisps of smoke coalesced into a cloud once more. There was an expectant silence.

'There's no way you can force us to get off the ship, you know,' went on the voice, calmly. 'So you might as well accept the situation; turn this thing round and head for home. Yes?'

'No,' said the overseer.

He was sweating heavily now.

He hadn't wanted to come in the first place. When he'd joined the company, all those years ago, he'd seen his future career developing in an entirely different direction. After five years or so loading sides of bacon on to the ships and sailing them from Copenhagen to Dover, he reckoned, he'd have proved himself the sort of man they could use in marketing. There would follow an orderly progression, from sales representative to assistant sales manager, then regional sales manager, then sales director, and so on until he was given overall responsibility for the whole Danish operation in Albion. And here he was, ten years later, trying to cajole a boatful of deported supernatural entities into colonising New South Cambria. Something, somewhere, had gone wrong.

'Please?' he said.

There was a swirling of mists and fogs the length of the ship that left him feeling dizzy. He could feel the roof of his mouth getting dry.

Two thousand longships; each one crammed to overflowing with minor divinities. There were river-gods, wood-nymphs, fire-spirits, elves, wills o' the wisp, pixies, chthonic deities, earth-mothers, thunder-demons, even a few metaphysical abstractions huddled wretchedly at the back and insisting on soft lavatory paper. As part of the dismantling of the magical culture of Albion, her entire population of supernatural bit-players had been rounded up and sent to Van Demon's Land.

The overseer dug his fingernails into the palms of his hands and took a deep breath. 'Come along now, people,' he wheedled, 'you'll like it once you get there, promise.'

'Nuts.'

'But there's rivers,' whined the overseer. 'Majestic, awe-inspiring torrents, crashing over dizzying water-falls, winding lugubriously through ancestral forests. There's deserts. There's rock formations any red-quartzed troll'd give his right arm to live in. There's bush fires that make Hell look like a camping stove. What in God's name are you complaining about? It's a bloody spook's paradise out there.'

'There are also,' said the spokeswraith, 'spiders.'

There was a soft thunk as the overseer's jaw dropped on to the studded collar round his neck. 'What was that?' he gasped.

'And snakes.'

'And mosquitoes.'

'And,' added the spokeswraith meaningfully, 'it's not as if it's exactly got vacant possession, you know. The whole place is absolutely crawling with . . .'

With a massive effort, the overseer hoisted his jaw back into place. 'Yes?'

'You know,' replied the smoke-cloud diffidently. 'Things. It's really *creepy* out there, you know?'

'They go around singing all the time,' ventured a voice from the last bench but one. 'It's enough to give you the willies.'

'Bloody unsocial hours, too,' added a scratching, grinding sound from somewhere near the middle of the ship. 'Dream-time-and-a-half, that sort of thing.'

'Let's get this straight,' said the overseer, with an ever so slightly unbalanced lilt in his voice. 'All you ghouls and ghosts and things that go bump in the night are refusing to get off the ship because you think the place is *haunted*?'

'Yes.'

'Be reasonable,' added the scratching sound – a fever-wraith from the Plumstead Marshes – 'they're natives, they're used to living here, we're not. They'd have us for breakfast. If you turn us off the ship, it'd be mass murder. Exorcism. Whatever.'

The overseer lowered his head, stuck his hands in his pockets – where, inevitably, he found a small piece of string, a half-eaten apple and two small bronze coins of purely nominal value – and thought about it for a while; then he retired into the helmsman's cabin and banged his head against the ship's wheel for a while. Oddly enough, it helped, because when he emerged he knew exactly what he was going to do.

And it worked. It was, of course, bitterly unfair on the indigenous paranormals; and it has to go down as one of the biggest stains on the superhuman rights record of the English nation. Now, however, it's far too late to do anything about it, because within five years of the arrival of the deported spirits from Albion, the native deities had been completely wiped out, leaving the entire continent empty to receive the newcomers. In due course, they settled in, adapted themselves to their new environment and evolved an entirely original lifestyle of their own which bore no resemblance whatsoever to the culture they had left behind them, and which survived for seven hundred years before being completely destroyed by the coming of the First Fleet.

Which, so the aborigines say, served the buggers bloody well right.

'Tho what did they actually *do* to the native thpiritth?' the Timekeeper demanded. Lamorak winced. He hated this part of the story. It was, he had always felt, enough to make one ashamed of being Albionese.

'They methylated them,' he replied quietly. 'Well, it's been really nice meeting you,' he said, 'and I look forward very much to having met you before, but unless we make a start immediately we're going to be very, very late. Ciao.' He picked up his rucksack, slung it on his back and advanced purposefully towards the unicorn.

'That'th horrible,' said the Timekeeper, and shuddered. 'But it thtill doethn't ecthplain about the apron and the unicorn.'

'Very true,' replied Lamorak over his shoulder. 'Right then, Per, you grab hold of the rope while I push.'

'The apron,' said Pertelope, 'was a talisman belonging to one of the deported spirits. It has magical powers of its own. We managed to track it down, through newspaper reports of unexplained happenings which could only have been caused by the apron, and it turns out to be owned by a maiden of unspotted virtue living in Sydney. Hence the unicorn.'

'I thee,' murmured the Timekeeper. 'At leatht I think I thee. What thort of unecthplained happeningth?'

Lamorak smiled unpleasantly. 'It's kind of hard to explain,' he said.

The Timekeeper was not amused. 'Try me,' she said.

'Football results,' said Pertelope. 'The apron plays merry hell with the results of Australian Rules football matches. All we had to do once we knew that was to plot all the results on a big graph and wait until a significant mutation in the sine curve became apparent.'

'And?'

'Paramatta Under-Twelves 22, Sydney 0,' Lamorak growled. 'Which was as good as putting up a big neon sign saying OVER HERE.' He paused and scowled. 'I can explain the mathematics of it in very great detail if you want me to,' he added.

'No thankth,' said the Timekeeper, and Lamorak noticed that her eyes looked as if someone had accidentally slapped three coats of weatherproof varnish over them. 'Actually,' she went on, 'it'th time I wath getting along, tho . . .'

'Of course. We quite understand. Right, Per, when I say heave . . . Per? What the hell are you staring at?'

Pertelope was standing bolt upright, his face contorted into an expression of terminal sheepishness. He swallowed once or twice, raised his left arm and waggled his fingers.

'Smile, Lammo,' he hissed out of the side of his mouth. 'I think we're on television.'

Faster than the speed of light is very fast. And, it goes without saying, dark.

'Ouch.'

'Sorry.'

'That was my foot.'

'Yes, all right, I said I'm sorry.'

'Well, mind where you're going next time.'

Sleek, streamlined, virtually frictionless and as devoid of light as six feet up a drainpipe, the mighty starcruiser pounced like a giant cat across the vastness of space. Far below – so far that distance became just another deceptive illusion – the earth spun on its languorous axis, while Time found itself dragged inexorably up the down escalator.

'For crying out loud, George, watch what you're doing with that bloody kettle.'

'Sorry.'

'You'd have thought the dozy cow would've been back by now. I'm *starving*.'

'So are the rest of us, Simon. The difference is, *we* don't make such a great big performance out of it.'

'Oh yes? And who asked for your opinion, Priscilla?'

'I'm not Priscilla, I'm Annabel.'

'And I'm Priscilla. You just put your teacup down on my head.'

'God, sorry, Priscilla.'

'I'm not Priscilla, I'm George.'

Aboard the starship *Timekeeper*, there are three levels of Time: earth time; relative time; and the time they'd all been cooped up on this small, cramped and above all *dark* spaceship. The third variety had the weirdest properties of all. It seemed to last for ever.

'Look, this is hopeless. I'm going out for a pizza. Anybody else fancy coming?'

'Listen, George . . .'

'Trevor. I'm George.'

'Listen, Trevor, you just can't do that. This is a scientific experiment, right? We're playing sillybuggers with the fabric of causality as it is; I mean, God only knows what damage we're doing just by being here. If you suddenly touch down in the middle of the twentieth century and start stuffing yourself with a deep-pan quattro stagione, there's no limit to what could happen. So just sit down and shut up, okay?'

There was complete silence.

'I said *okay*, Trevor?'

'I'm not Trevor, I'm Nick.'

'Where's Trevor, then?'

'How the hell am I supposed to know that, Louise? There's no light in here.'

'Actually, I'm not Louise, I'm Angela. Who the hell is Louise, anyway?'

Meanwhile, the second escape capsule roared away across the indescribable magnitude of Nothing, piloted by a ninety-seven-year-old child, straight as an arrow towards where he remembered the best pizza restaurant in the world used to be. The problem was that it wasn't open yet; it wouldn't be open for seventy years.

There was complete silence, except for the unicorn. It raised its head, saw the maiden of unspotted virtue, blushed, and said 'G'day' awkwardly, and started chewing the cud ferociously.

Then, very slowly, Lamorak reached out for Pertelope's pack, took out the sponge bag and found the oil of cloves; then he drank it, wiped his mouth on his sleeve, and smiled.

'Hello there,' he said.

'Actually, Lammo,' Pertelope hissed, 'you're not supposed to drink it, you're supposed to—'

'Shut up, Per, I know what I'm doing.' Lamorak stood up, brushed dust off his trouser-knees and walked up to the maiden of unspotted virtue.

'Swap,' he said. 'My unicorn for your apron. How about it?'

The maiden of unspotted virtue stared at him. 'Have you gone out of your tiny mind?' she said.

Lamorak raised an eyebrow. 'I'm sorry,' he said, 'I don't quite follow. Straight swap. You get your award for best nature programme, I get the apron, everybody's happy. Where's the problem in that?'

There are many cold places on earth, but few of them are as cold as two feet away from the maiden's eyes. 'Listen, whoever you are,' she said. 'I'm trying to make a serious film here. If I go home and tell my producer I've got ten minutes' footage of live unicorns in the can, I'm going to spend the rest of my career filming the weather forecast. Now will you please both go away? You're frightening the kangaroos.'

For perhaps the first time ever, Lamorak was at a slight loss for words. After considerable effort, he managed to say, 'But it's a *unicorn*.' The maiden of unspotted virtue sighed.

'Buster,' she said, 'I don't care if it's a performing woolly mammoth. I have my credibility as a serious wildlife presenter to think of. Understood?'

'But it's a—'

'Quite.' The maiden pursed her lips. 'That's fine. You take it along to the satellite boys, they'll probably give it its own chat show. Meanwhile, some of us have work to do, so if you wouldn't mind . . .'

Lamorak said nothing. Even if he could have found any words appropriate for the situation, he'd have had difficulty saying them with his lower jaw hanging loose like a second-hand drawbridge. He shook his head in disbelief, turned away and sat down under a rock.

'Excuse me,' Pertelope said.

'Well?'

'I think,' Pertelope said, 'there may have been a slight misunderstanding here. You do have the apron, don't you?'

'What apron?'

'Ah. So you're not a maiden of unspotted virtue?'

A moment or so later, Pertelope picked himself up off the ground, rubbed his jaw and joined his colleague under the rock.

'Something must have gone wrong,' he said.

Lamorak nodded. 'Wrong bloody maiden,' he replied. 'I mean, how the devil was I supposed to know there were *two* of . . .?' He broke off. A horrible thought had just occurred to him.

'Oh *shit*,' he said. 'Of course. Why didn't I realise?'

Pertelope looked up at him. 'What do you mean?'

'The football results. We must have misinterpreted them. Here, hand me your rucksack, quick.'

Pertelope did as he was told; and, while the maiden of unspotted virtue and her camera crew raced off into the distance, with a doomed kangaroo a mere ten yards in front of them, he thumbed through the Sports section of *What's On In Sydney*.

'Per,' he said at last, closing the book, 'you might have told me that Lightning Darren O'Shea had signed for the Paramatta Under-Twelves.'

Pertelope registered dismay. 'Oh drat,' he said. 'Yes, that does put rather a different complexion on it, I suppose. What do we do now?'

The Timekeeper leant over the rock and cleared her throat. 'We could eat,' she suggested.

'Not peaches, please,' Lamorak sighed. 'Not right now, I couldn't face it.'

The Timekeeper grinned. 'All right,' she said, 'how doeth thcallop chowder, chicken with bathil and oregano and apricotth in brandy thtrike you?' By way of explanation, she opened her shopping bag and produced three large tins. 'I'll just thet up the tholar-powered microwathe and we're in buthineth.'

Lamorak smiled wryly. 'Why not?' he replied. 'And afterwards, could you give us a lift in this spaceship of yours? Otherwise it's going to be a long walk.'

'Thure thing.' The Timekeeper took a small tin cube from her pocket, pressed a knob on the back, and held it at arm's length. It grew into a microwave oven.

'Only don't tell anyone you'the theen one of thethe, becauthe they haven't been invented yet,' she added. 'You could thet off a complete Dark Age with one of thethe thingth.'

'No problem,' Lamorak replied. 'You keep stumm about the unicorn, we'll forget about the technology.'

The Timekeeper laughed and set to work with a tin-opener. It was some time since she'd used it last, and she nearly burnt a hole the size of a large geological fault in the landscape before she got the atomiser beam properly adjusted, but there was no harm done.

'That still doesn't explain things, Lammo,' Pertelope was saying, and his voice sounded remarkably like the buzzing of a fly against a windscreen.

Lamorak shook his head and said, 'Not now, Per. Later, perhaps.'

Pertelope scowled at him. 'But Lammo,' he said, 'it

doesn't matter about Lightning Darren O'Shea, because it says here his brother Norman is now playing
for the Melbourne Werewolves, and that means the
x-coefficient no longer reciprocates the reflected tan-
gent of pi—'

'Later, Per.' Lamorak closed his eyes, settled his
head against his rucksack and lay back. You know, he
said to himself, I could get to like failure after a while.
It's so much more relaxing . . .

And then he sat bolt upright again, and grabbed for
the book.

'Told you,' Pertelope was saying. 'And of course we'd
have to recalculate the differential shift in the y-axis.'

Lamorak wasn't listening. He was staring at the
Timekeeper; who had opened the tins and emptied
their contents into little plastic bowls, which she was
loading into the machine.

'Nearly ready,' she said.

'Great,' Lamorak replied, trying to sound calm. 'Tell
me, when it was your turn to go shopping, why did you
come here?'

'It'th where my tholks came throm, originally,' she
replied. 'Of courthe, I don't thuppothe it'th anything
like it'll be in their day, but . . .'

'I see,' Lamorak said. 'Um, that's a nice pinny
you've got on, if I may say so.'

The Timekeeper smiled. 'You think tho? Actually,
it'th been in my thamily for yearth. Nithe embroidery
round the edgeth, look. Thlowerth and thingth.'

The two knights exchanged glances. Then Lamorak
drew Pertelope to one side.

'All right,' he said, 'you're obviously thinking the
same as me.'

'It'd explain the distortion in the base coefficient, certainly,' Pertelope replied. 'It's a very interesting effect, actually, because—'

'Yes, all right, I believe you.' Lamorak drew in a deep breath, then let it go. 'Look,' he said, 'one of us is going to have to ask her, and I think it's probably your turn. Okay?'

'Ask her what, Lammo?'

'Never mind,' Lamorak replied. 'Forget I spoke.'

The Timekeeper shut the oven door and twiddled the dial a couple of times. 'It'll be about three minuteth,' she said. 'Tho that'th a unicorn, ith it? I've alwayth wanted to thee a real unicorn.'

'Bingo,' muttered Lamorak under his breath. At her age, *and* with those braces on her teeth, I don't need to ask, I just *know*. 'Can I just have a closer look at that apron thing for a moment?' he asked.

There are two ways of landing a spaceship escape capsule on the surface.

The first way is to ease your way down through the upper atmosphere and sidle back into gravity with the aid of your stabiliser rockets. The alternative method is to keep on going until you hit the ground. This technique should on no account be confused with crashing, although the net result is more or less the same.

Fortunately, anything that happens to the landscape of the Great Victoria Desert is almost certain to improve it, and Trevor would no doubt have been only too pleased had he known that in years to come (long after he was born, in fact) the enormous crater brought into being by his textbook Method II landing would be flooded with water and turned into Australia's first inland surfing park, with tides automatically stimulated by a huge solar-powered turbine.

As he dragged himself out of the remains of the cockpit, however, all he could think of was the rather depressing fact that his spacecraft had had its chips, which meant that unless he could find the foraging party, he was going to have to stay here for the rest of his life. Quite apart from the fact that he seemed to have landed in a distinctly unprepossessing spot, he faced the horrible prospect of reverting to the normal life-pattern of a surface-dweller, with all the morale-sapping repetition that would entail. It's bad enough turning thirty once in one's lifetime. Having to do it twice is enough to make anybody very depressed indeed.

And even that unattractive prospect, he realised, was going to be pretty remote unless he found something to eat. Quickly.

He had been trudging generally eastwards for about half an hour when the smell of something edible floated past him on the sluggish desert breeze. He stopped in his tracks and concentrated. About thirty seconds of intense inhaling satisfied him that it wasn't some sort of olfactory mirage. If the smell was simply a product of his imagination, then his imagination wouldn't have put so much garlic in it. He walked quickly in the direction he guessed the scent was coming from, later breaking into a run.

'It's not for me, you understand,' Lamorak said hastily. 'It's for a friend of mine.'

The Timekeeper continued to stare at him. 'A friend

of yourth,' she repeated. 'A friend of yourth who liketh drething up in women'th clotheth.' She shot a glance at Pertelope, and then added, '*Another* friend of yourth who liketh drething up in women'th clotheth. I *thee*.'

'Now hang on a minute,' Pertelope started to say, but Lamorak ignored him. 'It's not like that,' he said. 'Look, we're on this quest, right, and we've got to recover the Holy Grail, okay, which means that—'

The Timekeeper raised her ladle threateningly. 'I'd thtay right there ith I wath you,' she hissed. Or rather hithed.

'Now look . . .' Lamorak began to say; then he broke off, bent double and clutched his jaw. 'Now look what you've done,' he mumbled.

'He's got toothache,' Pertelope explained. He was like that, of course; he was also perfectly capable of explaining that you were getting wet because it was raining, and that you'd just broken your leg because you'd fallen off your ladder.

'Nethertheleth,' replied the Timekeeper grimly, and swung the ladle demonstratively. You don't get to stay a maiden of unspotted virtue for long on a pitch dark spaceship without knowing how to handle heavy kitchen implements. She backed away, didn't look where she was going, and tripped over the unicorn.

Startled out of its narcotic dreams (in which, behind a bush with a gang of other unicorns, it lay in wait for a maiden of tarnished virtue to be attracted by a tethered kangaroo), the unicorn started, kicked against the ropes restraining its legs, and succeeded in loosening them.

'Right, you bunch of Pommy woofters,' it started to say; and then the Timekeeper fell on it, knocking it out cold. It subsided into a heap, taking up its dream where it had left off.

'Don't just stand there, you pillock,' Lamorak shouted. 'Grab the bloody apron.'

Pertelope hesitated. On the one hand, he was a Knight of the Table Round, and he distinctly remembered the bit in the rule book about succouring damsels in distress. He mentioned this.

'So?'

'So I should be succouring, shouldn't I?'

'Right,' Lamorak snarled. 'And the thing to remember about succouring is never to give them an even break. Now move!'

'Oh,' Pertelope replied. 'That's what it means. I always thought it meant—' He got no further than this, because the Timekeeper belted him across the head with her ladle.

Lamorak said something under his breath – it rhymed with *pit* – and made a half-hearted sort of lunge. He was hampered by the fact that he was trying to shield his jaw with his body, and only succeeded in putting his foot in the Timekeeper's discarded armour. There was a crash, and he landed heavily.

'Thcumbag,' the Timekeeper yelled, and raised the ladle above her head. Then she froze.

'If it's any consolation,' Lamorak said after a while, 'I really don't feel good about doing this.' He waggled the Timekeeper's revolver, which had somehow found its way into his hand when he landed. 'One, it's unchivalrous. Two, it's an anachronism. Three, these things terrify the life out of me. On the other hand . . .'

The Timekeeper wasn't listening. She was looking at something over Lamorak's left shoulder, while trying to do high-level semaphore with her eyebrows.

'Don't give me that,' Lamorak sighed. 'Oldest trick in the book, that is, pretending to see something so's I turn round, and then you hit me with—'

Then he too fell silent, as Trevor thumped him hard on the side of the jaw with a rock.

The true origin of the Apron of Invincibility will probably never be known.

One school would have it that the apron was worn by the head chef at Belshazzar's feast, and the distinctive red marks down the front are all the remains of the venison casserole, spilt there by the chef when he saw a huge hand materialise out of thin air and start writing graffiti on the walls of his newly decorated taverna.

Others claim that the red marks are the stains left by the particularly virulent Algerian beaujolais served to the guests at the wedding at Cana just before the wine finally ran out. This view is substantiated to a certain extent by the fact that generations of owners have done their best to bleach them out, but without success.

Still others say that the red marks are just red marks, and that the Apron is a seventh-century Byzantine forgery; although what it's a forgery of, nobody even pretends to know.

Whatever the truth of the matter is, the fact remains that the Apron has curious properties which cannot be explained in rational terms. For example; the touch of its hem cures certain extremely rare varieties of scrofula (not a particularly useful property, this, since the bacteria in question are so rare that they count as protected species, and anyone harming them is liable to a substantial fine); it mucks up Aussie Rules football like nothing else on earth; and a sponge cake baked by a person wearing it will invariably turn out as hard as millstone.

After a while, Lamorak came round. He shook his head and gathered together the splinters of his memory.

He realised that he was feeling a lot better.

Something sharp was digging into his neck. He fished around inside his shirt, and found a dislodged tooth. He seemed to recognise it from somewhere.

'Ah,' he said. 'Good.'

He looked up, and saw the barrel of the revolver. Behind it stood the Timekeeper and another figure, similarly dressed, male, its jaw moving steadily.

'Threethe,' rasped the Timekeeper. 'Or Trethor here'll drill you full of holeth.'

It'th okay,' Lamorak replied, 'don't thoot. Oh thit,' he added, rubbing his swollen jaw. 'You'the got me at it now.'

'What the hell's going on here, anyway?' Trevor enquired, with his mouth full. 'The fight. The unconscious guy in the frock. The horse with a flagpole up its nose. I mean, what is this?'

Lamorak grinned painfully. 'Let me ecthplain,' he said.

'I'the got a better ...' The Timekeeper growled impatiently, opened her mouth, and pulled out two little strips of shiny metal. 'That's better,' she said, stuffing them in her pocket. 'The hell with dental consistency. I've got a better idea, Trevor. Let's tie these two idiots up and get back to the ship, okay?'

Trevor shrugged. 'Please yourself,' he said. 'What'll we tie them up with?'

Lamorak coughed politely. 'Ith I may make a thuggethtion,' he said.

The Apron of Invincibility, torn into thin strips, produced enough material to keep the knights securely bound for six hours; at the end of which they were released by a party of wandering Fruit Monks on their way to replenish the cache of tinned lychees at Ayers Rock.

On their return to Albion, the knights entrusted the job of restoring the Apron to the Sisters of Incongruity, an even smaller and more secretive order who devote themselves to prayer, meditation, needlework and spot-the-ball competitions (from which source is derived the fabulous wealth of the community). Three months of round-the-clock work resulted in an Apron that was almost, but not quite, as good as new. True, it no longer affected the outcome of football matches; on the other hand, it developed a quite staggering knack of turning anything left overnight in its pockets into small balls of disintegrating paper, discarded fruit-gum wrappings, delaminated metro tickets and de-monetised fifty-lire coins.

4

'Admit it, Turkey,' said Bedevere, 'we're lost.'

You can tell of the Hanging Gardens of Babylon, or the Colossus of Rhodes; if you're looking for the world's great wonders, try a knight of an ancient order of chivalry coping with a statement of the painfully obvious.

'I know we're lost,' Turquine replied cheerfully, folding the road map and shoving it under the seat of the van. 'We're supposed to be lost. If we weren't lost, we'd be going the wrong way.'

Bedevere looked at him.

'After all,' Turquine went on, 'we're looking for a lost city. *The* lost city. Therefore . . .'

'Yes,' said Bedevere patiently, 'point taken. But right now, we aren't looking for Atlantis, we're looking for the M6.'

Turquine grinned. 'Not necessarily,' he replied.

When Bedevere made an uncharacteristically impatient gesture, Turquine went on: 'You don't seem to have tumbled to it yet, young Bedders. We're talking mysticism here.' He broke off to avoid and swear at a T-registration Allegro which had churlishly insisted on its right of way on the roundabout.* 'You remember what old Beaky Maledisant used to say about mysticism.'

Bedevere confessed that he'd forgotten. Turquine nodded.

'Thought you had,' he said. 'I seem to remember you spending the Wisdom lessons looking out of the window at the girls from the—'

'Anyway,' said Bedevere.

Turquine changed gear noisily. 'The point is,' he said, 'if you're looking for a lost city, or a lost priory, or a hermit's cell under an enchantment of oblivion, anything like that, it's no good going through the index at the back of the *A–Z*; you've got to get lost yourself. Then it sort of finds you. That's,' he added proudly, 'logic.'

Bedevere raised an eyebrow. 'Logic?' he asked.

---

*By right of his position as Seigneur de Montcalm and Earl-Banneret of Belfort, Turquine had a hereditary right of precedence over traffic feeding in from the right on roundabouts; and, being Turquine, insisted on exercising it even against articulated lorries and bulk tankers. His ambition was to cause an accident and get charged with reckless driving, so that he could stand up in court and produce the original charter, bearing the seal of Uther Pendragon. Unfortunately, all the drivers he pulled out in front of without warning either had hair-trigger reflexes or ABS brakes.

'Well,' Turquine replied, shrugging, 'theology, then. All those that are lost shall be found, or words to that effect. Hell fire and buggery,' he added, staring at a road sign, 'that's the Stirchley turn-off. How the devil did we get here?'

Bedevere smiled wanly. 'Theology, probably,' he said. 'That and taking the wrong exit back at Brownhills. You want the A37.'

'Give me the map a minute,' Turquine said. 'I know a short-cut that should . . .'

Bedevere was about to protest, from long experience of Turquine's short-cuts, when it occurred to him that all that stuff about being lost on purpose sounded uncomfortably reasonable. 'Great,' he said, therefore, and even added, 'Good idea.'

Turquine's short-cut, predictably, took them up a single-lane cul-de-sac terminating in a deserted farmyard. They always did. In fact, Bedevere had often felt, if only one took the trouble to get out of the car and have a look, it would probably turn out to be the same farmyard each time. Which made sense, somehow . . .

'Right,' he said, releasing his seat-belt and opening the door, 'we're here.'

Turquine looked at him.

'What on earth are you doing?' he asked.

'Following your premise to its logical conclusion,' Bedevere replied, grabbing his haversack from the back of the van and putting on his hat. 'Coming?'

'But . . .'

Bedevere smiled nicely, slammed the door and set off towards the farmhouse. After a moment's therapeutic blaspheming, Turquine followed him.

'You see,' Bedevere explained, as they squelched

through the slurry, 'if you've got to be lost in order to find a lost city, it follows that you've got to be as lost as humanly possible. I think a farmyard up a five-mile lane with grass growing up the middle of it is about as lost as we can get without actually poking our eyes out with a stick, don't you?'

He smiled and knocked at the door. Surprisingly quickly, the door opened.

'Good afternoon,' Bedevere said. 'We're looking for Atlantis. Can you put us on the right road?'

The woman who had answered the door looked as if she probably could, in a sense. She struck Bedevere as the sort of woman who has a son called Oak and two daughters called Skychild and Mistletoe, and she was wearing rather a lot of that peculiar silver jewellery that nobody ever buys at craft fairs.

'Sorry?' she said.

'Atlantis,' Bedevere repeated. 'You know . . .'

'Oh,' said the woman, 'yes, right. You don't look the type, that's all. You'd better follow me.'

She led the way into the house, and Turquine and Bedevere exchanged looks.

'That's probably the nicest thing anyone's ever said about me,' whispered Turquine under his breath. 'God, this place smells a bit.' He sniffed distastefully. 'Looks like they go in for the old wacky baccy around here.'

The woman opened a door and stepped aside.

'In here,' she said. 'You know what to do.'

It was an odd room, in context. It was, Bedevere decided, exactly like the more fashionable sort of building society, except that there were no girls in uniform sitting behind the computer screens. Not a pentangle or a cabalistic sign in sight.

'If you need anything,' the woman said, 'we're all in the scullery, meditating.' She closed the door, and the knights could hear the plopping of her bare feet in the corridor.

For about a minute, neither of them spoke. Then Bedevere shrugged.

'All right,' he said, 'maybe we should have gone left at the Shard End underpass.'

Turquine sat down behind one of the screens. 'Not at all,' he said. 'I think I'm getting the hang of this. Neat,' he added, with a hint of admiration. He closed his eyes, flexed his fingers like a concert pianist, and dabbed the keyboard at random.

'After all,' he said, as the screen went blank and the machine beeped a couple of times, 'there's lost, and there's lost. Now, then.'

'Do you know how to work one of those things?' Bedevere asked.

'Previous experience is not essential,' Turquine replied. 'Think of a number.'

'Seven.'

'And why not?' Turquine tapped a key. 'For example,' he went on, 'when was the last time you had any dealings with the Inland Revenue?'

Bedevere blushed. 'I . . .' he said.

'All right,' said Turquine, 'the telephone people, DVLC, British Gas, any of that mob. People who use computers a lot.'

'They all have screens at the office,' said Bedevere, the insurance salesman.

'And,' Turquine went on, 'what's the commonest explanation for things getting cocked up?'

'Lost in the computer, of course,' Bedevere said automatically, and then bit his lip. 'Oh,' he said, 'yes. I think I see what you're getting at.'

Turquine smirked. 'Took your time, didn't you?' he said. 'How to lose something while still permitting it to exist. Feed it into the computer. Easy. I mean, it'll be in there somewhere; it's just lost, that's all, along with half a million renewal notices, paid parking tickets, standing orders, estimated meter readings and revised assessments. And all you need to do to get it back again is type in the magic word.'

Bedevere smiled, full of admiration. 'Which is?'

'Ah,' Turquine wheeled round on the swivel chair. 'There you have me. Still, we're almost there.'

Bedevere slumped a little; then he perked up. 'Absolutely,' he said. 'Allow me.'

He pushed Turquine gently out of the chair, sat down and rubbed his hands. 'They do this at the office,' he explained, 'whenever the wretched thing has a bit of a paddy and nobody can get anything out of it. You're not meant to, of course . . . Ah, here we are.'

He found the button he was looking for and pressed it. The screen went blank and a floppy disk popped out of a slot. He pressed it back in, pressed the button again and smacked the side of the console with the flat of his hand.

There was an interval while the machine swore at him in morse code; then the screen went completely blank. Bedevere was just about to start feeling a complete idiot when letters appeared on the screen.

ALL RIGHT, YOU WIN

'Bingo!' Bedevere exclaimed. 'Right, let's see.'

He typed in a message, one-fingered, and the screen went blank again.

'What was that you just—?' Turquine started to ask, but Bedevere shushed him.

READY TO TRANSMIT

'Brace yourself,' Bedevere whispered. 'This could be a bit disconcerting.'

'How do you mean, brace myself? Brace myself against what?'

'Ssh!'

TRANSMITTING

The world vanished . . .

The question, 'How did people manage before there were fax machines?' is fortunately academic.

There have always been fax machines, but they have gone under other names, and some of the experimental models bear as much relation to the modern versions as, say, a pair of cocoa tins connected by a piece of string bears to a cellular carphone.

For example; the Pyrolex IV Turbo, which had a passing vogue in the Near East around the time of the Pharaoh Rameses II of Egypt, operated by a primitive form of fibre-optics, whereby concentrated beams of light were conducted through the upper air in the form of radio waves, collected by a rough and ready trans-ducer – the leaves of a rare variety of palm tree, now long since extinct – and then focused on to the receiving medium through an organic lens formed by the tree's blossom.

The fax was, of course, known to the Romans, who used it to communicate with the gods. The Lector Lucius model favoured for this purpose was reliable but slow; the message was relayed into the DNA of a flock of sacred chickens, and was read by cutting open a chicken chosen at random and having a look at its entrails.

Albion used a form of fax technology very similar to our own; but after the fall of the Albionese kingdom we enter a period known to information-technology historians as 'the long dark winter of the postcard', during which only a vestigial form of fax was available.

The exception, of course, was Atlantis, where the fax machine has been known since the very earliest times; so much so that the seminal text of the Atlantean Apostolic Church, *The Gospel According to St Neville*, begins:

'In the beginning was the Word, and the Word was with God, and by the time it reached the other end of the line the Word was Gnzd.'

which suggests that at the time the Gospel was first reduced to writing, the Atlanteans were still using the Mark IVc.

Where the Atlanteans outstrip all other fax-using nations, of course, is in their ability to transmit more than mere facsimiles of the written word . . .

'Bedders?'

The word hung for a moment in the empty air,

glowed like embers, and died away. Then there was nothing but the faint howling of the wind that blows round the stars.

'Is that you, Turkey?'

The same, except that these letters flickered with a pale blue fire, and crackled in the thin air like sparklers.

'Where are you?'

'Over here.'

'Where's here, for God's sake?'

'I don't know, do I? Turkey, what's going on?'

And then they both felt the message; felt, not heard or saw. The message was:

There is no here or there. There is only information.

Two disembodied voices started speaking at the same time. It was a bit like Guy Fawkes Night.

Shut up and listen, then, came the message. *There is no here or there, up or down, you, me, they, he, she, now, then, right, wrong, fat, thin, black, white, yellow, green, alive, dead. There is only information. Transmitting.*

'All right,' the blue fire traced irritably. 'Transmitting what?'

You.

There were a few spurts of inchoate orange fire, and then a blaze of virtually illegible pyrotechnics. From the fact that most of the words spelt out were extremely vulgar, one can hypothesise the presence of some part of Sir Turquine.

Look at it this way, suggested the message. *You know how heavy gold is, right? And all money, broadly speaking, is gold. And you can send money by telegraphic transfer, right? Well, then.*

The orange flames flickered testily but got no further

than a bad-tempered incandescence. Then everything went black.

Two enormous rollers grinding out a roll of paper; except that it isn't paper. It has one dimension too many for that.

Sir Turquine and Sir Bedevere emerged from between the rollers as two-dimensional silhouettes, flopped out and gradually began to take shape, like balloons being blown up. Not until they were fully inflated did they animate; but as soon as that part of the process was over, Turquine at least was profoundly animated.

'Right,' he said, grimly. 'Nobody shoves me head first through a wireless set and gets away with it.' He rolled up his sleeves and looked round for somebody to take the matter up with.

'Turkey,' whispered Bedevere urgently beside him.

'What?' said Turquine, not looking back. 'Don't try and talk me out of this, Bedders. Somebody is going to get their heads punched for this, and—'

'Turkey.'

'What?'

'Look down, will you?'

Reluctantly, Turquine obeyed. He noticed that they seemed to be standing in a ploughed field. The earth was a pale reddish sort of colour, like clay. Very pale. Almost pink.

'Turkey,' said Bedevere, 'we're standing on some-body's finger.'

It's very hard to get yourself accustomed to truly enormous scales. The eye can only take in a certain amount of information, and the brain can only process a certain amount of the eye's input. You need to be able

to eke these resources out with a lot of imagination if
you want, for example, to identify a twenty-five-foot-
wide strip of ground as a finger.

'Oh yes,' said Turquine quietly, 'so we are.'

Welcome, purred the message, *to Atlantis. Do you
want to be enlarged?*

'I think so,' said Bedevere, 'don't you, Turkey? I
think that'd be a jolly good idea, if it's all the same
to—'

*Then we'll have a bit less of it from both of you, and
particularly him. Understood?*

'Understood.'

The finger shrank, until it became a hand, and it
shrank and it shrank and it shrank until the hand
closed over Bedevere's fingers and shook them warmly.
It was attached to an arm which connected it to a
round, bright-eyed, middle-aged man in a dark grey
suit.

'Let's get one thing straight, sir, shall we?' he said,
smiling. 'Here, we do things the civilised way. No
heavy stuff. All sanctions strictly economic. Got that?'
And he gave Turquine a look. Turquine growled and
nodded.

'Splendid,' said the round man. 'In that case, sir, let
me introduce myself. I'm Iophon, and this' – and the
two knights noticed another, identical man standing
beside him – 'is Pallas. We're from Exchange Control.'

'I'm sorry?' said Bedevere.

Iophon smiled. 'We're here to make sure that only
permitted amounts of authorised currency come in or
out,' he said. 'You can't be too careful, you know.'

'Excuse me,' said Bedevere. He pulled Turquine
aside by the sleeve and whispered to him for a moment,

and then turned back to Iophon, who was writing something on a clipboard. 'I think perhaps there's been a slight misunderstanding here.'

'I hope not,' said Iophon cheerfully. 'Now then, if you'll just let me have your amounts, denominations, account numbers and sort codes, I can pay you straight in. You're expected, you see.'

'Yes,' said Bedevere, 'like I was saying, a misunderstanding. You see, we're not money, we're people.'

Iophon grinned a little. 'That's all right, sir,' he said. 'People are accepted at more than two billion outlets galaxy-wide. People, if you'll pardon the phrase, sir, will do nicely. Just sign here, and we'll have you debited in no time.' He held out the clipboard. Bedevere backed away slightly.

'I don't think you quite understand,' he said. 'We don't want to ... to be cashed. I think we'd probably bounce. We just want to see someone about ...'

The other man, the one referred to as Pallas, stepped forward. There was something extremely unsettling about him. Bedevere explained it later as his having the air of someone who'd grab you by the scruff of the neck, shove your head under a spring-clip and slam the till shut on you without a second thought.

'Look, sir,' he said, 'you can either be paid in or' – and he made an unpleasant little gesture – 'paid out. Which is it to be?'

Turquine, meanwhile, had had enough. He was not, to put it mildly, as sensitive as Bedevere, and as far as he could see, here they were being threatened by two middle-aged men, the taller of whom came up to his breast pocket. He pushed past Bedevere and reached for a handful of lapels.

When he came round he was lying on his face. Whatever had happened to him, he hadn't enjoyed it. Bedevere, he noticed, was still on his feet, and his face had that Never-seen-him-before-in-my-life expression he remembered so well from their mutual schooldays. He groaned.

'Right,' Pallas was saying, 'that does it. Take them away and put them on deposit.'

Turquine groaned and loosened his belt.

'I mean,' he said 'it's inhuman. There's something about this in the Geneva Convention, isn't there – unusual or degrading punishment?'

'I think that's the American constitution,' Bedevere replied. Somewhere at the back of the cell there was a dripping noise. There always is in prisons. They have worse plumbing than hotels.

'Four stone in two days!' Turquine burst out, and pointed to his stomach, which had slopped over his waistband and was threatening to run down his legs. 'For God's sake,' he said bitterly, 'if this goes on any longer, even my socks won't fit. And,' he added desperately, 'they haven't even given us anything to eat.'

Bedevere nodded sadly. He'd never been exactly slender himself – he was one of those people who only have to look at a chocolate biscuit to start thickening up around the tummy – so it wasn't quite so bad for him; but Turkey, he knew, had always been quite fanatical about keeping his figure. Even, he remembered, at school; not that there'd been any danger of running to fat on half a loaf and a mug of stale mead a day. He smiled wanly – and, since it was pitch dark in the cell, pointlessly – and tried to think of something cheerful to say. He couldn't.

It's no fun being put on deposit. You ask a five-pound note.

Bedevere stirred about in the straw, finding to his distress that there was rather more of him than he was used to, and that it took quite a lot of effort just to move it about. 'You never know, there might be something clever we could do. Let's just stop a minute and think, shall we?'

'Fine.' Turquine glowered at him, or at least where he remembered seeing him last. It was very dark in the cell. 'Let's take stock of the situation, okay? We're in a cell in the depths of some sort of castle . . .'

'Vault,' said Bedevere.

'All right then, it's a bloody vault, so what? We're chained to the wall, in a vault, and . . .'

'In a bank,' Bedevere went on, talking more or less to himself. He'd found over the course of a long acquaintance that when one has nobody but Sir Turquine for company, quite often talking to oneself is the only way to get an intelligent conversation. 'In a bank,' he repeated.

'Fine,' Turquine growled, 'in a bank, if it makes you any happier. Chained to a wall, fat as pigs and getting fatter by the second . . .'

'And heavier.'

'Thank you, Mr Tactful. And, as you so perceptively say, heavier. And . . .'

Bedevere opened his eyes. 'Yes,' he said quietly. 'Heavier, and in a bank vault. On deposit. Yes, I think we're on to something here.'

'My God,' Turquine went on, ignoring him, 'I hate to think what this is doing to my arteries. They must be

so hard by now you could use them for gun barrels.
Ten years of eating high-polyunsaturated marge gone
for nothing.'

'Turkey,' said Bedevere, 'shut up whingeing for a
moment, and listen to me.'

Turquine stopped in mid-complaint. There was
something about the boy Bedevere – he'd half-noticed
it a few times over the years – that made you listen to
him when he sounded like that. Not that he ever said
anything remotely sensible, of course; usually he'd
come up with some remark like, 'I think we're lost,' or,
'It's late, perhaps we should be heading for home now,'
or even, 'Hitting people doesn't really solve things, you
know.' The trouble with young Bedders, if the truth
were known, was that there was a lot of good ware-
house space standing idle between his ears.

'Right,' Bedevere said calmly, 'I want you to stand
up.'

Ah well, thought Sir Turquine, why not? Nothing
else to do. He stood up.

'You standing up, Turkey?'

'Yes.'

'Thank you. Now walk forward until you reach the
end of the chain.'

'Is this some sort of aerobics, Bedders? Because if it
is, I've tried all that, and . . .'

Bedevere shook his head. 'Just do what I say, old
man, all right? Thanks. You there yet?'

'Yes.'

'Great. Now, then,' said Bedevere, 'I want you to fall
forwards.'

There was a faint clink in the darkness. 'What did
you say?'

'Fall forwards, there's a good fellow,' said Bedevere. 'As if you were trying to fall flat on your face. Just try it, would you, please?'

'Are you feeling all right, Bedders?' Turquine enquired cautiously. 'Starvation isn't getting to you, is it? Because I've heard stories, not eating makes you go all light-headed. You aren't seeing things, or anything?'

'No, thanks all the same,' Bedevere replied calmly. 'Now then, I'll count to three. One. Two.'

On the count of three, there was a grinding noise, and the sound of unhappy stone.

'Ah,' said Turquine, catching his breath, 'I think I see what you're getting at. You think my increased weight will mean I can pull the chain out of the wall. Good thinking.'

Bedevere, masked by the kindly darkness, made an exasperated face and counted quietly up to five. 'That's it, Turkey. Give it another go, why don't you?'

It took seven goes before finally there was a loud crash and a vulgar expression, muffled by having Sir Turquine's bulk on top of it. Then a small whoop of joy.

'Right,' said Bedevere, 'how are you doing?'

'Fine,' Turquine replied. 'Chain came out of the wall like a cork out of a bottle. My God, Bedders, I must have put on a hell of a lot of weight to manage that!'

Bedevere sighed. 'Splendid,' he said. 'Stout fellow, if you'll pardon the expression. Now, come over here and help me with my chain.'

With two extremely tubby knights yanking away at it, the staple holding Bedevere's chain to the wall didn't stand a chance. Bedevere would have preferred it if his comrade-in-arms hadn't landed on top of him when the staple gave way, but you can't make an omelette, as they say. He struggled out, stood up and dusted himself off.

'Now,' he said, 'we're getting somewhere.' He reached out with his foot and felt something cold, small and heavy. A pile of them. He nudged, and there was a heavy clunk, like a lead brick falling.

'Like I said,' he muttered to himself, 'a bank vault. Hey, Turkey, did you know that we were in a bank vault?'

'You may have mentioned it, yes.'

'And do you know what we're going to do next, Turkey? Well,' said Bedevere, smiling to himself, 'we're going to rob it.'

There was a silence broken only by that blasted drip. If ever I get out of here, Turquine thought to himself, I'm going to beat the pudding out of the first plumber I meet.

'What did you say?' he asked.

'We're going to rob the bank, Turkey,' Bedevere said cheerfully. 'What's up, got wax in your ears or something?'

Time, Turquine said to himself, to get a few things sorted out; such as priorities. 'Look,' he said, 'a place for everything and everything in it's place, that's what my old mother used to say. Let's get out of here first, and then we can think about—'

'You're an idiot, Turkey, do you know that?' said Bedevere, highly pleased about something. 'Listen. This is what we're going to do.'

Deputy Cashier Callistes woke from his doze and pulled on his helmet. Bells were ringing all over his office. Either the world was coming to an end or someone was robbing the vault; which, in the circumstances, was six of one and half a dozen of the other.

With his five deputy clerks at his back and a big wooden club with nails in it clutched in his right hand, he tiptoed down the corridor, opened the safe door and went in. The deputy clerks, who were also brave men, followed him.

Once they were all inside, somebody with no sense of fair play hit them over the head with gold bars, took the keys, locked them in the safe and ran away. By the time they were rescued by a SWAT team of trained auditors, they were all so fat that it took hydraulic lifts to move them.

Because they were native Atlanteans, with their biorhythms linked by the central computer to their current accounts, their short spell on deposit meant that each of them came out of the vault not only many stones heavier but many millions of dollars richer; and they were therefore taken directly from the vault to the courthouse, tried and found guilty of embezzlement. Under Atlantean law there is only one possible penalty for such a terrible crime. They were loaded on to a lorry, taken to the Till and cashiered.

'I knew a bit of exercise would get the fat off,' gasped Turquine, leaning on a doorframe and wiping the sweat from his eyes. 'Look!' He pointed to the waistband of his trousers.

'Good job too,' Bedevere panted in reply. 'Only I don't think it's the exercise, somehow.'

He was, of course, right. By leaving deposit without filling out the necessary withdrawal slips, both the knights had become hopelessly overdrawn, which accounted for the fact that they could barely stand up. It was probably just as well they didn't know what was happening to them; or that if they hadn't been picked up by a patrol fifteen minutes later, they would have been hit by massive bank charges and killed outright.

'Where the hell are we?' Turquine asked.

And that's bloody typical of the man, Bedevere thought, as he leant on the doorpost and tried to coax some air into his traumatised lungs. I mean, Turkey, how am I supposed to know where the hell we are? You think I nip over here on my days off for a spot of being hunted or something?

'Lord knows,' he replied. 'Look, is this actually getting us anywhere?'

Turquine stared at him. 'Say that again,' he said.

Bedevere put his back against the wall and slid down until he was crouching on his haunches. 'Running away,' he said. 'I mean where's the bloody point? It's not as if we know where the door is. Why don't we just . . .?'

'Well?'

Bedevere shrugged. 'Forget it,' he said. 'Don't mind me, I'm out of condition. Leave it to you.'

Turquine made no reply, and Bedevere suddenly realised that he – Turkey, of all people – was more or less at the end of his rope. Probably as a result of his habit of absent-mindedly eating the leftover pizzas.

'Stuff it,' said Turquine. 'I vote we stand and fight. Or stand, at any rate. Better still, let's sit down and fight.'

He sat down, let his head fall forward, and fell asleep.

About ten minutes later, the men from the Chief Clerk's department arrived. They were clearly intended to be the heavies. You could tell this by the way the pencils in their top pockets all had rubbers on the ends.

'Okay,' said Bedevere, 'it's a fair cop. I'm easy, but I think my friend here wants to hold out for a better exchange rate.'

The clerks looked at each other, and Bedevere noticed that they were, in a curious way, all trying to stand behind each other. Then one of them was propelled forward, politely but firmly, and cleared his throat.

'Resistance is useless,' he said.

'I know,' said Bedevere.

'Well, all right, then,' said the clerk, nervously. 'Try anything, buster, and you're history. You got that?'

'Absolutely.'

'Good.'

Nobody moved. It was all rather embarrassing, and Bedevere found he had this very strong urge to offer them all a cup of tea or something.

The spokesman made another soft, throat-clearing noise. He was standing on one foot now.

'We can do this the hard way,' he whispered. Or—?

'Sorry,' said Bedevere. 'Do you think you could speak up a bit?'

'Yes, certainly. We can do this the hard way, or we can do it the easy way. If that's all right with you,' he added. One of his colleagues gave him a shove. He turned round.

'All right,' he said, 'I've had enough, you hear? And I don't give a monkeys what they said at the office party.' He threw his clipboard to the ground, trod on it, slowly and rather majestically walked to the very back of the small knot of clerks and stood there with his arms folded.

Bedevere had had enough, too. 'Excuse me,' he said. 'I don't want to be a pest or anything, but perhaps you could see your way clear to taking me to your leader.'

'Right,' squeaked a voice from the middle of the posse. 'And no tricks, okay?'

'No tricks,' Bedevere sighed.

One of the clerks pointed to Turquine. 'What about him?' he said to his comrades.

'He looks so peaceful just sitting there.'

'It seems a pity to wake him, doesn't it?'

'No law against sleeping.'

'Doesn't look dangerous to me. Does he look dangerous to you, George?'

Oh for crying out loud, Bedevere thought. 'Please,' he said abruptly, 'can we make a start, if it's all the same to you? Only—'

'Cool it, all right?' snapped a small clerk, and then ducked behind the shoulder of the man next to him. Bedevere came to a decision.

'Actually,' he said, 'I expect you're all quite busy, really. Perhaps it'd be easier all round if you just showed me the way – draw a map or something – and then you lot could get on with whatever it is you're supposed to be doing. I mean, there's no point all of us trooping around, is there?'

The clerks looked at each other.

'Sounds all right to me,' one of them said.

'Great.'

'Fine.'

'Thank you.' Bedevere reached down and pulled Turquine by the ear.

'Go 'way,' Turquine growled. ''Nother ten minutes.' He lolled forward and began to snore.

'Turkey!' Bedevere shouted. 'Wake up!' He turned round. 'Sorry about this,' he said.

'Quite all right.'

'Don't mention it.'

Bedevere nodded amiably and kicked Turquine hard on the knee.

Ten minutes or so later, they were sitting in an office.

Quite a nice office, if you like them tidy, with matching matt-black in-tray, out-tray, anglepoise lamp and desk tidy. The chairs were comfortable, at any rate.

'Pleased to meet you,' Bedevere said.

'Likewise.'

The Atlantean was different, somehow. He was tall, young, with short hair and big ears. He looked at home in his surroundings; in fact, you could well believe that he was chosen to go with the decor.

'Allow me to introduce myself,' he said. 'Diomedes, Chief Assistant Technical Officer, at your service.'

'Thank you,' Bedevere replied, and gave Turquine a savage nudge in the ribs. Turquine simply nodded and went back to sleep. Diomedes smiled.

'Don't worry about it,' he said. 'It takes some people like that, being put on deposit. Especially if you're not used to it.'

'Um . . .'

'Exactly. And now,' Diomedes went on, 'I expect you'd like to know what Atlantis is all about, wouldn't you?'

'Yes,' Bedevere lied. 'Absolutely.'

'Right.' Diomedes nodded, and pulled a jar of paperclips towards him. As he spoke, he linked them up to form a chain.

'In a sense,' he said, 'Atlantis is a bank.'

He stopped speaking, and gave Bedevere a keen look. Oh hell, thought the knight, he wants me to say something intelligent. 'In a sense,' he hazarded.

'Spot on,' Diomedes replied, nodding vigorously. 'That is, in the same way Mussolini did his bit for the Italian railways, and Jesus Christ had his City and Guilds in carpentry, Atlantis is a bank. It's also something else, something rather special.' Diomedes smiled, catlike, and folded his fingers, by way of saying, Wow, this is going to curdle your brains.

Bedevere was uncomfortably aware that his right leg had gone to sleep.

'Atlantis,' Diomedes said, 'is a repository for money.'

'Right.'

'Precisely.' The smile widened, until it was in danger of losing itself behind Diomedes' ears. 'You're starting to get the point now, aren't you?'

At this point, Turquine woke up.

He blinked, rubbed his eyes, and then leant forward.

'Hello, Trev,' he said. 'What are you doing here?'

Diplomats must feel this way, Bedevere thought. You spend hours in airplanes, hotel rooms, bloody uncomfortable conference rooms with hard seats and nowhere to stretch your legs out; and just when you think you've got something lashed together that might just possibly work, some idiot of a basketball player defects and you might as well have stayed in bed.

Leave them to it, he said to himself.

'It *is* Trev, isn't it?' Turquine was saying. 'Trev Hastings, used to be behind the counter at the Global Equitable in Perry Bar? You remember me, I used to deliver pizzas. Yours was always ... Hold it, I never forget a pizza. Double pepperoni and—'

'That,' said Diomedes coldly, 'was a long time ago.'

In retrospect, Bedevere couldn't remember actually moving from his seat, but he would have sworn blind he jumped about a mile in the air.

'Perry Bar?' he said.

'We have many offices,' Diomedes said. 'It's a big organisation.' Something about the juxtaposition of his eyebrows and the bridge of his nose passed messages to Turquine's brain.

'Anyway,' said Turquine, 'long time no see. Sorry, you were saying?'

Diomedes relaxed his eyebrows. 'Money,' he said. 'What *is* money?'

Before Turquine could reply, Bedevere gave him a smart tap on the shins with his toe. Then he lifted an eyebrow and said, 'Ah!'

It was the right thing to do. 'I mean,' Diomedes went on, 'we all know what it does. Great. So the Son of Man was quite capable of knocking you up a perfectly decent Welsh dresser. But that's not what he was all about, is it?'

Turquine, to Bedevere's great relief, seemed to have got into the swing of it, because he scratched his ear, nodded and said, 'Precisely.' He spoilt it rather by winking at Bedevere immediately afterwards; luckily, though, Diomedes didn't notice.

'Gold 337,' Diomedes said. He reached across the desk and caught hold of one of those Newton's cradle things. 'This continent is built on it. It's anti-magnetic. Anti-magnetism makes the world turn. Okay so far?'

Bedevere nodded. 'Sure,' he said. He shrugged nonchalantly. 'Everyone knows that. Tell me something I couldn't get from the Sunday supplements.'

'Right,' said Diomedes, and just then, Bedevere realised that yes, this man *could* be called Trevor. In fact, he probably was. 'So gold is money, okay?'

'Okay.'

'And money is magic.'

In another part of the building, the bell rang for the afternoon history lesson.

Two junior Atlanteans took their place at the back of the class. One of them had a mouse in his pocket. Just as some flowers did manage to grow between the trenches in Flanders, so the schoolchildren in Atlantis do have mice.

They catch them. They build little hutches for them out of shoe-boxes. They feed them on breadcrumbs and bits of apple-core. Then they sell them.

By the time they reach the sixth form, some Atlanteans have already made their first million just from dealing in mouse futures.

The teacher, a tall lady with deceptively thin arms, rapped on her desk.

'Good morning, children,' she said.

'Good morning, teacher.'

'Open your history books,' said the teacher, 'and turn to page 58.'

She took a deep breath, and hesitated for a moment. She'd been teaching for twenty years, and this bit still gave her the willies.

'Now then,' she said. 'Which of you can tell me what money is?'

The usual bewildered silence. The usual rustle at the back of the class as a mouse changed hands under the desk. The usual blank faces.

'Well?'

'Please, miss.'

Isocrates Minor, the teacher noticed. Ten and a half years old, and already he's got a cellular phone strapped to the handlebars of his bike. The teacher nodded approvingly and made a mental note to ask him about moving heavily into short-dated gilts after the lesson.

'Please, miss,' said Isocrates Minor, 'money is magic, miss.'

'Well done, Isocrates Minor. Now then . . .'

'Miss.'

The teacher frowned. There is such a thing as showing off. 'All right,' she said. 'Questions later.'

'Yes, but miss . . .'

'Later! Now then, money is magic. What does magic do, anyone?'

'Miss!'

'No, someone else this time. Diogenes, let's hear from you for a change.'

A small face crumpled at the back of the room, as a daydream of a nationwide chain of mousebroking offices faded away and was replaced by panic.

'Don't know, miss.'

'Anyone else? Laodicea?'

A small girl stood up and smirked. 'Magic,' she recited, 'is the name commonly given to the technology based on the exploitation of the remarkable properties of the gold isotope Gold 337. Gold 337 was discovered by Simon Magus . . .'

'Yes, thank you, dear.'

'. . . in the year 4000BC,' continued Laodicea, 'when he was hoeing his turnip field. He quickly grasped the immense potential of—'

'Thank you, dear,' said the teacher. 'Now, as soon as the early Atlanteans realised how special gold was, they started digging it up and making magical things out of it. Now, can anyone give me an example of the sort of things . . . yes, Lycophron?'

The small boy blushed under his freckles. 'Buttons, miss?' he suggested.

The teacher sighed. 'No, not buttons.'

'Waste-paper baskets.'

'Catapults.'

'Space rockets.'

'My uncle's got gold buttons, miss, on his blazer. He showed me . . .'

'The ancient Atlanteans,' said the teacher magisterially, 'made *coins* out of the gold they found in the earth. When they'd got lots of these coins, they put them in a bank . . .'

A hand shot up. 'Please, miss.'

'Yes, Nicomedes?'

'Why, miss?'

The teacher braced herself. 'To keep them safe, of course. Now . . .'

'Why didn't they put them under the bed, miss?'

'That's not terribly safe, is it, dear? Now . . .'

'My dad keeps all his money under the bed, miss.'

The teacher felt her knuckles tightening up. 'Well, I don't think that's a very sensible thing to do, dear. Now . . .'

'My dad says he doesn't trust banks. He says if he put his money in the bank, Mummy would see the statements and know how much money he's got. What's a statement, miss?'

'A bank,' said the teacher firmly. 'And then the bank would lend money to people so that they could start up businesses, and so the money was all put to work, and the country prospered. But then something very peculiar started to happen. Now, does anyone know what that was?'

Silence again. This time, the teacher decided, just tell them. Then we'll all be home in time for tea.

'What happened,' she said, therefore, 'was that all the magic in the coins in the bank started *leaking out* – ' She said it well. Several of the more nervous and imaginative children went quite pale. '– leaking all over the place. It got so bad that the rooms in the bank where they kept all the coins stopped being square and became round.'

Several hands shot up, but she ignored them. She didn't want to explain; it wasn't very nice to think about. When she'd been a student, she'd had to read the description of it by a clerk who'd got trapped in the vault overnight. The bit where he described what the gold ingots did to each other when they thought nobody was looking still made her feel ill to this day.

'Quite round,' she said. 'And that wasn't all, not by a long way. So the wise elders of Atlantis decided that they'd have to do something about it. Now, does anyone . . .?'

A mistake. But it was too late by then.

'Please, miss.'

'Yes, Hippolyta.'

Hippolyta cleared her throat. 'The Atlanteans founded the Central Research Institute (AD 477), whose principal objects were research into the relationship between the gold's powerful anti-magnetic field and the rest of the world, which is of course attuned to positive magnetism, miss. Their researches revealed that if too much anti-magnetic material was released into the outside world, it would have drastic effects on the stability of the planet, miss. They . . .'

My God, thought the teacher, that girl will probably be Chief Cashier one day. She shuddered.

'Very good, Hippolyta,' she said. 'In other words, if any more gold left Atlantis, it would be very bad indeed. So the gold had to stay where it was, buried underground, and all the gold they'd dug up and made into coins had to be put back. *Alcibiades, what are you doing with that mouse, bring it here immediately*!'

The mouse safely locked in her desk, the teacher pulled herself together and hurried through the rest of the lesson . . .

How the Atlanteans realised that the unique relationship between their gold deposit and the similar deposit on the moon would be jeopardised by further gold exports . . .

How this was a problem, because the entire civilization of Atlantis was now based on the exploitation of money. How the Atlanteans thought about it, and came up with a way of trading in money which didn't actually involve the money ever leaving the earth's crust; a way of getting lots of money in but never paying any money out ...

How they renamed the gold 'capital' and invented financial services ...

'Now then,' said the teacher, and looked at her watch. In exactly five seconds, the bell would go, the children would run out into the playground to play football, swing on the swings and form mouse-holding syndicates, and she would retreat to the Common Room for a cigarette and a large sherry.

'Any questions?' she said.

For maybe twenty seconds, which is a long time, nobody said anything. Eventually, Turquine closed his eyes, shook his head and laughed.

'Come on,' he said, 'this is a wind-up, isn't it? You always were a bloody comedian, Trev, like the time you got that girl on your reception to swear blind you'd ordered a deep pan Cheese Banquet with double pepperoni and ...'

It was Diomedes' turn to look bewildered. He frowned, as if someone had just suggested to him that the sun was a huge practical joke.

'Are you saying you think I've made all that up?' he asked.

'Well,' said Turquine, still smiling jovially, 'you have, haven't you? All that cod about the moon being made out of gold ...'

'It is not,' said Diomedes coldly, 'cod.'

'I mean,' Turquine went on, oblivious to the danger

signals, 'if you'd said made of *silver*, or maybe if you'd said it was the *sun* that's made of gold, yes, you might have had me going there for a minute. But . . .'

Turquine's voice did roughly the same thing as a pint of water might do if spilt in the middle of the Kalahari Desert. 'Trev?' he asked.

'I must ask you,' said Diomedes, 'not to call me Trev.'

Turquine bristled. 'Why not?' he demanded. 'It's your name, isn't it?'

'Was.'

'Bloody good name, too,' Turquine went on. 'If ever I saw a born Trev, that's you. All young men with big noses and ties like road accidents who work in building societies are called Trev; it's a well-known fact. Like all dogs are called Rover,' he added sagely.

'Please . . .' said Diomedes. Tiny red spots appeared behind the lines of his mouth, and Bedevere came to the conclusion that it was time he intervened. Idiots are all very well in their place, but one mustn't let things get out of hand.

'We're just a little – well, taken aback,' he therefore said. 'I mean, it's a bit of a shock, finding out all of a sudden that the world revolves because of money on the moon, and . . .' Something occurred to him. 'Mind you, it explains things, though, doesn't it? Are interest rates linked to the tides, or something? And what about inflation?'

Diomedes sighed. 'Look . . .' he said.

He got no further; because Bedevere, having drawn him off guard with his questions, now chose what was, after all, the perfect moment to hit him very hard with the base of the anglepoise lamp. Diomedes made a little gurgling noise, and fell forward across the desk.

'You see,' Bedevere said calmly, standing up and reaching across the table for a bunch of keys he'd spotted some time earlier, 'it's all a matter of finesse. Sure, we thump the bastards. But we use our heads, too.'

Turquine grunted. 'Speak for yourself,' he replied. 'Tried it a couple of times, had a headache for weeks, cut my forehead. Look, you can still see the scar.' He pointed. 'Mind you,' he conceded, 'one of the little perishers was wearing a helmet at the time.' He pushed the stunned Atlantean away from the desk, rolling his swivel chair aside, and started to go through the desk drawers.

'Calculator,' he said, 'another calculator, *another* calculator . . . Hey, what's this?'

'What?' Bedevere was looking through Diomedes' briefcase. 'Oh, that. It's a small solar-powered calculator that looks like a credit card.' He frowned. 'Hold on, you don't even know what we're looking for yet.'

'Yes I do,' replied Turquine. 'We're looking for the Personal Organiser of—'

'It's not going to be here, is it?' said Bedevere impatiently.

Turquine scowled at him. 'And why not?' he said. 'It's in Atlantis, young Snotty said as much. This is Atlantis. Ergo . . .'

Bedevere was surprised. 'Where d'you learn expressions like ergo, Turkey?' he asked.

'There was a radio in the van,' Turquine replied. 'What are we looking for, then?'

'Food,' Bedevere replied. 'I'm starving.'

* * *

When they got out into the corridor, unfed and disguised as dangerous fugitive knights, they heard the PA yelling, 'Warning! Warning! Unauthorised intruders! Accept no cheques without a banker's card!' This worried them until they found that the noise stopped if you ripped the speakers off the wall and jumped on them.

Actually, that was Turquine's idea. One of his better efforts.

'We're not really making ourselves popular around here, are we?' Bedevere muttered, as they ran along yet another identical passageway.

'Bloody touchy, this lot,' Turquine agreed. 'You were right saying we should try the softly-softly approach.'

He paused to bang together the heads of two passing actuaries, and then added, 'Mind you, it doesn't seem to be working.'

'True,' Bedevere replied, and he kicked a third actuary in the groin. 'You know, I have this feeling we're going about this in the wrong way.'

Turquine nodded. 'I vote we—'

But he was interrupted. A hidden door opened in the wall, and a face materialised and grinned at them.

'This way,' it said. 'Quick.'

Turquine hesitated for a split second. 'Why?' he said.

'Why not?' the face replied. 'Come on.'

The two knights looked at each other.

'That's the best reason I've heard for anything since we got here,' said Bedevere. 'After you.'

It was dark, and cold. The walls were bare stone. In the

shadows, water dripped and a rat scuttled.

'This is more like it,' said Turquine enthusiastically. 'You know, that place was starting to give me the creeps. All that carpet...'

The owner of the face beckoned, and they followed.

'Really bad for the nerves,' Turquine went on, 'all that carpet. You get to thinking, My God, if all the sheep that got sheared just to make this lot were lined up nose to tail, they'd probably reach from' – he made a wide gesture with his arms – 'Paddington to Euston. But this, it's more like, well, homely.' He stopped to admire a skeleton hanging from chains on the wall. 'My dad had one of those,' he said. 'Bought it at a wagon boot sale. Said it made him feel all baronial.'

Bedevere quickened his step and drew alongside their guide.

'Where is this?' he asked. The guide chuckled, and the sound echoed away into the darkness, where something probably ate it. 'We're just passing under the main bourse complex,' he said, 'midway between the Old Exchange and the Rialto. We're about five hundred feet beneath cash level. Are you having trouble breathing?'

'No,' Bedevere replied.

The guide shrugged. 'Well,' he said, 'it takes all sorts. This way.'

He disappeared through a low archway; the sort of opening Jerry the mouse might have built if he'd had access to explosives. Turquine, who was too busy looking about him and sighing happily to look where he was going, banged his head and swore.

'Along here,' the guide was saying, 'we're going directly under the registered office itself, so watch where you're going. Reality can be a bit iffy...'

As he spoke, the floor and ceiling vanished. When it came back again a few seconds later, Bedevere had the distinct impression that everything had moved about a yard to the right.

'It does that,' the guide explained. 'It's because of the registered office's main relocation matrix.'

'Ah,' said Bedevere, 'of course.'

The guide grinned at him. 'Which works like this,' he said. 'Because, you see, Atlantis is what you might call an offshore tax haven. In fact, *the* offshore tax haven.'

'Gosh.'

'Quite true. Now,' said the guide, 'I expect you've often thought that one day, what with one thing and another, all the money in the world is gradually going to get sifted and slipped offshore, till there's nothing actually left to spend. Right? Thought so. Well, that already happened. A long time ago.'

'Um.'

'In fact,' the guide was saying, 'that's what Atlantis is all about. You see, Atlantis is where money started...'

'Um, yes,' Bedevere said. 'Someone just told us.'

'I wouldn't be at all surprised,' said the guide. 'They love telling you all about it, don't they? Mind your head, it's off again.'

In the two or three seconds when all the dimensions were up for grabs, Turquine yelled and said something very vulgar. This was because he hadn't ducked, but the world had. They were now four and a half metres lower than they had been.

'The registered office,' the guide was saying, 'is not

only offshore, it keeps dodging about. Brilliant, really. How can they ever assess you to tax if you never stay still for more than thirty seconds running?'

'Absolutely,' Bedevere agreed. 'Look, are we nearly out of that bit, because . . .'

The guide laughed. 'Depends, doesn't it?' he said. 'You never know. I've known days when the registered office just sort of follows you about. Ah, that's better, we're clear of it now.'

They had come out under a broad dome; the sort of thing Justinian would have put on Saint Sophia if he'd had peculiar dreams and lots of money. Far above them was a tiny point of light.

'That's the blowhole,' the guide explained. 'What with all the magical money directly underneath us, and the registered office darting about like a mouse in a maze, there's got to be some way the excess pressure can find its way out. It's the only point where Atlantis is open to the sky. We tend to like it in here.'

'Pardon me asking,' Bedevere asked, 'but who's we?'

The guide smirked at him. 'Thought you'd never ask,' he said. 'We're the hackers. The Atlantis underground, so to speak.'

'Right,' said Turquine. 'So you hate the little bastards too, do you?'

'Right on,' said the hacker. 'That's why we're helping you.'

Turquine extended a massive paw. 'Put it there,' he said. 'Right, let's get the little . . .'

The hacker smiled sadly. 'Good idea,' he said, 'but not practical. Instead, we just try and get as far up their noses as we possibly can.'

Turquine shrugged. 'So why are you called hackers?' he asked.

'Partly,' the hacker replied, 'because we live by tapping into the natural energy discharges of the money reserves and turning them into food. Partly because if ever we catch any of the Topsiders down here, we hack their—'

'Fine,' Bedevere interrupted, 'point taken. You were explaining.'

'Was I?'

Bedevere glanced quickly at Turquine, on whom all this talk of hacking was probably having a bad effect. 'Yes,' he said firmly. 'So how does it all work?' he went on. 'How come Atlantis can't be found from the outside?'

The hacker beckoned. 'This way,' he said. 'It's very simple, really. Atlantis is a corporation, right? And the address of a corporation is its registered office. That's where all its official letters and faxes are sent to, that's where its books of record are kept, and the place where the registered office is decides which tax jurisdiction it falls under. Follow?'

'I think so.'

'Well,' said the hacker, 'the registered office of Atlantis moves every thirty seconds, so it follows that Atlantis isn't anywhere, or at least not anywhere in particular. It's mobile. It's flicking backwards and forwards all over the place. It therefore has no geographical reality; just a fax number. That's how you got here, isn't it?'

They were looking at a huge steel column which ran up from the ground into the roof. It was humming slightly, and when Turquine tried touching it he pulled his hand away quickly, yelped and sucked his fingers.

'That,' said the hacker, 'is the main matrix coil. It controls the movement of the registered office; sort of generates the field which bobs it around. If we could only cut through that . . .'

'Yes?' said Turquine, enthusiastically.

'But we can't,' continued the guide. 'Nobody can. That thing's driven down into a five-kilometre-thick layer of molten Gold 337, and it sort of pipes magic up into a network of conductors that runs through the whole structure. We've tried dynamite, we've tried diamond-tipped drills, we've tried walloping it with big hammers, but all we manage to do is have a really good time and break a few tools. It's magic, you see. Can't touch it without magic of your own.'

'I see,' said Bedevere, thoughtfully. 'And what would happen if you did manage to . . .?'

The hacker grinned. 'God only knows,' he said. 'Probably the world would come to an end. Who cares? Come and have a coffee.'

He led the way to a little lean-to propped up on the side of the pillar, where a small group of people – more hackers, presumably – were boiling a kettle over a fire of what Bedevere recognised as thousand-dollar bills. The hackers grinned at them and waved.

'Hiya,' said one of them. 'Grab a mug, sit down, help us blow up the world.'

Over a mug of truly awful coffee – Bedevere learnt later that it wasn't coffee at all but an *ersatz* made out of deutschmarks steeped in radiator oil – Bedevere tried to find out a bit more about their new hosts.

The hackers, it turned out, had been here almost since the beginning. They were, in fact, dissenting

shareholders, who had refused to accept the recom-
mended offer when Atlanticorp was taken over by
the present holding company Lyonesse (Atlantis)
plc . . .

'Lyonesse?' Bedevere asked suddenly.

'Who else?' replied a friendly, red-faced hackeress.
'Been in charge around here for – what, getting on for
eighteen hundred years since the big takeover bid. We
were all on the wrong side, of course. We held out for
the rescue package offered by the White Knight—'

'Thought we had 'em, too,' interrupted a large, hairy
hacker with a lot of scars on his neck. 'Got it referred
to Monopolies, full investigation, the works. Then they
mounted a dawn raid.' He shuddered.

'We're the ones who got away,' went on the hackeress. 'Most of us didn't, though.'

Bedevere tried to look sympathetic. 'Killed?' he
asked. The hackers started to laugh.

'God, no,' said their guide. 'Atlanteans don't die.
We're all companies, see, and you can't kill a company.
You can only wind it up.' He made a horribly ex-
pressive gesture with his hands. 'They're all up there
somewhere,' he said, 'in the Receiver's Department.
Being wound up.'

The hairy hacker nodded. 'We calculated the other
day,' he said, 'that if you attached a propeller to one of
them and let him go suddenly, he'd probably fly from
here to Jupiter before he ran out of —'

'Ah,' said Bedevere. 'So, er, what is it exactly that
you're hoping to, well, achieve?'

The hackers gave him a funny look.

'We don't want to achieve anything,' said their
guide, after an uncomfortable pause. 'Bugger achieve-

ment. We want to get our own back on the bastards. Pity, really,' he added.

'We're into impotent resentment, mostly,' explained a thin hackeress. 'We harbour grudges, too, but mostly we resent. That and a bit of conspiracy.'

Bedevere was thinking. 'This White Knight,' he said. 'Anybody I'm likely to have heard of?'

The hackers looked at each other. 'Come to think of it,' said the guide, 'that's a very good question. Anybody here know who . . .?'

'It was a consortium,' said the red-faced hackeress. 'An international consortium negotiating a management buy-out.'

'No it wasn't,' replied the hairy hacker. 'It was the original shareholders on a rights issue. They issued a Declaration of Rights. I've got a copy of it.' He patted his pockets. 'Somewhere,' he added.

'You're both wrong,' broke in a tall, freckled hacker, 'it was a market-led refinancing programme backed by the Bank of Saturn.'

'It was the Martians. They were trying to break into the oxygen-based lifeform market, and they wanted a way round the tariff barriers . . .'

'I always thought it was us,' said a small, dumpy hacker. The others stared at him, and he went bright red.

'Anyway,' said the guide, 'it was them. Have some more coffee?'

'No thanks,' said Bedevere. 'Anyway, there was this takeover, and these people – the Topsiders, you called them – they took over?'

'Absolutely,' said the guide. 'They had new sorts of magic, you see. New ways of making the gold do what they wanted. We were decimalised.'

'You mean decimated.'

'I meant,' said the guide grimly, 'what I said. Anyway, that's enough about us. What can we do for you?'

Bedevere kicked Turquine quickly on the shin and then smiled.

'Actually,' he said.

5

Midnight.

The last tourist had long since gone, the bookstall was closed, the curator had locked up. The place was empty.

Well, almost.

In the back room – in his day it had been a sort of secondary scullery – the immortal remains of William Shakespeare sharpened a pencil, licked his lips and turned over a handbill about guided tours of Warwickshire.

Amazing, he said to himself, the cavalier attitude they have towards paper these days. The nerds. They only use one side of it, and then as often as not they screw it into a ball and chuck it on the floor. He sighed as his insubstantial fingers smoothed the paper out. Don't know they're born, the lot of them. In my day, he muttered under his breath, you wanted to write something, first you had to get a sheep, then you knocked it on the head, peeled off the wool, scraped the thing down with a whacking great knife ... Made you choose your words that bit more carefully. But now...

Uncharacteristically, he hesitated for a moment before getting down to work and looked around him. This had always been a good room for writing in, he remembered; which was just as well, seeing as how it was the only one he could ever get any peace in. Then, of course, the fact that it was only just big enough for a man to sit down in and close the door had been a problem. Now, it didn't matter very much.

He shook his head. Youth, he said to himself, ah, youth! You can stuff it.

A quick glance at the clock reminded him that time was getting on. Not that he'd ever had difficulties in meeting deadlines; far from it. Still, they'd been most insistent, and he had been in the game too long not to know that you're only as good as your word. He lowered his head and, his lips moving rhythmically, he began to write.

Scene Four, he wrote. *The Rovers Return. Bet is checking the mixers while Alec puts the float in the till.*

Well, yes. Structurally speaking, the situation demanded it, and these days, of course, you didn't have to bother about giving them time to change the set. You could have any scene you liked. Have a scene at the North Pole next, if you wanted to. Long live progress!

Bet: Jacko's late again.

Alec:

He scratched his head and thought hard. There was something about Alec; perhaps he hadn't yet got the voice properly fixed in his mind. It just wasn't coming; the true Alec hadn't yet come to life. He rubbed his chin thoughtfully and tried to think about the motivation behind the character. Here we have a man, he thought, apparently successful, in the prime of life, happily married, popular in the community. But something is lacking; and that which should accompany old age (honour, love, obedience, troops of friends) he cannot look for . . .

Ah! Gotcha.

Alec: (snorts) Typical! If he spent less time supping ale down the Legion and . . .

Just then, there was a faint but distinct noise from the old back parlour, as of somebody walking stealthily in the dark and barking his shins on the firedogs.

Burglars!

It had to be burglars. Nobody else was likely to be about at this time of night. He bit his lip, screwed his courage to the sticking point and reached for the poker.

If you're hunting burglars through a deserted and darkened house, it helps to have been born there and to have spent the last four hundred years haunting it. You tend to know the more important facts about the place, like where the chairs are. You aren't liable to walk straight into a . . .

'Sod it!' he howled, rubbing his toe and hopping up and down. 'What bloody fool put that there?'

There were sounds of hurried movement from the back parlour, and a sliver of light appeared under the door. Voices, speaking urgently and low. More than one of them.

In situations like these, one has a choice. One can seek the bubble reputation, even in the cannon's mouth. Or one can hide in the grandfather clock.

There was a faint oath as something insubstantial but fragile collided with the pendulum, and then the door of the clock swung shut, just as the back parlour door flew open. They have their exits and their entrances, you might say.

A woman was silhouetted against the light; a tall, slim woman. Light flashed on a loose coil of golden hair. Behind her, the shape of a man loomed ominously. Inside the clock-case a mouse, searching for a light supper for herself and her nest, bumped into something she didn't recognise, squeaked in terror, and started to climb for all she was worth, until she banged her head against the escapement, staggered, and darted back.

For the record, the clock struck one. Life is full of these little coincidences.

'Hell's bells,' said the woman testily, 'is it that late already? Come on, we'll leave it for now. Time we weren't here.'

It was difficult to tell from inside the clock what was going on; there was a series of bleeps, a whirring sort of noise, and then a sort of peculiar ringing. Then the sound of tiny rollers feeding something. Then another bleep. Then silence.

After about five minutes of the silence, the door of the grandfather clock swung open and nothing emerged carefully from it. This time he was properly dematerialised. Like the man said, discretion was the better part of valour.

A brief investigation showed that the funny noises had indeed come from the back parlour, which the tourist people used as a sort of office. The room was empty, but the strange white machine that sat by the telephone was

winking its little red light at him. He sat down on the desk
and looked at it. It was the thing he always thought of as
the paper-wasting machine, in that during the day,
whenever it was used, the tourist people were always
complaining about bits of paper not feeding in properly
and getting screwed up. A crying waste.

Just then, it bleeped once more and started to churn
out a little slip with some numbers on it. He waited
until the rollers had quite finished, shook his head
sadly and pulled the little slip clear. You could get ten
or twelve lines on that, if you wrote small. He folded it
neatly, switched out the light, and went back to the
scullery.

Transmitting . . .

The Queen of Atlantis, Managing Director of the
Lyonesse group of companies, stepped out of the fax
and walked briskly towards her office. Behind her came
her seven personal assistants, carrying the luggage.

The Queen sat at her desk, kicked off her shoes and
looked through the sheaf of While-you-were-out notes
that had gathered like a drift of wind-blown leaves in
her absence. Some she put to one side, the rest she
distributed like a sort of Royal Maundy among her
PAs.

'What's this?' she demanded. 'Unidentified trans-
mission from – where? I'll swear that woman's handwriting is getting worse.'

'Stirchley, Your Majesty.'

'Stirchley . . .' The Queen bit her lip and pondered
for a moment. 'What's at Stirchley, somebody?'

The PAs looked at each other for a while, until the
faint tapping of long nails on the leather of the desktop

goaded one of them into action.

'Nothing, Your Majesty,' he said. 'Or at least, nothing much. We maintain a small transmitting station there as part of the network, but it's never used.'

The Queen swivelled round in her chair and smiled at the unfortunate spokesman. 'Well,' she said brightly, 'somebody's been using it recently, haven't they? Perhaps you'd be awfully sweet and find out what's been going on.'

The PA blanched, bowed swiftly and hurried backwards out of the room, and his colleagues heard the sound of hurried footsteps climbing the stairs. The Queen, meanwhile, was looking at a security report and frowning.

'Listen to this,' she said. 'Apparently, someone's been duffing up the cashiers while we've been away. Fancy! And what's more, two intruders were put on deposit but escaped. I didn't know it was possible to escape from deposit. One of you' – she swept the remaining PAs with a smile like a prison-camp search-light – 'be a dear and look into that for me, will you?'

The smile stopped at the second PA from the left, who set his jaw, swallowed hard and dashed away. That just left five of them.

'Honestly,' the Queen was saying, 'one pops out of the office for five minutes and everything gets into such a tangle! Who was duty officer, someone?'

A PA consulted the register. A name was mentioned. The PA was ordered to be an angel and have a quiet word with him. Trembling slightly, the PA hurried off. It's a filthy job, he said to himself as he went, but somebody's got to do it.

'Otherwise,' the Queen said at last, 'everything seems to be in order and running nicely. Good. Perhaps now we can get down to some work. My briefcase please, someone.'

She had just started dictating a long memo about unit costings when the door flew open and the PAs reappeared. In defiance of some of the leading laws of physics, they all seemed to be trying to stand behind each other. The Queen looked up.

'Well, boys?' she said, smiling at them over the top of her reading glasses. 'Any luck?'

'Um.' The PAs had had an informal ballot, and the loser had been elected spokesman. 'Not as such,' he said. 'At least, we do seem to have found out who the intruders are, but not where they are. Not,' he said, and his voice withered like a daffodil in a furnace, 'strictly speaking, that is. Or at least, we think there's a chance they may be . . .' He gulped and pointed at the floor.

The Queen took off her glasses and nibbled one earpiece thoughtfully. 'Go on,' she said. 'You were saying who these people might be.'

'Um.' A small globe of sweat bounced down the PA's nose. 'We, um, did a credit search on them while they were on deposit, and they seem to be a couple of, ah, knights.'

'Knights?'

'Um.'

'Knights,' enquired the Queen, 'as in Arabian, or knights as in shining armour?'

'Knights as in shining armour, ma'am. Bedevere and Turquine, Your Ma—'

There was a tiny brittle sound, caused by the

snapping of the earpiece of a pair of dainty gold-framed spectacles. 'Dear me,' said the Queen, 'how extremely tiresome.'

'Yes, Your M—'

'Drat.'

'Yes, Your—'

'And in the . . . in Thing, you say?'

'Yes, um . . .'

The smile, bright as the oncoming headlights to a dazzled rabbit, flicked from one pale, drawn face to another and finally came to rest.

'Be an absolute sweetheart, one of you,' said the Queen, 'and go and fetch them.'

'It's not fair.'

By way of emphasis, the lantern swayed violently, revealing a narrow spiral stone staircase. A worn brown chain running up the central column provided the only handgrip. It was spooky.

'Shut up.'

'Yes,' replied Iphicrates, senior assistant Assistant to the Queen of Atlantis, 'but why's it always us, for crying out loud? It's not as if she hasn't got about fifty thousand other bloody gophers who could—'

'Shut up.'

The lantern wobbled violently. 'Don't you tell me to shut up, you crawler,' Iphicrates snapped. Above his head, something whirred, and if this was a hotel rather than the bowels of Atlantis City, you'd have sworn someone had just had a bath. 'Oh hell. Freeze, everybody.'

The staircase disappeared, only to rematerialise a moment or so later three feet to the right. The lantern, which had gone out, lit up again as several million confused photons groped their way through the stonework towards it.

'And that,' said Iphicrates firmly, 'doesn't help matters, does it? I mean, how the hell are you supposed to keep a sense of direction around here when the whole place keeps going walkabout? I mean, how do we know this staircase still goes anywhere, for a start? We could spend the rest of our lives—'

'Look.' A hand tightened on Iphicrates' ear. 'For the last time, be quiet.'

Iphicrates shook himself free. 'No,' he said angrily. 'The hell with you, Androcles. This is a lousy, dangerous job and I'm damned if I'm going to go chasing around in the basement among the hackers for a bunch of lunatic burglars, just because Madam's got her knickers in a twist again. Bloody good luck to them, I say.'

'Shut—'

'No,' said Iphicrates, firmly, and there was a grating sound as he put the lantern down. 'Go on, you tell me, why should I?'

'Because,' hissed a voice in his ear, 'Her Majesty is just behind us on the stairs. All right?'

'But don't mind me,' sang the proverbial silvery voice from the darkness. 'You boys just carry on with what you were doing and pretend I'm not here.'

There was a profound silence; then the sound of a lantern being picked up and somebody nervously humming the national anthem. The procession continued on its way.

It was a very long staircase.

'Er, chaps . . .'

The lantern stopped. 'What's up?'

'Have you, sort of, noticed something?'

'Like what?'

Pause.

'Like,' said the voice from the back – and if there had been any light it would have been possible to see the speaker looking extremely self-conscious – 'put me straight if I'm not on the right lines, but we are going *down* the stairs, aren't we?'

'So?'

'So, why are the stairs going *upwards*?'

Pause.

'Not that I'm the slightest bit bothered myself, one way or the other,' the voice continued. 'All the same to me, really. Just thought I'd . . .'

Grating sound of grounded lantern. A distant scraping sound, which could be a man scratching his head.

'You know,' said Iphicrates, 'he's got a point there, hasn't he?'

Shuffling of footsteps, and the sound of seven people waiting for somebody else to be the first one to say something. Eventually—

'Excuse me.'

'Yes, Your Majesty?'

'Someone be terribly sweet and pass me the lantern. Ah yes, got it, thanks ever so much. Now then, let's just have a quick look, shall we?'

The lantern flickered and then started to blaze out light like a beacon. It showed up seven very nervous men, a composed but frowning woman with golden hair, and a spiral staircase. Going up.

'Perhaps,' suggested Iphicrates, 'it would help if we all turned round. Then surely . . .'

Then the world disappeared. As the perceptible

parameters of reality faded away, there was an audible sigh of relief. The lantern went out.

'Has anybody got a match or something?'

Fumbling in pockets noise. Scraping sound. The hiss of flaring sulphur.

'Oh look,' said the Queen, 'we would appear to be in a corridor. Now, anyone, how did that happen?'

Before the light died, it had a chance to explore a patch of what looked like a straight, flat passageway with tiled sides. Perfectly normal looking for, say, a walkway in an Underground station; but a bit counter-intuitive for a staircase, unless you're very heavily into lateral thinking.

Pause.

'Oh well, everybody, looks like we're here. Anybody mind if I lead the way?'

There was a muffled chorus of Fines and Greats and, rather more accurately, Right behind you, Your Majestys, and then a sparkling flash of yellow light as the Queen of Atlantis lit the end of her sceptre and walked purposefully down the corridor.

Transmitting . . .

There was a grinding noise, rather like a crate of milk bottles being run over by a road roller, and then a bleep. Turquine, Bedevere and ten hackers fell out of the fax machine and on to a plain rough plank floor.

The fax machine whirred on for a moment, gave its customary hiccup, and wound out its little slip of paper. Then it realised what it had done, and whimpered.

'Well,' said Bedevere, picking himself up and brushing a fair quantity of dust off his knees. 'It worked, then.'

Nobody seemed to be listening. The hackers were staring with open mouths and eyes like compact discs at this small, unfurnished, bare-walled, scruffy room. Turquine was feeling in his pocket for something.

'Got it,' he said, producing a rather grubby peppermint. 'Knew I'd lost one in there a while back.' He popped it in his mouth and crunched it.

'So this is it,' Bedevere was saying. He was aware that, for all intents and purposes, he was talking to himself; but what else could you do if you wanted an intelligent conversation around here? 'Pretty smart thinking on my part, that, I thought. Yes,' he agreed, 'a neat piece of detection, though I say it myself as shouldn't. Now then.'

He looked around. Apart from the fax machine, himself, eleven men, an empty styrofoam milkshake carton and a small cardboard box, the room was empty.

'The way I saw it,' Bedevere went on, 'it was all down to relativity. Relativity? Yes, relativity. Because although you could say that the world stays still and the registered office moves about, you could also say that it's the registered office that stays still and . . .'

Turquine had picked up the milkshake carton. He looked into it, turned green and dropped it.

'And then you said,' Bedevere went on, turning to one of the hackers, who wasn't listening, 'that nobody had ever found the door to the registered office. They'd looked hard enough, you said, but never actually *found* it. Almost, you reckoned, as if it only existed on the outside, not the inside. And it was that, you see, that set me thinking.'

Turquine drew a finger along a wall until the build-up of dust grew too thick to be ploughed any further. 'This place could do with a good clean,' he observed. 'Not like any office I've ever been in before, really. No phones, for a start.'

'And what I thought was,' Bedevere continued, staring hard at the cardboard box, 'if nobody's ever seen the door, maybe there isn't a door. And what do you know,' he concluded triumphantly, 'there isn't a door.'

Nobody was listening; but that didn't mean to say he wasn't right. There was no door. No window, no ventilation shaft, no cat-flap, nothing. Just four walls of immaculate integrity.

Bedevere knelt down and felt in his pocket for a penknife to cut the string which held down the lid of the cardboard box. 'Like the man said,' he muttered, 'eliminate the impossible and you're left with the truth. I wonder where the light's coming from, in that case.'

The room went suddenly dark.

'The map, somebody.'

In the corridor, it went very quiet.

'One of you,' said the Queen, sweetly, 'did remember to bring a map, didn't you?'

'Did you say something, Bedders?'

Bedevere, who couldn't find his penknife, grunted. It was that strong nylon string that burns your hands if you try and break it.

'Something,' Turquine went on, 'about the light.'

Around him, Turquine could hear strange, soft noises coming from the hackers. At the back of his mind, he could understand why; after all, they were in the registered office, the holy of holies of all Atlanteans. And they'd just found out that it didn't have a door. And it was dark.

'Odd,' Turquine went on, thinking aloud as much as anything, 'the way there's no way in or out of here, just walls. Makes you think, really.' He passed his tongue round his mouth, searching for a tiny residual taste of peppermint. Nothing. 'Not surprising nobody's dusted it in yonks, I mean, how'd they get in, let alone get a hoover up here as well. In fact,' he added, 'makes you wonder how the air gets in. I mean, those walls look pretty airtight to me . . .'

In the darkness, a hacker choked.

'Well, then, a compass maybe. Any of you boys got such a thing as a compass on you?'

No answer. The Queen tutted briskly.

'Well really,' she said, 'no offence, but isn't that a bit feeble on somebody's part?'

In a dead straight, level, tiled corridor that stretches away for miles in either direction, there is only one place to hide; behind somebody. Without apparent movement, the rest of the PAs formed an orderly queue behind Iphicrates.

'Sorry,' he said. The Queen looked at him and smiled until he could feel the skin start to peel on his cheeks.

'That's all right,' she said. 'We all make mistakes. Well, anybody, what do we do now? Any bright ideas?'

The Queen waited for a moment, tapping her nails very gently against the tiled wall of the corridor, until you could find yourself believing that the whole place was vibrating like a drumskin.

'Nobody? Pity.' she licked her lips. 'Well,' she said, 'it's just as well I'm here, then, isn't it?'

The PAs relaxed slightly. Terrifying she undoubtedly was, and nobody much liked the idea of having her along – why was she here, by the way? – but there was no question that Madam would get them out of the tunnel somehow. The dodgy bit was what would happen afterwards.

You can get to like it down a tunnel.

'How would it be,' the Queen said, 'if we all had a cup of tea?'

Bedevere's teeth were in remarkably good shape, considering.

At school, of course, they'd made fun of him. Hidden his toothbrush. Put chalk in his dental floss. But he'd stuck to it – he'd promised his mother – and now he understood why she'd been so insistent.

'Gotcha!' he said, and spat out a few strands of nylon thread. A moment later, he found the lid of the box, and opened it.

This is not going to be easy to describe.

At the root of the problem are the lingering effects of the catastrophic outbreak of Adjective Blight which hit the Albionese-speaking world shortly after King Arthur was deposed. Remarkably little known, the blight (later found to be transmitted by fleas carried on the back of the Lesser or Journalistic Cliché) did to descriptive prose what phylloxera did to the French vineyards. Whole classes of similes were wiped out. Generations of authors have been left poking awkwardly at raw wounds in the collective subconscious where extinct metaphors once grew.

Anyway, here goes. As the lid folded back, something like light in that it was bright and insubstantial and assisted vision, but unlike light in that it jumped out and rushed around the room banging into people, hopped out and whirred through the air like a released balloon. Wherever it made contact with anything it left a big orange phosphorescent glow. It smelt awful.

Air swelled up out of the box like the biggest extrusion of bubble-gum you could possibly visualise, and whacked the hackers and Turquine smack up against the wall. Oddly enough, it didn't seem to affect Bedevere. Perhaps that was because he was still holding on to the box.

Time . . . You want to know what Time looks like? Time that's been trapped inside a one-time baked-bean carton ever since prehistory, and which is then suddenly released into an atmosphere rich in carbon dioxide, looks rather like a very expensive Roman candle. Having burnt out, it leaves behind a floating, sparkling yellowy-red ash, rather like gold dust.

Time is money.

Time is, of course, also of the essence. It is the first, the only pure element. Everything else is made up of Time, in one form or another. When Time burns in carbon dioxide, however, it precipitates deposits of that extremely rare and highly volatile element known as Gold 337. Which is why the fax machine suddenly started to glow, steamed, melted and changed shape. It became a jar.

Bedevere, kneeling beside the box and wondering what on earth was going on, slowly began to understand. Gosh, he said to himself, as simple as that . . .

He turned back to the box, which contained a heavy

metal seal, a sheaf of share certificates and some old-fashioned ledgers. He picked out a ledger at random, opened it, and began to read. From time to time he smiled knowingly.

'Excuse me,' Turquine said, 'but when you've quite finished, some of us are being squashed to death over here.'

Bedevere looked up. 'Sorry,' he said, 'I was miles away. It's not here.'

'What isn't here?'

'That personal organiser thing,' Bedevere replied. 'All we've got here is the statutory books of Lyonesse Ltd. Tremendously interesting stuff, all of this, but not what we're actually after. Shall we be getting along?' He stopped talking and lifted his head, with an expression on his face like Archimedes seeing the pattern of the universe in a damp bath-mat. 'Oh,' he muttered to himself, 'I think I see.'

Turquine tried to reach out a leg and kick Bedevere, but a lot of air got in the way. 'Look,' he said.

'All right,' replied Bedevere, engaged in the ledgers once more, 'you lot go on ahead and I'll catch you up.'

Exercising more self-control than he ever imagined he possessed, Turquine replied, 'How?'

'Sorry?' said Bedevere. 'Oh, yes. Why not try going out of the door and turning left? If I've got my bearings right, that should bring us out—'

'What door?'

Bedevere pointed to where the fax machine had been.

'Excuse me,' Turquine answered, 'but that is not a door.'

Bedevere grinned. 'Bit slow today, aren't we, Turkey

old man? Correct, that is not a door. When is a door
not a door?'

'Oh I *see* . . .'

As if by magic; or rather, by magic, the air pressure
dropped away to normal, and Turquine slid himself off
the wall, squared his shoulders, took a brief run-up and
gave the jar one hell of a kick.

'Happy?'

'Yes,' replied Turquine from the corridor. 'Coming?'

Bedevere smiled. 'In a minute,' he said.

The main thing to remember if you are ever offered tea
by the Queen of Atlantis is that you should accept,
without question or hesitation. Never mind if you can't
take the tannin or if you'd rather have coffee; when the
Queen offers you tea, you have tea.

Six of the seven PAs knew this. The seventh had no
objection to tea, but didn't quite understand where it
was going to come from, seeing as how they were
standing in a bare, deserted corridor that extended as
far as the eye could see. In the grip of what, with
hindsight, he identified as a subconscious urge to self-
annihilation, he pointed this out.

The Queen smiled.

'Gosh,' she said, 'aren't you the clever one. You're
quite right, we'll have to improvise.' She closed her
eyes, clenched her elegant white hands and said:

'Let there be tea.'

And tea there was, in Snoopy mugs, with a matching
milk jug, sugar bowl and biscuit jar.

'There,' said the Queen, 'it's surprisingly easy so
long as you aren't too ambitious to start with.'

Closer inspection revealed that there were seven mugs for eight people. That, as even the PA could recognise, was a Hint.

When they had finished their tea, the Queen beamed at them, vanished the mugs ('Saves washing up,' she explained) and rapped hard on the biscuit jar with her sceptre. There was the necessary quantity of blue light and burning sulphur, and the jar turned into a door in the wall.

'Explanations wanted, anyone?' she said sweetly. Silence. 'Fine,' she said, nodding in approval, and loosed off a small but powerful burst of personality at the doubting PA. 'After you,' she said.

Some are born brave, others achieve bravery and some are forced into acts of great courage by the unimaginable terror of what might happen to them if they refuse. The PA closed his eyes, reached for the door handle, turned it and pushed.

Nothing. Wouldn't budge.

'I think you'll find it opens better if you pull,' said the Queen.

The number of native-born Atlanteans who have been inside the registered office is small, but not nearly as minute as the number who've ever wanted to be inside it. As to the number of those who have ever got out again, there are no reliable statistics. The PA smiled sheepishly at the Queen, mumbled something about a far, far better thing and preferring to be in Philadelphia, and stumbled in.

'Name.'
  'John Wilkinson.'
  'Occupation.'

'Tax inspector.'

'Thank you, please take a seat over there, we'll get back to you in just a moment. Right then, next, please. Name.'

'Stanislaw Sobieski.'

'Occupation.'

'Revenue official.'

'Thank you, please take a seat over there, we'll get back to you in just a moment. Right then, next, please. Name.'

'Li Chang-Tseng.'

'Occupation.'

'Customs officer.'

'Thank you, please take a seat over there, we'll get back to you in just a moment. Right then, next, please. Name.'

'François Dubois.'

'Occupation.'

'Revenue official.'

'Thank you, please take a seat over there, we'll get back to you in just a moment. Right then, next, please. Name.'

The fourth man smirked.

'Guess,' he said.

The desk clerk didn't look up. She had another twelve thousand, five hundred and seventeen more management trainees to deal with, and already she could feel a headache coming on. 'I don't guess,' she said. 'People tell me. Name.'

'Weinacht,' said the fourth man. 'My name is Klaus von Weinacht.'

'Occupation.'

Von Weinacht laughed. He laughed so loud you

could hear him all over the reception area, and twelve thousand, nine hundred and ninety-nine revenue officials looked up and stared. What they saw took them back an average of thirty years . . .

. . . To a child, half-delighted, half-terrified, peeping out from under the blanket at the knife-blade of light under the door. To the sound of silence audible, darkness visible, stillness palpable; and a half-imagined clattering of hooves and clashing of bells in the unspeakable enigma of the night.

'Well now,' von Weinacht said, throwing back his hood, 'how about delivery man?'

The Queen stood in the doorway and stared.

'You!' she said.

Bedevere looked up and smiled vaguely. 'Yes,' he said. 'Long time no see.'

For a moment, the Queen hesitated; then she turned and yelled for the guard. Bedevere shook his head.

'Sorry,' he said, 'but it isn't going to work. You know your trouble? Bloody awful management relations.' He indicated the stunned PA curled up by the door. 'All the rest have scarpered,' he said, 'and I don't think *he's* in a fit state to be of much use to you. I hit him,' he added, 'with the door.'

The Queen looked down and saw a few shards of smashed porcelain. Then she smiled.

'Never mind,' she said, 'plenty more where that came from.'

'Doors or heavies?'

'Both,' replied the Queen, 'although I was thinking more of the jar. Actually, I was rather fond of that one. Been in the family for ages and . . .'

Bedevere was impressed. 'That old, huh?' he said. 'Oh well, never mind. You can't make an omelette, as they say.'

The Queen laughed lightly. 'Very true,' she said, and sat down on the cardboard box. 'Now then,' she went on, 'what can I do for you?'

Bedevere looked at her, and his face seemed to have undergone something of a transformation. Gone was the slightly sheepish look that always reminded Turquine of the last thing but one he saw in his mind's eye before going to sleep; in its place was an expression of gentle but hard determination, such as you might find on the face of someone who will break both your arms if necessary, but with a fitting sense of gravity and decorum.

'I want my money back,' he said.

The Queen's mouth fell open, and for the first time since the groat was demonetised she couldn't think what to say. 'I'm sorry?' was the best she could do.

'So you should be,' replied Bedevere sternly. He was silent for a moment, and then added, 'You don't remember, do you?'

The Queen shook her head. 'Frankly,' she replied, 'no.'

Bedevere frowned. 'A castle,' he said, 'in the middle of a waste and desolate plain, somewhere in the middle of Benwick. A dark and stormy night, with the rain lashing down and lightning playing about the battlements. A young and innocent knight, hopelessly lost on his quest to pay the month's takings from the family dye works into the bank in Rhydychen. The knight sees the castle, murmurs "Thank God!" and craves the right of hospitality. The chatelaine of the castle invites him in, makes him welcome. There is light, and warmth, and food. And then . . .'

A brief spasm of pain shot across Bedevere's face and then his jaw set, as firm as a join in a superglue advertisement.

'In the morning,' he said, 'the castle has gone. So has the money. The knight awakes on the cold fell, with nothing but his armour and a share certificate for twenty thousand Lyonesse Goldfields plc three-mark ordinary shares. He returns home. He explains as best he can. Stunned silence; then the reproaches, the recriminations, how could you *do* such a thing . . .?'

Bedevere shook his head and sighed. There were tears in the corners of his eyes, but his face remained as grim as death.

'The young knight was me, of course,' he said. 'Of course, you don't remember, how could you? Another day, another sucker. But we were different. We couldn't afford it. Dammit, it was hard enough being in trade as it was. God, when I think how they scrimped and saved just so that I could go to the Ecole des Chevaliers! It ruined us, you realise, completely ruined. My father had to get a job as a fencing master. My mother had to go out posing for illuminated manuscripts. *And kindly have the courtesy not to powder your nose when I'm talking to you!*'

The Queen closed her compact with a firm click and looked up. 'Sorry,' she said, 'I was miles away. Did you say something about wanting some money back?'

Unable to trust himself to speak, Bedevere reached inside his jacket and pulled out a folded paper, which he tossed contemptuously on the ground. The Queen leant forward and picked it up.

'Gosh,' she said, 'haven't seen one of these for years. Twenty thousand shares!' She giggled, then composed herself rapidly. 'At the time,' she said, 'a greatly fancied investment. I believe they tried to put together a rescue package.'

'Be that as it may,' Bedevere growled. 'My money back, please. Now.'

The Queen raised an eyebrow. 'Terribly sorry,' she said, 'no can do. It's this thing – terrible bore, but a fact of life nevertheless – called limited liability. It means that—'

'I know what it means, thank you very much,' said Bedevere, his voice ominously soft. 'It means you can do something and get away with it scot free.'

The Queen nodded brightly. 'Exactly,' she said. 'Keystone of the enterprise economy, that is.'

'Because the company has ceased to exist.'

'That's right.'

'Fine.' Bedevere stood up. 'Now then,' he said quietly, 'on the same principle, how would it be if this company of yours ceased to exist? For the sake of argument,' he added, picking up the ledgers he'd been sitting on. 'Unlikely, but possible. If, for example, all the statutory books went missing? No, that wouldn't work. How about if the company secretary and major-ity shareholder took it into her head to wind the whole thing up, just like that?'

The Queen laughed shrilly. 'Now, then,' she said, 'why on earth would I want to—'

'And if she did,' Bedevere went on, 'I wonder what would happen to all this?' He made a sweeping gesture with his free hand. 'This ... this *remarkable* set-up you've got here? The registered office that nobody can find, and which keeps dodging about, so that it's never in any one jurisdiction long enough for the courts to dissolve the company. Or the strong magical field that keeps the whole enterprise hidden, so that the only way to get into it is by fax? All it would take is one special resolution of the shareholders, with a straight seventy-five per cent majority vote.' He held the register of shareholders open. 'I notice,' he said, 'that you hold ninety-nine per cent of the shares, so all you need to do is vote yes, and that's that.'

'Quite true,' said the Queen, very calmly. 'I hold ninety-nine per cent.'

Bedevere reached inside his jacket again. 'And I,' he said, 'hold this very sharp knife.' He grinned. 'Ready?'

The Queen started to back away towards the jar of pickled onions that had appeared out of nowhere in the corner of the room, but Bedevere simply laughed and threw the register at it. It smashed into a thousand pieces, and no door came.

'Ready?' he repeated. 'In the Articles of Association, which I've just been reading, it says that only a director can move a special resolution.' He advanced slowly, holding the knife very steady in his right hand. 'I think,' he said, 'there's just been a vacancy on the board.'

The Queen's eyes were glued to the knife. 'Surely not,' she said. 'I'd have been the first to know.'

'Not in this case,' Bedevere replied. 'Your friend there,' and he nodded at the recumbent PA, 'resigned just before he passed out. I heard him. You believe me, don't you?'

The Queen nodded. The knife caught the light and glittered.

'In which case,' said Bedevere, 'you've just proposed me for the post of –' he chuckled '– director in charge of takeovers and mergers. Bloody, foul and unnatural mergers. All those in favour say yes. Say yes.'

'Yyy.'

'Great. Now then, I vote that Lyonesse (Holdings) plc be wound up forthwith. All those in favour . . .'

The Queen started to scream, but Bedevere curled his lip. It was a long time since he'd last had occasion to do anything so melodramatic – not, in fact, since he'd been the Second Roman Soldier in the sixth-form mystery play – and as a result, parts of his moustache went up his nose. He sneezed.

'Save your breath, please,' he said. 'Nobody can hear you, and even if they could, what good would it do? Nobody can get in here, remember? Nobody can even find it. It moves about. Unless you know the trick with the jar, the only way in here is by fax, and I've cut the bloody thing's flex. And once you're in here,' he added, 'magic, even Gold 337, doesn't work, because of your extremely clever insulation system. I'm sorry,' he continued, moving the knife, 'but this is a cut-throat business. All those in favour.'

The Queen's tongue darted round the circuit of her lips but could do little to moisten them. She tried to speak, but nothing came out except a small, creased whimper.

'Ready?'

'No!' The Queen could feel her shoulder-blades against the wall. 'You can't. You're a knight, remember; knights can't kill damsels in distress. It's . . .'

'Unethical?' Bedevere smiled. 'Three points, briefly. One, you're not a damsel, you're a sorceress, and they're fair game, all year round, with or without a permit. Two, we're inside the registered office of the Lyonesse Group, which is outside all recognised jurisdictions, so nobody will ever know. Three ...' He grinned. 'Three is, what the hell, rules were made to be broken.' He grinned savagely, and the Queen instinctively raised her arm in front of her face.

'There is, of course, an alternative ...'

'Excuse me,' said the assistant cashier, 'but you can't go in there.'

Von Weinacht turned and stared at him. 'Sorry?' he said.

There was a brief moment when their eyes met; and the cashier remembered that he had a son, and the son wanted a mountain-bike and a Teenage Mutant Accountants Playset more than anything in the world, and that if he didn't get one ...

'No problem,' the cashier mumbled hoarsely. 'Where to?'

'The Forbidden City, I think it's called.'

'Third on the left,' the cashier said. 'Follow your nose, you can't miss it.'

'Is there?'

Bedevere nodded. 'Absolutely,' he said. 'Just give me my money back and,' he added, as nonchalantly as he could, 'the Personal Organiser of Wisdom, and we'll say no more about it. All right?'

Don't you just know, immediately and instinctively, when you've said the wrong thing? Like asking someone how his girlfriend is, just as you notice out of the corner of your eye that half the furniture is missing, and the picture of a dog burying a bone which he'd always told you he hated has vanished from the wall? And all the magic of the Great Pentagram won't drag the words back into your mouth, or do anything to mitigate the joint-cracking embarrassment of it all.

'So that's what it's all about, is it?' the Queen replied.

'Um.' Bedevere bit his lip. 'That's beside the point,' he said, 'and the point is very sharp, very sharp indeed, so . . .'

'Very well, then,' said the Queen, folding her arms and sticking her chin out. 'Kill me then, see if I care.'

Bedevere frowned, and then turned the frown into a scowl. 'Don't push your luck,' he growled; but the growl came out about as menacing as the mewing of a kitten.

'Go on.'

'Look . . .'

'Scaredy-cat!'

'Don't you—'

'Cowardy cowardy custard!'

'Damn!'

With a grunt of pure rage, Bedevere swung the knife up and hurled it into the floor, where it quivered like a violin string. Then he sagged, like an ice-cream skeleton in a microwave.

'I thought so,' said the Queen. 'You never had the faintest intention, did you?'

Bedevere scowled at her. 'Don't sound so damned disappointed,' he said, and slumped into the corner. 'Anyway,' he added, 'I had you going there for a moment, didn't I?'

The Queen had her powder compact out again.

'Certainly not,' she said to the mirror. 'You knights are all mouth and vambraces. You'll be hearing from my legal advisers about this, by the way.'

But Bedevere had made up his mind. One moment he was in the corner, about as taut and poised as a bag of old shoes; the next moment he was on his feet and grabbing the Queen's organiser bag with both hands.

'Hey!' the Queen squealed. 'Get off, will you?'

The strap broke – it was a fiendishly expensive bag, with one of those flimsy gold chain straps, and Bedevere weighed close on thirteen stone without armour – and the bag flew open. One of the things that landed on the floor was a small, leather-covered thing like a book. Before the Queen could move, Bedevere was standing on it, with a smirk on his face you could have built a trading estate on.

'And sucks to you too,' he said.

'You've got no right . . .'

'Granted,' said Bedevere. Then he stuck his tongue out.

The Queen shrieked and grabbed the hilt of the dagger, but it was too firmly stuck in the floor. So she called Bedevere a rude name instead.

'Sticks and stones,' replied the knight, and he stooped quickly, picked up the book, and stowed it carefully away.

'Now then,' he said, 'about my money . . .'

Just then, a chimney appeared in the corner of the room; and in the mouth of the chimney, a pair of boots . . .

'What the hell's keeping him?' said Turquine irritably.

The hackers looked at each other.

'Ten to one he's got lost,' Turquine continued, picking at the sleeve of his coat, where a loose thread was beginning to unwind itself. 'No more sense of direction than a tree, that man. Got us lost on the way here, and that was just on the ring road.'

The hairy hacker coughed meaningfully. 'Look,' he said, 'I know this isn't going to be easy for you to accept, but people . . .'

'What?'

The hacker flushed under his superabundance of facial hair. 'When people go in . . . in *there*,' he said, 'well, coming out is the exception rather than the norm, if you see what I mean. Like, your friend is probably . . .'

'Balls,' Turquine replied. 'He's just got lost somewhere, that's all. Come on, you dozy lot, I suppose we'd better go and get him.'

The hacker shrugged; a what-the-hell, Light-Brigade, last-one-into-Sebastopol's-a-sissy shrug.

'All right,' he said. 'Wait for us.'

'Freeze,' said a voice from the fireplace.

Bedevere and the Queen turned and stared. The boots kicked, like the feet of a hanged man, and there was a vulgar expression from about where the mantelpiece should have been. Then a lot of soot and what looked rather like a dead bird fell into the grate, followed by a man in a somewhat grubby red cape.

'Hold it right there,' he said. 'Don't even think of moving, either of you.'

He extracted himself from the fireplace, brushed a good deal of soot off himself, and straightened his back. He was very tall and broad, and he had eyes like little red traffic lights.

'Where you made your mistake,' he said to Bedevere, turning round and tugging at something still lodged in the chimney, 'was in assuming that there was no other way into this room. Well, you were wrong. I can get in *anywhere*.'

Bedevere turned to the Queen. 'Excuse me,' he said, 'but do you know this gentleman?'

The Queen mumbled something and nodded. Good Lord, Bedevere said to himself, she's terrified. Then a tumbler fell in the combination lock of his mind.

'Just a moment,' he said, 'aren't you . . .?'

Von Weinacht snarled at him. 'Don't say it,' he said. 'Don't make things worse for yourself than they already are.' He tugged, and a sack came down into the grate with a heavy crunch. From it, von Weinacht produced a transparent cellophane package with a brightly coloured piece of cardboard at the top. Bedevere recognised its contents as one of those plastic swords given to children by parents who don't value their neighbours' daffodils. The Queen gave a little shriek.

'Now,' said von Weinacht, 'to business.' He tore off the cardboard and took out the plastic sword. 'Two birds with one stone. You,' and he nodded his streaming white beard at Bedevere, 'are searching for the Holy Grail. You aren't going to find it. And you . . .' He gave the Queen a long and unfriendly look. 'You and I go way back. I'll deal with you later.'

'Excuse me,' Bedevere interrupted, 'But how did you know . . .?'

Von Weinacht laughed. 'I know everything,' he said,

with conviction. 'I know the ground-plan and floor layout of every house in the world. I can read the minds of every parent and every child ever born. Of course I know what you're up to, and you aren't going to get away with it. Now, give me that book before I take it from you.'

He pulled off the plastic scabbard and threw it on to the ground, revealing a horribly shiny steel-blue blade. If that's plastic, Bedevere realised, then I'm Sir Georg Solti.

'Sorry,' he said, 'no can do.'

Von Weinacht grinned repulsively, then roared like a bull and swung his sword. There was a disturbance in the air where Bedevere's head would have been if he hadn't moved it; and at the same moment, a patch of honey appeared on the wall, followed by a door, which opened to reveal Sir Turquine. He was slightly out of breath and holding a two-foot-long adjustable spanner.

'Oh good,' he said, 'fighting. That's more like it.'

Von Weinacht wheeled round and scowled at him. Turquine did a double-take.

'Just a tick,' he said, 'I know you. You're that burglar.'

There was a moment of perfect stillness while two memories rewound many hundreds of years . . .

. . . To the Yuletide Eve before Turquine's seventh birthday, when he'd been sleeping peacefully in the hall at Chastel Maldisen and this burglar had tried to break in through the smoke-hole in the roof. Ugly customer, dressed all in red for some reason, carrying a whopping great swag-bag on his shoulder. Luckily, Turquine's father had bought his son a crossbow for Yule, and hadn't hidden it very carefully . . .

... To that nightmare back in the Chastel Maldisen, when some horrible little child had kept him holed up in the roof for ten very long minutes by shooting arrows at him while he clung to a rafter and yelled frantically for reindeer support ...

Turquine was the first to recover. 'It's been a constant source of aggravation to me, that has,' he said, 'the one and only time I've ever had a burglar and I kept missing. Mind you,' he added, 'bloody thing wasn't properly shot in, kept pulling to the right ...'

'You didn't do so badly,' von Weinacht hissed, and he drew back the sleeve on his left arm to reveal a long, white scar. 'Three birds,' he added. Then the sword flashed in the air like a blue firework.

Turquine parried with the spanner, and there was a ringing sound like a fight in a belfry. The head of the spanner fell to the ground.

While von Weinacht was celebrating with a horrible gloating cry and whirling the sword round his head for a final devastating blow, Turquine very shrewdly kicked him in the nuts, belted him with what was left of the spanner, and ran for it.

Von Weinacht recovered quite remarkably quickly, screamed like a wounded elephant and followed.

Bedevere shrugged and turned to the Queen. 'Anyway,' he said, 'time I was going. Thanks for everything.'

The Queen tried to hit him with the register of shareholders but missed, and he darted out of the door just before it healed up and vanished. Bedevere stood in the corridor and caught his breath. A long way away, he could hear running feet and curses. That way, he decided.

He was running flat out, one hand clamped on the book, the other pumping rhythmically at his side, when the corridor turned back into a spiral staircase.

Of course, he came the most terrific purler. First he banged his head on the ceiling, then he bounced several times off the walls, and then the steps got him. As if that wasn't enough to put up with, he had just managed to arrest his rapid progress by sticking his legs out when a stunned PA came down on top of him, landing a sharp elbow in his midriff before rolling away into the darkness.

Come on, Bedders, pull yourself together, this isn't getting you anywhere.

He hauled himself on to a step, rubbed his head to make sure he wasn't bleeding, and breathed in a couple of times. Nothing broken, as far as he could tell. Splendid.

Down below, there was the most appalling racket, rather as if a lot of people were falling down on top of each other and swearing a lot. Grinning ruefully, Sir Bedevere got up and began walking carefully down the staircase.

The Queen had emptied her bag out on the floor. It must be here somewhere. She always had one, for just such emergencies as these.

Lipsticks. No. Nail varnish. No. Purse, credit cards, tissues, calculator, notebook, diary. No.

Ah . . .

She took the small jar of cold cream, drew back her arm, and let fly . . .

Von Weinacht had, apparently, knocked himself out

cold on the stone pillar at the foot of the staircase. Under him, squashed flat and moaning slightly, was a PA. Various semi-conscious hackers lay about untidily. Bedevere smiled, feeling ever so slightly superior, and stepped over them.

'Turkey?' he called. 'You there, Turkey?'

'Over here,' came the reply, and Bedevere followed the sound of the voice under a low doorway. There was Sir Turquine, sitting astride a large oak chest, trying to lever off the lid with von Weinacht's sword.

'Not now, Turkey,' said Bedevere. 'I think it's time we left, don't you?'

Turquine shook his head. 'Haven't got it yet, have we?' he replied. The sword broke.

'What makes you think it's in there?'

'What makes you think it isn't?' Turquine replied, hammering at the padlock with the sword-hilt. 'I'm just being thorough, that's all.' The padlock broke.

'Well,' said Bedevere, 'is this what you're looking for?' He produced the notebook and held it up. If Michelangelo had ever wanted to do an allegorical statue of Smugness, he couldn't have found a better model.

Turquine looked up and grinned. 'That's it, is it?' he said.

'Reckon so.'

'Good lad.' He got up off the chest and threw back the lid. 'Might as well have a look in here anyway, while I'm here,' he said. 'Good Lord, it's full of diamonds and things. There's a turn-up.'

Bedevere shook his head affectionately. 'Hurry up, then,' he said, 'and then we'd better be off. And don't take any gold.'

Turquine nodded. 'Because of buggering up the earth's axis, I know,' he replied. 'Load of old socks if you ask me. Just the sort of thing you'd expect from a lot of bankers. Want some?'

Bedevere thought of twenty thousand gold-mine shares and nodded. 'Why not?' he said. 'Just to show willing, you understand.'

'Exactly,' Turquine agreed. He scooped out a double handful of emeralds and handed them to his friend, who stowed them away in his pockets.

'Ready?'

'Almost,' Turquine replied, scrabbling about in the chest. 'I think this one's rather nice, don't you?' He held up an enormous ruby, then kicked the lid shut.

'It's not stealing,' he added, 'because in return, they can have *this* back.'

He threw down a piece of paper and stamped on it. Bedevere recognised it, and smiled.

'Lyonesse Goldfields?' he asked.

'Worse,' Turquine replied. 'Lyonesse Capital Growth Trust Income Units. When I told my dad what I'd done he nearly flayed me alive.'

The knights grinned at each other.

'Time we weren't here,' said Turquine. 'Now then, this way.'

Bedevere shook his head. 'Not unless you want to see the boiler room,' he replied. 'Follow me.'

'But I think there's a short-cut—'

'Follow me.'

As they walked, Bedevere asked Turquine what had kept him.

'I like that,' Turquine replied. 'Honestly, Bedders, you've got a nerve. If it hadn't been for . . .'

Bedevere shrugged. 'I knew I could rely on you, Turkey. You just cut it a bit fine, that's all.'

Turquine nodded. 'I know,' he said. 'As soon as you didn't follow, I guessed something was up. No, finding the spanner was easy, it was just finding a jar . . .'

'You tried the kitchens?'

'Yes, and . . .'

'You stopped for a sandwich.'

Turquine blushed. 'I was *starving*, Bedders. It wasn't like this in the old days. There were always pages and squires and things you could send down to the baker's while you waited for the dragon to come out. I don't hold with progress, personally.'

'It's a bit overrated, certainly,' Bedevere replied. 'Now then, left here, and we should be . . .'

They stopped. The Queen was standing in the doorway, and behind her were about seventy heavily armed clerks.

'Hello, boys,' she said.

Bedevere blinked. 'How the hell did you get here?' he said.

'Simple,' the Queen replied, 'I used the lift. Grab them, somebody.'

'Well,' said Turquine, 'this is extremely jolly, isn't it? Right, who's going to be first?'

There was something about his tone of voice which the clerks seemed to find quite remarkably eloquent. They just stood there, in fact, listening to him, as if he were Maria Callas.

The Queen made a little clicking noise with her teeth, rather like someone loading a rifle. 'Come on, boys,' she purred. 'Let's not be all tentative about this. Grab them.'

That was even more eloquent; as if Maria Callas had been elbowed out of the way by Elizabeth Schwartzkopf and Joan Sutherland. The clerks shuffled forward in an unhurried but determined phalanx, while Turquine reached behind him and, as if by magic,* wrapped his hand round thirty inches of scaffolding pipe. It made a soft, heavy sound as he patted it against the palm of his left hand.

'Excuse me,' said Bedevere.

Nobody was paying the slightest attention. One does one's best to take the heat out of the situation, and one might as well have stayed in bed. He frowned, and then pulled something out of his pocket.

'Excuse me,' he repeated, and this time everyone stopped what they were doing and looked at him. It was so quiet you could hear a pin drop. And, shortly afterwards, they did.

'It's all right,' Bedevere went on, displaying a grenade prominently in his left hand. A rather superior example, admittedly; if Fabergé had ever made grenades, they would have looked like this one. 'So long as I don't let go of this lever thing,' he said, trying to sound extremely reasonable, 'it won't go off. Now . . .'

Turquine nudged him so hard that he nearly drop-

---

*As if? Who are we trying to fool?

By a quirk of magic and genetics, all the first-born males in Turquine's family had the knack of being able to put their hands on heavy blunt objects suitable for use as weapons whenever they needed to. Which probably explains why so many of them became warriors, and so few of them went into catering, stockbroking or graphic design.

ped the bomb, and whispered, 'Where in God's name did you get that from, Bedders?'

Bedevere turned to him and smiled gently. 'You gave it to me, Turkey. From that big chest you broke open, remember? Now then . . .'

Turquine's hand flew to his pockets, which clinked faintly. 'Mine aren't,' he said. 'Mine are all diamonds and sapphires and . . .'

'Really?' Bedevere clicked his tongue. 'You always did have rather a limited imagination, though.' He turned back to the clerks, just in time to stop them drifting away.

'Now then,' he said, 'playtime's over, so if you all pay attention we can get this all sorted out and then we can get on with what we're supposed to be doing instead of playing at cowboys and Indians. Happy?'

Happy probably wasn't the word Flaubert would have chosen, but at least he had the audience's attention. He held up his hand – his other hand – and cleared his throat.

'Gather round now, please,' he said. 'Thank you. Right, first things first. This is indeed a real hand grenade, which I made out of a diamond about ten minutes ago, with the help of . . .' he dipped his right hand in his inside pocket and pulled out the leather-bound book. 'This. The Personal Organiser of Wisdom. Note the tiny gold clasp; made, of course, from Gold 337; hence the transformation from a decorative but useless form of carbon to a highly practical firework. Neat, yes?'

The clerks shuffled their feet. If it's possible to be scared out of your wits and ever so slightly bored at the same time, they were.

'Second,' Bedevere went on, 'we mean you no harm, honestly. All we want is this little notebook thing. It's not for us, it's for a friend. I know it'll mean removing a minute quantity of Gold 337 from Atlantis, and yes, that'll mean a slight wobble in the earth's axis. So what? By my calculations, it'll mean a small contraction in the orbit pattern, and we won't have to bother with leap-year any more, and that'll—'

'Hey,' Turquine interrupted, 'it so happens I was born in a leap-year.'

Bedevere turned to him irritably. 'So what?' he said.

'So I'm still four hundred and sixteen,' Turquine replied. 'Just thought you might be interested, that's all.'

Bedevere nodded, and turned round again. 'Be that,' he said, 'as it may. If we leave, it'll be no skin off your noses and you can get back to fleecing the greedy and making money, we can press on with our job, nobody gets hurt, big anticlimax but really the best solution in the circumstances. If you try and stop us leaving, we'll throw this bomb at you. Anybody here feeling lucky?'

Nobody, apparently. Bedevere nodded, and pointed to the Queen. 'Right,' he said. 'To make things easy, you lead the way.'

The Queen gave him a look you could have put on dandelions and started to walk. She didn't get very far.

With a roar like the sound of a dinosaur having a filling done, the Graf von Weinacht appeared in the corridor behind them.

'Oh drat,' Bedevere sighed. He released the handle of the grenade, counted to three, shouted 'Catch!', and tossed the grenade at the Graf, who caught it one-handed and popped it in his sack. A moment later there was a soft, distant thump.

Followed, shortly afterwards, by a louder, nearer thump as Turquine wiped the smile off his face with the scaffolding pipe and bolted, followed closely by Bedevere, the Queen and the clerks.

For the record, Klaus von Weinacht woke up about ten minutes later, looked at the footprints all over his cape and the scorched hole in the side of his sack, and decided to call it a day. He produced a fireplace, climbed up it and vanished. When, many hours later, the Queen went to bed, she found on her bedside chair a large stocking filled with scorpions and a card with 'Happy' crossed out and replaced with 'Really miserable'; both of which she placed in the waste-disposal system.

'I liked him,' Turquine said as they ran. 'No mucking about, straight to the point. If he had better reflexes he'd be quite handy.'

Bedevere had no breath with which to reply, which was probably just as well. They were in another corridor; but this one was carpeted and there were doors with frosted glass windows in them leading off it at regular intervals. In other words, they were back Topside again.

'Let's try this one,' Turquine suggested.

Bedevere, who could run no further in any case, nodded, and they leant heavily on the door and fell into a small office.

If they'd had time they would have seen the writing on the window, which said:

COMPLAINTS

The Atlantean financial services industry prides itself on the fact that it has never yet received a complaint from one of its clients. There are three reasons for this:

1. All Lyonesse Group financial packages are tailored to meet your exact requirements by a team of dedicated experts with more than two thousand years of experience in all forms of monetary planning behind them.

2. The Lyonesse Group investment management team continually monitors all investment and insurance portfolios on behalf of their clients and advise immediately when a change in investment strategy is desirable.

3. Under the doormat in the Complaints Department there's this trapdoor thing that leads to a soundproof dungeon.

'Turkey.'

'Yes?'

'It was you who said Let's try this one, wasn't it?'

'Yes.'

'Fine. I was worried there for a moment that I was losing my grip.'

'No, it was me.'

'Fine.'

A rat hesitated in the doorway of its hole, lifted itself on to its back paws, and sniffed. Something didn't smell right.

With a flick of his tail he retreated, demonstrating that animals are far more sensitive to atmosphere than human beings. If he had been so foolish as to go much further, there can be little doubt that Turquine would have caught him and eaten him.

'I'm famished, Bedders,' he said for the seven hundredth time. 'I mean, prison's one thing, you can't really squeal when you land up in a dungeon, it's all part of the game. They capture you, Dad comes up with the ransom, you go home, finish. But they're supposed to feed you while you're here. It's in some convention or other.'

Bedevere stirred uneasily. He had tried to keep his friend off the subject of why they were there, for fear it might upset him.

'Turkey,' he said quietly, 'I don't think you quite realise what's going on. I don't think this is the sort of dungeon you're meant to get out of.'

Turquine laughed. 'Don't be an ass, Bedders,' he replied. 'There's no such thing as a dungeon you're *meant* to get out of. That's the whole point about dungeons. They're containers for the thing contained, like shoe boxes.'

'Up to a point,' Bedevere replied, staring up at where the roof should be but seeing only darkness. 'Only, with your ... your conventional dungeon, you're only kept there for a limited time – you know, till the ransom's paid or until you've served your time or whatever. Somehow I don't think this is one of those.'

'Why not?'

'No door,' Bedevere replied. 'The only way in is through that trapdoor thing we fell through. I think you more, sort of, stay here.'

Turquine shuffled about on the straw. 'Surely not,' he said. 'I mean, don't take any notice of there not being a door. They don't seem to hold with doors in this place. Reminds me of an office I delivered a couple of pizzas to once, there was just this sort of partition thing and—'

'No, hold on a moment,' Bedevere interrupted. 'You see, I'm basing my theory on all the, er, skeletons.'

'Skeletons?'

By way of reply, Bedevere rattled together a couple of tibias. 'I don't think they were on diets, Turkey. I think nobody fed them. Not for ages and ages.'

'Oh.'

'In fact,' Bedevere went on (and as he spoke, he had the feeling that if he was trying not to alarm his friend unduly, he had probably gone about this the wrong way), 'not at all. Do you follow?'

'Sort of,' Turquine replied. 'Bit unsporting, that, don't you think?'

'Absolutely.'

'Not on, really.'

'Yes.'

Turquine found one of the skeletons, and amused himself by pretending to be a ventriloquist; something that Bedevere found somewhat irritating. Still, he said to himself, if it takes his mind off things it's all right by me. Turquine's mind, as he knew from long experience, was a bit like nuclear war; when he got an idea into it, things were often very noisy and unpleasant for a while, but it was soon over. He lay on his back and tried to think of something clever.

A human pyramid to reach the trapdoor? No, not enough manpower.

Magic, perhaps? He felt in his pocket for the Personal Organiser, but the gold clasp wasn't even warm. No magic down here that he could detect, or if there was, it wasn't compatible. Probably the place was insulated, like the registered office.

He was just weighing up the possibility of using some of the bones to build a makeshift ladder when Turquine's ventriloquist's dummy started to laugh hysterically. Better put a stop to that straight away, he thought, or else the poor chap'll be right off his trolley in no time, which won't help matters.

'All right, Turkey,' he said, as gently as he could, 'Pack that in, will you? It's starting to get on my—'

'Um.'

'Turkey?'

'Bedders.' There was a note in Turquine's voice that Bedevere had never heard before, in all the years they'd known each other. Fear. Say what you liked about old Turkey, he never seemed to get the wind up. If you asked him what the word fear meant, he'd probably think for a bit and say it was the German for four.

'Turkey?'

'Um, could you come over here and ask this, er, lady to stop talking? She won't listen to me, and . . .'

That's it, said Bedevere to himself, the poor idiot's finally flipped. My fault for letting him play with the thing in the first place.

'Now don't be silly, Turkey,' he said, edging over across the straw on his hands and knees. 'You know it's you doing the voice and not the skull at all, so just—'

There was another peal of laughter, and Bedevere winced. Laughter like that meant only one thing. And then something occurred to him.

Turquine was talking to the skull in his own voice, asking it – begging it, even – to shut up. And the skull was still laughing. Either Turkey was a damn sight better at ventriloquism than he thought (and he wasn't;

there's no 'g' in 'bottle') or else it actually was the skull talking . . .

'Turkey,' he shouted, 'pack it in, you hear me?'

'Leave him alone.'

Silence. The only sound in the echoing dungeon was that of the rat banging the rathole door and jamming a piece of coal against it.

'Sorry?'

'I said leave the poor boy alone, you big bully.'

'I . . .'

'Go and pick on someone your own size.'

Great, thought Bedevere, absolutely spiffing. Now I've gone round the bend too. If ever I get out of here, I'm going to kick young Snotty's arse all the way from here to Benwick.

'Excuse me,' he said.

'Yes?'

'Who am I talking to, please?'

There was more of the laughter, and Bedevere found that he was getting a bit tired of it. He coughed meaningfully.

'Don't you get on your high horse with me, young man. I'm old enough to be your grandmother.'

'Actually,' Bedevere couldn't resist saying, 'I doubt that, rather.'

'Don't you answer me back.'

'Sorry,' Bedevere said, 'but I do happen to be well over fifteen hundred years old.'

There was a click, like rolling dice or – but it didn't do to think too hard about it – a skull's jaw falling open.

'Don't you try being funny with me, young man, because—'

'Really,' Bedevere said. 'I used to be one of King Arthur's knights, you see, and I'm here on a—'

'King *Arthur*?'

'Yes.'

'Oh. Oh I see.'

'Good.'

'No disrespect intended, I'm sure.'

'Not at all.'

'My name's Mahaud, by the way.'

'Sir Bedevere de Haut Gales.'

'I've heard of you. Aren't you the knight who used to—'

But Bedevere interrupted. The name was familiar, and the voice – ye gods, how could he ever forget that voice? But no, surely not. It wasn't possible.

'Did you say Mahaud?' he said.

'That's right,' Mahaud replied. 'Mahaud de Ville-hardouin.'

Bedevere's voice quivered as he spoke. 'Matron?'

The skull laughed again, and this time Bedevere laughed too.

'You remember me, Matron,' Bedevere exclaimed. 'I was in the same year as Aguisant and Bors and Gaheris Minor.'

'Of course I remember! You kept beetles in a shoe box in the junior dormitory.'

'Look . . .' It was Turquine, and there was just a hint of peevishness in his voice. 'I hate to interrupt, but aren't you going to introduce me?'

There was a puzzled silence and then Bedevere said, 'Sorry, Turkey, I forgot. Matron left the term before you arrived. Matron, this is Sir Turquine le Sable. He was at the old Coll too, but after your time.'

'Pleased to meet you.'

'Likewise. Look, Bedders, do you know what's going on here, because—'

'Shut *up*, Turkey, there's a good chap. Sorry, Matron. How are you keeping, anyway?'

There was a long silence. 'I'm dead.'

'Surely not?'

'I most certainly am.'

'I see. Oh I am sorry to hear that, Matron. I . . .'

Bedevere stopped in mid-sentence. Was it just him, or was something turning out a bit counter-intuitive here? 'Dead?' he repeated.

'As nail in door,' Matron replied. 'And I'm not at all pleased about it, let me tell you.'

'I'm not surprised.'

'I mean to say,' Matron went on, 'when I retired, the Coll was *extremely* generous – much more than I expected, really very moving – and so of course I wanted to invest my little nest-egg for my old age. And then I met this charming young lady, said she was the elder sister of one of the boys at the Coll . . .'

Bedevere felt a lump rise in his throat. 'Lyonesse Capital Growth Trust units?' he asked.

'Lyonesse Managed Income Bond, actually,' Matron replied. 'And not six months after I'd taken out the policy, I got this letter saying the whole thing had gone into liquidation and how sorry they were. It made my blood boil, I can tell you. So I came straight down here and . . . Well, here I am. And if ever I get my hands on that wicked little chit of a sales girl, I'll . . . Well, she'd better watch out, that's all.'

'That's awful, Matron,' Bedevere said. 'Cheating you like that and then murdering you as well. That's –

well, awful. They really shouldn't be allowed to get away with it.'

'Hear hear,' muttered Turquine, and added something about it needing no ghost come from the grave, which Bedevere thought was in rather poor taste. He shushed firmly, and then scratched his head.

'Excuse me asking,' he said after a moment's thought, 'but how come you can still, well, talk? I thought you needed to be . . .'

The skull clicked its teeth. 'Some people may let themselves run to seed when they retire,' Matron said. 'Not me. Like I always used to say to you boys at the Coll, the important thing is willpower, willpower and determination. I was *determined* not to let myself get out of shape, and it's worked.'

'I can see that,' Bedevere replied, and added, 'Good for you.' But he still felt there was something lacking. An explanation, for instance. Still, it was bad manners to keep on, and Matron had always been most particular about things like that. He changed the subject, and they chatted for a while about the other boys in Bedevere's class. This kept them entertained for a while; except that all of them were dead, and there was a risk of the whole thing getting a touch morbid; not to say repetitive. Very carefully, he reverted to the earlier topic.

'Matron,' he said, 'do please excuse me if this is a bit, well, personal, but I'd always understood . . .' Inspiration! 'When I was at the Coll, Sir Giraut taught us that when a person's sort of dead, that's it, you know . . .'

'Giraut!' snapped the skull, contemptuously. She has no lips to purse now, Bedevere reflected; otherwise . . . 'The man was a charlatan. Used to leave applecores behind the radiators.'

'I never liked him much.'

'Good for you,' Matron replied. 'What did he know about being dead? Just because he'd got a fancy degree from some university somewhere, that doesn't mean to say he's got the right to pick the middle out of the bread.'

Bedevere nodded, not that anyone could see him. 'So what's it really like, then?' he asked. 'Death, I mean. I've always wanted to know.'

'Well,' Matron said, after a moment's reflection, 'I can only speak as I find, you understand. You won't catch *me* pontificating about things I know nothing about, like some people we could mention. But personally, I find it's quite like being alive. Of course, the magic makes a difference.'

'I see,' Bedevere said. 'The magic.'

Matron laughed. 'I can tell *you* didn't pay much attention in class, young Master Bedevere. Too busy playing Hangman with that Ector de Maris, I'll be bound.'

Bedevere flushed, for nobody likes to be maligned; but he repressed his indignation and said, 'About the magic, Matron. What does it do?'

'Magic,' Matron said, in that slightly plonking voice of hers, 'is a by-product of the decay of the gold isotope Gold 337. It's a form of radiation. All radiation can make living things mutate; it influences molecular structures, you see. But magic radiation is extremely powerful. It can make living things mutate very quickly – turn you into a frog, for example – or it can affect inanimate objects, such as vases of flowers or the flags of all nations; make them pop out of top hats, that sort of thing. It can also, well, raise the dead.' Matron hesitated for a moment. 'No, that's not strictly true. More a case of making death a bit more like life, you might say. No, that's still not quite right. More the other way round.'

'Make life seem like death, you mean?' Bedevere enquired. This was like GCC Philosophy with Dr Magus; and then he remembered, very faintly, that Matron and Dr Magus used to take long walks down by the archery butts. Under cover of the friendly darkness, he grinned.

'Exactly,' Matron was saying. 'If there's a lot of magic about – and there's plenty down here, I can tell you; if you don't believe me, ask the rat to show you his conjuring tricks – then a person can be dead and alive at the same time. That's to say, she's alive, but her body is dead. It's all a bit spooky, really,' she added, 'but you get used to it after a while.'

'I see.'

'Not,' Matron continued, 'that it's the slightest bit of use to me being alive if the rest of me is nothing but a lot of old bones. In fact it's the worst of both worlds, except that I don't get toothache any more. One must be grateful for small mercies, I always say.'

Bedevere sat in silence for a while. Turquine, for his part, was surreptitiously trying to fit together the bits of the skeleton that he'd started to use to make a set of stumps and a cricket bat with.

'How would it be,' Bedevere said at last, 'if we all got out of here? I mean what would happen, do you think? Would you – well, stop being half alive and be wholly dead, or would you stop being half dead and be . . .?'

'I really couldn't say,' Matron answered. 'Mind you, either would be an improvement. I never could be doing with shilly-shallying, you know that.'

'Fine,' Bedevere said thoughtfully. 'So if we could get out of here . . .'

'If, young man. As we used to say when I was a girl, if ifs were horses, beggars would ride.'

'Quite,' Bedevere agreed. 'But you've been down here a long time. Haven't you, well, noticed anything?'

The skull mused for a moment. 'Not a great deal, no,' it said. 'From time to time, people drop in, they die, we talk for a while, then usually we fall out and they sulk, and they give up the power of speech. Some people can be so petty.'

'So you haven't got any suggestions about how we might . . .?'

'Well.' A long silence. 'There is something. I tried it with a young man who dropped in fifty years or so back, but I'm afraid he made rather a muff of it. No backbone, you see.'

'Ah.'

'Especially after he fell off the wall.'

'Right.' Bedevere scratched his ear thoughtfully. 'I'm game,' he said. 'What about you, Turkey?'

Turquine looked up. He was having difficulties. Beyond the basic principle that the leg bone connecka-to the thigh bone, he was no anatomist.

'You know me,' he said, 'I'll try anything once. Er, Bedders, do you know anything about knees?'

'This isn't going to work,' said Turquine. 'Don't ask me how I know, I just do.'

'Shut up, Turkey,' Bedevere grunted.

'All right, I'm just saying, that's all. Don't blame me if—'

'Boys!' said the skull sharply. 'No getting fractious, please.'

'Sorry,' said Turquine. 'It's just—'

'That'll do, Master Turquine,' the skull said. 'Oh, by the way, did you have a cousin called Breunis?'

Turquine raised an eyebrow. 'That's right,' he said. 'Breunis Saunce Pitie. Come to think of it, he was at the Coll, too.'

'I knew you reminded me of someone,' said the skull. 'He was a *horrid* little boy.'

Many years ago, Lyonesse Market Research discovered that market penetration for Lyonesse financial services among the Giants of South Permia was less than 18½ per cent, and a major marketing drive was launched. It was quite successful, and, as a result, the Giants (who were basically personifications of glaciers and could trace their ancestry back to the Second Ice Age) were soon extinct.* One such Giant, Germadoc the Violent, had taken out an offshore roll-up sterling assets bond which went yellow on him about ten minutes after the ink was dry on the policy document, and he had come straight across to Atlantis City to complain. The customer service people had had to fire catapults at him just to stop him moving about. Then they tied him up and put him in the dungeon. In sections.

Being a Giant, his femurs were a touch over twelve feet long. The trapdoor was very slightly more than eighteen feet above floor level.

---

*Giants are nothing if not single-minded. If you tell a Giant that if he dies he stands to make thirty thousand marks, he doesn't hang about.

'I saw someone at a circus do this once,' Turquine was saying. 'Garcio the Magnificent, they called him, he was very good. Mind you,' he added, 'he had proper stilts, with little ledges you put your feet in and hand-grips and everything.'

Bedevere, clinging on to an enormous bone for dear life, nodded impatiently. 'Are you there yet?' he demanded.

'Not sure,' Turquine replied. 'It's so dark, you see . . . Ah, what's this?'

The stilts swayed alarmingly, and Bedevere was nearly swept off his feet. He braced himself against the wall and hugged the bone to his chest. This had jolly well better work, he was saying to himself, other-wise . . .

'Gotcha!'

And then a loud cry and an oath, and suddenly there wasn't any weight at the top of the stilts any more. Bedevere yelled 'Turkey!' and tried to peer upwards, but it was pointless. There were some grunting noises.

'Turkey!'

'It's all right,' came a strained voice from above. 'There's a handle or something, I'm hanging on to it. If I could just loosen this catch . . .'

And then there was a flood of light.

And then things in the dungeon got a bit fraught.

Germadoc the Violent was very good about it all, considering. Once Bedevere and Matron had explained, and he'd understood that he was alive again and it really wasn't their fault at all, he'd helped them all up out of the cellar – Bedevere was amazed how many of them there had been – and then led his fellow-complainants away to find somebody to complain to. They could hear them doing it, far away in the distance.

'Well,' said Turquine, 'that's that. Piece of duff, really.'

Matron smiled. Once she got the flesh back on her bones, Bedevere saw that she hadn't changed a bit.

'Thank you, both,' she said graciously. 'Very much obliged, I'm sure. It was very perceptive of you, young Bedevere, to realise that we weren't dead at all, and it was just the magic in the dungeon all along.'

Under normal circumstances, Bedevere would have explained that Sir Giraut at the dear old Coll had explained to him that since death is final, anything that permits the patient to carry on talking must be something else. But he remembered the apple-cores behind the radiators and contented himself with a bashful smile. 'That's all right,' he said.

'And you, Master Turquine,' Matron continued, 'that was very brave of you. Well done.'

Turquine, unused to compliments, blushed. Usually when he was brave, the only witnesses were the people he was being brave against, and they tended to be hyper-critical.

In the distance there was a crash which made the floor shake, followed by a lot of cheering. That was probably Germadoc, complaining. By the sound of it, he had decided against putting it in writing.

'Well,' Bedevere said, 'we've got the Personal Organiser, the Atlanteans don't seem to be about, I think it's time we were on our way. Can we drop you off anywhere, Matron?'

Mahaud de Villehardouin smiled. 'Thank you,' she

said, 'that would be most kind. Would Glastonbury be out of your way?'

Glastonbury ... Bedevere knew the name from somewhere, but although the bell rang in his mind, nobody came to answer it. He assured her that that would be fine, and together they went in search of the fax machine.

It was hard to find. Although under normal circumstances Atlantis City is crawling with faxes, just then none of them seemed to be working. In fact, most of the office equipment was out of order, one way or another, which only goes to show that a good concerted complaint can make itself felt.

Eventually they tracked one down in a snug little room with comfortable chairs and a calendar with pictures of kittens on it. Something told Bedevere that this was probably the Queen's office.

'Here we are,' Turquine said, thumbing through the directory. 'Any number of places in Glastonbury are on the fax. Any preference?'

Mahaud shook her head. 'I expect it's changed rather a lot since my day,' she said. 'And besides, I won't be stopping.'

Glastonbury. The town of the Glass Mountain.

Bedevere did his best not to stare; he managed to get by with just glancing out of the corner of his eye as he dialled in the number. If she was going into the Glass Mountain, that meant that she was ...

She was smiling again. 'You are a sharp one, Master Bedevere,' she said. 'You're quite right. Not in my own right, though; just by marriage, so to speak.'

The last piece dropped into place in the jigsaw of Bedevere's memory. Dr Magus and Matron had, of course, both left in the same term. All those long walks.

'How is Dr Magus, by the way?' he asked, as nonchalantly as he could.

'Simon?' Matron beamed. 'Very well indeed, thank you, or at least he was when I last saw him. That was some time ago now, of course, but I don't imagine he'll have noticed. A brilliant man, of course, but something of a dreamer. I expect I'll find fifteen hundred years' worth of washing-up waiting for me in the sink when I get home. I'll tell him you were asking after him; he always said you were rather brighter than you looked.'

Bedevere was going to say something, but then it occurred to him that from what he had heard, time in the Glass Mountain is rather different, somehow.* Rather like life, he remembered someone telling him once; you only get out of it what you're prepared to put into it. Something like that, anyway.

'Here goes,' he said. 'Hold tight . . .'

Transmitting.

---

*The best way to describe Glass-Mountain time is to consider the analogy of first- and second-class post. Both get to exactly the same place eventually; but whereas one of them usually arrives within twenty-four hours, the other can take a great deal longer, is far more prone to get lost on the way, and somehow always arrives at its destination tatty, heavily stamped on and via Preston.

6

In the stables of the Schloss Wei-
nachts, the reindeer were restless.

Because the Graf has distinctly
idiosyncratic requirements in trans-
port, the stables are twice the size of
the rest of the castle; and the rest
of the castle is rather larger than,
say, Tuscany.

There are sports reindeer, touring reindeer, four-
leg-drive reindeer, turbo-charged reindeer with six
stomachs and extremely antisocial digestive systems,
reindeer with red go-faster stripes down their flanks;
even a few with 'My other reindeer's a Lappland Red'
stickers on their rumps. And then there is Radulf.

Radulf and the Graf go way back; right back to when
he started out as a Finno-Ugrian storm-deity with
responsibility for punishing perjury and collecting the
souls of the dead. They have seen some high old times
together, howling through the midwinter skies with the
wind in their hair and the world splayed out below

them like a spilt breakfast. It wasn't Klaus and Radulf then, of course; it was Odin and Sleipnir – and there have been other names, too, which the race-memory has been only too glad to forget. All the stuff with the red dressing-gowns and the sleigh bells is comparatively recent, the result of one of the biggest balls-ups in theological history.

Radulf is virtually retired now, and only rides the winds once a year. He hates the Americanised form of his name, and the song and the greetings cards make him sick. The slight discolouration of his nose (he prefers to think of it as a snout, anyway) is an honourable wound, the red nose of courage; a lasting memento of a desperate ten minutes with the Great Frost-Bear, back when the world was young, violent and not nearly so damn soppy.

Retired from flying, anyway; there's plenty of work for him to do on the ground, what with all the various jobs that need to be done under the terms of the Great Curse. There are toy catalogues to be pored over, order forms to make out, deliveries to supervise, and mountains and mountains of requisition chits to be sorted through as the requests from every family in the world come cascading through. And last, but definitely not least, there are the preparations for each year's Ride; itineraries to plan, architects' plans to study, ingenious methods of breaking into chimneyless houses, converted windmills and blocks of flats to be worked out.

'Radulf!'

A girl's voice, echoing melodramatically in the vastness of the stables. The old reindeer lifted his snout, took off his reading glasses and mooed softly. He knew the Graf didn't hold with the Grafin coming down to the stables. Not safe for a young girl, he said, and he was right. Some of the reindeer were special thoroughbreds, wild and savage, with antlers like pneumatic drills and tempers to match; and the Grafin was young and silly. She carried sugar-lumps in the pocket of her dress. Not sensible.

'Radulf, the phone for you!' she was saying. It sounded like she was down among the drag-racers. Radulf flicked his left ear apprehensively. Give a sugar-lump to one of those high-octane monstrosities, you could have an explosion.

He mooed loudly to her to stay where she was and not feed anything, then sprang to his hooves and padded silently through the rows of stalls. He knew the layout of the stables as well as a taxi driver knows Bayswater. He should do, by now.

'There you are, Radulf,' said the Grafin, and handed over the portable phone. 'It's Father. He says it's urgent.'

Radulf nodded his head, and the dim light of the chandeliers high above under the rafters glinted on the tinsel wrapped round his horns. He put the receiver to his ear and mooed into it.

'Moo. Moo. Moo. Moo? *Moo*? Mo ...' The antlers nodded a couple of times, and Radulf hung up. 'Moo,' he explained.

'Oh dear,' said the Grafin. 'I suppose we'd better get back to the house, then.'

'M.'

'I expect he'll need plenty of hot water and band-ages.'

'M.'

They left the stables, switching out the lights as they

went. For a while, the enormous building was silent – except, of course, for the shuffling of innumerable hooves and the quiet whinnying of the reincalves.

Then a voice spoke in the Number 2 hayloft.

'Are you sure this is the right place?' it said.

There was a sharp intake of breath next to it, and a muffled click as a torch was switched on.

'Be quiet, Gally, I'm trying to think.'

'Please yourself.'

In the hayloft, Boamund was turning the situation over in his mind; or at least he was trying to. Something – he hadn't the faintest idea what – kept getting in the way. His companion, Galahaut the Haut Prince, had gladly abdicated any participation in the decision-making process at a very early stage, and was filing his fingernails. Toenail was cleaning the boots.

'Who was that?' Boamund asked suddenly. Galahaut shrugged, and so it was left to Toenail to reply.

'Looked like a bloody great big deer, boss,' he replied. 'Domesticated, too, by the looks of it.'

'Thank you,' said Boamund, with what he hoped was irony. 'Actually, I meant—'

'It's amazing the things you can train animals to do,' Toenail went on. 'Cousin of mine, worked in a circus, used to tell me how they trained the lions—'

'Toenail.'

'Sorry.'

Boamund leant his chin on his cupped hands. 'That girl,' he said. 'I don't remember there being anything about a girl . . .'

Toenail pointed out that they had heard her speak of somebody, presumably the Graf, as Father, and suggested that she might be his daughter.

'Don't be silly, Toenail,' Boamund replied. 'Whoever heard of the Graf von Weinacht having a daughter?'

'Whoever heard of the Graf von Weinacht?' Toenail
answered.

Boamund clicked his tongue. 'Not under that name,
maybe. But – well, surely you've twigged by now. It's
him. You know . . .' Boamund rubbed his stomach and
said 'Ho ho ho!' with a sort of manic jollity. Toenail
smiled tactfully.

'Yes,' he said, 'I'd managed to get that far, sure.
What I mean is, all this –' he waved his arms in an
encircling gesture '– doesn't actually fit in with what
you might call his public image. I mean,' he went on
ruefully, 'the barbed wire. The dogs. The searchlights.
The mines. The moat full of piranhas . . .'

He glanced down at his boots, which had nibble-
marks where the toecaps had once been. Boamund
nodded.

'I think I see what you're driving at,' he said. 'You
mean, he isn't really like how he seems to us.'

'Exactly,' Toenail replied, relieved. 'The image and
the man. It turns out that we don't know anything
about the real Santa . . .'

Boamund put his hand over the dwarf's mouth and
hissed. 'Not here, you clown. I don't think you should
say that name here.'

'Why not?' asked Toenail through a gag of fingers.

'I don't know,' Boamund replied. 'I just have this
feeling, all right?'

'About the real Graf von Weinacht, then,' Toenail
said. 'I mean, the person with the sack and the sleigh
doesn't have a daughter, admittedly, but then, I've

never seen a Christmas card with claymore mines and attack dogs on it, have you?'

Galahaut yawned. 'You mean,' he said suddenly, 'we should abandon our preconceptions?'

The other two looked at him.

'Forget about stereotyped role-perceptions,' he continued. 'Look for the real persona behind the image. Fair enough.'

For the seventy-third time since they'd set out, Toenail gave his master that Why-did-we-have-to-bring-him look. Boamund shrugged and grimaced back. Galahaut, for his part, was completely engrossed in dealing with a potential whitlow.

'So,' Boamund said, 'you reckon that girl was his daughter, then?'

'Could be.'

'Right.'

Boamund lowered his chin back on to the palms of his hands and sat for a while, completely still. If this was a cartoon, Toenail said to himself, he'd have a big bubble with 'Thinks' in it coming out of his head.

'Anyway,' said Boamund at last, 'I reckon it's about time we got on with the job in hand. Right.' He nodded his head purposefully and punched the palm of his hand to register decisiveness. Boamund, Toenail decided, would have been a great success in the silent movies.

He waited.

'So,' Boamund said. 'First things first, eh? Let's . . .' He bit his lip thoughtfully. 'How'd it be if . . .?'

The dwarf looked at him expectantly. An X-ray of his head, he said to himself, would show up completely blank at this particular moment.

'Sorry to interrupt,' Toenail said, therefore, 'but if I could just break in here . . .'

Boamund registered the democratic attitude to supreme command and nodded. Toenail thanked him.

'What I was thinking was,' he said, 'we want to get inside the castle proper, don't we?'

'Correct.'

'Just off the top of my head, then,' Toenail went on, 'wouldn't you say our biggest problem was getting past the gates?'

The gates. They'd seen them already, of course. They made you feel vertiginous half a mile away. The two flanking towers were black needles of masonry soaring up into the sky, and the gates themselves were cliff faces in hobnailed black oak.

'Tricky, certainly,' Boamund replied. 'I thought we might actually give the gates a miss and try the wall instead.'

Toenail couldn't help shuddering. Eighty metres high at least, and built of polished black marble. Probably best, he decided, to try and divert the boss's mind away from that one.

'Good idea,' he said, 'I hadn't thought of that. Yes, that's much better than what I had in mind.'

Boamund raised his eyebrows, registering his willingness to listen to any suggestion, however puerile. 'What were you thinking, then?' he said.

'Oh, it was just . . . No, it was silly.'

'Out with it.'

'I thought,' Toenail said, 'we could pretend to be postmen.'

Boamund's face clouded over. 'Postmen,' he said.

'That's right,' said Toenail. He waited for what he

judged to be the right moment, psychologically speaking, and added, 'Didn't you notice the letterbox, then?'

'Letterbox?'

'In the gate,' Toenail said artlessly. 'Well, not in the big gate, of course. I meant the little side gate we passed when we were trying to find a place to cross the moat.'

'Ah,' Boamund said. 'The *side* gate.'

'That's it,' Toenail said brightly. 'You remember. I kept trying to point it out to you and you kept telling me to shut up, so I guessed you must have noticed it for yourself. Well, it had a letterbox in it, so it stands to reason . . .'

'Yes,' Boamund said, 'of course. I was wondering when you were going to . . .'

'Of course,' Toenail continued, 'to begin with, I was puzzled how the postman gets to the letterbox, what with the moat and the piranhas and everything. Had me thinking there, I can tell you.'

'I bet!'

'And then,' Toenail went on, 'I saw what you'd seen.'

'Oh good.'

'The little boat,' said Toenail, kindly, 'tied up under the weeping willow. Of course, you with your trained eye, you saw that like a shot.'

Boamund managed to register smugness.

'And then I wondered, Why did he make us paddle across the moat on that floating log when there was a perfectly good boat just sitting there? Pretty slow on the uptake, wasn't I?'

'Oh, I don't know,' said Boamund feebly. 'It takes a

special sort of mind, I always think.'

'Anyway,' Toenail said, 'it wasn't till after we were across the moat and in the potting shed and I was putting TCP on where the piranhas—'

'Um . . .'

'Then,' said the dwarf, 'I realised. Of course, I said, we couldn't have taken the boat, or else it wouldn't have been there for the milkman, and he'd have raised the alarm, and . . .'

'Ah,' said Boamund. 'Just out of interest, what was it put you on to there being a milkman?'

'Same as you, I expect,' said Toenail, maliciously.

'Good man.'

'The empty milk bottles outside the little gate, I mean.'

'Splendid,' said Boamund, and he laughed. 'Make a general of you yet, we will.'

'Thank you,' said Toenail. 'Must be marvellous to think of things the way you do.'

'It's a knack.'

'So,' Toenail said, 'my idea was that we wait until the postman comes along in the morning – that'll be after the milkman's been and gone, of course – and then one of us knocks on the door, as if there was a parcel . . .'

'Or a registered letter,' said Boamund, excitedly.

'Yes, even better,' said Toenail resignedly. 'And then, when somebody comes to answer the door, we thump him and get in.' He paused for a moment. 'Pretty silly idea, really.'

'Oh, I don't know,' said Boamund slowly. 'I mean, put like that . . .'

'I thought you said something about the wall.'

'Oh, just thinking aloud,' Boamund replied. 'Got to

consider every possibility, you know. Actually, I was coming round to the postman scenario myself. Neat, I thought.'

'One of your better ideas?'

Boamund registered modesty. 'Simple, anyway,' he said. 'What do you think?'

Toenail smiled. 'I don't know how you do it, boss,' he replied.

The sleigh howled through the night sky, the clanging of its bells drowned by the shrieking of the wind.

Klaus von Weinacht, head down over the console to reduce the coefficient of drag, stared out through the driving snow for the first glimpse of his battlements. On the instrument panel, the compass stopped its crazed spinning and jammed dead.

Nearly home. Good.

He ran back through the timings in his mind. If they had all left the Grail Castle at the same time then, allowing for pack ice in the Nares Straight and contrary winds over Permia, then it would still be two or three days before they were due to arrive. Plenty of time. He laughed cruelly.

The reindeer pounded the clouds with their hooves.

'Ready?'

Toenail, concealed behind a bush, nodded, while Galahaut yawned and picked bark off the branch they had found for a club. Boamund took a deep breath, and knocked on the gate.

'Let's just run through it once more,' he hissed. 'The porter opens the door, I distract his attention. Galahaut, you hit him. Toenail . . .'

There was the sound of heavy bolts being shot back, and the door opened.

'Hello.'

Galahaut gripped the club and started to move. Then he stopped.

'Er ... hello,' Boamund was saying. He had gone a very pretty shade of pink.

'Was there something?' said the girl, nicely.

For four seconds, Boamund just stood there, irradiating pinkness. Then he smiled idiotically.

'Postman,' he said.

'Oh good,' said the girl. 'Something nice, I hope. Not more horrid old bills. Daddy gets so bad-tempered when it's bills.'

Toenail had covered his face with his hands. The worst part was not being able to do anything.

'Letter,' Boamund gurgled. 'Registered. Got to sign for—'

'How exciting!' said the girl. 'I wonder who it's from.'

There was a moment of perfect equilibrium; and then it dawned on Boamund that he didn't have about his person anything that looked like a registered letter.

Toenail had to admit that he coped as well as could be expected in the circumstances. After he had made a right pantomime of patting all his pockets and rummaging about in his knapsack, he said, 'Damn, I seem to have left it in the van.' It could have been worse, said the dwarf to himself, just conceivably.

'Never mind,' said the girl. 'I'll wait for you here.'

In retrospect, Toenail realised that there was a funny expression on her face, too. At the time, though, he put it down to a complete absence of brains.

'Right,' said Boamund, rooted to the spot. 'I'll just go back and, er, fetch it, then.'

'Right.'

They stood for a moment, gazing at each other. Then Boamund started to walk slowly backwards. Into the bush.

'Be careful!' the girl called out, too late. 'Oh dear, I hope you haven't hurt yourself.'

Toenail, who had broken Boamund's fall very neatly indeed, could certify that he hadn't. But the fool just sprawled there. It was only natural that the girl should come and look . . .

'Oh,' she said.

Boamund grinned feebly. Galahaut tried to hide the club behind his back, and waved.

'Actually,' said Boamund, breaking a silence that was threatening to become a permanent fixture, 'we aren't postmen at all.'

'Not . . . postmen?'

My God, thought the dwarf, and I thought *he* was a pillock. He tried to wriggle the small of his back away from the sharpest roots of the bush.

'No,' Boamund said. 'That was a ruse.'

'Oh!'

'Actually, we're—'

'Knights,' Galahaut interrupted. 'Knights of the Holy Grail. At your service,' he added.

Boamund gave him a filthy look.

'Knights!' the girl squeaked. 'Oh, how *exciting*!'

The hell with this, said the dwarf to himself, things can't get any worse, they just can't. With a tremendous wriggle, he extricated himself from under Boamund, shook himself free of leaves and bits of twig, and tugged at his master's sleeve.

'Boss,' he said.

Boamund looked round. 'What?'

'The plan, boss. You know.'

'Go away, Toenail.'

Dwarves cannot, of course, disobey a direct order. He shrugged his shoulders and drifted away to the shelter of a wind-blasted thorn tree, crossed his legs, and sulked.

The girl's eyes were shining. 'This is so thrilling,' she said. 'What are you doing here? Or is it a secret?'

'We're ...' A tiny spark of common sense flared up in Boamund's brain. 'It's a secret,' he said. 'A quest,' he added.

'Gosh!'

'And you mustn't tell a soul.'

'I won't.'

'Promise?'

'Promise.'

A long silence followed, as the girl gazed at Boamund, Boamund and Galahaut gazed at the girl, and Toenail darned a sock. It could have gone on for ever if it hadn't been broken by the sound of a door slamming.

The girl gave a startled squeak and looked round. The gate had blown shut.

'Oh *aear*!' she wailed. 'And I've forgotten my key again.'

Toenail closed his eyes and counted under his breath. One, two ...

'Never fear, fair damsel,' Boamund said. 'We'll have you back in there in two shakes, won't we, Gally?'

(Three, said Toenail, opened his eyes and returned to his darning.)

'Absolutely,' said Galahaut. 'No trouble at all.'

Wearily, Toenail picked himself up, put the sock carefully away, and walked over. He took his time. Why hurry? Where's the point?

'You'll be wanting the rope now, then,' he said.

Boamund's eyes were fixed on the girl. 'Rope?' he said.

'The rope I just happen to have with me in this holdall,' Toenail continued resignedly. 'And goodness me, what's this? Gosh, it's a grappling hook and some crampons. Talk about coincidence, eh?'

Boamund nodded, with all the animation of a hunting trophy. 'Right,' he said, 'this won't take a jiffy. We, er, take the hook like *so*, we pass the line *behind* the hook to make sure it doesn't tangle, then we swing the hook one, two, three and . . .'

The hook soared into the air, hung for a moment like a strange steel falcon, and came down again, precisely where the girl would have been standing if Galahaut hadn't moved her.

'You idiot!' Galahaut shouted. 'Give me that hook.'

'Shan't.'

There was a tussle. Both knights fell over and started pulling each other's hair. Toenail finished off the sock and started on another.

Eventually, Galahaut won control of the hook, stood up and dusted himself off. 'Like this,' he said. 'Watch.'

He threw the hook, and far above their heads there was a faint chink of steel on stone. Toenail stared in amazement.

'All *right*,' he said.

Not long afterwards, the gate opened and the four of them passed through. They didn't, however, pass unnoticed. On the main security monitor in Radulf's stall, a green light began to wink ominously. The old reindeer narrowed his brows, studied the screen and shóok his head until the tinsel in his horns swayed.

Then he sounded the alarm.

'Pass the salt.'

'Sorry?'

'I said pass the salt, there's a good fellow.'

'There you are. Sorry. I was miles away.'

Aristotle shrugged, salted his kipper and turned to the sports pages. There is a difference, he always said, between not being one's best in the mornings (which was something he could respect) and being dozy. His mood wasn't improved when he read that Australia had gone down thirty-seven to three against the All Blacks.

'Typical!' he said.

On Aristotle's left, Simon Magus looked up from the letter he was reading and said, 'What is?'

'Huh?'

'You said something was typical.'

'Oh.' Aristotle closed the paper. 'The bloody Newzies have walked all over us again, that's all. We've been no good ever since they capped that idiot Westermann.'

Simon Magus looked at his neighbour over the tops of his spectacles. 'By us, I gather, you mean the Australians,' he said. 'I never knew you came from those parts, Ari.'

'Certainly not,' replied Aristotle severely. 'As a philosopher, I am above nationalism. On the other hand, I am logical. There is no point following rugby football unless you support a particular team. On purely rational grounds, I selected the Australians.'

Simon Magus grinned. 'I did that once,' he said. 'At five to one on. Never again.'

Aristotle frowned at him down the great runway of his nose, and reached for his toast.

'Beats me why you want to follow sport anyway,' Simon Magus went on. 'Complete waste of time, if you ask me, a lot of idiots running about chasing things. When I used to be a teacher we had to take it in turns to be referee. I loathed it.'

'You,' Aristotle replied, 'are not a philosopher. If one has any pretensions to philosophy, one must cultivate understanding. I study humanity. Humanity is obsessed with sport. Therefore, if I want to understand humanity, I must study sport. It's purely scientific, you see.'

Simon Magus grinned. 'It wasn't entirely scientific a couple of months back,' he said, 'when you made us have the telly on all day in the Senior Common Room for Wimbledon. I distinctly remember you standing on the table waving a bloody great flag round your head and chanting *There's only one Boris Becker* every time the other one fell over. It was embarrassing.'

'Research,' Aristotle mumbled through a mouthful of toast. 'Just research, that's all.'

'Or what about that time after the World Cup when you made that big statue out of wax, and you called it Maradona and threw teacups at it? You can still see the marks on the wall.'

'One has to try and enter into the spirit . . .'

'Spirit, maybe,' Simon Magus replied, 'but there was no need to throw a brick through Dante's study window just because he supports Italy.'

Little red spots appeared in the corners of Aristotle's cheeks. 'It *was* offside,' he snarled. 'I've got it on video, you can see if you like. And Dante had the ... the *infernal* nerve to suggest ...'

Simon Magus chuckled. 'I'll say this for you,' he said, 'I do believe you've got into the spirit of the thing. Have some more coffee?'

Aristotle, offended, waved the pot away and returned to his newspaper. Still chuckling, Simon Magus leant back in his chair and called to the small, wizened figure sitting on the other side of Aristotle.

'Merlin,' he said. 'More coffee?'

'Sorry?'

'Would you like some more coffee?'

'I do beg your pardon, I was miles away. No, no more coffee for me, thank you. Two cups are quite sufficient.'

Simon Magus nodded and turned back to his letter. He had read it seven times already, but he wasn't bored with it yet, not by a long way.

... Such a charming young man, though inclined to be a little bit hot-headed. Sir Bedevere also wishes to be remembered to you. You always did have a very high opinion of him.

And now I must close, dear heart, and trust that it will not be too much longer before we are together again. All my love, and do remember to wrap up warm!

Your very own,

Mahaud

P.S. I almost forgot. While I was talking to him, young Bedevere happened to mention that he had seen the Graf von Weinacht while he was in Atlantis! Such a coincidence, don't you think! I wonder how the poor dear Graf is these days. They say that they can do wonders with drugs and leeches and things nowadays, but perhaps he is beyond help.

As he read the final paragraph, Simon Magus's brows gathered in a slight frown. Perhaps it was indeed all a coincidence, but perhaps not.

He lifted his head and looked out of the window – easy enough, since all the walls, floors and ceilings of the Glass Mountain are windows of a sort. Far away, he could see the earth, twirling gracefully and apparently aimlessly on its axis like an enchanted and very stout ballerina. He looked at his watch. Only another two hours to go . . .

To keep himself from being impatient, Simon Magus turned his thoughts to the Graf von Weinacht. A sad case, certainly; understandable, too, very understandable. In his position, anyone would probably react the same way. And a brilliant man, too, before it happened, although even then people were saying some very strange things about him.

The hall steward removed his plate and he sat for a moment, letting his mind relax. Nice to know that young Bedevere had finally made something of himself. Always a lot of promise there, he had often thought, just waiting for an opportunity to get out. No, that's not quite right; waiting for a situation in which he would be forced to take charge and make sure the job got done. Without that extra little bit of pressure, he could never achieve anything. Well, then.

He pushed back his chair, nodded affably at Nostradamus and Dio Chysostom, and strolled through into the library in search of the latest issue of the *Philatelic Monthly*. Instead, he found himself stopping in the Astrotheology section and taking down a very big, extremely dusty book that nobody had moved for quite some time.

Simon Magus pulled up a chair, crossed his legs and began to read.

Klaus von Weinacht knelt in the snow and howled at the sky.

Five hundred and twenty miles north of Nordaustlandet, in the middle of the bleakest, wildest, most inhospitable of all the desert places of the earth, is no place to break down. The nearest telephone box is in Hammerfest, five hundred miles the other way, and it's usually out of order. Besides, the chances of getting a garage to come out this far on a Sunday are practically nil.

Having vented his rage on the howling winds, von Weinacht opened the toolbox, took out a cold chisel, a wrench and a very big hammer, and set to work on the broken runner.

'Bloody – cheapskate – Far – Eastern – gimcrack –' he snarled in time to the hammer-blows. 'Ouch,' he added. He paused, sucked his throbbing thumb and calmed himself down. Now then, Klaus, he could hear his mother saying, you'll only make things worse if you lose your temper.

He picked up the wrench and set to work. Last time

he allowed himself to be talked into buying a stinking Japanese sleigh. No idea of craftsmanship, just thrown together any old how, Friday afternoon job. Anger surged up inside him, and he stripped a thread.

'Sod!' he roared at the flat horizon. Then he hurled the wrench to the ground and jumped on it.

Permafrost may be thick, but there are limits. There was a cracking sound, like the earth's crust yawning, and the Graf jumped clear just in time to avoid going down a ravine. The wrench, however, was gone for good.

'Right,' said the Graf. 'Let's all keep absolutely icy calm, shall we?' He went back to the toolbox, found another wrench, and continued with the job.

He ached all over. If ever he caught up with that misbegotten bloody knight – what was the bastard's name? Something sounding like turquoise. Any bloody knight, come to that. They're all the same, knights. Scum, the lot of them. Without realising it, he picked up the hammer and started to beat the hell out of the oilcan.

An hour later, he had managed to destroy a complete set of tools, smash the sleigh quite beyond repair, and frighten fifteen heavy-duty Trials reindeer into a stupefied trance. He threw down the hammer, lay on the ground and beat the ice with his fists.

Then he got up and pulled the walkie-talkie out of the saddlebags.

'Radulf,' he shouted. 'Beam me up.'

'Gosh!'

'Yes, miss,' said Toenail automatically. His head

swivelled from side to side, looking for somewhere safe. Optimism is another dwarfish characteristic.

'What's that funny ringing noise?' asked Galahaut.

'That's the alarm,' the girl replied. 'Do you think somebody could have broken in?' She shivered a little.

Brill, said Toenail to himself. 'I'm already lumbered with two idiots, now it looks like I've got a third one to look after as well. Any more, while I'm at it? Bring out your idiots.

He nudged Boamund in the ribs.

'Boss,' he said, 'don't you think we ought to be, well, getting along? You know . . .'

Boamund looked at him blankly for a moment. 'What?' he said. 'Oh, I see what you mean. Yes, good idea.' He remained where he was. In fact, the dwarf noticed, the three of them together looked remarkably like the legs of a table.

It was, in fact, the girl who broke the spell.

'Do excuse me,' she said, 'I'm completely forgetting my manners. Would any of you care for some tea?'

The early history of the Grail is surrounded by legends, most of which were put about by the PR department of Lyonesse back in the tenth century to create artificial runs on Byzantine long-dated government stock.

When the emperors of Byzantium ran into financial difficulties, they raised money by hocking sacred relics – the Crown of Thorns, the True Cross, the shin-bone of St Athanasius, and so forth. The record of the Empire in those days is not so much history as pawnography.

The value of these relics was determined by the market, which in turn was influenced by supply and

demand. So complete, however, was the Empire's col-
lection of holy bits and bobs that it very nearly consti-
tuted a full set. There was only one worthwhile relic
missing; but it was also the big one. So long as it was un-
accounted for, the market could never crystallise, for
fear of what might happen if it should ever reappear.

Clearly, as far as the market-makers were concerned,
this was a situation that had to continue, if they were
to have any hope at all of controlling the market. And
in order that the Grail should stay missing, it stood to
reason that they had to find it themselves, quickly.
Then they could arrange for it to get permanently and
definitively lost.

The result was the massive outburst of knightly
energy which swept Christendom, playing a major part
in the fall of Albion. In due course, Atlantis did indeed
find the Grail, and re-lose it so thoroughly that it has
stayed lost ever since. Just in case, however, the Chief
Clerk made a secret note of its whereabouts, which he
then put in a safe place; to be precise, in the library of
Glastonbury Abbey.

After the Dissolution of the Monasteries, however,
the library was dispersed; and a certain manuscript
found its way into the hands of one Gabriel Townsend,
bookseller of Stratford-upon-Avon. When Townsend
fell into debt and was sold up by the bailiffs, a local
man called John Shakespeare was attracted by the
picture of naked angels illuminated on the flyleaf and
bought it. To prevent his wife finding it, he wrapped it
round the pendulum of his clock.

Where, of course, it has remained to this day.

It's all right for them, Toenail muttered to himself.

They can sit there stuffing themselves with Bakewell
tart and digestive biscuits, because they've got no
imagination. They can't see what's going to happen
when we get caught.

He gritted his teeth and returned to the job in hand,
which was sewing a button back on Galahaut's pyjama
jacket.

'Are you sure you won't have another biscuit?' the
girl was saying. 'Go on, there's plenty.'

Boamund, who had eaten seven biscuits, three slices
of fruit cake and a scone, all washed down with four
cups of tea, shook his head politely and subconsciously
longed for a nice slab of cold roast ox. Galahaut, who
had a digestion like a cement mixer, helped himself to
a coconut pyramid.

The girl tried to think of something to say. In her
dreams, of course, it had all been much simpler; it always
is. All her life she had known that one day, a handsome
young knight would call in on this gloomy old castle on
his way somewhere, and Father would happen to be out,
and she would offer the knight tea, and they would talk
. . . She had insisted on having this room converted from
a subsidiary boiling-oil store into a nice little sitting
room with flowery pink curtains and frilly cushions. She
had spent hours – thousands of hours – baking and icing,
so that when the moment came there would be plenty of
fresh, home-made things to eat to go with the tea. She
had thought of everything; except, of course, what she
was going to say. That, she had somehow assumed,
would come naturally.

'It must be wonderfully exciting,' she said, 'being on
a quest.'

'Oh, it's not as wonderful as all that,' Galahaut

drawled, leaning back in his chair and hoping the light through the arrow-slit would catch his profile. 'Most of it's just plain, hard slog. Hours in the saddle, out in all weathers, nights under canvas or just huddled under a blanket against the rain . . .'

Toenail snorted, but nobody heard him. Had the girl chosen to ask him, he could have pointed out that the Haut Prince refused to spend the night anywhere that didn't have at least two stars and a southerly aspect, and insisted on his own private bathroom. And the fuss he made if the bed wasn't properly aired . . .

The girl nodded eagerly. It was hard to decide which of them was the more romantic, really; the world-weary thin one with the pimple, or the strong, silent one with the pink face. On the whole, probably the pink one; but it was too early in the story to choose.

'This quest,' she said, 'I bet it's terribly dangerous.'

'Um,' said Boamund. 'Hope not.'

The girl laughed prettily. 'Oh, you're so modest,' she replied. 'I'm sure you're not the least bit scared.'

Boamund fidgeted with the tablecloth, while Galahaut broke in and said that without fear you can't have courage. That did for the conversation what a damp towel does for a burning chip-pan, and the girl offered them another cake.

'That bell's still ringing,' the girl observed. 'I wonder what on earth it can be.'

The two knights glanced at each other. 'Probably just a loose connection in the wiring,' Galahaut said. 'Always going wrong, burglar alarms. We used to have one at the Castle, but next-door's cat was always setting it off so we took it down again. Nobody ever takes any notice of them, anyway.'

The girl looked surprised. 'Don't they?' she said.

Galahaut shook his head. 'Not usually. This is delicious angel cake, by the way. Did you make it yourself?'

Inside Boamund's heart, a great coiled spring of anger was being compressed, slowly and painfully, until he felt sure that he could stand it no longer. Damn Gally, he thought. I never liked him. Why did I bring him with me? Why couldn't it have been Lamorak or Turquine or one of the others? Old Turkey would have wandered off to look for the socks by now, and I could have . . .

'Actually,' he said – it was the first thing he'd said for ages – 'I think it's time we were going. Come on, Gally.'

Galahaut raised his eyebrows. 'What's the rush?' he said.

'You know perfectly well.'

'No I don't,' Galahaut replied. 'You must excuse my friend,' he said to the girl. 'So impatient.'

Boamund had gone bright red. 'Thank you, Sir Galahaut,' he said, as stiff as a newly laundered shirt. 'I don't need you to make my apologies for me.'

'Someone's got to do it,' Galahaut replied, grinning. 'Pretty nearly a full-time job it can be, sometimes.'

'What do you mean by that?'

'You understand plain Albionese, I take it.'

The girl's heart beat faster. They were going to fight! And because of her – yes, of course it was, knights only ever fight among themselves because of a lady. How marvellously, unspeakably thrilling!

Toenail edged across to the coal-scuttle, climbed in and shut the lid firmly.

'By God,' Boamund was saying, 'if there wasn't a lady present, I'd have a good mind to jolly well . . .'

'Jolly well what?'

'Jolly well ask you what you meant by that.'

'Well then, I'll save you the trouble of asking. I mean you're a liability, young Boamund. Can't take you anywhere, never could. Do excuse him,' he said to the girl. 'He always gets a bit over-excited if he eats too much chocolate. I remember once at school—'

'Sir Galahaut!'

'Sir Boamund. If only you could see how ridiculous you look.'

Boamund reached slowly into his pocket and drew out a glove. Actually, it was a woolly mitten with the fingers cut off, but it would have to do.

'My gage,' said Boamund. 'If you will do me the honour . . .'

'What do you want me to do with your glove, Bo? You lost the other one again, have you?'

'Sir Galahaut . . .'

'Always were a terror for losing gloves. At school Matron made you tie them round your neck with a bit of string.'

'Very well.' Boamund picked up the glove and slapped the Haut Prince across the cheek. 'Now, sir . . .'

'Don't do that, Bo, it tickles.'

Oh God, thought Toenail. I suppose I'd better do something, before they hammer each other into quick-fry steak. Carefully, he raised the lid of the scuttle and lifted himself out. Then he tiptoed across the room to the door, opened it, and left.

'Don't pretend you don't understand,' Boamund

was saying. 'That is unworthy of you.'

'Honestly, Bo, I haven't the faintest idea what you think you're talking about. Please stop drivelling, you're upsetting the lady.'

'I . . .' Boamund was lost for words. All he could think to do was to take out the other mitten and dash it in the cur's face.

'There,' Galahaut said, 'it was in your pocket all the time.'

'That does it. I demand satisfaction.'

The Haut Prince giggled. 'You what?' he said.

'You heard. You're a knave, a cad and a blackguard, and . . .' Boamund delved back into the archives of his mind, 'you cheated in falconry.'

A red curtain of rage swept unexpectedly across Galahaut's consciousness, obscuring everything else. 'What did you just say?' he gasped.

'You heard,' Boamund snarled. 'At the end of the summer term back in '08. You bought a cage of white mice from the pet shop, and you—'

'It's a lie!'

'It's not,' Boamund retorted. 'I found the receipt in your tuck box.'

'And what were you doing looking through my tuck box?'

'That's beside the point. You used those mice to—'

'So that's where my Aunt Ysoud's fruit cake got to!'

'You used those mice—'

'Greedy pig!'

'Cheat!'

The girl looked at them, puzzled. Well, at any rate, they were definitely going to fight.

★ ★ ★

Von Weinacht jumped down from the sleigh and called for his axe.

It had taken two hours – *two hours!* – for the pick-up sleigh to arrive, and then the tow-rope had broken, one of the reindeer had escaped, and they'd flown the wrong way over the Harris Ridge. The Graf took the axe from a trembling page and advanced towards the malfunctioning sleigh. He'd give it metal fatigue!

He noticed the alarm, and snapped his fingers imperiously.

'All right,' he yelled, 'I'm back now, you can turn that God-awful racket off!'

Radulf, who had come out to meet him, was trying to tell him something, but von Weinacht couldn't be bothered right now. All he wanted to do was give that worthless heap of Nipponese junk a service it would never forget.

'Excuse me.'

Something was tugging at his sleeve.

The Graf looked down and saw a dwarf. He frowned. Years since he'd seen a dwarf about the place. The last one, he remembered, had handed in his notice and gone south to work in the diamond mines. Funny.

'Excuse me,' the dwarf repeated, 'but could you possibly spare a moment? You see, two dangerous knights have broken in, and—'

'Knights?' Von Weinacht scooped the dwarf up in one enormous hand and held him about an inch from his nose. 'Knights?'

'Yes, sire, two knights. Boamund and Galahaut, sir. They're in your daughter's sitting room. Having tea.'

'Tea!' Von Weinacht roared, dropped the dwarf, and

broke into a run. Toenail picked himself up, rubbed his elbow vigorously, and followed.

He just hoped he was in time, that was all.

'Will these do?' the girl asked.

It was odd, she was saying to herself, I thought knights always had their own swords. In all the books she'd ever read, a knight didn't go anywhere without at least one sword, sometimes two. Still, there it was. Sometimes, she felt that she didn't really know an awful lot about real life.

'Thanks,' Boamund said gruffly. 'That'll do fine.'

'I found them,' the girl was saying, 'in Father's study. He's got lots of swords and things in there. I think he collects them or something. I brought swords, but there's axes and flails and maces and daggers too, if you want them.'

'Just swords will do fine,' Galahaut said. 'Unless, of course, Sir Boamund wants a shield or anything. He always insisted on having a shield at school.'

'I did *not*.'

'And if he couldn't have one, he used to burst into tears.'

'At least I didn't put an exercise book down my front when I was tilting.'

'What do you mean by that?'

'You heard.'

'There are some books in the library,' the girl put in helpfully, 'if anyone wants one.'

Boamund drew his sword from its scabbard. It was very cold. 'Shall we get on with it?' he asked. 'That is, if Sir Galahaut is ready.'

'Perfectly ready, thank you.'

'After you, then.'

Von Weinacht stood outside the sitting room and caught his breath.

'In there?'

Toenail nodded.

'Right.'

One kick from the Graf's enormous boot sent the door flying open. But the room was empty.

Oh God, Toenail thought, I was too late. They've gone off to fight it out; there'll be nothing left but torn clothes and a hundredweight of minced knight. Bugger.

'I thought you said . . .'

'They must have left, sir,' Toenail replied. 'Gone somewhere else, I mean.'

'Somewhere else?' There was an extra edge to the Graf's voice, which implied that it was bad enough their being there at all without them moving about like a lot of migratory wildfowl. 'Where?'

'Somewhere where there's plenty of room, I expect,'

Toenail replied. 'You see, they were wanting a fight . . .'

The Graf lifted his head and roared with laughter.

'A fight,' he repeated. 'Well, they've come to the right place, then, haven't they?'

'Yes, sir. Only we haven't.'

'Apparently not.' The Graf turned to his pages and shouted, 'You lot! Search the castle, understood. Two dangerous knights. Jump to it.'

Then something thudded into place in von Weinacht's brain, and he swung down a hand and grabbed the dwarf.

'You,' he growled. 'Who are you supposed to be, then?'

'Toenail, sir. I'm a dwarf.'

'I can see that.'

'Attendant on the knights, sir. I came with them from Albion.'

'I see.' Von Weinacht breathed out fiercely through his nose. 'And why are you betraying your masters to me?' he asked.

Toenail squirmed slightly. 'Oh, no reason,' he said. 'I just thought, blow this for a lark, all this mending things and cleaning things. I have nothing to lose but my chains, I thought, and—'

'What chains?'

'Figuratively speaking, sir.'

'Right,' said the Graf. 'I'll deal with you later. Follow me.'

He released the dwarf, smashed up a coffee table for good measure, and strode out of the door. Toenail didn't follow him at once; he darted back to his knapsack, retrieved something from it, and then followed as fast as his legs could carry him.

'Will this do?' the girl asked.

They were standing in the main courtyard. Because the entire staff was occupied in searching for intruders, the place was empty except for an abandoned and rather beat-up looking sleigh.

'Yes, that's fine,' said Boamund. 'I suppose we'd better get on with it.'

Although he was still burning with pent-up fury and rage, he was doing it rather more sheepishly than he had been a few minutes before. True, Sir Galahaut had wronged him quite unforgivably, and the shame would have to be washed out in blood; nevertheless, when you thought about it, it was a dashed silly way to settle an argument, chopping the other fellow's head off. Or getting your own chopped off. And a fellow you'd been at the dear old Coll with, into the bargain. He couldn't help feeling, deep down, that there might be a better way of dealing with situations like this. A really aggressive, hard-fought game of squash, for example.

Galahaut had taken off his jacket and was doing flamboyant practice sweeps with his sword. The girl was sitting on the sleigh. She had picked up a box of chocolates from somewhere, and was eating them avidly.

'Ready?' Boamund asked.

'Just a tick,' Galahaut called back. 'Um – got a bit of cramp in the forearm, I think. You don't mind if I just loosen up a bit, do you?'

'Not at all.'

'Jolly decent of you, old man.'

'Not a bit of it, Gally. Have as long as you like.'

The Haut Prince did a few more practice sweeps, and then some arm-flinging exercises. Not, he assured himself, that he wasn't eager to get on with it and give young Snotty the hiding he'd been asking for ever since he could remember; but there wasn't any rush, was there? All the time in the world.

'Excuse me,' said the girl, 'but why haven't you started yet?'

The knights looked at her.

'We aren't ready yet.'

'Can't rush these things.'

'Wouldn't be sporting.'

'Oh.' The girl shrugged. 'I see. Sorry.'

The knights circled gingerly. Once or twice they tried a few very tentative lunges, but not without asking the other fellow whether he was ready first. The Grafin, meanwhile, finished her chocolates and started clapping. Slowly.

In desperation, Boamund attempted a double left-hand reverse *mandiritta*, a fiendishly complex and difficult manoeuvre which, as he remembered only too well once he'd started, he'd never quite managed to master. It involves a duplex feint to the right side of the head, a slow pass to the left body, and finally a long lunge, executed by the fencer on one knee with his left hand passing behind his back until it touches the inside of his right knee.

'Help,' he said. 'I'm stuck.'

'Oh, hard luck,' exclaimed Sir Galahaut, sheathing his sword and helping him up. 'Better?'

'I think I've sprained my wrist.'

'That does it, then,' said Galahaut quickly. 'No earthly good fighting if you're not feeling a hundred per cent. Wouldn't be right.'

'Absolutely.'

'Pity,' Galahaut went on, 'but there it is. We'll have to call it a draw, I suppose.'

'Good thinking.' Boamund levered himself to his feet, winced, and put up his sword. 'Just when we were getting back into the swing of it, too.'

'Can't be helped,' said Galahaut sympathetically. 'Hey, where's that dratted girl gone?'

They both looked round. They were alone.

'Got bored, I expect,' said Boamund with contempt. 'That's girls for you, of course. I never did meet one who was really interested in Games.'

When the Graf came thundering down the main staircase into the Great Hall, he found his daughter sitting on the steps of the dais crying into a small lace handkerchief. He dropped his axe and hurried over to her.

'What's the matter, precious?' he said. 'Tell Daddy all about it.'

'It's those silly knights,' the Grafin sniffed. 'They won't fight. They're just standing there chatting.'

'There, there,' said the Graf. 'Don't upset yourself over a couple of silly knights. They're not worth it really.'

'And I thought they were both so brave,' the girl went on. There were little tears, like pearls, on her cheeks. She blew her nose loudly.

'Huh!' The Graf snorted contemptuously. 'Knights! They don't know the meaning of the word.'

'And they just left me sitting there,' the Grafin said, 'after I'd given them tea and everything.'

'Young blackguards,' said von Weinacht. 'I'll soon teach them a thing or two.'

The girl's eyes lit up and she smiled.

'I love you, Daddy,' she said.

'I love you too, Popsy,' muttered von Weinacht, gruffly. 'Right, where are those knights? Dwarf!'

Toenail, who had been standing on a chair and looking out of the window at the courtyard, jumped down and ran over to him.

'Yes, sir?'

'You got any idea where those knights are?'

'In the courtyard, sir. Not fighting,' he added, thoughtfully.

'Where's that dratted dwarf got to?' said Boamund. 'Always wandering off somewhere, I've noticed.'

'Typical,' Galahaut said, putting on his jacket. 'Especially when there's work to be done.'

'And he's got the luggage.'

The two knights looked around the huge courtyard.

'Could be anywhere,' Galahaut said at last. 'Big place, this.'

'Gloomy, though.'

They started to stroll towards the main hall.

'I vote,' said Galahaut, 'that we find this Graf von Weinacht, make him tell us where the Socks are, and buzz off. How does that sound to you?'

'Pretty shrewd,' Boamund replied. 'Where shall we start?'

'How about over there?'

'Good idea.'

They pushed open the doors of the main hall and walked in. They stared.

'Toenail?' they said, in unison.

In front of them, sprawled on the hearthrug like a pile of bright red bedclothes, was the Graf von Weinacht. An enormous Danish axe lay by his right hand. Standing over him, grinning and holding an aerosol can of chemical Mace, was the dwarf.

'I suppose,' the Graf said, 'I'd better begin at the beginning.'

It had been a long day. Acting on the information received, he had gone dashing off to Atlantis in search of Grail Knights, had been beaten up twice and rolled down a spiral staircase, crash-landed his sleigh in the middle of nowhere, arrived home to find the place knee-deep in knights, been Maced by a dwarf and tied up with his own dressing-gown cord. It was enough to make you spit.

'Is that necessary?' yawned Galahaut. 'Only . . .'

'Yes,' the Graf snapped. 'Absolutely essential. All right?'

'Fire away, then,' replied the Haut Prince. He leant back, put his feet up on a stuffed bear, and helped himself to a big, fat bunch of grapes.

Simon Magus turned the page and settled his reading-glasses comfortably on his nose.

The Pitiful History, he read, *of the Count of Christmas.*
He reached for his notebook.

It was a hell of a story. If it wasn't quite the greatest story ever told, that was just because the Graf wasn't quite in the mood to give it the full treatment.

. . . About how, getting on for two thousand years

ago, he packed in his promising career as a weather-god to study astrology at the University of Damascus. About how he and three of his fellow students, looking through the University's electron astrolabe, discovered what at first they took to be a bit of dirt on the lens, and then realised was an entirely new star.

About how they set off to observe it from the University's hi-tech observatory near Jerusalem. About how there was the inevitable cock-up with the hotel bookings, which meant that they arrived in Galilee one cold, wet night to find that their rooms had been given to a party of insurance salesmen from Tarsus, and they were going to have to doss down in the stables.

And how, just as they were squelching across the courtyard and muttering about suing somebody, young Melchior happened to look up and notice that the star was slap-bang over their heads; and that the group of shepherds who'd just come out of the stables were looking very worried indeed . . .

'And another thing,' said the shepherd, grinning insanely. 'I don't know if you're superstitious or anything, but if you are, don't go in there. The place is knee-deep in angels, okay?'

'Angels?'

'I don't want to talk about it.'

The shepherds hurried away, leaving Caspar, Melchior, Balthazar and Klaus standing in the rain.

'Did that man just say the Angels were in there, someone?' Balthazar asked.

'I thought so.'

They groaned. As if they didn't have enough to put

up with without sharing their sleeping accommodation with a gang of greasy, leather-clad, foul-mouthed, camel-riding hooligans.

It was dark in the stable. The oil lamp flickered atmospherically in the slight draught. Suddenly, all four of them felt this very great urge to kneel down.

'Hello,' Balthazar called out. 'Anybody here? Hey, lads, I don't like this, it's kind of spooky in here . . .'

It grew lighter; there was a soft golden glow coming from the far manger.

'Hush,' said a woman's voice, 'he's asleep.'

It was Melchior who spoke first. Very gently, he crept forward towards the crib, peeped into it, and then rocked back as if he had been stunned. Then he knelt down and covered his head with the hem of his cloak.

'Lady,' he said.

The woman's face was in shadow. 'Welcome,' she said. 'Blessed may you be for ever, for you are the first to look on the face of the Son of Man.'

Melchior rocked backwards and forwards on his heels. 'Lady,' he said again, 'is it permitted that we might offer gifts to your son?'

The woman smiled, and nodded, whereupon Melchior searched in his satchel and produced a small, shiny box. The woman nodded, as if she had been expecting it.

'Gold,' Melchior explained. 'Gold is a fitting gift for a king.'

The woman took the box without looking at it and laid it down beside the crib. Caspar stepped forward, fell on his knees and offered the woman a little alabaster jar.

'Frankincense, lady,' he said shyly. 'To anoint Him who shall be crowned with thorns.'

The woman nodded, and put the jar down by the box. Balthazar, his knees trembling, now stepped forward, knelt, and held out a silver phial.

'Myrrh, lady,' he whispered. 'To embalm Him who shall never die.'

Again, a trace of a smile crossed the woman's lips. She took the phial from Balthazar's hands, looked at it for a moment, and put it with the other gifts.

Why didn't they tell me, Klaus muttered to himself. The bastards. Why didn't they *say* something?

There was a moment's pause, while the other three looked at him. He decided to improvise. He grabbed something out of his satchel, tore a page out of a book to wrap it in (the book was a treatise on ornithology, and the page he had selected had little pictures of robins on it) and stepped forward.

'Um,' he said, and thrust the parcel into the woman's hands.

She gave him a long look, then slowly unwrapped the parcel.

'Socks,' she said. 'Just what He always wanted.'

The expression on her face told a different story as she held up two knee-length stockings to the light. Klaus winced.

'They're probably a bit big for him right now,' he said, as lightly as he could, 'but never mind, he'll grow into them.'

The woman gave him another long, hard look; then she rolled the socks up into a ball and dropped them. 'You may go,' she said.

'Thank you,' Klaus mumbled, backing away. 'Oh

yes, and a happy ... happy. The compliments of the season, anyway.'

He banged his head on a rafter, reversed out of the door, and ran for his life.

'A fortnight later,' the Graf went on, breathing heavily, 'I got a parcel. It contained a pair of socks, and a letter. It was delivered by an angel.'

He hesitated, closed his eyes, and continued. 'The letter wasn't signed, but then, it didn't need to be. I won't bore you with the first three paragraphs, because they were mostly about me. What you might call the business part of the letter came in the last few lines.

'To cut a long story short, I was cursed. For the rest of Time, it said, until the Child comes again to judge the quick and the dead, it would be my job to deliver presents to all the children in the world, every year, on the anniversary of my ... on Christmas Eve. Presents as inappropriate, unwanted and futile as the present I had seen fit to choose for the King of Kings. And, just to drive the point that little bit further home, just in case I hadn't quite grasped it by now, on each ensuing Christmas Eve every child in the world would henceforth see fit to hang at the foot of its bed the longest, woolliest sock it could find, as a perpetual reminder.'

There was a long silence.

'Yes,' said Galahaut, pulling himself together, 'be that as it may, what about these Socks?'

'Socks?' Klaus von Weinacht looked up at him and laughed. 'Haven't you worked it out yet? The socks you and your friend here have been looking for are *the* Socks. Hence,' he added with a bitter chuckle, 'the name. Do you seriously believe that I can hand them over to you, just like that?'

Boamund set his face in what he hoped was an impassive expression. 'You'd better had,' he said, 'or it'll jolly well be the worse for you.'

Von Weinacht turned his head and looked at him.

'Please?' Boamund added.

'No.' The Graf curled his lip. 'You don't think I wouldn't be delighted to see the back of them, do you? I hate the very sight of them. But they aren't mine to dispose of. Certainly not,' he added, 'to you.'

Boamund became aware of an urgent digging in his ribs and glanced down.

'What is it?' he said. 'Can't you see we're busy?'

'It won't take a moment,' Toenail replied. 'Just come over here, where he can't hear us.'

Boamund shrugged and got to his feet. They walked over to the fireplace.

'He's not telling you the whole story,' Toenail said, 'I'm sure of it.'

'Really?' Boamund raised an eyebrow. 'It must be a pretty long story, then, because ...'

Toenail shook his head. 'It's true all right, about the Socks and that. But there's more to it. I know there is.'

'Do you?'

'Yes.'

Boamund considered. He had always known that everybody, even servants, knew much more about everything than he did, and that was the way it should be. A knight has far more important things to do than go around knowing things. The way he saw it, if your head's full of knowledge, it'll get too big to fit inside a

helmet. Nevertheless, wasn't the whole thing supposed
to be a secret?

'How do you know, exactly?' he asked.

Toenail looked round. 'I just do, that's all. Maybe
it's because I'm a dwarf.'

'How does that come into it?'

'Race-memory,' Toenail replied. 'That and it's easier for dwarves to keep their ears to the ground. Look,
just ask him about the Grail, see how he reacts. Go
on.'

Boamund nodded. Great heroes, he knew, had
faithful and wise counsellors, invariably of lower social
rank, but dead clever nonetheless; and the good part of
it was that *their* names tended to drop out of history at
a relatively early stage.

He turned to the Graf, narrowed his brows to
indicate thought, and walked slowly back across the
hall.

'You're keeping something back, aren't you?' he
said. 'Come on, out with it.'

'Drop dead.'

'Don't you take that tone with me,' Boamund
replied. 'What about the Grail, then? You tell me that.'

By way of response, von Weinacht roared like a bull
and struggled furiously with the dressing-gown cord
that held him to the chair. Galahaut frowned and
reached for the rolling pin he'd found in the kitchens.

'Now cut that out,' he said. 'Honestly, some people.'

'Knights!' Von Weinacht spat. 'Bloody knights! Always the same. If I ever get my hands on you two . . .'

Galahaut hit him with the rolling pin. It seemed to
have a mild therapeutic effect, because he stopped

roaring and confined himself to looking daggers. Boamund nodded.

'Thanks, Gally,' he said.

'Don't mention it, Bo. It was a pleasure.'

Boamund drew up a chair and sat down. 'Let's start again,' he said. 'Now then, about the Grail.'

Von Weinacht made a suggestion as to what Boamund might care to do with the Grail as and when he found it. The rolling pin moved through the air once more.

'The Grail,' Boamund repeated. 'What about it?'

This time von Weinacht remained resolutely silent, and the two knights looked at each other.

'Don't think you can hit him just for not saying anything,' Galahaut remarked. 'Probably. What do you think?'

'Probably not,' Boamund agreed. 'Pity, but there it is. What do we do now, then?'

Galahaut shrugged his shoulders. 'Find the Socks, I suppose. Hey, you,' he said, leaning down and placing the rolling pin under the Graf's nose. 'Socks. Where?'

Von Weinacht tried to bite the rolling pin and Galahaut removed it quickly. 'I wonder what he's got against knights,' he mused. 'Is it just us, or knights *per se*, or what?'

'Don't think he likes anyone very much,' Boamund replied. 'Odd, that, given the line of work he's in. You'd think somebody who spends his whole time delivering Christmas . . .'

Von Weinacht howled like a wolf. The knights exchanged glances.

'Seems like he doesn't like you to mention a certain word,' Galahaut remarked.

'It does, rather, doesn't it?' said Boamund. 'Christmas!' he hissed in the Graf's ear, and then jumped back, startled. He wouldn't have believed a human being could make such an extraordinary noise.

'Well now,' said Galahaut, with a malicious grin on his face, 'that changes things rather, doesn't it? Doesn't it?' he shouted in the Graf's ear.

'Get knotted.'

'I think,' Galahaut said, 'it's time for a sing-song, don't you?'

It was a scene that Toenail would never be able to forget until the day he died. The Graf, twisting and squirming in his chair and roaring until you thought his voice would crack; and on either side of him, the two knights, singing *The Holly and the Ivy*, *Silent Night*, *Away in a Manger*, *God Rest Ye Merry Gentlemen* and *Rudolf the Red-Nosed Reindeer*. It was the last of these that finally did the trick.

'All right,' the Graf sobbed. 'You swine, you inhuman swine. I'll talk.'

Radulf grabbed the walkie-talkie impatiently.

'Moo,' he grunted into it; then he slammed the aerial down and nodded his horns. Three pages armed with halberds at once set off down the stairs.

They must be somewhere. Two knights and a supernatural being can't just vanish off the face of the earth . . .

Use your brains, Radulf. What are the knights here for? Suppose – just suppose – they've managed to overpower him somehow and forced him to show them the secret hiding place. Of course! That must be it.

The only problem being that the secret hiding place is – well, secret . . .

★ ★ ★

'In here?'

Von Weinacht nodded. 'And the very best of luck,' he added.

Boamund didn't quite follow that, but following things wasn't his forte, unless they happened to be hounds. He was quite good at that, provided there weren't too many gates and things in the way.

He grabbed the handles of the drawer and pulled.

Socks. The drawer was *full* of socks ...

'My God,' said Galahaut, in an awed voice, 'there must be several hundred pairs in there.'

Von Weinacht chuckled dryly. 'One thousand and forty-one,' he said. 'A good idea, no?'

'I don't suppose,' Galahaut said, 'that you care to tell us which pair is the right one?'

'Correct.'

Galahaut grinned. 'Did you ever hear the one about Good King Wenceslas?' he enquired. But the Graf was ready for him. With a sudden movement, he broke away from Galahaut's grip and dashed his head against the frame of the door, knocking himself out cold.

'Hey,' exclaimed the Haut Prince, 'that's cheating!'

Boamund lifted a heaped handful of socks and let them fall again. 'Just look at them all,' he said. 'I've never seen so many socks in all my born days.'

'Nor me.'

'Oh well,' Boamund sighed. 'I suppose we'll just have to take the lot, and try and sort them out later. Toenail, get us a very large sack.'

The dwarf made a resigned gesture with his shoulders and wandered off. Between them, Boamund and

Galahaut pulled out the drawer and emptied its contents on to the floor.

'I expect we can discount the ones with St Michael written on the label,' Galahaut said. 'Although he might have had a false label sewn in as camouflage. He's a clever devil, I'll say that for him.'

Boamund nodded. 'We'd better take all of them, Gally,' he repeated. 'Gosh, though. Who'd have thought socks could be so heavy?'

'So's sand,' Galahaut replied, 'in bulk. Did you follow all that stuff about Atlantis and offshore banking?'

'Not really,' Boamund admitted, 'all that sort of thing goes right over my head. But I sort of gathered that he'd had the Grail at one time, and then this Joseph person—'

'Joseph of Arimathea.'

'You know,' Boamund said, 'I've heard that name before somewhere. Anyway, this Joseph took the Grail himself and disappeared with it, so we're not much further forward in any event. Not that it matters, really. Once we've got the Apron and the Personal Organiser, and we've sorted out these socks, it won't really matter very much, will it?'

'Hope not,' Galahaut said. 'I prefer things to be as simple as possible. Where's that wretched dwarf got to?'

They looked round.

'Wandered off somewhere, I expect,' Boamund said. 'They do that.'

'Shouldn't be any problem finding a sack in this place,' Galahaut said. 'One thing you'd expect to find, a sack. Probably full of presents. I remember one year,

I was resting, I got a job as a Father Christmas in one of those big department stores. Of course, there was nothing in the sack except old newspapers and bits of cardboard.'

Boamund looked across at the stunned figure on the floor. 'We could try waking him up, I suppose. Sing some more, that sort of thing.'

'We could try,' Galahaut agreed, but with just a touch of hesitation. It wasn't that Boamund's voice was *flat* exactly – it was certainly no worse than a pneumatic drill – but there was no guarantee of results, and he didn't want to get another one of his headaches.

'Or,' he suggested, therefore, 'we could find someone else who's in on the secret. Must be someone,' he added.

'Such as?'

'Well,' replied Galahaut diffidently, 'there's that awful bloodthirsty girl, for a start.'

'The one who doesn't appreciate Games?'

'The impatient one, that's right. Bet you anything you like she knows which pair of socks it is.'

Boamund nodded fervently. 'Brilliant,' he said. 'Where is she?'

Galahaut was just about to say that he hadn't the faintest idea, when the door opened and the girl herself came in.

She was simply but attractively dressed in an organdie-print blouse with pin-tucks and a Peter Pan collar and a Liberty cotton skirt in pale lilac, and she was holding an assault rifle.

Aristotle was losing his temper with the pinball machine.

'It's rigged,' he muttered, fumbling in his pocket for change. 'Every time you get beyond three hundred thousand, a little gate opens down there and the ball sort of trickles down into it.' He gave the side of the machine a hard blow with the heel of his hand.

'You aren't using your upper flippers properly,' Simon Magus observed quietly.

'What the hell do you know about anything?'

'Sorry,' Simon Magus replied, 'just trying to be helpful. You haven't seen my wife anywhere, have you?'

'No.' Aristotle pulled back the handle and put the first ball into play. There was a short, tense interval while he pressed both buttons about a hundred times in the space of ten seconds, and the ball ran unerringly down the table and into the jaws of the machine.

'She's wandered off somewhere again,' Simon Magus said. 'Funny creatures, women.'

Aristotle glowered at him. 'Exactly,' he replied. 'Not really appropriate on campus, either, if you ask me.'

'Then I'll make sure I don't,' Simon Magus replied. 'Thanks for the warning.'

Aristotle grunted and launched into the second game, while Simon Magus wandered through into the coffee room. Nobody in there had seen Mahaud, either.

Eventually he ran her to ground on the balcony. She had a big pair of binoculars and was looking out in the general direction of the North Pole.

'Something,' she said, 'is going on.'

'Yes,' her husband replied. 'I know.'

She looked round at him. 'You do?' she said. 'What? Is it anything to do with that quest young Bedevere was on?'

'You might say that, yes. Lend me those glasses a moment, would you?'

He focused them, and stood for a while; then he lowered them and bit his lip thoughtfully. 'Oh well,' he said. 'Too late to do anything about it now, I suppose.'

'What do you mean?'

'It looks rather like I chose the wrong man for the job,' he replied. 'Do you remember a boy called Boamund? One of the Northgales kids, tall, gangling, unfortunate manner.'

'Of course I do,' Mahaud said. 'Snotty, the other boys called him. Not a very agreeable name, but apt.'

'Well,' Simon Magus said, 'he was one of my Sleepers. This spot of business that's going on now, I put him in charge of it. He was doing all right, too, until . . . Oh well.'

Mahaud took the glasses back. 'What's happened?' she said.

'Girl trouble.'

'Oh dear. I never thought he was the type, really.'

'They're the worst sort, usually,' Simon Magus replied. 'Anyway, it's not that sort of trouble. Oh *damn*,' he added peevishly.

'Never mind,' said Mahaud briskly. 'Can't be successful every time.'

'Suppose not,' replied the magician, philosophically. 'A great pity, though. I'd rather set my heart on this one coming off.'

'Put a lot of work into it?'

'Rather a lot, yes,' Simon Magus said. 'And I thought I'd made sure it was fairly idiot-proof. Still, there are idiots and idiots.'

Mahaud thought for a moment. 'It's never too late

to – well, give him a helping hand, you know.'

Simon Magus looked at her. 'But that's unethical,' he said. 'Once they've started and everything. Most improper.'

'Nobody would ever know.'

'I would.'

'Oh.' She stood for a moment, playing with the binoculars. 'Fair enough,' she said. 'Fancy a quick game of Scrabble?'

Simon Magus studied his wife for a moment.

'Mahaud,' he said, 'you're up to something.'

'Nonsense.'

'Come on, I know that expression. You're not to interfere.'

'I wouldn't dream of it,' replied his wife innocently. 'You know that.'

'Well, then.' He glanced at his watch. 'Blast,' he said, 'I must dash. I said I'd give Merlin a game of dominoes.'

'You run along then,' Mahaud said. 'See you later.'

It was an awkward moment.

'Hello again,' Galahaut said. 'We were just going to come and look for you.'

'Oh yes?'

'We were just,' Galahaut went on, 'helping your father have a really good sort-out of his sock drawer.'

'Really.'

'And then,' Galahaut persevered, 'he said he felt a bit tired and went to sleep, and so we thought we'd come and find you. But here you are anyway.'

The girl gave him a look. 'I don't believe you,' she said.

'You don't?'

'No, I don't'.

'Oh.'

'I think,' the girl said, 'that you're trying to steal Daddy's special Socks. I think you're *burglars*.'

'What makes you think that?'

'You are, aren't you?' the girl said. 'I think you tricked your way in here pretending to be knights, but really you're just sock-thieves. Probably,' she added, remembering a phrase from a book she'd been reading, 'an international gang.'

'Oh, we're knights all right,' Boamund interrupted. 'There's no question of that.'

The girl sniffed. 'Knights fight fair,' she said. 'Knights don't tie people up and go emptying drawers out on the floor. Burglars do that.'

'Knights do too, sometimes. It's all a matter of what's right in the particular circumstances.'

The girl shook her head. 'Daddy told me to be specially on the look-out for burglars,' she said. 'And he told me that if ever I saw any, I was to get this gun from his study and shoot them.'

'Gosh,' Boamund said. Galahaut smiled.

'And you always do what Daddy says?' he enquired.

'Always.'

'What a terribly dreary life you must lead.'

The girl frowned. 'What do you mean?' she asked.

Galahaut raised an eyebrow. 'I mean,' he said, 'I don't suppose you get out much, do you? No going to parties or anything like that.'

'Certainly not.' The girl looked pensive as she fidgeted with the safety catch of the rifle. Pensive but extremely dangerous.

'Can't be many people of your own age around here,' Galahaut went on. The girl nodded.

'None,' she said. 'Except for some of the pages, of course. Some of them are quite nice, or at least one of them . . .' She hesitated for a moment. 'But Daddy says I'm not to talk to the pages. He says . . .'

Galahaut raised his eyebrow a little bit more. It was very eloquent. But the girl suddenly shook her head.

'What's that got to do with burglars?' she said.

'Um . . .'

'You're just trying to confuse me,' the girl went on. 'That's a typical burglar trick, trying to confuse people. Knights wouldn't do that. They'd think it wasn't chivalrous.'

Slowly, she raised the rifle towards her shoulder, and Boamund shut his eyes. This didn't fit in with his preconceptions about damsels in distress at all.

A moment later he heard a hissing noise and a thump. At first he guessed the thump must be his own dead body collapsing to the floor; but after a few seconds he revised this opinion and opened his eyes again.

The girl was lying on the floor, snoring gently, and Toenail was putting an aerosol can back in his satchel.

'Knew it'd come in handy,' said the dwarf. 'Marvellous stuff, Mace. Works wonders with large dogs, too. I couldn't find a sack, by the way, but I thought a couple of pillow cases might do instead. Is that all right?'

Galahaut, who had gone a very funny colour, extricated himself from the corner of the room, into which he had backed, and grinned.

'Jolly good timing, that,' he said shakily. 'Nice work.'

'Thank you,' Toenail replied, rather taken aback. He tried to remember if anyone had ever thanked him before; good question. 'I met this woman out in the laundry room who said I was needed back here, so I came in.'

'What woman?' Boamund asked.

'Dunno,' Toenail replied. 'Just a woman. Appeared out of nowhere holding a pair of binoculars, gave me a message about you two being in the ... you two wanting me for something, and vanished again. Might have been a hologram, even.' He opened a pillow case and began filling it with socks.

'We still don't know which pair is which, though,' Boamund observed. 'You know, I do think it'd be a good idea if we found out. Otherwise ...'

The other two looked at him.

'Bo,' Galahaut said, 'I don't want to seem slapdash or anything, but if it's all the same to you, I'd rather we escaped with our lives first and saved the underwear-sorting part of it till later. If that's all right with you, I mean.'

'I wonder who that woman was. She might have known.'

'Who?' Toenail asked, looking up from the pillow case. 'The hologram, you mean?'

'That's if it really was a hologram,' Boamund said. 'What is a hologram, anyway?'

Toenail was about to explain when a sound outside the door checked him. The sound, if he wasn't very much mistaken, of hooves. Feet, too. Lots of them.

'Oh God,' he said, 'more of them.' He reached for the aerosol, shook it and made a face. 'Not much left in there,' he muttered. 'May I suggest that you hide?'

'Where?'

Toenail nodded towards the fireplace. 'You could try the chimney,' he said.

'Good Lord,' Simon Magus said. 'How on earth did they manage that?'

Mahaud looked up from her Scrabble pieces. 'Manage what, dear?' she said.

'That young Snotty and the other one,' said the magician, putting the binoculars down. 'They've got away from that lunatic girl after all. There's more to Boamund than I thought, apparently.'

Mahaud smiled. 'That's nice, dear,' she said. 'Now, what can I make with this lot?'

She studied her hand carefully. There was a C, an H, an E, an A and a T.

'Is there such a word as theac?' she asked.

It was windy up on the roof.

'Hand me up that other pillow case,' Boamund called down the chimney. 'Careful now, don't drop it. That's the way.'

A moment later Galahaut emerged. He was very sooty, and he'd broken a fingernail.

'Pity we had to leave the dwarf,' he said. 'Still, never mind.'

'We'll just have to wait till we get home,' Boamund said. 'Still, it is a shame. I hate polishing shoes and sewing on buttons. It's so fiddly.'

A sleigh was floating in the air a few feet from their heads, tethered to a ring on the side of the chimney-stack. There was a full team of reindeer in the shafts.

'That's handy,' Boamund said. 'I was wondering

how we were going to escape.'

'Something always turns up,' Galahaut replied. 'Do you know how you drive one of these things?'

'Not really,' said Boamund. 'Still, I expect it's not too difficult once you've got the hang of it. Probably an ordinary flying spell will do.'

'I forgot,' Galahaut said, 'you know all that magic stuff for getting about and things. I could never be doing with it, personally.'

Boamund hauled himself up into the sleigh, took the pillow cases from Galahaut and gave him a hand up into the cockpit. 'Now then,' he said, 'we just say the magic words, and then we're away.'

He said them. Nothing.

'What's wrong?'

'It isn't working, that's what.'

Galahaut, the actor, sniffed. 'Try putting a bit more *feeling* into it. Motivation, that's what you need. Come on, let me try. What's the spell again?'

Boamund told him, and he sat for a moment, thinking himself into the part. Then he said the spell.

'Gosh,' Boamund said. 'That was very good.'

'Thanks.'

'We still aren't moving, though, are we?'

'Probably a bit too melodramatic,' Galahaut admitted. 'A bit too Olivier, maybe. I'll make it a bit more Marlon Brando this time, shall I?'

'Who's Marlon Brando?'

Galahaut said the words again. The sleigh continued to bob gently in the breeze.

'That's a bit tiresome,' he said. 'Are you sure you've got the right words?'

'I think so.' Boamund muttered them over to himself

under his breath. They sounded all right.

'Perhaps magic doesn't work here,' he suggested. 'I've heard that there are places like that.'

Just then, Galahaut noticed that an arm had appeared over the edge of the chimney-pot. He drew his sword, and then stopped.

'It's all right,' he said, 'it's only the dwarf.'

Sure enough, Toenail's head appeared a moment later. They helped him up on to the sleigh.

'Sorry you got left behind,' Galahaut said, 'only, well, it was you or the socks. Couldn't carry both, you understand.'

Toenail understood all too well. Still, it had been all right, just about. He had a nasty antler-gouge in his leg, and his neck ached where a page had thrown a teapot at him, but otherwise he was all right. All the Mace had gone, though.

'Would it be a good idea if we left now, please?' he suggested. 'Only, they were saying something about following us, and . . .'

'Easier said than done,' Boamund replied. 'We can't get this thing to budge. We've tried the magic spell, and it won't work.'

Toenail looked down at the console.

'It might help,' he said, 'if you took the handbrake off.'

'Running away,' Boamund said, 'is just not *done*.'

'I've done it,' Toenail interrupted, 'lots of times. It's quite easy once you get the hang of it.'

'But it's not right,' Boamund protested. 'Sir Lance-lot never ran away from people.'

'Maybe not,' Galahaut retorted, as they skittered

over a patch of turbulence. 'Maybe the fact that everyone was shit-scared of him had something to do with it. I don't think that lot are terribly frightened of us, do you?'

He waved an arm behind them. Boamund looked over his shoulder. In the distance he could just make out the figure of von Weinacht in the leading pursuit sleigh – there were ten of them – standing up in the box and wielding his big Danish axe. He certainly didn't *look* frightened.

'That's beside the point,' Boamund objected, ducking to avoid a passing skua. 'I mean,' he added, 'they'll never be scared of us if we keep running away, will they?'

'I don't think they'll be all that scared if we suddenly decide to keep still,' Galahaut replied. 'Just rather surprised and very pleased.'

The sleigh rocked as a thermal hit it, and Boamund grabbed the rail. 'I still don't think ...' he started to say, and then caught sight of the world, a very long way below. 'Gosh,' he said.

The pursuers were gaining on them. In the shafts of von Weinacht's sleigh, there was a very big reindeer with a red nose and grey hairs round its muzzle, the tinsel on its antlers cracking in the wind. It looked rather unfriendly.

Toenail, who had been exploring the glove compartment, tugged Galahaut's sleeve. 'Look at this,' he said, 'I think it's some sort of instruction manual.'

Galahaut took the booklet and glanced at it. 'Hey,' he said, 'that's not bad, is it? Here, Bo, how about a compromise? How'd it be if we ran away and fought them at the same time?'

'Talk sense, Gally,' Boamund replied, resolutely not looking down. 'How can we do that?'

'Look,' Galahaut said. 'Apparently this sleigh's got, like, built-in optional extras. I wondered what it was doing tethered up there. It must be the old Graf's escape sleigh. According to this, it can do some pretty antisocial things if you want it to.'

Boamund looked at him. 'Such as?'

'Well,' Galahaut said, 'apparently, this button here . . .'

There was a whooshing noise directly under them, and two vapour trails appeared behind the sleigh. A moment later there was a loud explosion in the sky to their rear.

'Heat-seeking rockets,' Galahaut said, 'disguised as gift-wrapped golf umbrellas. And this . . .'

He got no further with his sentence; the air was filled with thick, rolling black clouds which billowed away into their slipstream. Toenail finished the sentence for him.

'Smoke screen,' he said. 'Now, which of these is the machine-guns, and which is the rear wash-wipe?' He shrugged and pressed both.

When the smoke cleared, there were only seven sleighs following them. Boamund grabbed the instruction manual and started flicking through it.

'Jet boost,' he said. 'Hey, Gally, what does that . . .?'

Before Galahaut could answer, the sleigh was hurled across the sky like a fast leg-break. Boamund only managed to stay in it by clinging on to the strap of a sleigh-bell.

'Nice one,' Galahaut said, as he hauled him back into the cockpit. 'Won't be long before they've closed in, though. They're pretty nippy, those sleighs.' He looked at the dwarf thoughtfully. 'We're carrying too much weight,' he said. 'We could do with lightening this thing up a bit, really.'

Toenail didn't speak; he put his arms round one of the bags of socks and set his face into a grim expression. Galahaut shrugged, said that it was just a suggestion, and looked over Boamund's shoulder at the manual.

'Anti-aircraft mines,' he read. 'Don't see that myself, do you?'

'Does no harm to try.'

'All right.'

They pressed the button together, and at once the rear cargo-door of the sleigh flew open, scattering hundreds of little brightly wrapped parcels which hung in the air on tiny individual parachutes. A few minutes later, as the lead pursuit sleigh passed through the floating cloud, they found out how that one worked.

'That's about it,' Galahaut said wistfully. 'And there's still five of them following us.'

'There's still this button here.'

'I'd leave that alone if I were you.'

'Ejector seat,' Boamund read aloud. 'I wonder what that does?'

Toenail hit the surface of the ice, and bounced.

The sackful of socks burst under him, scattering its contents, and he slid for a while on his stomach until he came to rest in a snowdrift. He picked himself up slowly and examined the punctured sack. There was just one pair of socks left in it.

Then he lifted his head and looked up at the sky.

Without the dwarf's weight, the knights' sleigh was moving faster, drawing rapidly away from its pursuers. He stood and watched as the chase screamed away over the skyline.

Oddly enough, in the middle of the ice floe there was a signpost.

Hammerfest 1200 km, it said, and pointed.

The dwarf put his hand down into the pillow case and drew out the remaining pair of socks. Slowly he unravelled them, found the label and read it. The lettering was faint, worn away by incessant laundry, but after a while he was able to make out the words.

MADE IN SYRIA. 100% COTTON. HAND-WASH ONLY.

He grinned, stuffed the socks into his satchel, and began to walk.

Von Weinacht reined in his sleigh, leant forward and shook his fist at the tiny speck on the horizon.

'Next time, you bastards!' he yelled. 'Next time!'

8

Exit Ken Barlow, pursued by a bear.

The ghost looked at the page in front of him, wrinkled his broad, insubstantial forehead, and crossed out what he'd just written. No good; start again.

The Rovers Return. Alf Roberts and Percy Sugden are leaning against the bar.

Alf: The way I see it, Percy, there's a tide in the affairs of men which, taken at the flood, you understand, well – you could be on to a good thing there.

Percy: I'm with you all the way there, Councillor. I was saying to Mrs Bishop just the other day, if you don't grab hold of your opportunities in this life, you're bound in shallows and in miseries, like.

No. Something lacking there. Not punchy enough.

The ghost drew a line through it and noticed that the sheet of paper was completely full. He scowled irritably; a perfectly good sheet of A4 down the plughole, and nothing to show for it.

In the hall, the old clock whirred, hesitated for a moment and struck thirteen times.

Funny, the ghost reflected, how it did that. It always had, ever since he could remember, and it had always aggravated him beyond measure. Ironic, really, that the only piece of original furniture in the whole place should be that knackered old clock. Why they couldn't get one of those smart new digital affairs was beyond him.

He wrenched his mind back to work, bit the end of his pen, spat out a fragment of quill, and wrote:

The Rovers Return. Vera, Ivy and Gail sharing a table.
Vera: Well, here we all are again, like. Raining cats and dogs outside, an' all.

Another thing which had always annoyed him was the way his concentration tended to waver when he came to a sticky bit. Instead of pulling himself together and getting down to it, he had this tendency to let his mind wander away from the job in hand to quite irrelevant and unimportant things, like why that bloody clock had never worked, not since the day . . .

He strolled into the hall, trying to hear Vera's voice in his head. What would the confounded woman be likely to say? She's come home after a hard day, gone down the pub, run into her best friend and her best friend's daughter-in-law . . .

Maybe it was the pendulum. It wasn't the escapement; he'd had that out and in pieces all over the kitchen table that time he'd had a block with *Titus Andronicus*. But the pendulum was something he hadn't considered. If the poxy thing was out of true – the weight not balanced right, or whatever – that might well account for it.

Maybe he shouldn't start the scene with Vera at all. Maybe two courtiers . . .

First Courtier: They say Jack Duckworth's been off his feed lately.

Second Courtier: Perhaps he hasn't heard that their Terry's in trouble with the police over that vanload of stolen eiderdowns that was found round the back of Rosamund Street . . .

Nah.

He opened the door of the clock and looked inside.

There were his initials, where he'd scratched them on the case when he was twelve. There was the stain where he'd hidden the rabbits he'd had off the Squire's back orchard, the night Sir John Falstaff's men had got a warrant to raid the place. Happy days.

He reached in and located the pendulum. Seemed all right, not loose or anything. Maybe it's the . . .

The ghost raised an immaterial eyebrow. There was something wrapped very tightly round the pendulum and tied on with a bit of binder cord. It had plainly been there some time. Maybe Dad had tried to adjust the timing by packing the pendulum. That could account for it; a good sort, Dad, but not mechanically minded. Didn't hold with machines of any sort, which was why he'd refused to fork out when there was that chance of being prenticed to the instrument-maker. The ghost shook his head sadly; still, it didn't do to dwell too much on lost opportunities. Things hadn't worked out too badly in the end.

The something tied round the pendulum turned out to be a sheet of old-fashioned parchment. Swept away by nostalgia, the ghost removed it carefully, smoothed it out, and studied it. Marvellous stuff, parchment;

miles better than this squashed-tree rubbish you got these days. Once you'd finished with it, all you had to do was get a pumice-stone and you could wipe off all the old writing and there you were.

He closed the door of the clock and wandered slowly back to his desk, squinting at the writing on the parchment. Pretty old-fashioned writing, even by his standards. Pictures, too; *naughty* pictures. A piece fell into place in his mind, and he remembered Dad coming home from the Fair one night, when he was quite young … saying something about – that was right, about fixing the clock. But it didn't need fixing, Mum had said. I'll be the judge of that. Soon have it right. And the blessed thing had been up the pictures ever since. Hardly surprising, really.

Fancy that, the ghost muttered to himself. After all these years, and it was a bit of porn round the pendulum all the time.

The words, he realised, were in Latin, which was a closed book as far as he was concerned; and the pictures weren't as naughty as all that. Good piece of parchment, though, keep you going for weeks if you were careful and didn't rub too hard. He smiled and nodded his head, then put the parchment down and went off to the bathroom to look for a piece of pumice.

'Great,' said Sir Turquine. 'Now what do we do?'

They had cleared the table in the Common Room of shirts, empty pizza boxes and Lamorak's angling magazines, and had mounted a sort of trophy.

An apron, a small leather-covered book and a pair of socks. The silence in the Common Room was tainted with just the tiniest degree – one part in a hundred thousand – of embarrassment.

'Maybe I'm just being more than usually obtuse here,' Turquine went on, 'but speaking purely for myself, I don't see that we're *that* much closer to finding the Grail. Do you?'

Pertelope had taken a biro from his top pocket and used it to poke the socks experimentally.

'They don't *look* old,' he said. 'You sure that ruddy dwarf got the right pair?'

'Positive,' Boamund replied.

'Why?'

'Because.' The other knights looked at him, and in a disused compartment of his mind Boamund began to speculate as to why 'Because' wasn't as convincing a reason as it had been when he was a boy.

'Maybe it's an acrostic or something,' Lamorak suggested.

There was a brief moment of silence, as six knights tried to make sense out of the initial letters of the items before them.

'No,' said Bedevere, 'I think there's more to it than that. I mean, if it was that we wouldn't actually need the things themselves. I think there must be, well, clues in there somewhere.'

'Clues,' Turquine repeated.

'Like,' Galahaut suggested, 'some common factor, maybe?'

Six pairs of eyes rested on the exhibits; an apron, a leather book and a pair of socks.

'Animal, vegetable or mineral?'

'Shut up, Turkey, I'm thinking.' Bedevere rubbed his nose with the heel of his hand and picked up the apron. 'I'm asking myself,' he said, 'what does an apron say to me?'

'Not a lot,' Turquine replied. 'Not unless you've been out in the sun again.'

Bedevere ignored him. 'Apron,' he said. 'That suggests housework, cleanliness, tidiness, cookery . . .'

'Kitchen floors,' said Lamorak, whose turn it was to clean it. 'Fruit cake. Rubber gloves. Persil. I don't think we can be on the right lines here, somehow.'

'Maybe we're missing the point,' Galahaut interrupted. 'It's not just aprons, it's this apron in particular. Has anyone examined it? In detail, I mean?'

'Well, not as such,' Boamund said. 'I mean, an apron is an apron, surely.'

'Not necessarily,' Galahaut replied. 'Give it here, someone, and let's take a closer look.'

He took the apron in his hands and stared at it for a while. 'It's just an apron, that's all,' he said.

'Brill,' Turquine said. 'The fundamental things apply, and so on. If you ask me, someone with a very odd sense of humour's had us for a bunch of mugs.'

'We're approaching this from the wrong angle,' Pertelope interrupted. 'There you all go, trying to understand things. That's not what we're for; if they wanted things understood, they'd have given the job to a bunch of professors instead of us. As it is, we're doing it; and what are we good at? Being brave and socking people. Therefore . . .'

Bedevere held up his hand for silence. 'Per's right,' he said. 'That's got to be it, hasn't it? I mean, the thing about knights is, they're fundamentally – well, stupid, aren't they? I mean we. Obviously, what we're meant to do is take these things, ride forth for a year and a day and have adventures, and then it'll just happen. Stands to reason, really.'

'What's *it*, Bedders?' Lamorak asked.

'It,' Bedevere replied. 'Thing. Finding the Grail. I mean,' he said, waving his hands about, 'that's the way it's always been done. You set forth, you meet a wise old crone by the wayside, she gives you a scrotty old tin lamp or a bit of carpet or a magic goldfish, and next thing you know you're in business. You've just got to have a bit of patience, that's all. Leave it to them.'

'Them,' Turquine muttered, 'we, they, it. You're nothing but a pronoun-fetishist, Bedders.'

'What's a pronoun?'

'And who are you calling stupid, anyway?'

Galahaut, frowning, banged the table with his fist.

'I vote we give it a shot,' he said. 'I mean, can't do any harm, can it? And if all that happens is that we wander around for a year and a day having a good time, then so what? We can start again from scratch, no skin off our noses.'

'He's right,' Bedevere said. 'Whoever heard of knights having to organise things? It's just a matter of getting on with it.'

Boamund nodded suddenly. 'Bedevere is right,' he said decisively. 'Put all that stuff in a bag, somebody, we're going questing.'

Toenail, who had been curled up in a cardboard box under the table polishing the sugar-tongs, jumped up, loaded the three treasures into a plastic carrier, and stowed them in his knapsack. He had come to this conclusion half an hour ago.

'Ready?' he asked.

'I'll just do my packing,' said Lamorak. Toenail pointed out that he'd done everyone's packing that morning, while they were all having breakfast. The cases were in the hall, he said.

'Right,' said Boamund happily, 'that's settled. Let's get on with it, shall we?'

Thus it was that three minibuses set off from three very different places at precisely the same moment.

The first – an ex-British Telecom Bedford, property of the Knights of the Holy Grail – headed off down the Birmingham ring road towards London, with Sir Pertelope driving and Sir Turquine doing the map-reading. Perhaps because of the human chemistry involved, it missed all the relevant turnings and ended up on the A45 to Coventry.

The second – an Avis eight-seater Renault nominally on hire to the Faculty of Experimental Mythology skittles team – left Glastonbury, joined the M5 north-bound to Bristol and the Midlands, made good time and stopped at the Michael Wood service station for a cup of tea and a go on the Space Invader machines in the front lobby.

The third – a brand new, jet-black Dodge with tinted windows, fat tyres, diplomatic number plates and a sticker in the window saying 'Tax Disc Applied For' – materialised on the M40 at its junction with the M25 and drove like a bat out of hell northwards, staying in the fast lane all the way and flashing the cars in front with its lights until they pulled over and let it pass.

'No,' said Aristotle, '*I* had the iced bun, *Dio* had the Black Forest gateau, *Merlin* had the toasted teacake, *you* had the croissant and the black coffee, so *you* owe *me* thirty pee.'

The soi-disant skittles team glowered at each other. Nostradamus, who had the bill, took a pencil from behind his ear and began to do sums.

'Actually,' Merlin said, 'I just had a cup of tea. It was, er, Mrs Magus who had the . . .'

Simon Magus glanced at his watch. 'All right,' he said, 'I'll treat you. I'll pay. Can we go now, please?'

The magi looked at him.

'There's no need to take that tone,' Aristotle growled. 'It's perfectly simple. I gave Nostradamus a fiver—'

'We haven't got time, Ari,' Simon Magus growled. 'Let's sort it out in the van, all right? Mahaud – oh God, where's she got to now?'

'I think she went to the shop to buy some peppermints,' Merlin said. 'She said that sucking a peppermint stops her feeling travel-sick.'

'Oh for crying out loud,' Simon Magus exclaimed. 'Dio, be a good chap, go and tell her . . .' But Dio Chrysostom, who was adamant that he'd had nothing but a hot chocolate and a digestive biscuit, folded his arms and pretended not to hear. Things were starting to get just a little bit out of hand.

Simon Magus frowned. On the one hand, here were eight of the finest minds in the whole of the Glass Mountain, the final repository of the wisdom of the world, the fountain of magic, the shield and pillar of mankind. On the other hand, they made the Lower Shell back at the Coll seem positively rational by comparison. He cleared his throat meaningfully.

'Right,' he said. 'The bus leaves in three minutes.

Anybody not back by then gets left behind. Clear?'

He jingled the keys and stalked off across the car park.

'Oh bother,' said the Queen of Atlantis, frowning slightly. 'That *is* a nuisance. Get out and change it, somebody.'

There was a certain degree of shuffling in the body of the bus, but otherwise nobody moved.

'Don't tell me,' the Queen said. 'There isn't a spare wheel in this thing.' She smiled glacially. 'Am I right?'

'There, um, wasn't room,' said a foolhardy young PA. 'You see, we had to strip out everything that wasn't absolutely essential so's we could fit the surveillance devices and the mobile fax transceiver in, and . . .'

'And somebody decided that a spare wheel wasn't essential.' The Queen pursed her exquisite lips. 'More a sort of luxury, I suppose, like a built-in cocktail cabinet. I *see*. Well then, did we also discard the puncture repair kit as the last word in Sybaritic self-indulgence, or have we still got that somewhere?'

'Oh yes, we've . . .'

The searchlight eyes homed in. The wire-guided smile locked on target.

'How simply splendid,' the Queen said. 'Out you get, then.'

Reluctantly, like a toreador going out to meet a bull with nothing but a bunch of flowers and a toothpick, the foolhardy young PA stood up, banged his head on the roof of the bus, and shuffled across to the door.

'Now then.' The Queen turned her head and turned the smile up to saturation level. 'While we're waiting, let's just see what else we've forgotten, shall we?'

Fortunately, the phone rang.

'Turkey.'

Sir Turquine looked up from his map. By his calculations they should be in Hertfordshire by now, which meant that some damn fool had moved Coventry a hundred miles to the south. 'What?' he snapped.

'Are you *sure* this is the right way?'

'Look . . .'

Boamund, who had been fast asleep ever since Perry Bar, woke up with a jolt and said, 'Stop the van!'

'Sorry?'

'I said,' Boamund repeated, 'stop the van.'

Turquine looked at him and shook his head. 'You can't,' he said, 'it's a main road. You'll have to wait till we pass a Little Chef or something.'

'Not that, you fool,' Boamund snapped. 'We're here. This is it.'

Pertelope shrugged. 'You're the boss, Snotty,' he said. 'There's a lay-by just ahead. Will that do?'

'Yes,' Boamund said impatiently, 'that's fine, just pull over.' He was frowning – a bad case of concentration, by the looks of it, as if he was struggling to keep something large and slippery in his mind.

'You all right, Bo?' Bedevere asked. 'You look all funny.'

'Actually,' Boamund replied, 'I had a dream.'

'Hello,' Turquine said, 'here we go. Young Snotty's been at the glue again.'

Boamund waved his hand angrily. 'Shut *up*, Turkey,' he said. 'This dream was important, and I'm trying to remember it. It's not easy, you know.'

The van stopped, and the knights jumped out. It was cold, and a fine shower of rain was falling. Beyond the post-and-wire fence, mist was blurring the edges of a large pine wood.

'That's it,' Boamund said, pointing. 'That forest over there. The other side of those trees, there's a lake. That's where we've got to go.'

Bedevere had managed to get hold of the map, and was examining it carefully. 'He's right, you know,' he said. 'At least, there's flooded gravel pits all round here. At least,' he added, lowering the map and nodding northwards, 'if that's Meriden over there, then there's gravel pits behind those trees. Otherwise, we could be anywhere.'

He stopped and looked down. Toenail was tugging at his sleeve.

'Did you say Meriden?' the dwarf demanded excitedly.

'Yes,' Bedevere replied, 'that's right. Why?'

'Meriden,' the dwarf repeated. 'Where the bikes come from.'

Bedevere raised an eyebrow. 'What's he going on about bikes for, anybody?' he said. Galahaut nodded.

'The old Triumph factory was at Meriden,' he said. 'What of it?'

The dwarf grinned. 'Nothing,' he said. 'Only, Meriden happens to be the exact geographical centre of Albion, that's all.'

Galahaut frowned. 'How extremely interesting,' he said. 'Now puddle off, there's a good little chap, because . . .'

'Say that again,' Bedevere interrupted.

'Meriden,' the dwarf repeated, 'is the exact centre of

Albion, geographically speaking.' He winked at Bedevere. 'Just thought I'd mention it,' he added.

'Thanks.' Bedevere twitched his nose a few times and looked at the map. 'You know,' he said, 'that's rather interesting, if you think about it.'

Lamorak looked at him quizzically. 'Is it?' he said. 'Personally, I could never get the hang of geography. What's the capital of Northgales, all that stuff. I mean, who wants to know?'

'In the exact centre,' Bedevere said, as much to himself as to anyone else. 'Well, I'll be blowed.'

'Your Majesty.'

'Mmmm?'

'I think you'd better pull over, Your Majesty.'

The Queen glanced in her rear-view mirror, sighed, and slowed down, while the PAs looked at each other and grinned. They were going to enjoy this.

The policeman who walked over and tapped on the window was young, tall and red-haired. In fact, the Queen said to herself, it's funny how young they all look these days. She wound down the window and smiled.

'Good afternoon, officer,' she said pleasantly.

The policeman didn't react to the smile; or if he did, he didn't show it.

'Do you realise,' he said, 'you were doing over a hundred and ten miles per hour back there, madam?'

'Gosh!' the Queen replied. 'How frightfully exciting! It didn't feel like that at all.'

'Please get out of the van, madam.'

'But it's raining.'

The policeman's face remained impassive. 'Out of

the van, please,' he said. 'Now I'm going to ask you to blow into—'

'Sorry?'

'I'm going to ask you rivet rivet rivet rivet,' said the small green frog; and then it seemed to notice that something was different. It hopped up and down on the spot once or twice and then it just sat there with its mouth open. The Queen shook her head sadly and beckoned to the other policeman.

'Officer,' said the Queen, 'I'm going to turn you into a frog, too.'

The policeman stared at her.

'Please don't take it personally,' the Queen went on, 'because I know you're just doing your job, and really it's not your fault, it's just the way things are. It won't hurt, I promise you.'

She smiled, and a second frog appeared at her feet. Very carefully, so as not to damage the little creatures' fragile legs, the Queen picked the two amphibians up and put them on the palm of her hand.

'Now then,' she said. 'One day, a princess will come along this road. Probably,' she added, 'doing a hundred and twenty and towing a horsebox. If you're terribly nice to her and don't ask to see her driving licence, she may kiss you and then you'll be back to being policemen. If not, try mayflies. I'm told they're a bit of an acquired taste, but well worth persevering with. Ciao!'

She put her index finger gently behind the frogs' back legs to encourage them to jump off her hand, smiled once more and got back into the van.

'Right,' she said.

★ ★ ★

'Where?'

Boamund scowled. It had been such a vivid dream, the sort you know you're going to remember, and now all there was in his mind was a sort of sticky silver trail where it had once been.

'It's about here somewhere,' he said. 'A lake. All misty. You know the sort of thing.'

Turquine shook his head. 'No sign of a lake here, Snotters,' he said. 'I mean, a thing like a lake, it's not easily overlooked. You must just have imagined it.'

'I did *not* imagine it,' Boamund shouted. 'It was a lake, and it was *here*.'

'Isn't here now,' said Turquine, and he smirked. 'Just a lot of trees, and this.'

He waved his arm at the small, exclusive, half-finished development of executive starter homes and shrugged. The other knights, unusually sensitive to their leader's embarrassment, said nothing.

'We could try over there,' Boamund suggested; and Bedevere was reminded of a cat he'd once known who had the habit of going to each door and window in turn every time it rained, presumably on the off-chance of finding one where it was sunny. 'It must just be hidden by the mist. I'm sure if we looked *properly* . . .'

'Come on, now,' Turquine was saying, in that unbearably aggravating let's-be-reasonable tone of his. 'We've given it a jolly good go, there's no lake here, so let's say no more about it and—'

There was a splash. Turquine had found a lake all right.

The ghost read back what he'd written and knew that

it was good. You get that feeling sometimes, when you're a ghost.

He looked at the clock, which was now keeping perfect time, and saw that it was just on half past nine. Just time to fax it through before everyone at the Manchester studios went home.

As the ghost strolled through the abandoned house, he wondered to himself what he'd found so difficult. As soon as he'd cottoned on to the idea of having Mike Baldwin start off the scene, it had just come; as if someone somewhere had been feeding it directly into his head. He'd just sat down, grabbed the paper, never blotted a line.

For the first time, he noticed what he'd been writing on; it was that funny piece of parchment he'd found in the clock. Without thinking he'd pumiced away the pictures and the initial capitals, but he hadn't touched all that silly Latin writing. Still, too late to do anything about it now.

A brief spasm of curiosity took hold of him, and he sat down on the lid of a chest and squinted at the manuscript. Years now since he'd tried to read any Latin, thank God – bloody silly language, anyway, with half the words ending in -us and the rest ending -o. The handwriting was small and cramped, too, which didn't help.

Historia Verissima de Calice Sancto, quae Latine vortit monachus Glastonburiensis Simon Magus ex libello vetere Gallico, res gestas equitum magorumque opprobria argentariorumque continens . . .

. . . A very true history of the holy something or other, which Simon the Magician, a *monachus*, that's monk, yes, monk of Glastonbury something-ed to

Latin; the verb's at the end of the line; containing, containing, oh yes, containing the things done of horsemen and magicians and the *opprobria*, opprobrious things of somethings, *argentariorum*, people who have something to do with money . . .

Load of old cod. As soon as I've faxed my copy in, the ghost promised himself, I'll take the pumice to this lot, and then maybe I can write something worth reading on it. Opprobrious things of people who have to do with money indeed! Who on earth would want to read about that?

He went into the office, dialled the number into the fax machine and fed the sheet of parchment into the automatic feed. There were the usual strangled-duck noises, and the parchment started to twitch spasmodically into the little plastic jaws. When it had finished transmitting, he pulled it out, carefully removed the little record slip, and went in search of pumice.

'Boamund.'

'Yes?'

'I don't want to appear personal, but you know that leather book thing, you know, the one we got back from Atlantis?'

'Yes?'

'There's a ruddy great piece of paper coming out of it.'

Danny Bennett yawned, reached for his coffee cup, found it empty, and swore.

Nine thirty. It had been a long day. Still, the new documentary was coming along, the ideas were flowing, the adrenaline was starting to move. Now, if only he could find some way to connect the Highland and Islands Development Board in with the Massacre of Glencoe, he'd really have something here.

He pulled the diagram towards him and gave it a good long stare. Like all his conspiracy charts, it was drawn out in at least seven different colours – blue for the CIA, green for the FBI, red for MI6, purple for the English National Opera, and so on. There was a pleasingly kaleidoscopic nexus round the escape of Bonnie Prince Charlie, and a straight orange line linking that with the North Sea oil franchises; all it needed now was some frilly pink bits up in the top right-hand corner. What was pink? Oh yes, the Public Lending Rights people. There was definitely something going on there. But what?

Down the corridor, in the part of the building where the soap opera people lived, he could hear a fax quietly chuntering away. Soaps! The scum of the earth. Opium of the masses. Why didn't *he* ever get any faxes, anyway?

Still, you had to say this for commercial television, they had a better class of felt-tip pen than he'd been used to at the BBC. If you inadvertently bit into the stem of one of these little babies during the throes of composition, you didn't go around for the next three days with a bright green tongue.

Something was disturbing his concentration. He tried to block it out of his mind, but it wouldn't go away; a persistent whining noise, like a machine in pain. It was that fax down the corridor, he realised; jammed, probably, and all those lazy sods in Soap Opera had gone home long since. Reluctantly – for he had seen a way to get the pink to join up with the yellow without crossing the blue – he got up and went down the corridor to sort the blasted thing out.

Predictably enough, the paper feed had jammed. A few sharp blows with the side of his hand soon put the thing out of its misery, and he pulled the paper out, dumped it down on the desk and turned to leave. Then he frowned and turned back.

What in God's name were the soap people doing getting faxes in Latin?

Sure, it started off in English – and whoever had written it was truly awful at spelling – some sort of rubbishy drama script about people called Alf and Deirdre. But then, where the handwriting finished, there were ten or so paragraphs of tiny handwriting in what Danny was sure was Latin, if only he could make it out. Odd, to say the least. Very odd.

It was – oh, fifteen years, twenty even, since they'd stopped trying to teach him Latin at school; but Danny's mind was like the boot of the family car. Things that nobody wanted and which they were certain they'd chucked out ages ago tended to congregate there, hiding, waiting to pop out when nobody expected them. To his surprise, he found he could just about make it out . . .

Without realising what he was doing, he sat down on the desk and began to read.

'What's it doing, Bedders?' Boamund demanded.

'Printing out,' Bedevere replied, startled. 'Gosh, Bo, it looks like that thing's got a built-in miniature fax in it, Clever!'

'What's a . . .?'

Bedevere was examining the narrow strip of paper

emerging steadily from the side of the Personal Organiser of Wisdom. 'It's a magic thing,' he said. 'It means you can send letters and documents and things right across the world in a matter of seconds.'

'Oh, one of *those*,' Boamund said, relieved. 'Only, where's its wings?'

Bedevere raised an eyebrow. 'What do you mean, wings?' he asked.

'In my day,' Boamund replied, 'when you wanted to send a letter from one end of the world to another in a matter of seconds, you used a magic raven. Where's its wings?'

'They've improved it,' Bedevere said, his attention on the paper in his hands. 'All done with electricity now. That's why they call it wingless telegraphy. You know, this could be interesting. We've got a crossed line here, and . . .'

In spite of themselves, the knights gathered round and peered over his shoulder; all except Turquine, who was too busy wringing out his shirt and shivering. The small group fell silent.

'Well well,' said Lamorak at last. 'Interesting's putting it mildly, I should say. Fancy that, Ken Barlow and Liz McDonald . . .'

'Not that bit,' Bedevere said. 'The bit after that. My God . . .'

'But it's in Latin, Bedders. I was always useless at Latin.'

Bedevere was a quick reader, and his finger had already arrived at the foot of the page.

'Hell,' he said, 'The rest of it's missing. Still, it's a start. How the devil did that come to be passing across the airwaves, I wonder?'

Boamund interrupted him impatiently. 'What does it say, Bedders?' he demanded. 'And if it hasn't got wings, then how come . . .?'

Bedevere, however, wasn't listening. Instead, he was smiling.

'I see,' he said, slowly. 'Oh, very clever, very clever indeed. So that's what this thing was for all along.' Then he seemed to notice the rest of the knights, and turned to face them. 'What we've got here,' he said, 'is the first part of a contemporary account – well, near as dammit contemporary – of the losing of the Holy Grail.' His face melted suddenly into an enormous grin. 'And you're never going to guess,' he added, 'who it's written by.'

They were going to be absolutely livid, Simon Magus told himself, especially Mahaud. Still, he had warned them, and one can't make an omelette, et cetera. He'd probably be better off on his own, anyway.

He glanced down at the map on the seat beside him, but it was too dark to see. He'd have to rely on memory, and it must be at least eight hundred years since he'd been this way last. Luckily, he had a good sense of direction.

'Coventry,' he said aloud. Good idea, these new-fangled road signs; saved you all that stopping and asking the way from gnarled old rustics. He leant forward and switched on the radio. *Round Britain Quiz*; oh good. He liked that. Mildly entertaining, didn't have Robert Robinson in it.

Quite understandable that he was feeling slightly nervous. This job had been a long time coming to fruition, and a lot of work had gone into it. He glanced at the speedometer and eased his foot off the accelerator. No need to rush, and it would be stupid to be stopped for speeding.

('Rivet rivet rivet,' croaked a frog on the hard shoulder as the van swished by.)

As he drove, he went over in his mind the various things that still remained to be done. There was plenty that could still go wrong, but that was always the way. There came a time when you just had to sit back and let them get on with it. They were a pretty sound bunch of lads, if you didn't expect too much out of them, and they had the dwarf to make sure they didn't get themselves into too much trouble.

After *Round Britain Quiz* came the weather forecast – remarkably accurate, Simon Magus noted with approval; they do a good job, considering how abysmally primitive their technology is – followed by a repeat of a gardening programme. Simon Magus yawned and switched the thing off. Should be nearly there by now, anyway.

The shape of the country was definitely familiar, and Simon Magus turned off the motorway on to the A45. He could almost hear it, calling to him . . .

'Magus!'

He looked up, and saw Aristotle's face in the rear-view mirror. Blast! He'd forgotten to switch the damn thing off.

'Hello, Ari,' he replied. 'I warned you. Three minutes, I said.'

'How could you?' Aristotle said, white with rage. 'Just leave us here, I mean, in the middle of nowhere . . .'

'I'll pick you up on my way back,' Simon Magus

replied. 'Look, why don't you just go and have a cup of tea and a go on the electronic games, there's a good lad. And, er, tell Mrs Magus I was called away suddenly or something, will you? Thanks.'

He reached up and flicked a little switch behind the mirror. Aristotle disappeared, and was replaced by the distant prospect of a Daf truck.

Well. If he'd forgotten anything, it was too late now.

The knights were getting wet.

'So,' Bedevere was saying, 'it's all very straightforward, really. Albion isn't Albion at all, it's a sort of . . .' He racked his brains for the right term. 'It's what you might call a financial institution,' he said, lamely. He knew it was all wrong, but never mind. There was no point in trying to understand; all they had to do was get on with it, and everything would be fine.

'I see,' Boamund lied. 'So what do we do now, then?'

'I've got a travelling backgammon set,' said Lamorak.

Boamund considered that. 'All right,' he said. 'And then what?'

'Well, by then someone will have turned up and we'll know what we're meant to do, I suppose. You heard what Bedders said, Bo. We've got to be patient.'

It turned out, rather inevitably, that Lamorak had mislaid the dice, so in the end they sat down under the intermittent shelter of a tree and played Twenty Questions. It was pitch dark by now, and the mist was starting to swirl round them in clouds.

'Your turn, Bo. Think of something.'

Boamund knitted his brows for a moment. When he

said 'Ready,' there was something in his voice which made Bedevere wonder; but he kept his thoughts to himself.

'Two words,' said Boamund. 'And it's mineral.'

'Mineral,' Galahaut repeated. 'Is it something you'd expect to find about the house?'

Boamund considered for a moment; it was almost as if he was listening to a voice telling him the answer. 'Yes,' he said, and he sounded rather surprised. 'That's one.'

'Bigger or smaller than a football?' Turquine asked.

'Bigger,' Boamund replied. 'Gosh,' he added. 'Two.'

'Is it made of metal?'

'Yes,' Boamund said, and then frowned. 'No,' he corrected. 'No, it's not, actually. Three.'

'A household object, not made of metal, bigger than a football,' Pertelope mused. 'Is it mechanical?'

'No. Four.'

'Not mechanical, right. Would you expect to find it in the kitchen?'

Boamund waited for the answer. When it came, it seemed to amaze him. 'Yes,' he said. 'Five.'

'Right,' Galahaut said. 'Mineral, not metal, bigger than a football, not mechanical, you'd find it in the kitchen. Dustbin?'

'No. Six.'

'Vegetable rack?'

'No. Seven.'

'Is it,' asked Lamorak, 'made of plastic?'

Boamund listened, and his mouth opened for a moment in wonder. 'Yes,' he said. 'Eight.'

'Pasta jar?'

'That's not bigger than a football, idiot.'

'Some of them are,' Turquine replied. 'I went into this shop once . . .'

'It's not a pasta jar,' Boamund said quietly. 'Nine.'

'Kitchen scales,' Pertelope suggested. 'No, that's mechanical, I take that back. I know, it's a large tupperware cake box.'

'No. Ten.'

'Mixing bowl?'

'No. Eleven.'

'God, we're so *close*,' Lamorak said. 'Let's see, it's a large plastic kitchen utensil, not mechanical. Plate rack?'

'No. Twelve.'

'Tricky one,' said Galahaut. 'Can't be a flour jar, 'cos that'd be pottery, not plastic. Lammo, what do we keep in the cupboard under the sink, just behind the blender?'

There was a tense silence. Bedevere looked up, and saw that it had stopped raining.

'How about a sink tidy?' Pertelope suggested. 'We haven't had that yet, have we?'

'It's not a sink tidy, and that's thirteen,' Boamund said. 'What's a sink tidy, anyway?'

'How about a bucket?' suggested Galahaut. 'You know, for doing the floor with?'

'Fourteen.'

'Let's recap,' Turquine suggested, and while they were doing it, Boamund stared (so to speak) at the sharp, clear picture in his mind. It couldn't be . . .

'Dustpan and brush,' said Galahaut, the spokesman. 'I mean, you could keep it in the kitchen if you didn't have a cupboard under the stairs.'

'Fifteen,' replied Boamund, absently. The image in his mind refused to fade; if anything, it grew brighter.

'I'm trying to think,' Turquine was saying, 'what they've got in the kitchen at Pizza To Go.' He shook his head. 'But it's not mechanical. I dunno, it's a good one, this.'

'Lampshade,' Lamorak broke in, and there was a hint of desperation in his voice. But Boamund simply shook his head and said, 'Sixteen.'

'I know,' Pertelope said. 'Silly of me not to have guessed. It's a plastic colander.'

'Seventeen.'

'Salad shaker.'

'Eighteen.'

'In the *kitchen*, for God's sake.'

'Cutlery drawer.'

Boamund shook his head again. 'Nineteen,' he murmured.

The knights looked at each other; and then Bedevere, who had been looking up at the sky and noticing that the clouds were breaking up and the stars were coming out, cleared his throat.

'I think,' he said, 'it's the Holy Grail.'

'That's right,' Boamund said. 'Twenty.'

9

Before anyone had a chance to speak, there was a soft cough behind them, and a man stepped forward.

'Good evening, gentlemen,' he said.

A thousand-year-old instinct brought the knights smartly to their feet.

'Good evening, Mr Magus, sir,' they chorused.

Simon Magus looked down at his clothes and sighed. He had done his best to disguise himself as an aged woodcutter, but fancy dress had never been his cup of tea.

'Ready?'

The knights looked at each other. 'Yes, sir,' said Boamund. 'All ready.'

'Splendid,' Simon Magus replied. 'In that case, Boamund, if you'd care to follow me? The rest of you, stay here till I call.'

There was a faint rumble of murmuring from the

knights – something mutinous about it not being fair, and a certain person being the teacher's pet. When Simon Magus turned round and looked at them, it died away completely.

'Be good,' Simon Magus said. Then he walked away.

'You'll need this.'

Boamund had been wondering what was in the canvas bag. It could have been fishing rods, or drain rods even, or a small collapsible easel, or possibly a photographer's tripod. But it wasn't.

'Mind out,' the magician warned, 'it's sharp.'

Boamund, who had already discovered this, sucked his finger. Very sharp and remarkably light, and it seemed to shine of its own accord in the pale moonlight.

'Excalibur,' said Simon Magus casually. 'Been up on the top of my wardrobe for years now, so I said to myself, I'm never going to get any use out of it, might as well pass it on to somebody who will.' He looked at it wistfully.

Excalibur! Someone or something with just a little more imagination than Boamund – a rock, say, or the root of a tree – might have imagined that the dim flame of light dancing on the blade of the sword flickered at the sound of the name. Boamund bit his lip.

'Um,' he said, 'are you sure, sir? I mean, I always thought that the King sort of chucked it in the lake.'

Simon Magus grinned. 'He did,' he replied. 'That's how I got it. Look.'

He pointed to a small group of letters engraved in gold on the ricasso of the sword; and as he did, one could have been forgiven for thinking that they glowed brightly for a fraction of a second.

SHEFFIELD, they said.

'Anyway,' Simon Magus went on, rather self-consciously, 'put it away for now and let's hope we won't need it. Should all be perfectly straightforward ...'

'Halt!'

Out of the darkness, a figure loomed. Moonlight glinted on blued steel.

'All right,' said Simon Magus patiently, after a relatively long pause. 'We've halted. What can we do for you?'

'Um.' The silhouette turned its head and whispered something urgently into the bush from which it had emerged. A couple of other silhouettes emerged rather reluctantly and stood behind it. 'You may not pass,' it said.

'Why not?'

'You can't. Go away.'

Simon Magus and Boamund exchanged glances.

'Can I?' said Boamund hopefully.

'Go on, then,' Simon Magus replied. 'But don't get carried away.'

With a whoop of delight, Boamund drew the sword from the canvas bag, swung it round his head so fast that Simon Magus nearly lost an ear, and lunged into the darkness. There were a few loud but very musical clangs, and Boamund came back.

'They ran away,' he said. It was almost a whimper.

'Never mind,' the magician replied. 'There'll be others, I expect.'

Boamund nodded stoically and sheathed the sword.

'Perhaps,' he said eagerly, 'they'll ambush us.'

Simon Magus shrugged. 'Actually,' he said, 'I rather think that was meant to be an ambush just then. I don't think they've had an awful lot of practice at this sort of thing.'

'Oh.' Boamund sounded surprised. 'You know who they are, then?'

'I've got a pretty good idea,' Simon Magus replied. 'I think they're independent financial advisers. That or portfolio managers. Come on.'

They walked on round the edge of the lake. In a tree above their heads, an owl hooted. Boamund got something in his eye and paused to get it out again.

'Excuse me asking,' he said tentatively, 'but was it you who was that hermit I saw when I woke up, the one who said I should go and do this quest?'

Simon Magus nodded. 'That's right,' he said.

'Oh. I didn't recognise you.'

'I was in disguise. It wouldn't have done for you to know, you see. Actually, it was a pretty terrible disguise. I'm surprised you didn't see through it.'

Boamund considered this revelation for a moment. 'So you've been behind the whole thing, then? Me going to sleep and all that.'

'That's right.' He hesitated, and then added, 'You didn't mind, did you? I mean, you weren't about to do something else, or anything like that?'

'No, not at all,' Boamund replied.

'Good. I was a bit worried, you know, that I'd messed you about rather.'

A shadowy figure with a knife in its mouth dropped from a tree. Unfortunately, it had mistimed its descent. There was a thump; and when the shadowy figure came round, there were two men standing over it solicitously.

'Are you all right?' asked Simon Magus.

'I'th cut my mouf on this thucking dagger,' the assailant replied. 'Thod it.'

'You should be more careful, then, shouldn't you?' Simon Magus replied. 'Here.' He gave the assailant a handkerchief.

'Thankth.' He wiped his face, spat out a tooth and crawled away into the bushes.

Simon Magus shrugged. 'Something tells me we're up against the B-team tonight,' he said. 'Never mind. Bit of an anticlimax, though.'

They walked on in silence for a while, and then Boamund asked:

'I know about the personal organiser, but what about the socks and the apron? I mean, are they *for* anything, or . . .?'

Simon Magus made a clicking noise with his tongue. 'Me and my memory,' he said. 'Good job you reminded me. Have you got them with you?'

'They're in my satchel.'

'Good lad. Now,' said Simon Magus, lowering his voice, 'let's just duck under this tree where it's nice and—'

'Ouch,' said a masked assassin tetchily.

'Sorry.'

'Why the hell don't you look where you're going?'

'Sorry,' Boamund replied, 'it's dark. Have at you?' he suggested hopefully.

The masked assassin scowled at him. 'Not bloody likely,' he said, getting to his feet and hopping a few paces. 'You've done enough damage as it is.'

Muttering to himself, he limped away into the gloom.

'Right,' said Simon Magus. 'Put on the socks and the apron, there's a good lad.'

Boamund frowned. 'Have I got to?' he said.

Simon Magus looked at him. 'Of course you've got to,' he said.

'Oh,' Boamund replied. 'Only I'll feel such a twit wandering about the place in a pinny with flowers on it.'

'You can put it on under your coat if you like,' said the magician tolerantly. 'Just hurry up, that's all.'

Boamund knelt down and unlaced his shoes. 'They're important, are they?' he asked.

'Vital, absolutely vital. Get a move on, will you? We haven't got all night.'

'They're tickling my feet.'

'Look . . .'

There was a bloodcurdling cry just behind him, and Simon Magus spun round.

'Sorry,' he said, 'but can you just hang on a tick? We aren't quite ready yet.'

The hooded thug froze in mid-swing. 'What?' he said.

'Won't keep you a moment,' Simon Magus replied. 'The lad's just changing his socks.'

'His *socks*? Now just a minute . . .'

'It's all right, I'm ready now,' Boamund said, and there was a sudden flash of blue light as Excalibur swished out of the canvas bag. 'Lay on!' he cried happily, and he darted forward. There was a metallic note, approximately D sharp, followed by the sound of someone in armour tripping over his feet and falling into a bush.

'That's not fair,' said a voice from the undergrowth. 'I wasn't ready.'

'Tough,' said Simon Magus. 'We ambushed you.'

'No, you've got it all wrong, *I* ambushed *you*.'

Simon Magus grinned. 'Didn't make a very good job of it, then, did you? Come on, Boamund, we'd better not be late.'

They walked on a few paces. 'That wasn't very fair, was it?' Boamund said. 'I mean, if he waited for us, then surely . . .'

'Nonsense,' replied the magician firmly. 'An ambush is an ambush. If he doesn't know that, then he's not fit to be out on his own.'

'*I* didn't know that—'

'Ah,' replied Simon Magus, 'but you're not on your own, are you?'

'Oh, I see.'

They had come to a sort of jetty or landing-stage, and Simon Magus stopped and looked about him.

'I think we're here,' he said. 'Well, best of luck and all that. Don't forget what I told you.'

Boamund's face fell. 'You're not leaving me, are you?' he said. 'Only I thought . . .'

''Fraid so,' the magician replied. 'Any further intervention on my part would be most irregular, and I don't want the whole quest set aside on a technicality.'

'Oh,' Boamund said. A light breeze began to blow, rippling the surface of the lake. 'What do I do now, then?'

'You'll find out,' said the magician through a curtain of blue fire. 'Cheerio.'

'Cheerio, then,' Boamund replied. He turned and looked at the lake. 'Oh, sir.'

'Yes?'

'What was it you told me that I'm supposed to remember?'

'I've forgotten,' Simon Magus replied, and his voice was hollow and indistinct. His immortal half was already thousands of miles and hundreds of years away. 'It probably wasn't important. Keep your guard up, remember to roll your wrists, something like that. Good luck, Boamund.'

The blue pyramid flared up briefly and faded, leaving only a few lingering sparkles and an empty crisp packet. The wind started to blow harder, rustling the leaves of the trees round the lake. The moon came out. It was getting colder.

'Good evening.'

Boamund spun round. Standing beside him – he hadn't been there a moment ago, unless he'd been very heavily disguised as a small ornamental cherry tree – was what Boamund took to be a hermit.

'Hello,' Boamund replied. 'Are you a hermit?'

'Yes,' said the hermit. 'How did you guess?'

'I just sort of did,' Boamund replied. 'Excuse me, but what do hermits actually do?'

The hermit scratched the lobe of his ear. 'It depends, really,' he said. 'In the old days, we used to meditate, pray, fast and converse with spirits. These days, though, most of us sit in lay-bys on main roads with a big painted board saying "Strawberries". You've probably seen us.'

'Well, no, actually,' Boamund replied. 'You see, I've been asleep for rather a long time, and—'

'So you have,' the hermit replied. 'I forgot. Well now, young Boamund, I expect you're rather excited.'

'Um,' said Boamund, 'yes. Quite. Are you going to tell me what happens next?'

The hermit shook his head. 'I'm afraid not,' he said. 'My role is what you might call a nice little cameo. Very cameo,' he added, with a touch of bitterness. 'All I'm supposed to do is tell you something true but misleading. You don't mind if we spin it out a bit, do you? Only I've been waiting fifteen hundred years for this, and I'd hate to rush things. I mean,' he added, 'it's not as if I've got a great deal to look forward to, is it?'

'Is it? I mean, haven't you?'

'Not really, no,' the hermit said. 'I'm booked in at that terribly dreary Glass Mountain place. Have you ever been there?'

'No.'

'You haven't missed much,' replied the hermit. 'That's why I volunteered for this job, actually, just to have an excuse to put it off for a while. It wasn't exactly a riot of fun sitting beside the A45 in the rain with twenty pounds of squishy strawberries for all those years, but anything's better than where I'm going next.' The hermit sighed deeply and brushed a fly off the tip of his nose.

'Oh,' Boamund said. He felt rather awkward. 'I'm sorry,' he said.

'Not your fault,' the hermit replied. 'That's where we go, you see, when we finally leave the world. They'll all be there, all the great magicians and sorcerers and hermits and anchorites, all sitting about yammering away or falling asleep in big leather armchairs. I expect I'll get used to it.' The hermit shook his head sadly. 'They all do, apparently, after a while. That's the really awful part of it, in my opinion.'

'I'm sorry,' Boamund replied. It was hard to know what to say.

'Thank you,' the hermit said. 'Now, the message is this. Only the true King of Albion will recover the Holy Grail. Good luck.'

A blue pyramid, smaller than the one Simon Magus had vanished into and somehow indefinably but perceptibly second class, formed over him, gave a few perfunctory twinkles and vanished. Boamund looked at where it had been and chewed his lip for a moment.

'Oh,' he said.

He turned to look at the lake; and then in the corner of his eye he caught sight of a stealthy shadow creeping furtively towards him. He whipped out the sword and sprang.

'Hold it,' said the figure. 'Have you just been talking to the hermit?'

'Yes,' Boamund said. 'Why?'

'Oh nuts,' said the figure. 'I'm late. Forget it.'

'But . . .'

'I'm sorry,' the figure said, 'my fault, I blew it. What I'm going to say to the bloody woman when I come back without a scratch on me I really don't know. Probably I'll be back behind the counter Monday morning doing car insurance. Still, there it is.'

Boamund frowned. 'You *want* me to thump you?' he said. The figure nodded.

'Still,' he said, 'no use crying over spilt milk. Thanks anyway. Be seeing you.'

Boamund moved to strike, but the figure had gone. He shrugged, and returned to his seat on the landing-stage.

'Gosh,' he said.

Where he'd been, there was now an enormous blue car – a Volvo – with a strange yellow object fastened to its wheel. Under one of its windscreen wipers was a scrap of paper. Boamund lifted it out, unfolded it and read:

WHOSO EXTRICATES THIS CAR FROM THIS CLAMP SHALL BE THE RIGHTFUL KING OF ALBION.

He scratched his head, and looked down at the yellow thing. It looked like some sort of trap or snare, and he wondered if the car was in pain. Perhaps it was dead; it certainly wasn't moving.

Rightful King of Albion . . .

'Well,' he said, 'here goes.'

Excalibur whistled in the air, and he struck with all his might. Because of a slight miscalculation – the blade was some six inches longer than he'd imagined – the net effect was that a tree immediately behind him lost the tip of one of its branches. He steadied himself, rubbed his wrist where he'd jarred it, and tried again. There was a clang, and the yellow thing broke in two and fell to the ground.

'Nice,' said a voice behind him. 'Very neat.'

It was a girl, wearing a blue and yellow uniform and holding a notebook. For some reason Boamund felt slightly apprehensive.

'It's all right,' the girl assured him, 'I'm purely allegorical, I'm not going to give you a ticket. You're supposed to get in and turn the key.'

'Oh,' Boamund said, 'right. Which key?'

The girl gave him a puzzled look, and then laughed.

'Sorry,' she said, 'I forgot, you've been asleep. Inside the car, there's a big wheel thing. Behind that on your right-hand side you'll find a small key. Give it a gentle turn clockwise and that'll start the engine. Clockwise is this way.' She demonstrated. 'Got that?'

'Thanks.'

'You're welcome,' said the girl and, rather to Boamund's disappointment, vanished. He climbed in, located the ignition and turned the key.

The car vanished.

Boamund sat up and felt the top of his head. There was something on it. A crown.

'Good Lord,' he said, and took it off. It was quite light and thin, and he had the feeling it was probably silver gilt; but it had little points like a saw-blade and a few rather small jewels set into it. He put it back on and tried to imagine being a king.

He looked up, conscious of a noise in the middle distance. It wasn't the sort of noise he had expected to hear beside a lake, somehow. It was, in fact, a telephone.

He looked round, and saw a hand breaking the surface of the lake, about a hundred and fifty yards from the bank. It was white, clothed in samite and holding a telephone.

Suddenly, Boamund wondered if the whole thing was a practical joke.

You know how it is with telephones. Whatever you're doing, however busy or preoccupied you are, sooner or later you give in and pick up the receiver. Boamund sighed and got to his feet. At the side of the jetty was a small boat – hadn't been there a moment ago; big deal, nothing surprised him about this caper any more – and sitting in it was a hooded figure holding the oars.

'Come on, will you?' said the hooded figure. 'I'm catching my death in here.'

Boamund scrambled down into the boat, sat down and began to sulk. The hooded figure dipped the oars in the water and began to row. The boat made no sound as it moved, and the water was as smooth as glass.

'Is it Thursday today?' the ferryman demanded suddenly.

Boamund looked up. 'Sorry?' he said.

'I said, is it Thursday?' the ferryman said. 'You lose track of what day it is when you're on nights.'

'I think so,' Boamund replied. 'Does it matter?'

'Because if it's Thursday,' the figure went on, 'then I've forgotten to set the video. *She* won't bother, of course, the dozy cow. Probably got her feet up, watching the news. You married?'

'No.'

'Very wise,' the ferryman said, and Boamund noticed that there was no face under the hood. 'Go on, then, answer it.'

Boamund hesitated. 'If I do,' he said cautiously, 'this boat isn't going to disappear, is it? I mean, the car did.'

'Get on with it.'

'All right, then.' He leant over and took the receiver. 'You're sure the boat won't disappear? Only . . .'

The hooded figure gave him a scornful, eyeless look, and he put the receiver to his ear.

'Hello?' he said.

The boat vanished.

Danny Bennett reached the bottom of the page and sighed.

A thousand-year-old, ecologically significant international insurance, tax and financial services scam, protected by offshore trusts, conspiracies in high places, corruption, intrigue, cover-ups and graft, implicating virtually every well-known figure in history from Julius Caesar to Spiro Agnew, the implications of which would cast entirely new light on the Princes in the Tower, the Turin Shroud, Easter Island, the Loch Ness Monster, the Fall of Constantinople, Alexander Nevski, the *Mary Rose*, Christopher Marlowe, the *Flying Dutchman*, Cortés and Montezuma, the Gunpowder Plot, the Man in the Iron Mask, the Salem witches, the escape of Bonnie Prince Charlie, the death of Mozart, the War of Jenkins' Ear, the *Marie Celeste*, Jack the Ripper, Darwin, the Hound of the Baskervilles, Ned Kelly, Rorke's Drift, Anastasia, Piltdown Man, the Wall Street Crash, the Lindbergh kidnapping, the Bermuda Triangle, the Reichstag fire, fifty tons of Nazi gold going missing near Lake Geneva in 1945, McCarthy, Suez, Watergate, decimalisation, the death of Pope John Paul I, Three Mile Island, the sinking of the *Belgrano* and the disappearance of Shergar.

'Load of old rubbish,' he said.

He screwed the pages into a ball and threw them in the bin. Then he went back to his desk and got on with his work.

'Well, hello there,' said a voice. 'Your *Majesty*,' it added, and giggled.

Boamund opened his eyes. It was true that his entire life had flashed before him in that terrible few seconds in the water; since he'd slept through most of his life, however, it hadn't been terribly interesting. He'd seen himself lying there, snoring, while his clothes gradually rusted.

'Where am I?' he asked.

The voice (female) giggled again. 'That's a very good question,' it said. 'Shall we start with something a bit easier, like the square root of two?'

Boamund tried to move but couldn't. From where he was lying, all he could see was ceiling. It was a sort of dark green and it moved about, and there was a fish where the lampshade should have been.

'Water pressure,' the voice explained. 'You've got tons and tons and tons of water on top of you, you see, and since you aren't used to it, it's squashing you flat.'

'Oh,' said Boamund. 'Did I drown?'

'Certainly not,' the voice replied. 'If you'd drowned, you'd be dead, silly. You're at the bottom of the lake.'

'Oh,' Boamund repeated. There was something sharp digging into the small of his back.

'Well,' the voice said, 'you got here, then.'

'Yes,' Boamund said. 'Um, am I on the right lines, or did I go wrong somewhere? I mean, am I *meant* to be here?'

The voice laughed. 'Absolutely,' it said. 'You've succeeded. Well done.'

Boamund reviewed his position, and decided that success was probably over-rated. 'What happens now?" he asked. 'And who are you, anyway?'

Suddenly he could feel the weight sliding off him, and he sat up with a jerk. He found himself looking at a woman; tall, slim, graceful, with golden hair and a portable telephone. She was sitting in a tubular steel chair wearing a silky cream blouse and lemon Bermuda shorts. A pike swam past her with a saucer in its jaws, and on the saucer was balanced a tiny coffee cup, which the woman lifted off and held between thumb and forefinger.

'Can I get you anything?' she asked. 'Coffee? A doughnut, perhaps? You strike me as the sort of person who likes doughnuts.'

Boamund blushed. 'No, thank you,' he said stiffly. 'You seem to be a person of importance, please explain what's going on.'

'Business before pleasure, you mean?' the woman said. 'Fair enough. My name is Kundry.'

Boamund looked behind him and saw what it was that he'd been lying on. He picked up the crown, which had been flattened, and tried to bend it back into shape. He felt extremely depressed, but wasn't sure why.

'Don't worry about that,' said Kundry. 'It isn't a real crown, actually; just something to be going on with. Allegorical.'

The word made a connection in Boamund's mind. 'I recognise you,' he said. 'You were that girl with the car.'

Kundry smiled. 'The traffic-warden, that's right. Also the hand with the telephone.' She lifted the portable handset off the smoked-glass table beside her. 'Also the hermit, the unpunctual assassin and the owl. Cast of thousands, in fact.'

'You're a sorceress,' Boamund said.

'Quite right,' Kundry replied. 'Actually, it's not illegal any more. Hasn't been, since Nineteen Fifty-Something. In my position, one has to be very careful.'

'Um,' Boamund said. 'What is your position, then?'

'I'm the Queen of Atlantis,' Kundry replied.

'Among other things, of course. I'm also the high priestess of New Kettering and the Grafin von Wei-nacht. Actually,' she added, 'that's not strictly true; I'm not supposed to use the title since the divorce, so my daughter Katya's the Grafin now. She's a horrid little girl, my daughter. Let's say, shall we, that I'm the Dowager Grafin von Weinacht. I'm not absolutely sure what Dowager means, but I think that after being married to the Graf for six hundred years I deserve some sort of title. A medal, even,' she added. 'Anyway,' she went on, 'none of that really matters as far as you're concerned. What you should be in interested in is me being Kundry.'

'Ah,' Boamund said. He beat about furiously in his mind and stumbled across a phrase which seemed to fit. 'You have the advantage of me there, I'm afraid.'

Kundry raised a beautifully pencilled eyebrow. 'You've never heard of Kundry?' she said.

'Um . . .'

'Good Lord. What *did* they teach you at school, I wonder?'

'Falconry,' Boamund replied. 'Also fencing, tilting, heraldry – actually it was the New Heraldry, you do it all with little diagrams – courtesy, magic with divinity and dalliance to Grade 3. And the flute,' he added, 'but I never got the hang of it properly. I can play *Edi Bi Thu* and *San'c Fuy Belha ni Prezada* if I go slowly.'

'It was a rhetorical question,' Kundry replied. 'You're not the least bit what I expected, you know.'

'Aren't I?'

'No.' Kundry drank some coffee and dropped the cup. A tiny roach darted up, caught the handle of the cup in its mouth and disappeared with a flick of its tail, while a perch retrieved the saucer. 'A moment ago you asked me where you were.'

'That's right,' Boamund said.

'Well,' Kundry continued, 'this is the registered office of Lyonesse (UK) plc, and we're in the exact geographical centre of Albion. You're sitting on it, in fact.'

Boamund shifted rather uncomfortably.

'Here,' Kundry went on, 'you're exactly half way between Atlantis and the North Pole. Does that mean anything to you?'

'Well, no, not really.'

'Doesn't it? Well, never mind. I expect you want to know where the Holy Grail is.'

'I would rather, yes.'

Kundry smiled. 'In that case,' she said, 'I think I'd better begin at the beginning. It all started a very long time ago . . .'

In the narrow street outside, a Roman legionary was leaning on his shield, looking out over the city of Jerusalem and doing his best to ignore the smells of cooking coming from the upper room of the house behind him.

He could smell garlic. He could smell lamb, basting in its own juices. He could smell coriander, and freshly baked bread, and thyme, and sea-bass being steamed with dill and fenugreek. It was sheer torture.

In the kitchen above his head, Bartholomew's girl-friend was stirring the sauce for the roast peacock with one hand, and turning the pages of a cookery book with the other.

'Cream the yeast with a little of the milk,' she said

aloud, 'and leave until frothy.'

She hadn't tried the recipe before, but it sounded wonderful – spicy buns with cinnamon and currants! Yum.

Bartholomew's girlfriend liked cooking, and so when someone had suggested that they have a slap-up meal to celebrate Simon Peter's birthday, she had volunteered like a shot. And when they'd told her that the Master would be coming – well, she'd been in a right tizzy for days. Just imagine it, her cooking for the Master!

After a lot of soul-searching and internal debate, she'd decided on the lamb. You couldn't go wrong with lamb, not at this time of year; and anyway, the marinade would cover a multitude of sins. Then Simon Peter had caught those really nice bass – say what you like about Si, his fish was always properly fresh, which was more than you could say for some – and Philip had been given a peacock by the nice Roman lady whose garden he did twice a week, so that had been all right. The little cinnamon cakes had been her own idea, though.

'Turn on a floured surface,' she read, and 'knead for eight minutes until smooth and elastic.'

It would have been nice, she reflected, if once, just once, one of them had the good manners to say thank you; but that was men for you. She smiled indulgently, thinking of the time when they'd brought all those people back, and nothing in the house except a couple of loaves and a few tiddly little mackerel.

Bartholomew was nice, she said to herself; a nice, steady young man, not likely to go dashing off and joining the army or disappearing for months on end with a caravan. She didn't mind waiting while he went through this religious phase of his – long engagements were a good thing, really, you got to know each other's little ways, so it didn't come as a great big shock when you finally did get married. Besides, it gave her plenty of time to make her dress.

As she made the glaze for the buns, she turned over in her mind the rather peculiar rumours that she'd heard in the Market that morning. Not that there could possibly be anything *wrong* with the Master; he was a holy man, they said, one of these prophets or something like that. But it was true that the Romans didn't really hold with prophets, and really, no good ever came out of antagonising the Romans. She'd have to be firm, she decided. Once they were married, she'd have to stop Bartholomew going to all these prayer meetings and things. If he was really serious about having his own little sandalmaker's shop one of these days, there wouldn't be time for hobbies, anyway.

'There,' she said, and closed the oven door. She wiped her floury hands on a towel, nodded with satisfaction, and started to arrange the flowers on the table. Thirteen to supper would have panicked a lot of girls her age, but she'd managed.

The first to arrive was James the son of Alphaeus. A shy boy, always knocking over ornaments. He helped her lay the table, but didn't say a word. Preoccupied, she thought.

Andrew, James and John all came at once.

'John,' she said bitterly, 'I do wish you'd learn to wipe your feet. Just *look* at my nice clean floor.' She scurried away for the mop; but as soon as she'd cleaned up, in came Simon Peter and Thomas, in their work-clothes too, and she had to do the whole thing again. Nobody noticed the flowers, although it had taken her half an hour to get them just right.

Matthew and Simon the Zealot left their muddy cloaks on the worktop and Judas the brother of James picked the decoration off one of the buns. She was quite rude to him.

Just when she was starting to fret about the meat spoiling, Philip, the other Judas and Bartholomew came in; but she couldn't scold them for being late because they had the Master with them, and Bartholomew got so upset and difficult if she said anything to him in front of the Master. Judas wiped his hands on one of her lovely Damascus napkins, and Philip's dog knocked over the hat-stand, but she didn't say anything. Her mother had always said that she had the patience of a saint.

She hadn't enjoyed the meal. Although the lamb had turned out just right, the peacock was delicious and the sea-bass just the way it should have been, nobody seemed to be hungry. They just sat there, picking at it; and the Master ate nothing but a few pieces of bread all evening. The conversation had been very gloomy and depressing, all about theology, and she'd got the impression that they were all rather on edge. Mind you, what with bringing in the food and clearing away the dishes – and nobody raised a finger to help, of course, although she should have expected that – she hadn't been in her seat for more than a couple of minutes together. And, of course, Judas Iscariot had to go and upset the gravy-boat, all over her mother's best table-cloth. Finally, to put the tin lid on it, nobody had so much as tasted the clever little cinnamon buns with the pretty decoration on them. For some reason, she got the impression that everybody thought they were in rather poor taste, but she couldn't for the life of her think why.

Eventually, Simon Peter looked at the water-clock and said something about it being time they were going, and they all stood up to leave. That was rather more than Bartholomew's girlfriend could take.

'Excuse me,' she said, 'but aren't you forgetting something?'

Andrew and Thomas gave her a filthy look but she ignored them. She'd had enough; and if Bartholomew cared for her even a little bit then he'd say something, surely.

'The washing-up,' she said. 'You aren't just going to walk out of here and *leave* it, are you?'

There was an embarrassed silence; then Simon Peter mumbled something about them having to dash or they'd be late.

'It won't take a moment,' said Bartholomew's girlfriend. 'Not if six of you wash and the rest of you dry.' And she went and stood in front of the door with her arms folded.

'Oh for Chri – for crying out loud,' said Matthew. 'Get out of the way, woman, we're in a hurry.'

'You're not leaving this room until you've done the washing-up,' said Bartholomew's girlfriend. 'I'm *fed up* with you lot trooping in and out at all hours of the day and night in your muddy shoes, expecting to be fed and cleaned up after and have your silly cloaks darned, and knocking things over, and bringing your horrid dogs and nets full of fish, and leaving saws and drills and things all over the place. It's too bad, it really is.'

And then she'd burst into floods of tears.

'Look,' said James, 'we'll make it up to you later, right? Only, really, it is kind of important that we split now, okay?' He'd tried to edge past her to the door but she stuck out an elbow. There was a highly embarrassing silence.

The Master, who hadn't said a word, then looked at her and beckoned. She stayed where she was.

'And as for you . . .' she started to say. But he wasn't listening. Instead, he turned on his heel, marched over to the sink and grabbed the little mop. When Simon Peter tried to take it from him, he gave him a very fierce look.

'*Whether is greater,*' he said in that voice of his, '*he that sitteth at meat or he that serveth?*' And he gave the drying-up cloth to Judas the brother of James. '*Is it not he that sitteth at meat?*' he went on, scrubbing vigorously at one of the roasting dishes. '*But I am among you as he that serveth.*'

Judas the brother of James dropped a dish, which broke.

It was typical, of course; the rest of them just stood there, gawping and putting the dried-up things away in the wrong places, while Philip's dog jumped up on the table and started to lick the gravy off the plates. It was, all in all, one of those evenings you'd like to forget.

When they'd finished, she stood aside from the door and they all trooped through, thoroughly sullen and bad-tempered. Bartholomew didn't even speak to her, which was just as well, because she was damned if she was ever going to speak to him ever again.

'I just hope you're satisfied, that's all,' Simon Peter said. 'Honestly! Women!'

When they'd all gone, she went to the sink and put the things away properly. It was then that she noticed that the old brown terracotta washing-up bowl was different. Something had happened to it. Instead of being brown and heavy it was light and a sort of pale blue colour. In her amazement, she dropped it; but instead of breaking, it bounced, spun round on its side for a moment and rolled behind the vegetable rack.

It was a miracle. Another one, just like that dreadful scene at cousin Judith's wedding at Cana, when everyone had got completely drunk and she'd had to call the watch out to them. As if she didn't have enough to put up with.

Kundry was silent for a moment, her face suddenly old.

'And?' Boamund asked. 'What happened then?'

'You can imagine how I felt the next day,' Kundry said, 'when I heard He'd been arrested, I mean. It was awful, really. I mean, none of our family had ever been in any sort of trouble with the police. I was just thankful my mother wasn't alive to hear about it. She'd have been horrified.'

'But . . .' Boamund stammered, 'you stupid woman, don't you know who that *was*?'

Kundry frowned at him. 'Of course I know,' she snapped. 'I found that out soon enough. An angel told me. I was *livid*.'

'Livid?'

'Absolutely furious,' Kundry said, tight-lipped. 'The unfairness of it all. Do you know what they did to me? They cursed me, that's what. They said that until the Son of Man should come again, and I was permitted – *permitted*, would you believe – to wash up for Him and all His fine friends as I should have done then, until then I was doomed to wander the earth for ever, lugging that horrid little plastic bowl around with me. Well, I told them—'

'That bowl,' Boamund interrupted, 'that's it, isn't it? The Holy Grail, I mean.'

'Of course it is,' replied Kundry, and the knuckles of her hands were white with fury. 'What did you think it was, you silly? *I* told them. I said that hanging around waiting was one thing, I was used to that, but lugging a cheap plastic bowl about with me was something else. Oh yes, I put my foot down there all right.'

Boamund stared at her. It was, he was saying to himself, rather a lot to take in, all in one go. After a moment, Kundry seemed to recover her composure, for she smiled and accepted an After Eight mint from a passing gudgeon.

'It wasn't long after that,' she said, 'that I met Klaus. He was still at the University in Damascus finishing his thesis, though he'd completely lost interest in it by then, and as soon as we discovered what we'd both suffered at the hands of that . . . that Person, we felt that we really had something in common, and so we got married. It was a mistake, of course, but neither of us was prepared to admit it. Instead, we just did our best to put up with each other.'

'That's Klaus von Weinacht, is it?' Boamund asked. 'I think I . . .'

'Yes,' Kundry said, with a hint of distaste, 'that was Klaus von Weinacht. Anyway, where was I? We'd been married about a year or so when Klaus decided he was going to leave the University and go back to Atlantis, where he'd originally come from. I went with him – I wasn't going to give up that easily, not without a proper settlement, at least – and so we both went to Atlantis.

He told me all about the magic gold and the moon and the rotation of the earth and so on, and I realised that there was a simply marvellous opportunity there for someone with a good head for business. I took charge of that side of it – I didn't tell Klaus what I was doing till much later, and he didn't find out, what with having to deliver all those presents and everything – and it wasn't long before the whole operation was well and truly under way. I expect you know all about that.'

'That's all this insurance stuff, isn't it?' Boamund said. 'I don't think I've quite got the hang of how insurance actually works yet, but never mind. You carry on with what you were saying.'

'It was about twenty years later,' Kundry said, 'that my Uncle Joe came to see me, all the way from Arimathea. He'd brought the washing-up bowl with him, and I was a bit taken aback when I saw it again, as you can imagine. But then he explained about all the marvellous things it could do, about tax and so forth – basic rate tax was three deniers in the sol tournois in those days, we didn't know we were born – and so I put it to good use right away. Uncle Joe stayed on and we gave him a seat on the board, and everything was fine for quite some time. Well, not fine, exactly; I mean, Klaus and I only spoke to each other during board meetings, and even then we quarrelled a lot. I had an idea that he was up to something, you see. There were a lot of rumours going around about him wanting to have me thrown off the board so that he and Uncle Joe could take the whole thing over between them. Of course, I wasn't having that. The very idea!

'I found out what they were up to, eventually. They'd worked out that this place – Albion, I mean –

had been built by the ancient Atlanteans to separate the two magnetic fields, years before my time, and that they could use it for a sort of tax fiddle. By the time I found out, actually, the whole thing was rather too far advanced for me to be able to nip it in the bud, but I got there in the end and plugged the loophole. They were sick as parrots about my spoiling their little plan, but there wasn't much they could do about it. The tiresome thing was that Uncle Joe had managed to get hold of the Grail – we might as well call it that, although personally I think it's a *silly* name for it, don't you? – and smuggled it out to Albion and hidden it. He knew where it was, and so did Klaus, and there was a monk or somebody like that in Glastonbury who was in on the secret too, but that was all. They couldn't use the Grail without me knowing, of course, but I couldn't use it either. It was a great shame and very silly, but that's men for you. Spiteful.

'Anyway, things came to a head and I divorced Klaus. He got custody of our daughter and took her away to the North Pole, where he built a whopping great big castle right on top of the magnetic iron ore deposit. I think he had some idea about using that to upset the balance between the two magnetic fields, purely and simply to get back at me, but he's never actually got around to *doing* anything about it yet. I think he's always too busy getting ready to do his delivery round. The population explosion in the last two hundred years has affected him very badly, you know. Serves him right.

'Uncle Joe just packed his bags and left, too. The last I heard of him was in this Glastonbury place; apparently, he just sort of vanished in a puff of blue smoke,

if you can believe that. I heard rumours some time later
that he'd taken a job teaching at a boy's school
somewhere, but I don't know if it's true or not.
Anyway, the long and the short of it is, he took the
Grail with him, and that's all I know about it. So I can't
help you any more. Sorry.'

Boamund sat for a while, his eyes as round as the full
moon.

'Thank you,' he said. 'You've been most helpful. I
think I know what's going on now.'

Kundry raised both eyebrows. 'Do you?' she said. 'I
don't. *Something's* going on, I know that, or else why
did Klaus suddenly turn up the other day chasing your
friends? I hadn't seen him for years. Good job, too.'

'I think I know why,' Boamund said. 'He knew that
Mr – that your Uncle Joe was helping us to find the
Grail, and he wanted to find out what we knew.'

'Uncle Joe?' Kundry stared at him. 'What's Uncle
Joe got to do with it? Like I said, I haven't seen or heard
anything of him for simply ages. In fact, I rather
thought he was dead or something.'

Boamund shook his head. 'No,' he said, 'not as
such.'

'Have you seen him?' Kundry asked eagerly. 'Do you
know where he is?'

'Yes,' Boamund said slowly. 'I know where he is. But
I don't know where to find him. If you see what I
mean.'

Kundry sighed. 'Not really,' she said. 'Oh, by the
way, your friends took something of mine the other
day. Would you be very sweet and let me have it back
when you've finished with it?'

Boamund nodded. 'Thanks again,' he said, and

added, 'I think it was a swizzle, too. About the washing-up and everything. But, well, sometimes you've got to put up with people – *important* people, if you know what I mean. It's like knights and dwarves, really. I mean, knights aren't particularly clever and dwarves help them out a lot with the thinking. And dwarves do all the housework and the cleaning and tidying up, and we do sometimes forget to say thank you. But that's because that's the way things are. They understand, and we do, too. Sort of.'

Kundry frowned at him. 'That's men for you,' she said. 'Typical.'

Boamund stood up. 'I'd better be getting back,' he said. 'Um, how do I get out of here?'

'I'll see to that,' Kundry replied. 'Give my regards to your friend Bedevere. I quite liked him.'

'Thanks.'

'Goodbye then,' Kundry said. 'Your Majesty.'

Toenail was sitting in the boat when Boamund finally surfaced. He held out a boathook and Boamund pulled himself aboard.

'Lucky I brought a change of clothes and some towels,' said the dwarf. 'When I heard we were going to a lake, I said to myself, someone's bound to fall in, so I'd better . . .'

Boamund wiped the water out of his eyes. 'I didn't say we were going to a lake,' he said.

'*You* didn't, no,' Toenail replied. 'You wouldn't have known, would you?'

Boamund shrugged and towelled his hair for a moment. The dwarf picked up the oars and started to row for the shore.

'Toenail,' said Boamund suddenly, 'whose side are you on?'

'Yours, of course,' said the dwarf. 'Why d'you ask?'

'Nothing,' Boamund replied. 'I was just puzzled, that's all.'

The dwarf veered the boat towards the jetty with the left-hand oar. 'We've always been dwarves in our family,' he said, 'it's a tradition. I told you, remember?'

'Did you?' Boamund noticed that he'd lost Excalibur; that's if it really had been Excalibur. 'Sorry,' he said. 'I probably wasn't listening.'

'Don't suppose you were,' said the dwarf. 'You've found out, then.'

Boamund looked up. 'Found out?' he repeated.

'About the Grail, and Mr Simon,' Toenail replied. 'Or didn't she tell you?'

'You mean you knew all along?' Boamund said.

'Sort of,' Toenail replied. 'It's called race-memory, you see. Like, all dwarves can remember everything that's ever happened to all the other dwarves who've ever lived. Just not all at once. Bits of it come back to you, when it's necessary.'

'Right,' Boamund said. 'I think I follow. Yes, she told me. Came as a bit of a surprise, actually.'

'Everything comes as a surprise to me, sir,' replied the dwarf. 'I prefer it that way. Here we are.'

The boat nudged gently against the jetty, and Boamund jumped off.

'Can you manage?' he asked.

'Course I can,' Toenail replied cheerfully. 'Why do you ask?'

'Oh, no reason,' Boamund replied thoughtfully. 'Now then . . .'

'This way,' Toenail said.

'Bet you ten to one he's got lost,' Turquine was saying. 'Never did have a sense of direction, young Snotty. He could get lost in a lift.'

'Or else something's happened to him,' Galahaut replied. 'Not exactly practical, our Boamund. Accident-prone, too. I think we should go and look for him, don't you?'

Turquine yawned. 'Why bother?' he said. 'To be honest with you, I've had just about as much as I can take of being ordered about by him, the jumped-up little tyke. Worst thing Mr Magus ever did, making him a prefect. Gave him ideas. He's never been the same since.'

'You know,' Pertelope broke in. 'I always wondered why he did that. Anyone less suited to being a prefect than Bo you couldn't imagine.'

They had lit a fire, and Lamorak had somehow managed to hit a rabbit with an improvised catapult. They were having a late supper.

'I expect he thought it would be character-forming,' Pertelope replied as he turned the spit. 'Make something of him, you know. Bring him out of his shell. Didn't work, mind. Just made him insufferable.'

'More insufferable, anyway,' Turquine replied. 'He always was a pompous little git, even at the best of times. I reckon Mr Magus has got a lot to answer for.'

'Someone taking my name in vain?' said a voice from the darkness. At once, the five knights jumped to their feet and looked guilty. Pavlovian reflex.

'Hello again, sir,' Turquine mumbled. 'Just wondering where Boamund's got to, sir. Have you seen him?'

'He'll be all right,' Simon Magus replied. 'Well now, young Turquine, what have we here? Roast rabbit?'

'Yes, sir.'

Simon Magus sat down and warmed his hands in front of the fire. 'Quite like the old days, really. I remember you were always breaking out of the Dorm in summer, young Turkey, poaching rabbits and having – let's say, having unofficial barbecues behind the stables. The farmers used to complain quite dreadfully.'

Turquine went a deep shade of mauve and said nothing.

'Was I right in thinking,' Simon Magus continued as he poked the rabbit with a stick, 'that you were discussing why I chose to make young Boamund a prefect at the end of the Third year? Or were my old ears deceiving me?'

There was an awkward silence, which Bedevere broke.

'We were a bit puzzled, sir, yes,' he said carefully. 'It did seem rather an odd choice, if you don't mind us saying so. He wasn't really very good at it, was he?'

'I think the rabbit's about ready now,' Simon Magus replied, and Bedevere noticed that he was staring into the fire, as if he could see something there, in the blue part of the flame. 'It was an unconventional choice, certainly, but I had my reasons. In fact, if you're patient, you can hear them for yourselves in a minute or two. Have you got your famous penknife handy, Turquine? Or is it still confiscated? I can't remember.'

Very slowly, Turquine took an old and extremely worn penknife out of his pocket and handed it over. It wasn't the first time, either.

'Ah yes,' said Simon Magus. 'Old Faithful.' He

began to carve the rabbit.

'Actually, sir,' Bedevere said tentatively. 'I was meaning to ask you. About this whole quest business, sir . . .'

But before he could finish his sentence there was a rustling in the bushes and Boamund emerged, with Toenail trotting behind him carrying a bundle of wet clothes. Simon Magus got up slowly, put down the rabbit and smiled affectionately. Then he knelt down on one knee and said:

'All hail King Boamund the First, rightful King of Albion.'

There was a silence you could have built a house on, and then Turquine made a sort of choking noise.

'Oh, for God's sake,' he said. 'He isn't, is he? Tell me it isn't true, somebody.'

Simon Magus stood up. 'It's all right,' he said, 'the office is purely honorary. There isn't a kingdom of Albion any more.'

'God, I'm relieved to hear you say that,' said Turquine. 'Just imagine what it'd be like, having that horrible face peering up at your from postage stamps.'

Boamund was standing quite still. He looked pale, although perhaps it was just a trick of the light, and he was looking at the old magician. He made no attempt to speak.

'Well now,' Simon Magus said, 'did you manage all right?'

Boamund nodded. 'Yes, thank you,' he said. 'I managed.'

'And do you know where it is?'

'No,' Boamund replied. There was a disdainful

noise from Sir Turquine, but Simon Magus held up his hand for silence.

'I don't know where it is,' Boamund went on, 'but I do know who does know, if you follow me, sir. That's right, isn't it?'

Simon Magus smiled; or at least, the corner of his lip lifted about a quarter of an inch. 'Splendid,' he said. 'Very well done. Come and have some rabbit.'

10

'He's asleep,' Bedevere said quietly. 'He was absolutely exhausted.'

'I'm not surprised,' Simon Magus replied. 'Any chance of a cup of tea, by the way? I'm parched.'

They went into the kitchen. Unusually it was fairly presentable. Bedevere took down the jar where the tea-bags lived, and sighed.

'Empty,' he said. 'That'll be Lamorak. He's always using the last one and not telling anybody. We have a big shop once a month, you see; we go round the supermarket with a couple of those big trolleys and get everything we need. But we never seem to get enough tea-bags, or enough sugar, come to that. Will coffee do instead?'

'Coffee will be fine,' Simon Magus replied. 'Where are the others?'

'In the Common Room,' Bedevere replied, 'playing pontoon. Galahaut cheats.'

When the kettle had boiled they sat down on either side of the kitchen table and looked at each other thoughtfully.

'Biscuit?'

'No, thanks,' Simon Magus replied. 'When you went in and looked, did he still have it with him?'

'Yes,' Bedevere replied. 'He was holding it, like it was a teddy bear or something.' He laughed, but without much humour. 'Fancy it being in the garage all the time, in that big cardboard box full of junk. We all thought it was one of those crates of tins without labels that Lamorak's always buying in the market.'

Simon Magus had the grace to look slightly abashed. 'It was the best place I could think of,' he said. 'The one place nobody would ever dream of looking. I was right, too,' he added.

'It was a bit thick, though, wasn't it, sir?' Bedevere burst out. 'I mean, you've made us all look complete chumps. Honestly, here we are, the Grail Knights, and all the time the wretched thing's in our garage, hidden in an old cardboard box. We'll be the laughing stock of chivalry if anyone ever finds out.'

Simon Magus grinned sheepishly. 'You must admit, though,' he said, 'it was a good hiding place.'

'Exactly,' Bedevere said. 'So *why*? I mean, why this quest and so on? If you wanted it to stay hidden, why did you make us go and find it? It doesn't make sense.'

Simon Magus stirred his coffee and smiled. 'You always were bright, Bedevere,' he said. 'Unusually bright, but singularly lacking in energy. A pity, really, but there it is. I don't believe in forcing people to do things if they don't want to, and I don't think you ever wanted to be anything but ordinary. Am I right?'

'Absolutely,' Bedevere replied. 'But that's rather beside the point, isn't it? I mean, why hide the Grail so carefully and then send us out to look for it? And why did you make it take so long?'

'Ah.' Simon Magus nodded approvingly. 'You're asking the right questions, as usual. You remember what I taught you about the right question?'

'The right question,' Bedevere recited, 'is a question that can have only one possible answer. But I don't see—'

'Then think,' Simon Magus replied sharply. 'Why did I hide it, why did I make you – or rather, Boamund – find it, and why did it all have to take so long? Come on, you're nearly there.'

Bedevere thought for a long time.

'Well,' he said slowly, 'you hid it because you didn't want it found.'

'Quite right, yes.'

'You sent Boamund to find it because you wanted Boamund to find it.'

'Right again.'

'And,' Bedevere said, lifting his head, 'it took so long because it had to be found at the right time. Yes, I think I'm beginning to see daylight.'

Simon Magus leant back in his chair and sipped his coffee. 'Go on,' he said.

'You hid it,' Bedevere said, 'because you didn't want the Atlantis people to find it; not, what's her name . . .'

'Kundry,' Simon Magus said. 'She's my niece, actually, but we were never very close.'

'You didn't want her to have it,' Bedevere went on, 'and you didn't want old Father Christmas getting hold of it either.'

'Quite right,' said the magician. 'Dreadful people, both of them. I knew them quite well back in the old days, and they were a bit unbalanced even then. Now they're both quite mad, of course; but immortal, the pair of them, because of the curses they're both under. It wasn't just a case of waiting till they went away, you see. On the other hand, it was a holy relic, the holiest true relic that existed, so I couldn't just destroy it. Somehow or other, it had to be hidden.'

'Right,' Bedevere said. 'So you took the Grail and you hid it where nobody would ever find it. And you set up the Order of the Grail Knights deliberately so that we *wouldn't* find it, and that way everybody would know for sure that it was lost. Because the one place nobody would ever dream of looking would be in the Grail Knights' own garage.'

'Very good,' Simon Magus said. 'Carry on.'

'But . . .' Bedevere put his head between his hands and thought for a moment. 'Right,' he said. 'And then you took a knight, a particularly dopey but idealistic and upright knight, and you trained him from a boy to be *really* dopey and *really* idealistic and upright, so that he'd be the sort of person who you could be certain the Grail would be safe with . . .'

'The Holy Fool,' Simon Magus agreed. 'Biddable, virtuous, stupid, extremely pompous; the sort of person who would never be afflicted by greed, megalomania or anything like that. The perfect Grail Knight, in fact.'

'I should have guessed,' Bedevere said, 'when I remembered that you and he arrived at the Coll in the same term, and you left the term after he did.'

'Perhaps.' He smiled. 'It would have been very

inconvenient if you had, you know.'

'Anyway,' Bedevere went on, 'you trained this knight to be exactly the way you wanted him to be; but that wasn't enough. To be absolutely safe, you put him to sleep for hundreds and hundreds of years, so that when he woke up, he'd be completely disorientated. He'd have no family, no ties, no place in society or anything like that; but instead, he'd have this really enormous sense of his own destiny, because that's the only way he could account for what had happened to him.' Bedevere paused for a moment. 'That was a bit – well, ruthless of you, wasn't it? I mean, not exactly fair on the poor chap. He's a bit of a duffer, I know, but there are limits.'

Simon Magus shrugged. 'Boamund was – and is – the perfect knight,' he said. 'Brave, honest and stupid. Chivalry is what he was born to, and this is the ultimate in knightly adventures. I honestly don't think he's been all that hard done by, do you?'

Bedevere considered. 'Maybe not,' he said. 'Anyway, when you reckoned that the right time had come, you woke Boamund up and guided him unerringly to where the Grail was. Actually,' Bedevere added, 'I'm a bit puzzled about the three quests. What were they in aid of? Were the actual things, the socks and so forth, necessary? Or was it all sort of incidental?'

'Purely incidental,' Simon Magus replied. 'Really, the whole point of those exercises was to notify Klaus and Kundry, as loudly and clearly as possible, that the Grail still existed and that someone was looking for it. It's essential that they know, you see; I'm going to put a stop to all this Atlantis nonsense once and for all, before they do a great deal of harm. You heard about

that task force which was sent to deal with them, I
suppose, and what happened to it. They've been a
menace for some time now, and that's why I acted
when I did. Besides, that dratted woman Kundry had
found out about that manuscript from Glastonbury
which told the whole story. That was careless of me,
leaving that lying about; but I honestly thought it had
been destroyed back in the sixteenth century. Then,
when I heard about the Lyonesse Group hiring the
back rooms of all those ancient monuments, I realised
that she was on the track of the wretched thing and
might very well find it if I didn't act quickly. It was a
close-run thing, actually.' And he told Bedevere about
the fax from Shakespeare's birthplace.

'I see,' Bedevere said. 'Anyway, now Boamund's got
the Grail and everything's going to be fine. It *is* going
to be fine, isn't it?'

'Oh yes,' Simon Magus said, 'or at least it should be.
Fingers crossed, anyway.'

'There's just one thing,' Bedevere said. 'What did
you need us for? I mean, why did we have to wait
around all this time? Couldn't Boamund have managed on his own?'

They looked at each other.

'No,' Bedevere said after a while. 'No, I suppose not.
He's a good sort, Bo, but . . .'

'Exactly,' said Simon Magus. 'Thanks for the coffee.'

'I still think,' Boamund said, 'that he might have
waited and said goodbye.'

It was cold on the hillside, and Bedevere shivered
slightly. 'He had to rush,' he replied. 'An urgent

meeting or something like that. But he sent you his very best wishes.'

Boamund nodded. 'Well,' he said, 'I'll see you back at the house later on. I've just got to, er, bury something in that cave up there, and . . .'

Bedevere started to say something; but he didn't manage it. Instead, he turned and walked briskly away down the hill. Boamund wrinkled his brow, then shrugged and looked down for the dwarf.

'Well,' Toenail said, 'here we are again. I've brought the spade like you said.'

Boamund nodded, tucked the black plastic sack that contained the Holy Grail (but only he knew it was that, of course) under his arm and set off uphill as fast as his long legs would carry him.

In the cave, everything was as it had been, not so long ago now, when he had woken up. There were still bits of rusty armour lying about, and a strong smell of must and penetrating oil.

'Clever of you to think of this place, Toenail,' he said. The dwarf avoided looking at him and muttered something about getting the cave tidied up.

'All right, then,' Boamund said. 'You do that while I just dig a hole.'

Ten minutes or so later, Boamund laid aside his spade, wiped his forehead and knelt down. The Grail fitted very nicely in its last resting place. He nodded respectfully at it, and then shovelled back the earth and patted it down.

'Gosh,' said Toenail, in a rather strained voice. 'I expect you're hot after all that digging.'

'I am, rather,' Boamund replied. 'I'd give a lot for a nice cool drink of milk right now.'

Toenail blushed scarlet and fumbled in his satchel. 'Just as well I remembered to bring one, then,' he tried to say, but his tongue seemed to get in the way.

'You're a marvel, Toenail, the way you think of everything,' Boamund said, after he'd swallowed a large mouthful of milk. 'Don't know what I'd do without you, really. I know I sometimes forget to say thank you, but ... Hey, now, there's no call to start bursting into tears, you know.'

'Hay fever,' snuffled the dwarf. 'Don't mind me.'

'Sorry,' Boamund said, and he drank the rest of the milk. 'You know something,' he said, 'all of a sudden I feel terribly, terribly . . .'

He lay back, and a moment later he was fast asleep. Toenail took the milk bottle from his hands and put it on one side; then he unslung the large canvas bag he'd been carrying over his shoulder. It was as tall as he was and very heavy.

'Fall for it every time, that old milk routine,' the dwarf said softly. He opened the sack and gingerly took from it a sword and a golden crown.

'Cheerio, then,' said the dwarf. He placed the crown on Boamund's head and the sword under his hands, and tiptoed quietly out of the cave. Then he stopped, took out the scrap of paper which Mr Magus had given him, and read out the words written on it in a loud, self-conscious voice. There was a great flicker of blue fire, and the cave vanished, as if it had never been.

Toenail stood for a while, not thinking of anything in particular; then he remembered that the rest of the knights would be wanting their tea before they set off. They had a long way to go, too; all the way across the sea to the Isle of Avalon, where there is neither autumn nor winter, where men do not grow old, and where (according to Simon Magus, at any rate) if you wanted a pizza, you had to go and collect it yourself. Turquine could hardly wait.

'They'll be needing a dwarf,' Toenail said to himself. He glanced back once more at the hillside where the mouth of the cave had been, stooped instinctively to pick up an empty crisp packet, and ran swiftly away down the hill.

OVERTIME

Tom Holt

Only in a Tom Holt novel can you discover the relationship between the Inland Revenue, the Second Crusade and God's great plan to build starter planets for first time life forms . . .

It all started for Guy Goodlet somewhere over Caen. One moment he was heading for the relative safety of the coast, aware that fuel was low and the Mosquito had more than a few bullet holes in it. The next, his co-pilot was asking to be dropped off. This would have been odd if Peter had still been alive. Since he was dead, it was downright worrying.

But not quite as worrying as when Guy found himself somewhere in the High Middle Ages – rather than in 1943 – in the company of one John de Nesle. Unsurprisingly, Guy's first thought was to get out and home sharpish. But then he saw John's sister, Isoud, and somehow found himself agreeing to help John, also known as Blondel, in his quest to find Richard Coeur de Lion . . .

Overtime is another riotously funny novel from the acclaimed author of *Ye Gods!* and *Flying Dutch*.

ORBIT BOOKS
FANTASY

HERE COMES THE SUN

Tom Holt

All is not well with the universe – entropy and the cutbacks have taken their toll, and the sun is dirty and late, thanks to being 30,000,000,000,000 miles overdue on its next service. And you just can't seem to get the personnel these days, what with all the older workers retiring rather than face the problems of another round of financial constraint. And none of the committees can agree on anything. Extreme measures seem to be called for.

But there's extreme, and there's recruiting mortals to help run things. The Chief of Staff is uneasy when the dapper Mr Ganger suggests it as a solution. But he's not half as uneasy as Jane, who, after a momentary fall from grace with three cream doughnuts, finds herself sitting next to a daemon offering her a very strange job, which involves tidying up after a certain carelessness with earthquakes and tidal waves, and responding to crises, such as when joyriders decide to try their luck with one of the more important heavenly bodies.

ORBIT BOOKS
FANTASY

FAUST AMONG EQUALS

Tom Holt

WELL I'LL BE DAMNED...

The management buy-out of Hell wasn't going quite as well as had been hoped. For a start, there had been that nasty business with the perjurers, and then came the news that the Most Wanted Man in History had escaped, and all just as the plans for the new theme park, EuroBosch, were under way.

But Kurt 'Mad Dog' Lundqvist, the foremost bounty hunter of all time, is on the case, and he can usually be relied upon to get his man – even when that man is Lucky George Faustus...

Faust Among Equals is Tom Holt at his exuberant, inventive best.

ORBIT BOOKS
FANTASY

☐	Expecting Someone Taller	Tom Holt	£4.99
☐	Who's Afraid of Beowulf?	Tom Holt	£4.99
☐	Flying Dutch	Tom Holt	£4.99
☐	Ye Gods!	Tom Holt	£4.99
☐	Overtime	Tom Holt	£4.99
☐	Here Comes The Sun	Tom Holt	£4.99
☐	Faust Among Equals	Tom Holt	£4.99
☐	Odds and Gods	Tom Holt	£14.99

Orbit now offers an exciting range of quality titles by both established and new authors which can be ordered from the following address:

Little, Brown and Company (UK),
P.O. Box 11,
Falmouth,
Cornwall TR10 9EN.

Alternatively you may fax your order to the above address.
Fax No. 0326 376423.

Payments can be made as follows: cheque, postal order (payable to Little, Brown and Company) or by credit cards, Visa/Access. Do not send cash or currency. UK customers and B.F.P.O. please allow £1.00 for postage and packing for the first book, plus 50p for the second book, plus 30p for each additional book up to a maximum charge of £3.00 (7 books plus).

Overseas customers including Ireland please allow £2.00 for the first book plus £1.00 for the second book, plus 50p for each additional book.

NAME (Block Letters) ....

....

ADDRESS ....

....

....

☐ I enclose my remittance for ....

☐ I wish to pay by Access/Visa Card

Number ⬜⬜⬜⬜⬜⬜⬜⬜⬜⬜⬜⬜⬜⬜⬜⬜

Card Expiry Date ⬜⬜⬜⬜